THE
GOOD
MARRIAGE

CARA KENT

The Good Marriage
Copyright © 2024 by Cara Kent

CHAPTER ONE

PROLOGUE

HANNAH ROY HAD WOKEN UP ON THE WRONG SIDE OF the bed—literally. She'd stayed up late planning lessons for her return from maternity leave, and her husband, Dev—usually a night owl—had gone to bed before her. By the time she'd finally joined him, he had rolled onto her side of the king-size mattress, and no gentle shove or under-her-breath hiss could wake him from his comatose slumber. This was a rare occurrence, and he worked hard, so instead of exerting herself and irritating him, she laid down anyway, hoping she was exhausted enough to pass out. She did not. Instead, she spent the night tossing and turning, the scent of his tea tree shampoo on the pillow overpowering.

Not long after she'd finally drifted off into dreamland, the baby began to cry, and the two older ones bounded into the room demanding pancakes and TV time. It was only 5 a.m., but hungry mouths waited for no one. So she rose, fed the baby from her breast while making batter, and then woke her husband to delegate the remaining tasks to him. With the baby back in her crib, the kids in front of the TV, and her husband cooking up a storm, she embarked on her favorite solo activity—her morning run.

She smiled as she tore down the rain-soaked street. It was always hard to motivate herself to take those first steps, especially when the weather was miserable, but once she got going, it was the most freeing feeling in the world. That's why she did it. That's why she turned up her music and upped the pace. She wanted to push herself.

She'd been increasing her speed for weeks and, despite being a newbie, was soon to conquer the ten-minute mile. The weight was falling off, too. She hadn't been this skinny since before she'd met Dev in college. Despite giving birth a mere twelve weeks ago, she could see definition in her abdomen for the first time in years. She was lucky it had been such an easy birth, and considering there would be no more babies as Dev was scheduled for a vasectomy, she was planning on a wardrobe overhaul for her upcoming birthday. Yes, Hannah Roy was feeling good.

As she continued running, she remembered what that stranger had said about changing her route, and she made a U-turn toward the park. It was good advice, she thought; the trees were much prettier than the rows of houses and parked cars. Even more elated than usual, she was practically gliding as she headed down the gentle slope. Then, she felt *it*—the feeling she'd been having for the past two weeks. The feeling of being watched or, worse, followed. She had to be imagining it. She was heading in the opposite direction after all, but it made her skin crawl, flesh prickle, and stomach churn nonetheless.

It was awful. It was sapping her energy. It felt like an accident waiting to happen. It felt like saying goodbye to your sickly mother and having the dreadful feeling that there wouldn't be another hello. So you go back to hug her, and the following day, you find out you were right. It felt like a harbinger of doom, and it didn't matter where she turned or what she did; she couldn't outrun the feeling. Yet, she didn't want to give up either. This was her thing. She needed this.

However, today, it felt particularly intense, as if it was breathing down her neck. She slowed, pulled her headphones off, and hung them around the back of her neck. She half expected someone to be right behind her, but looking around the streets, the houses, the alleyways, and the nearby park, everything seemed normal. It was empty and peaceful, and the birds sang as they always did. Yet her body said otherwise. She was not alone.

A dark alleyway in between duplexes caught her attention in particular, and she flipped the bird at the shadowy space before pulling her headphones back on. Determined, motivated by irritation, she regained her speed, and, in some ways, her fear was a good motivator.

Once in the park, even her exhaustion and lousy mood went away. After such a snowy winter, it was hard to feel stressed when surrounded by amazing greenery. It was beautiful enough to make her want to stop and appreciate it, but she didn't slow, just in case.

She was about to exit the other side of the park when something caught her eye. It was a brown, clearly female duck seemingly in some sort of distress. Considering it was February, she wondered if something had happened to her babies, and being a mother herself, Hannah decreased her speed to a jog.

Glancing once again over her shoulder and seeing that she was definitely alone, Hannah approached the duck and turned down her music. The duck seemed to be pleading with her as she approached, leading her to the edge of a manmade pond that had been drained for cleaning. At the bottom were five baby ducklings. Luckily, the pond was only about four feet deep, and Hannah, a lifelong gym junkie, was confident she could get in and out without assistance. So, she hopped down and lifted each squirming, fluffy baby up one by one before heaving herself up.

Though the duck couldn't verbally thank her, she seemed grateful as they all waddled away, and Hannah sat on the edge for a moment, watching them as they disappeared into the long grass. She chuckled. Then she screamed.

At first, she didn't know why she'd made the awful sound until she realized she was lying at the bottom of the pond and the back of her skull was pounding. Shakily, she put a hand to her head and felt wet pooling just above her ponytail. She turned to look at her attacker, but the sun was in her eyes, and her gaze was hazy. She didn't—or couldn't—recognize him, but it was definitely a him. The tall, solid stature made that apparent.

She screamed again as he jumped into the pond and scrabbled away, her headphone wires catching under her palms and the buds pulling from her ear canals. The surrounding sounds were no longer muffled, and she could hear him grunt as he stooped to grab her ankles. A fighter, not a fleer, she kicked hard, with all the force she had, and caught him in the groin with the heel of her sneakers. It was a good hit, and he instinctively let go to protect his manhood, allowing her to make her getaway.

"Bitch," the man growled, low and deep, as she slid along the sludgy ground.

He lunged forward again, but her legs remembered that they existed and weren't broken. With surprising vigor, she tucked her knees into her belly and sprung to her feet before running to the other side of the almost pool-sized pond. He hadn't been expecting that and faltered as she jumped, reaching the edge, arms folded on the top, and hoisted herself up. A hand swiped at her calves, and she kicked again, this time catching him in his face and feeling a crunch in her sole.

Instinctively, not having hurt anyone before in her life, she looked back to see if she'd broken his nose. Despite his clenching and agonized roar, it was hard to tell. He was wearing a balaclava. Which meant that whoever this was, he had been planning this. And she wasn't going to stick around to find out what 'this' was.

On solid ground, Hannah took off through the trees, but they were sporadically placed and didn't allow for much hiding, and soon enough, she heard him pumping after her, boots pounding the freshly mown grass. He was fast, faster than her.

4

Maybe it was because he was taller or because she was new to this, but he was catching up to her, and yelling only seemed to scare the birds and slow her down.

With no idea of where she was going, she ventured further into the park's wilderness and away from civilization. Then, she hit a wall—a literal one. One that surrounded a building probably used for park maintenance. It was brick, roughly eight feet, and possibly climbable, so she tried. In her mind's eye, she scrambled to the top without issue, but instead, she slid, the wet preventing the necessary adhesion, and before she could try again, his hands were around her throat.

His grasp was strong, his hands large, and not a wisp of air could be inhaled into her lungs. She was halfway to unconsciousness when he released her, and she thought he might be showing her mercy before he moved in again. He didn't want the game to be over. He wanted her to suffer. He wanted to play with his food.

With the veins in her forehead feeling as if they might burst, she tried to remember what she'd learned in self-defense class. It came to her in vignettes, but it came all the same, and she raised her hands to his, bent his pinky back sharply, and dislocated it with surprising ease.

The man bellowed and moved back, allowing her to turn and throw the first punch of her life. It connected, but it was weak and only seemed to make him angrier.

Then, it was his turn to hit, and he hit hard. Her knees gave out, and she was on the ground again, kneeling before him as he held the neck of her t-shirt in his fist and punched again and again and again until she could hardly see or breathe because of the blood.

When he let go, she saw an opportunity and fell sideways, pretending to be dead. She hoped that, at least, might prevent the real thing for long enough to formulate a plan.

It worked; he stopped hitting and kneeled beside her, stroking her silky black hair that had long since come loose of its ponytail. By some miracle, he didn't reach out to feel her pulse, and she stayed like that, holding her breath, until she heard him walk away. However, even once she was sure he was no longer around, she still didn't move. It was too risky. So, like an opossum, she remained, belly up, waiting for help, and hoping he hadn't left to get a shovel.

CHAPTER TWO

THE DETECTIVE

WITH A THUNK AND A SPLASH, THE BLACK CAB pulled into an overflowing gutter, and a wave the height of a toddler doused the left side of the vehicle. Heather didn't wait for it to settle before exiting. It was pouring outside; 200 millimeters was expected to rain down over the next twenty-four hours—nearly eight inches, she whispered internally to the sound of Gabriel's confused question that immediately rose in her mind, as if he was there with her and not half a world away back in Glenville. She was getting wet regardless and had something more important to contend with than being soggy—a terrible case of motion sickness.

The tumultuous flight and bat-out-of-hell driving style of the local 'cabbies' had made her violently nauseous, and she'd spent much of her initial time in London with her eyes closed. They were still closed now as she moved to the sidewalk, the world spinning. She didn't even thank the driver—though she heard Julius pick up the slack—and breathed deeply through her nose. The cool droplets were helping, and thankfully, her nausea subsided enough to squint as she heard the car drive away.

"Are you alright?" Julius asked.

"Mm-hmm," she croaked, her stomach finally settling.

She widened her eyes and smiled at the concerned expression. Her lids were heavy, begging to close again. She'd been so focused on keeping her awful plane food down that she hadn't realized how tired she was. It made sense. She hadn't slept on the plane. Nor had she slept at the airport. Not that she'd expected to sleep there, considering they only arrived forty minutes before takeoff. However, after numerous delays and cancellations, they'd ended up waiting around for almost ten hours. Had she known that from the start, she certainly would have attempted to nap on the floor.

"Let's get out of the rain," Julius said, smiling back and tilting his head to the side, redirecting her gaze.

Heather swiveled on her heels, and her jaw dropped when she saw their destination. Even in the shroud of midnight, the house was beautiful, narrow but tall, and conjoined with a dozen similar houses, all of which sat in a curved row facing a small section of a much larger park. It was a classic London townhouse, a sought-after piece of property for the uber-rich. It must've been worth anywhere from two to ten million pounds. Possibly even more, she considered, as it, being at the end of the row, was larger than the others and stood out in color and style.

While the rest were white and uniform, this one had been stripped back to reveal a pale red brick, and the door, which was rounded instead of square, was a beautiful duck egg blue. The stairs leading to it were wide at the base, curved into a taper, and flanked by hip-height white stucco walls. There were ivy-wrapped columns, too, holding up the awning, and, as if it wasn't beautiful enough, there were flowers on every windowsill and a perfectly groomed hedgerow bordering the modest, almost non-existent front yard.

"Welcome to Farfalla House," Julius announced, holding the little wrought iron gate open for Heather and ushering her through.

"This is…" Heather trailed off, dumbstruck. Julius's penthouse in Seattle may have been impressive in size, view, and glamour, but this was something else. This had a history and an elegance she didn't see often in America. For the most part, the phrase 'out with the old and in with the new' seemed a foreign concept here.

"I know," Julius replied, a little breathless himself as he jogged past her toward the front door, suitcases in hand. "I'd forgotten how great it is. Just wait until you see the inside. And the garden. Are you up for a tour?" he asked, calling back over his shoulder as Heather meandered.

"Only if you have a caffeine IV handy."

"I can offer you a cup of tea."

"Close enough."

Heather reached the top step, and stared back at the park while Julius fiddled with the keys. He tried three in vain before choosing correctly. "It's been a while," he explained. "Years, actually."

"How can you afford it? I know your salary is, well, much better than mine, but still. It must cost a fortune in upkeep alone."

"I rent it out to tourists, which somehow manages to turn a profit. I then use that to pay for Mum's care home and anything else she needs. Seems about right, considering she bought the place. She gave it to me five years back when her mind started to go."

"So this is all yours?" Heather asked in awe.

"All mine."

"Wow, lucky you. My nana has a similar place in Ipswich, but I don't think I have a hope in hell of inheriting it, considering I've only visited her twice. Not that I want to live in Ipswich, but still."

"Well, you can have this one when this old man croaks."

Heather rolled her eyes. "You're only ten years older than me."

"Which means you'll have a lovely decade in it when you're ninety."

Heather snorted. "Works for me. I probably won't retire before then anyway."

Julius pushed the door open and turned on the lights, and Heather's laughter broke abruptly as silent shock took over. The hall and stairwell were narrow but grand, and everything was bright white except for the mixture of classic and modern decor and the amazing rose-and-merlot-colored fish scale tiles that covered the floor.

"Are those original?" Heather asked, looking down, not wanting to sully them with her muddy sneakers.

"Ish," Julius replied. "They were put in in the 1930s, but the house was built in 1886."

"Over a century old," she whispered before clearing her throat. "Remind me to take photos in the morning to show my parents. They're going through an interior design phase and redoing their apartment in an 'Old English' style. I think it's mostly Mum's idea. The woman is obsessed with period dramas."

"Mine too," Julius chuckled. "Do you always call her Mum, or have I worn off on you?"

Heather paused to think but was too tired to remember. "Who knows. Maybe it's just being in London. I've found that I'm a bit of an accent chameleon. By the time we leave, I'll probably be a full-blown cockney."

Julius barked a laugh. "Oh, I'm looking forward to that."

Heather joined him as she shut the door and found that, unlike more modern buildings, the weather outside was hardly muffled. It was nice, though, and she closed her eyes again, nodding off while standing up like an overridden racehorse.

Julius tapped her arm, causing her to start. "Come on, let me show you around before you collapse."

Heather yawned and nodded. "Alright, but the tour better end with my bed."

"It will, I promise."

"Alright," she said, louder than before, slapping her cheeks and feigning a burst of energy. "Let's go."

Seemingly convinced by her performance, Julius strode past her and veered right through a hallway doorway. With him out of sight, Heather psyched herself up, cracked her neck, and jogged after him. She was soon glad she did. Every room—with tall ceilings, elegant furniture, and historical artwork—was better than the last. The kitchen, in particular, was breathtaking with its glass, greenhouse-esque ceiling and walls. She imagined doing the dishes while looking out at the adorable, walled garden with its koi pond, rose bushes, and firepit adjacent seating area, and thought that even chores might not be so bad in a place like this.

They ventured upward after thoroughly investigating the fully stocked walk-in pantry and the downstairs bathroom with its clawfoot tub and chain-pull toilet. Despite the beauty, Heather began to lag once more and hoped the tour was nearly over as they looked through the bedrooms.

Finally, they reached a particularly grand bedroom. It featured a four-poster bed, sage linens, a bay window book nook that overlooked the garden, and a vase filled with fresh roses. It seemed like the last stop, and Heather's hopes were confirmed when Julius said, "So, this will be where you're staying."

No sooner than he'd finished speaking, Heather was already sitting on the bed, pulling her shoes off and unclipping the gold hoops that Julius had given her for Christmas.

"Just one more thing," he said, extending a hand and pulling her to her feet despite her efforts to go limp and collapse.

"After I sleep," she protested.

"You'll like it, I promise. I had it done up just for you."

She narrowed her eyes and slowly rose. "Alright, but it better be worth it."

Julius smiled, smug. "Oh, it is. Come on."

Muttering and mumbling, she trudged after him once again, her socks leaving wet streaks on the floorboards as she shuffled. They reached the end of the hallway, and he pointed at one door, identifying it as the bathroom, before moving to another. "And this is," he declared as the door swung open, "Your office."

For the third time that day, Heather's jaw dropped. It wasn't like the rest of the house. Not at all. It actually bore a lot of resemblance to Julius's house in Seattle. It was dark, modern, and lit by a variety of warm-bulbed lamps. Most of the furniture was sleek and black, and what wasn't was made of reddish leather. There was a sizeable L-shaped desk in the right corner that hosted a state-of-the-art computer with two monitors, a printer, a fax machine, a landline phone, and a whole bunch of brand-new stationery, all still in their plastic packaging, ready to be unpacked and placed in their holders.

Of course, that was far from everything. There was also a series of filing cabinets pressed against the right-hand wall and a water cooler in the space between them and the desk. On the opposite wall was a roll-down projector screen, and the projector itself was mounted from the ceiling, likely connected to the PC via Bluetooth. As if that wasn't enough, next to a bookshelf, coffee machine, and day bed were a whiteboard and blackboard complete with pens and chalk.

Most importantly of all, right in front of her, in the center of the far wall, was an enormous corkboard. Beneath it was a metal table covered in manila envelopes and piles of paperwork, and pinned neatly to the center were two photos. One was of Katy Graham, the other of Lilly Arnold.

"Wow," was all Heather could say.

"Do you like it?" Julius asked, sounding a little nervous now as her eyes darted around the room. She'd forgotten that he was such a nervous gift-giver, and this was probably the biggest gift he'd ever given.

"It's amazing," he reassured him, turning to hug him before bounding forth into her new investigation space. It was as if he'd reached into her mind and extracted her dream office. It was amazing and far too generous. She turned back at him. "You know I would've been happy with a laptop and a folding table, right?"

"I'm sure you could solve the case sitting on the toilet, but I figured this was more appropriate for someone of your status."

"My status," Heather tutted, lips coiled in amusement. "Seriously, though, thank you. This is crazy. And are those..." she began to ask, gesturing at the paperwork.

"Everything I could get my hands on about Lilly."

"Wow. You know, I almost forgot this wasn't a holiday until now."

"I suppose it can be both. Especially once you solve the case."

"Well, it's definitely the most relaxed I've been staring at a murder victim," she agreed, looking at Lilly's sullen expression. From what Heather had seen of her, she wasn't much of a smiler, unlike the Instagram-obsessed, outdoors enthusiast Katy. Admittedly, the poor thing had little reason to smile. It seemed to Heather—from what little she'd gleaned thus far—that Lilly had been overworked and over-sexualized every day of her life adult life until the night she died. She didn't come from privilege like Katy. She didn't have the protection that lifestyle afforded.

Not that it mattered in the end. Both of them were dead, and it was very possible the same man had killed them. That's why Heather was here. She had to know for sure. She had to know whether her ex-husband, Daniel Palmer, was a killer. More than that, she had to bring these girls justice. She and the institution she belonged to owed them that much. Especially if she could have stopped the man who had done it.

She started flipping through the files, but Julius sidled up and gently removed the folder from her grasp. "Tomorrow," he said. "Bright and early. We'll have crumpets and marmite and get to work."

Heather grimaced. "I don't know about that last part, but tomorrow morning sounds good."

Julius clapped, and all the lamps faded to black, obscuring the women's faces. Heather nodded at them, making a silent promise, before moving toward the light of the hallway, ready to re-energize and begin.

CHAPTER THREE

THE PARTNER

HEATHER HAD ONLY BEEN GONE FOR A DAY OR SO, BUT Gabriel was already missing his biggest ally. It wasn't that he didn't get along with his other co-workers. For the most part, they were a copacetic group. But without Heather around, he found that they were increasingly demanding. Her resting bitch face provided a reflective buffer that his perpetual smile did not, and he was already up to his ears in odd jobs and paperwork.

This was particularly inconvenient considering he had a much more critical task, one that Heather had entrusted him with—the murder of Katy Graham. The plan was to investigate in tandem; he would tackle Katy while she looked into Lilly, and they would come together to figure out if Daniel was guilty of both, one, or neither homicides.

It was a colossal undertaking in and of itself but was made even trickier by the time difference and the secretive nature of the entire endeavor. They couldn't risk unjustly condemning Daniel or getting the media involved, so they were keeping this from everyone, including Tina.

Gabriel had drawn the short stick in this regard because while Heather operated under the guise of an overdue holiday, Gabriel was still working part-time and studying for the other part. Somehow, he was going to have to find the time to sneak up to Seattle and investigate remotely for the most part. Something that seemed downright impossible with everyone looking over his shoulder, making sure he was prioritizing their task and not anybody else's.

Speak of the Devil, he thought, as Amanda approached and clapped him on the shoulders. He hastily swapped tabs, but it was too late; even that gesture looked guilty.

"Looking at porn?" she joked.

"Yeah. Cop on cop. Sexy stuff."

"Gross," she muttered, leaning in to read.

Gabriel huffed, scooching away. Amanda needed glasses badly, and everyone knew it, especially when she was driving, but she always denied the fact. She said that glasses looked lame as if that was a valid excuse. It wasn't as if she was cool to begin with. She was frumpy, loud-mouthed, and lacked the ability to think before she spoke, and her idea of dressing nicely was a slogan t-shirt and cargo shorts. Worst of all, in Gabriel's opinion, was the staunch socks and sandals combo.

He admittedly felt terrible for thinking these things about a person who—while often rude—was never cruel. Still, it was hard not to when she mouth-breathed over his shoulder and ignored loud, clear, and frequently verbal requests for personal space.

"Daniel Palmer," Amanda read slowly. "Who's that?"

"Just an ongoing case in Seattle that caught my eye," Gabriel lied, hoping that would be enough.

"Caught your eye so much that you have..." She paused to count. "Six tabs open about him?"

"It's an interesting case."

"Uh huh," Amanda replied, not convinced but not yet dropping any pennies. "Is it interesting enough to justify not finishing that bike thief report yet?"

"Well, considering that was your case," Gabriel began sourly.

"You helped me catch him. You were there. You took the witness statements."

"But—"

"Dude, I'm drowning in road accident reports after the holidays. Don't make me beg."

"Yeah, yeah. I'll get it done tomorrow."

"So," Amanda said, pulling up a seat. "Tell me about this Daniel Palmer case."

"I thought you were busy."

"I can take five for something so 'interesting,'" she mocked.

"You don't have Google?"

"Come on, humor me. I'm bored. It's been nothing but speeding tickets around here since the Violet Kennedy case."

Gabriel groaned. "Fine. Seven months ago, Daniel Palmer went home and found the front door unlocked. He went inside and discovered his fiancée, Katy Graham, dead in their bed. She had been bound with a phone charger and manually strangled. He was obviously arrested, but there was no evidence, so they had to let him go."

"You're not much of a storyteller."

"I'm not trying to be," Gabriel retorted, wishing she'd go away.

"Any other suspects?"

"Not really."

Amanda faked a yawn. "Boring. He did it. It's always the partner. I can't believe you find this interesting. It's like homicide 101. I've seen it one thousand times."

"I guess I'm interested in unsolved cases."

"The door is interesting," Amanda admitted with a shrug. "It being unlocked implies whoever entered didn't do so by force."

She was right. The door *was* interesting, and he'd been thinking about it a lot. In some ways, an open door was Daniel's only saving grace. Without it, there'd be no doubt that he was the killer, even if he was dressed in jogging clothes. That sliver of entryway opened up an entire world of possibilities. Of course, he could have still done it, but somehow Gabriel believed him. Surely, if he had killed her and wanted to stage a break-in, he'd have smashed a window or busted the locks. Though, would that have drawn too much attention from the neighbors? Regardless, and no pun intended, Gabriel felt that the door held the key to the case.

"You didn't think of that, did you?" Amanda asked smugly, reaching over Gabriel and clicking on one of the tabs.

Before Gabriel could retort, he caught a flash of vivid red through the windows of the station and knew he'd found an easy out of this conversation hell. Betty Barber was waiting for him, wearing her favorite red wool pea coat. It matched her always-perfect lipstick, and upon seeing him, she flashed a movie star smile and bobbed up and down as she waved enthusiastically.

Her platinum blonde hair was in curlers, wrapped up with a silk scarf as it often was during the day. Usually, this was because she made her money on nightshift tips at Dottie's Diner and needed to look her best, but today, she was glamming up for a different reason. It was their one-month anniversary, and they were going on a date.

Gabriel felt like a cartoon with hearts for eyes. Betty was the most glamorous person in town by far. In fact, she was the only woman he knew, aside from Nancy Ellis, who wore high heels on a daily basis. However, Betty didn't wear them because of any sexist stereotypes; she wore them because she loved to dress up. Today, she was wearing black slingbacks with a pom-pom on the toe, and her legs were covered in the type of stockings with a black line down the back. He knew, from experience, that they were attached via a lacy garter belt, and he wondered how he ever got so lucky.

"Ugh, her again," Amanda grumbled, and Gabriel thought that maybe he'd been too harsh on himself for thinking bad thoughts about the woman. "She's always hanging around town, primping and preening. Who the hell is she even waving at? The receptionist?"

Gabriel thought to stop her, but the idea of utter humiliation was too sweet to resist, so he let Amanda keep going.

"I mean, who does she think she is? Better question: *where* does she think she is? We're not in Hollywood, honey, and you flip burgers for a living." Amanda scoffed. "She thinks she's so much better than the rest of us, but I'll tell you, girls like that can't hold down a man."

"Oh really?" Gabriel asked, winking discreetly at Betty, who stopped hopping to light a smoke while she waited.

"Oh yeah. High maintenance, but also cheaters. Can't cook either."

"You just said she cooks for a living."

"Fine, can't do laundry then. Bunch of princesses who peaked in high school. And if I'm honest—"

Gabriel decided to stop her there by standing abruptly. "Well, that's me done," he said. "See you tomorrow, Amanda."

Amanda furrowed her brow as she looked up at him. "Yeah, okay, weirdo."

Triumphant, Gabriel strode toward the exit, and once he was outside, he picked Betty up in his arms, twirled her around, and then laid one on her, not caring about the thick layer of lipstick. He heard cheers through the glass and turned before taking a bow in front of his co-workers. As she regained her balance, Betty curtsied and kissed him hard on the cheek.

Then, Gabriel waved at Amanda, whose reddened face competed with the smear of cosmetics on his cheek. He laughed and turned back to his girlfriend. This was their big debut. Next up was meeting the parents, which was a far more nerve-wracking affair. However, that was still a few days away, so he put it to one side. Today was just about them. With Heather safe and asleep in London, Gabriel had no cares in the world except to make sure their date was a perfect one.

Then, Tina pulled up beside them, adding to his list of cares. She eyed Gabriel suspiciously as she exited her vehicle, one eyebrow raised, and she kept her gaze on him as she approached Betty and stuck out her hand.

Betty shook it enthusiastically. "Hi, Betty Barber. Nice to meet you."

"Tina Peters. Nice to meet you, too. Beautiful coat."

"Thank you!"

Still hardly looking at Betty, Tina stepped toward Gabriel. "Mr. Silva. Knocking off early, are we?"

"I already told you," Gabriel said sheepishly. "Remember I came into your office on Monday? It's our one-month anniversary."

Tina glanced at Betty, softening, but her eyes were still narrowed. Betty didn't quiver or hesitate. "That's right, ma'am," she said. "This one's trying to make an honest woman out of me."

Tina's mouth curled, and though she tried to tamp it back down, Gabriel knew she was won over. "I think it's more the other way around," she replied. "I guess she's what's been distracting you these past couple of weeks?"

"Yup," Gabriel said a little hastily. Betty might've been pre-occupying, especially when it came to daydreams, but it was Daniel and Katy who were the real distractors.

"Well, try to keep the puppy love away from work, and I might just let you sneak out early for month two."

"Thank you," Gabriel exhaled.

"Yeah, yeah. Where are you two going tonight?"

"Dottie's, after we see a movie," Gabriel replied.

Tina tutted. "Doesn't she work there?"

"Yeah," Gabriel replied, understanding her point when hearing it said out loud.

Tina rolled her eyes. "Young men, I swear. My husband's away on business, and I forgot we had a reservation at Luigi's at 7:30. Take that. Tell Luigi it's a gift from me. Say you're employee of the month. Whatever. We've already paid for champagne for the table, so enjoy that too. Somebody might as well."

Tina seemed crabby, likely because she hated it when her husband was further away than a three-minute drive, but Gabriel was too excited to think much about her feelings, and both he and Betty erupted into thankfulness.

Tina waved them off. "Just make sure that damn bike thief report is on my desk tomorrow, and we'll call it even."

As Tina turned her back on them and went inside, he hugged Betty again and held her hand as they walked toward her car. This may have been puppy love, but it felt amazing. No wonder dogs were always so happy.

"So, back to your place so that you can do your hair?" he asked.

"Yep. We can throw on a movie in the meantime and then swing by yours so you can get changed. Do you have a suit?"

"I have two," Gabriel said, faux-proud.

Betty laughed. "Mr. Fancyman over here."

"So, what have you been up to today?" he inquired as he looked into the sunset-lined distance for his keys.

"I actually went on a jog, believe it or not. Mom got me this all-pink set for Christmas and some new kicks. I was winded as hell, but it was great."

"Where did you go?"

"Whitetail Park."

Gabriel's body language must have changed, or he squeezed her hand too hard because Betty slowed and looked at him. "What?"

"Maybe don't go jogging in the park or the woods alone," he responded, screwing his face up, his voice unusually high.

"Why?" she asked, almost laughing.

"I just..." he trailed off, the crime scene photos of Lilly Arnold, propped and posed in Hyde Park, a ribbon around her blue throat, seared into his brain. "It's not safe for a woman. Or for anyone," he hastily added.

"But I hate jogging on the road," Betty pouted. "And come on. I'm more likely to get hit by a car than murdered."

Not in this town, he thought but didn't say. Instead, he smiled and said, "I get it. But maybe bring me along. Or you can join this tracking app. My family uses it." He paused, knowing how it sounded. "Not because I'm jealous or anything. It's just I'm a cop. You know?"

Betty nodded slowly before perking back up. "Yeah. Let's start jogging together. That could be fun. But you're not allowed to make fun of how slow I am."

"Oh, I won't. You'll smoke me, I'm sure."

"Want to test it?" she asked, undoing her grasp and taking off her shoes.

He shook his head in disbelief, but before she could finish counting down, he took off, and she ran after him, cussing and blinding and calling him a cheater. Yet, sure enough, she smoked him.

CHAPTER FOUR

THE DETECTIVE

WHEN HEATHER EVENTUALLY REACHED SEMI-CON-sciousness—after a particularly bizarre dream had sent her running and screaming from dreamland—she had an eerie moment of not knowing or remembering where she was. Even her skin against the sheets felt wrong as she stretched out under the cool linen sheets, and it was only when she opened her eyes to look around the antique-laden room that it all came flooding back to her. She was in London, in Julius's family home. It was Sunday, the 4th of February, and it was an absolutely beautiful day.

She twisted to check the clock in order to continue grounding herself and instead gave herself a minor heart attack. It was already half past eleven. She prayed it was wrong, that no cleaner or guest had bothered to reset it in accordance with years' worth of daylight savings. Yet her body clock told her it was telling the truth. She checked her phone, and sure enough, she had overslept on day one of her investigation.

She stormed down the stairs in her pajamas and complimentary slippers, calling out for Julius, but there was no response. The house smelt faintly of coffee, and his shoes that had previously been in the rack by the front door were gone. He was clearly already up, but the question was: had he left without her?

A breeze whispered across her exposed ankles, and she turned the other way, facing the open kitchen door. She padded toward it, the tiles icy even through the slipper soles, and once inside, she looked out through the conservatory-style windows. There he was, sitting at the outdoor table, reading the paper and sipping from a mug of steaming coffee, fully dressed and groomed, his hair wet from showering.

Knowing there were plenty more slippers where these came from, Heather stepped outside onto the still-wet stone ground. The air smelled of petrichor and damp soil, the birds sang, Julius turned and waved as she stormed toward him. It was hard to be angry in a place so lovely, and she felt her rage dissipate with each stomp until she became mock furious, and he, in turn, deeply amused.

"Something wrong?" he asked.

"You let me oversleep!"

"Would you rather I woke you up? Because in my experience, jet-lagged, over-exhausted people often don't take kindly to that."

"Yeah, I probably would've ripped your face off, but still. Having no face beats missing half a day of work."

"I'm not sure I agree. Especially considering it's my face on the line. Besides, Helen isn't available to meet until 1 anyway."

"I could've started going through the files."

"You have plenty of time, I promise."

Heather grumbled as she collapsed onto the adjacent chair and sucked her teeth as cold rainwater soaked her pants. "Seriously?" she exclaimed.

Julius grimaced. "How about a pillow and a cup of tea before we head to Scotland Yard?"

Heather lit up. "Scotland Yard?" she asked. "I thought that was, you know, in Scotland?"

"Nope. It's right here in London, and today, we'll be meeting one of the most important people there. So, cheer up and be glad you look refreshed. Helen takes no prisoners when it comes to appearance. Or anything really."

Heather scrutinized him, realizing he looked different somehow. "Have you combed your hair?" she asked, noting the lack of curls and how much she missed them.

"As I said, Helen is quite formidable. Even more so than you."

Heather snorted. "I'm looking forward to meeting her. I've never seen you look so skittish."

"Once you meet her, you'll understand."

"Well, chop chop on the tea so I can make myself pretty, too."

Julius immediately rose to his feet and then stopped himself. "On second thought, maybe you could give her a run for her money."

Heather smirked and shooed him before putting her feet up and enjoying her surroundings. Despite the soggy backside, she could get used to this.

———

Scotland Yard, or rather New Scotland Yard, was not entirely what Heather had been expecting. Perhaps she was being a cliche American, but she'd anticipated something more stately with intricate historical architecture, golden lions, and water features. Instead, she was met with a very professional, borderline brutalist five-story office block that wouldn't have looked out of place in Chicago. Apparently, it was about a sixth of the size of the old New Scotland Yard, and the more Julius talked about the old, the new, and 'the great' Scotland Yards, the more Heather's head hurt. Jet lag, as it turned out, was hard to overcome, even with nearly half a day's worth of sleep.

Still, she let him babble, enjoying his reverence for the building and its stripped Classicism, Portland stone annex, and 1935 origins. It was older than Heather had expected—looking to her decidedly 1960s—but she supposed everything here was old, or at least older than the city she'd grown up in. That was, aside from the people and all their creature comforts.

"You know I left before they moved into this building," Julius added after regaling her with the architect's life story. "I've never even been inside."

"How do you know so much, then?" she asked as they approached the sliding glass doors that were clearly a new addition.

"I've been reading," he whispered as they stepped into the building, sounding very much like a kid in a candy store trying his best to remember his manners.

It was then that she realized that he missed London, and painfully so. She figured it must be similar to how she felt about Seattle but without all the horrible memories. There was something about where you were raised that was hard to let go of, and London, being so famously amazing, must be harder than most. Her father, Adrien, had also struggled to let it go despite loving American culture so wholeheartedly. He would become misty-eyed when discussing it, and she often wondered if her parents would have moved back if it wasn't for their desire to be close to her. Like Julius, her father had moved to Seattle for work, but now he was retired, she wondered if his yearning for greener pastures would spur another intercontinental move.

She would understand if he did. Though she wasn't in love with London yet, she had to admit it reminded her how much she'd missed being in a city. It was a little overwhelming, but there was so much life, so much to do, so much to look at. It was both overstimulating and absolutely awe-inspiring. She may have joked with Julius about selling everything and becoming off the grid, farming hermits, but if she was honest, what she wanted was a two-bedroom apartment in a spectacular city. Yet, somehow, that felt like even more of a fantasy.

They approached the front desk, but before Julius could so much as state his name, a booming, jolly voice called out, "Julius Tocci?"

Heather and Julius turned in sync and saw an elderly but stylish man approaching with a hand-rolled cigarette tucked behind his ear. He was wearing a cable-knit forest green sweater, brown corduroy pants tucked into thick socks, and a pair of worn-out combat boots. His face was kindly and covered in lines but had a youthful exuberance that Heather suspected disguised a much older age. This, too, was helped by the fact he still had all his hair—shock silver though it was—with no signs of receding, and his silver unruly beard covered half of his countenance.

"Jonno?" Julius asked, his face erupting into a boyish grin.

'Jonno' jogged forward and wrapped Julius up in a bear hug, which he reciprocated fiercely as if they were brothers reunited at long last. She thought for a second, perhaps they were, but no, the faces were not a match, and neither were their bodies. Where Julius was thickly built like a soccer player, Jonno was wiry to the point of being underweight, and his facial features were fine, pointy, and decidedly mouselike.

After they were done hugging, they turned to Heather, arms wrapped around each other's shoulders. "Heather," Julius declared, no longer whispering, "This is Dr. Jonathan Watkins. He taught me everything I know."

"Call me Jonno," the man rasped before sticking out a hand. Heather took it almost as eagerly as Julius had the hug. She wanted to make a good impression on what was clearly a beloved friend. His hand was calloused and warm and reminded her of old leather.

"You're a forensic pathologist?" she asked, fascinated.

"I am. Best in the biz, they tell me. Or at least I was until this one came along. And who might you be?" he inquired, fixing her with a fascinated expression and a cocked head.

"Heather Bishop," she replied.

"Detective Heather Bishop," Julius added, bragging for her.

"Ah, you're the one who's looking into the Lilly Arnold case," Jonno acknowledged sagely. "She told me you were coming. Though she didn't mention that our Dr. Tocci here would be joining you."

"Who's *she*?" Heather asked, gaze drifting as a striking woman emerged from an elevator.

The woman, at least five foot eleven in heels, wore a black tailored pantsuit and pointed-toe stilettos that looked like torture devices, yet she didn't look uncomfortable. Instead, she glided across the room, her sleek bob of silvery platinum hair shining in the light. What also caught the light was her dewy skin and high cheekbones. Like Jonno, it was hard to figure out her age. Her bone structure and sunken buccal area gave her the look of an aged supermodel, but a supermodel nonetheless. More than her looks, however, what stopped Heather from being able to look away was how everyone moved out of the woman's way as she walked through the busy lobby.

If this was a movie, she'd have her own theme song, Heather thought.

"The witch," Jonno clarified with a phlegmy cough. "Helen Slater." Julius's eyes grew wide, and he shook his head. The woman, unbeknownst to Jonno, was heading straight for them. He continued on despite Julius's evident warning. "Oh, come on, Julius, you haven't lost your sense of humor, have you? In fact, the way I remember it, you coined that nickname."

"That he did, Mr. Watkins," the striking woman, who must've been Helen Slater, answered, her voice clipped.

Jonno seized dramatically, feigning heart trouble. "She's right behind me, isn't she?"

Helen patted Jonno on the shoulder. "Haven't you got a body to attend to?"

"Indeed I do. Lovely to meet you, Heather. Stop by the shop when you can. I'm always there. I have much to discuss with you."

"Still in the same place?" Julius inquired.

"You know it." Jonno waved to everyone and spun to bow to Helen before walking backward to the doors. He popped his smoke in his mouth and lit it just as the door slid open, causing Helen to purse her lips.

"Detective Bishop," she said, smiling tersely as she slowly turned her gaze to Heather. "Welcome to London."

"Thank you for having me," Heather said before flushing. "I mean to Scotland Yard. Not London."

"Well, I'll admit, I said no to Julius at first," Helen responded, using his first name but with a degree of disdain rather than friendliness. "But I did my research and figured, why not give you a shot?"

"Well, I'm very grateful that you have. Maybe I can find something the original investigators missed."

"Considering I was the original investigator, I highly doubt that. But who am I to put ego over the good of a case?"

Julius snorted but disguised it as a sneeze. "Sorry, allergies."

Heather fixed him with a strange look. It wasn't like him to be rude and certainly not childish. Helen hummed and rummaged in her YSL bag, retrieved an allergy pill, and handed it over along with a metal bottle of water. Julius took both and chugged, making sure to get his mouth on the lip, and water ran down his beard as Helen's face shifted into disgust.

He looked self-satisfied as he handed the foil pack and bottle back, and she wiped the lip on her jacket sleeve. They were too overfamiliar for a typical work rivalry, and Heather, as usual, put two and two together. It was her job, after all, and her verdict in this case was sex. Sex that had happened a long time ago, likely without any love, and if there had been affection, it had long since been snuffed out. The fact that it was ancient history, however, did not make her any less jealous, even though she really had no right to be.

Yet, determined to be more professional than her complex but platonic companion, Heather brushed it off and addressed Helen with confidence and good posture. "If I do find a suspect, or better yet, solve the case, what do I do?"

"Well, you don't make an arrest, that's for sure. As far as everyone is concerned, you are a journalist to whom I have allowed access to the case. Suspects and Lilly's loved ones should also believe this. I have already sent your identity file to Julius, so you know what to say should anyone ask."

"Your name is Heather Singh," Julius said flatly, perhaps disappointed with the lack of undercover flair. "You went to Brown. You write for the New York Times."

"And much more," Helen said, with a hint of smugness. "And should you miraculously turn up anything new, you are to contact me with the evidence, and just maybe, I agree with you. Then, and only then, will further steps be taken."

"What if I'm right and you don't agree?"

Something glinted in Helen's steely gray eyes, something akin to fondness. "I didn't become superintendent because I don't listen to my officers. You're a smart girl. I'm sure you'll convince me. Now, you must excuse me; it's lunchtime."

"How about The Thistle & Pig?" Heather blurted. "My treat. You could, I don't know, walk me through Lilly's movements that night."

"My dear, I believe that's your job," Helen replied, but there it was again—that glimmer. It was respect but also gratitude. Here was a case the great Helen Slater had failed to solve, and here was someone ballsy enough to try again. It must've been eating her up inside, being forced to move on and try to forget. Heather knew obsession when she saw it, even when it was buried deep.

Helen checked the time on her Rolex. "I suppose I could change up my routine. I don't think I've had pub food in years, and it is my cheat day."

"Great," Heather said, though it was clear Julius didn't agree with the positivity of the sentiment.

That was where she and he differed. He dealt with the bodies, the facts, the statistics, the science, and the math. They already had all the files, including all the witness testimonies, so to him, that was enough. Yet, Heather knew it wasn't. She wanted to hear Helen's side. She needed to understand why this case was so hopeless, so easily written off after a mere seven years. Julius knew science, but Heather needed humanity, and when Helen took off without a word, Heather followed dutifully like a duckling, and Julius begrudgingly trailed behind.

CHAPTER FIVE

THE DETECTIVE

"A H," Helen exhaled, surprisingly satisfied by her cheap glass of Chardonnay. "This brings back memories."

"She used to come here back when it was first built," Julius informed Heather, his face deadly serious.

"Really?" Heather asked before realizing that he was joking. She'd seen the 'Est. 1864' sign when entering. She excused her shoddy detective skills due to the lingering jet lag and how dis-orientating it was to be back in The Thistle & Pig almost seven years later. It hadn't changed at all; it was still dark and glossy and smelled of an era pre-smoking ban.

"Are you familiar with the phrase 'people who live in glass houses shouldn't throw stones'?" Helen retorted wryly, politely ignoring Heather's question. "That is to say, you're no spring chicken yourself."

Before Julius could reply, Heather interjected, finding their dynamic unpleasant and hard to read. "So, you used to come here?" she asked, addressing Helen.

"I did. When I was young and fun."

Julius snorted. "I'm not sure *fun* is the word I'd use."

Helen ignored him. "But then I got promoted and was expected to drink where the higher-ups did. I'd come back, now and again, for nostalgia's sake, but ever since the investigation... Well, let's just say I try not to think about this place."

"I came here once on holiday," Heather noted, not mentioning that it was on the same day that Lilly Arnold had been murdered. "It's nice," she added.

"It's fine," Julius and Helen said in sync.

"I guess I don't really know much about pubs," Heather admitted, flushing as she sipped her room-temperature beer.

"It's turned into a bit of a nightclub on the weekends," Helen explained. "We get a lot of noise complaints."

"It is nice during the day, though," Julius added, sensing Heather's embarrassment.

"But it's a problem at night?" Heather asked.

Helen nodded. "And its 'popularity' was the first hurdle I ran into while investigating. So many men. Half of them were absolutely besotted with poor Lilly Arnold. The list of men banned from this place while she worked there was as long as I am tall."

"So, I'm guessing the list of suspects was equally long?" Heather asked, retrieving her notebook.

"Yes and no, Miss Singh," Helen said, using Heather's undercover name as the server dropped off their lunches of two fish and chips and a salad. "Honestly, I spent so much time diving into one man in particular that I barely began to touch on the others."

"But you have a list?"

Helen looked down her nose at Heather. "There's no sign-in sheet at a pub, Miss Singh. And considering most people paid with cash..." she trailed off, gesturing for Heather to finish the sentence.

"You have no idea who was there that night."

"Exactly."

As Heather attempted to continue her line of questioning, Helen held up her hand and swallowed down spinach and tomato. Then she cleared her throat. "Save your questions for the end. I don't have time for a back-and-forth."

Heather nodded, Julius grumbled, Helen sipped, and then the story began. On Friday, the 14th of July, Lilly Arnold—who'd been working at the pub since she turned 18 the prior year—had been working the night shift as she did four nights a week; she had a day job working in a second-hand shop and was a part-time student studying cosmetology. Plus, the tips were always better at nighttime, and she needed all the money she could get as she financially and physically supported her mother, Wendy, also known as Didi. Didi had ALS and later passed away in 2019. Helen had personally paid for her to have a live-in carer after her daughter died, and the subject was clearly sore as she moved on quickly.

That night, the 14th, Lilly had been working the bar with her two co-workers and manager, Liam Butler, Poppy Smith, and Greg Daley. The four were close and protective over Lilly, especially on that night, as regular pest Barry Watts had shown up, already drunk. He was particularly obsessed with Lilly but had somehow never overstepped enough to get him in trouble. Up until that night, at least. Though nobody heard what he said to her, it was bad enough to cause her to storm out crying, and Barry was promptly kicked out around 1 a.m., with instructions to never return.

Lilly then pulled herself together and finished the last hour of her shift before leaving at 2 a.m. Poppy and Greg stayed behind to clean up, but Liam left when Lilly did. According to his and Poppy's testimony, Liam had offered to walk her home due to the issues with Barry, but she'd denied the offer and had walked away, a little tipsy, and embarked on her usual journey home through the park carrying a bottle of red. Though the wine was a little out of character, her turning down his offer was not surprising. She considered herself a tough girl, and to her credit—despite being only 5'2" and roughly 115 pounds—she apparently packed quite the punch.

"Why was the bottle of wine out of character?" Heather asked.

"Apparently, Lilly wasn't much of a drinker."

"Maybe Barry got to her more than she wanted to admit."

"That's certainly one theory," Helen replied. "Though, according to her co-workers, she'd been 'off' all week."

"But no one knew why?"

"No. I have my theories, but I want you to make your own assessments. I'm sure if you speak to Dr. Watkins, you'll come to the same conclusion that I have."

"Okay," Heather said slowly, a little annoyed by the vagueness. "And what happened with Barry Watts?"

"Well, as I said, I'd like for you to make your own conclusions. Otherwise, you'll surely end up where I did, no?"

"I guess," Heather replied, trying to disguise her terseness but failing.

"To put it plainly, we had no evidence, witnesses, or DNA. Nothing. We would never have been able to get him in front of a jury."

"But you think it was him?"

Helen smiled coyly from behind her glass.

"Make my own conclusions. Got it," Heather muttered.

"She does this," Julius reassured Heather, patting her knee, half-jokingly. "It's like talking to the bloody sphynx."

Though Helen couldn't see his hand, she must've had x-ray vision, or a sixth sense, because she bristled despite the wedding ring on her left hand.

"All I'm saying," she asserted, chin tilted down, eyes up like a stalking predator, "Is that I don't want to lead such a prize-winning thoroughbred to water and force it to drink stagnant water. How is she ever supposed to discover something from hearing about my dead-end observations?"

"You're right," Heather said, mollifying. "What happened next?"

"Well, if you'll finish slurping your swill, we can do some show and tell."

They finished their lunches and drinks hastily—leaving half of their ample portions behind—and followed Helen once again as she crossed the road into Hyde Park.

"350 acres," Helen called out over her shoulder. "It's lucky that the jogger went so far off course; otherwise, we might've never found her."

Even though the park was blatantly huge, much was hidden by the trees, and Heather found herself taken aback by its measurements, especially considering it was in the middle of one of the most popular cities in the world. As she crossed the street, she also noted two things of interest: the lamps and the street vendors.

"Would they be here at night?" she asked, gesturing to the food trucks.

"They will, and they were. Most of them have been selling here for the past decade. They tend to close up around 4 a.m. when the drunks stumble home. And yes, I did ask, and yes, they did see her. She veered off into those trees there and didn't reemerge before they went home. Some thought she was having a late-night 'picnic' to cool down after work. It was warm that night, and the stars were visible, so it's certainly plausible. What gave me pause, however, was that one of the witnesses saw her checking her appearance in a mirror and applying lipstick."

"You think she was meeting someone?"

Helen shrugged her bony shoulders. "Maybe. No one has ever admitted to it, but it seems likely."

"Did she have a boyfriend?" Heather questioned as they, too, veered from the path and pushed through a dense row of trees.

"Not according to her best friend Poppy, and I suppose she would know. I suppose caring for your mother and working twelve hours a day doesn't allow for much romance."

"Yeah, I suppose it wouldn't," Heather said quietly, feeling awful for the young woman. Talk about being dealt a bad hand.

After ten minutes, they emerged into a small clearing that was completely empty, aside from a metal picnic table that was adhered to a circle of concrete.

"We found her just over there," Helen said, pointing but not looking at the edge of the clearing.

Heather recognized it from the crime scene photos, but it was so different in person. This is why she'd asked for Helen's guidance. Pictures were not the same as seeing something in the flesh. Now she knew how it smelled, how it sounded, how far off the beaten track it was, how poorly lit it was, and how it would rarely be busy. All of a sudden, she could see the body laid out before her, the blood tacky and touchable. It was almost a game before, but now she was transported to that night in 2017. It had been warm, she remembered, and sticky. The mosquitos had been out in droves, forcing them back to the hotel.

Heather wondered why Lilly had chosen this area with no toilets, streetlamps, or even a particularly comfortable place to sit. Was it to be truly alone, or had the person she'd met requested privacy? Maybe sex was the intention, or at least on the cards. That would certainly explain the aphrodisiac bottle of red.

"We found the wine bottle there," Helen said as if reading Heather's mind. She pointed to the concrete slab beneath the bench. "It was broken, but considering how little of it had pooled around the glass, it had been almost entirely consumed."

"And you found her at 5:45 a.m.?"

"That's correct. The assumed time of death is around 4:30 a.m. Just over two hours after leaving work."

"What kind of red was it?"

"Does it matter?" Helen asked.

"I think so."

"Cabernet Sauvignon. 14.5%."

Heather looked at Helen. "Could you drink a bottle of Cabernet on your own in two hours? In *ten*? Especially if you weren't a big drinker."

"No. I couldn't."

"What was her blood alcohol level?" Heather questioned, staring at the spot where the bottle had broken.

"You'll have to ask Dr. Watkins about that one, I'm afraid," Helen replied. "I'm sure you know about the ribbon and the nail polish?"

"Yes. And the makeup," Heather said, directing the information at Julius, who was listening intently. "When Lilly left work, she was wearing heavy makeup, had hoop earrings, and her nails were long, acrylic, and yellow. When they found the body, her makeup had been all but removed and replaced with a doll-like blush. Her earrings had been removed, as had her nose ring, and her nails had been clipped short and painted beige."

"They wanted her to look more natural," Julius said, frowning. "Who would have brought all of that to the park?"

"Someone who isn't an opportunistic killer," Heather said. "Someone who'd been planning this."

"If the killer was someone who was obsessed with her, why would they want to change her so much?" Julius asked. "Surely they liked her as she was."

"Some men get angry when women have autonomy," Helen retorted. "They don't like us for us. They like us for what we could be. They want to control us. Shape us. Save us."

"And if they can't have us, they take us," Heather finished.

"Or, at the very least, we become bitches, sluts, or... witches." Helen glared pointedly at Julius, who had the sense to look ashamed.

"Sorry," he muttered. "I was a stupid kid."

"Yes, you were," Helen said, smirking.

"And the ribbon, was it used to strangle her?" Heather inquired, trying hard not to picture the two of them together.

"No. It was a manual strangulation. He left a lot of bruising. He was likely holding on even after death. I believe the ribbon was used to hide the damage."

"Maybe he regretted killing her."

"Or he wanted her to be young forever," Helen responded, looking younger herself as enthusiasm tinged her expression. Though she quickly composed herself by clearing her throat, it was clear that she was enjoying revisiting her case with somebody new. "And before you ask, there was no blunt force trauma on her body from the bottle. We believe she must've used it self-defensively."

"Interesting," Heather muttered, jotting everything down in her notebook.

Helen checked her watch. "Well, that's my lunchtime over, but feel free to book an appointment with reception should you have any more questions."

"Thank you for your time. This has been incredibly helpful."

A smile flickered across Helen's tightly drawn expression before faltering. "Good luck, Detective. I truly wish you the best. But try not to be too disappointed should you fail."

Helen pushed back through the trees and vanished, leaving them alone with Lilly's ghost as it began to rain. It felt like a bad omen, but a mere storm could not dampen Heather's motivation. Though there was no hope for Lilly's story to have a happy ending, that didn't mean that it had ended. There was so much still unwritten, and she was eager to put pen to page and find a satisfying resolution.

CHAPTER SIX

THE PARTNER

R AIN HAMMERED THE WINDSHIELD OF GABRIEL'S 2018 Dodge Charger that his brother, Matías, had handed down to him as a Christmas gift. It purred like a dream, but either something was wrong with the weather or the wipers because Gabriel—hunchbacked, squinting, chin close to the wheel—couldn't see a thing through the windshield.

Fortunately, his destination was nearby, and he used his GPS to guide him through the monsoon-esque deluge toward Daniel's suburban prison. From what he could see through the persistent splatter, it was clear this was a pricy area. The houses were enormous and, though newly built, possessed a more classic style. This, however, did not answer Gabriel's question: why stay? Here, Daniel was persecuted, loathed, watched, and trapped in his home with the remnants of his dead fiancée. Was it stubbornness? Indignation? Or was he too grief-stricken to leave? Having never met Daniel, Gabriel lacked information, which was why he was there, using his day off to fill in the blanks on Heather's ex-husband.

He'd tried to extract some answers from Heather, but she had garnered very little about Daniel's post-divorce life. Everything she knew had been ascertained from their unpleasant meeting back in December and the news. He suspected her eagerness to go to London had everything to do with that one meeting. She wanted to hold Daniel at arm's length while still investigating him. A tricky task, but she was, as the movies put it, 'too close to the case.' Still, as more and more tourist photos came through, Gabriel feared once again that he had drawn the short straw. At least he had Betty, he figured, and it was important to not attempt long-distance right off the bat. Soon, it would be their turn to head overseas, once he finally got a raise, that was.

Eventually, Gabriel found Daniel's house—number 37—and pulled into the drive. As his car grumbled to a halt, Daniel moved to the window. It was a little unnerving seeing him in the flesh, breathing and moving. There was something nerve-wracking about it, reminiscent of going on Tinder dates after having only seen them in photos. Sometimes, the result was disappointing, but this was the other way around. Photos, especially mugshots, had not done Daniel justice. Julius had warned him about this when Heather popped into the bathroom at Sherwood's. He'd said that Daniel used his good looks for evil to manipulate others, especially women. He'd said this quietly, fearing being overheard, not wanting to offend Heather by implying that she'd been lured in by a pretty face. Julius admitted that even he had, at one point, been taken in by Daniel's charms. However, newer developments—such as his treatment of Heather and the discovery that Daniel had set up Julius's ex-wife with her new husband—had shattered the genteel illusion.

Gabriel ran from the car to the front door, shielding his face and hair from the rain with a notepad. He knocked, and for whatever reason, Daniel took his sweet time opening the door. When he finally did, Julius's warning only rang truer. Gabriel considered himself moderately handsome, Julius downright majestic, and Beau model-esque, but next to Daniel, he wondered why any of them bothered to make an effort. He was just too perfect. Eerily so, in fact. More like looking at a painting than a person. A boring painting at that, lacking character and intrigue, yet he still couldn't look away.

"Hello? Can I help you?" Daniel asked scathingly instead of beckoning his guest inside.

"Hi, I'm Gabriel Silva," Gabriel responded, shoving a wet arm and hand through the gap in the door.

Daniel pressed the door gently against Gabriel's arm, but he looked as if he wanted to apply pressure and crush Gabriel's arm to the point of amputation.

"I'm sorry, I think you have the wrong house," he said.

"Did Heather not tell you I was coming?" Gabriel asked, throwing her name out as a lifeline.

Daniel's expression softened somewhat, but he still held his mouth in a straight line. "She did not."

Dammit, Heather, Gabriel thought. "Oh, well, I'm her partner. Like at work. Not romantically."

Daniel quirked an eyebrow. "Uh-huh."

"I'm going to be helping her solve your case. You know, to find out who really killed Katy."

Daniel chuckled, his entire demeanor shifting as he opened the door wide. "Why didn't you just say that? I was starting to think you were here to rob me or something."

Gabriel looked down at himself and remembered that he wasn't in uniform. It was his day off, after all, but his heavy metal shirt and leather jacket didn't make him look any more reliable than the pimped-out vehicle from his boy racer brother. Still, he slightly resented the implication that he looked like a criminal, even if, next to Daniel, he sort of did.

Daniel, despite spending all day every day at home, was dressed in a crisp white button-up shirt, dark blue slacks, and dress shoes. Gabriel supposed that wearing pajamas 24/7 would get old quickly—for some anyway, not for him—but this was just plain disturbing. It was even worse than lounging around in jeans or wearing shoes on the couch. Gabriel couldn't think of anyone who dressed this formally in the privacy of their own home except for maybe Nancy Ellis, but at least she'd recently fallen in love with fluffy slippers. Even Betty wore sweats in her apartment, and Julius had turned out to be a dorky, matching pajama-set guy. He might've ironed them, but at least Gabriel could picture Julius unwinding, watching TV, and drinking wine. All he could imagine Daniel doing in his spare time was pacing or rigidly standing in a corner like some sort of business ghost.

Gabriel dripped onto the entry mat as he pulled the door shut behind him and looked around the entryway. Heather had told him to expect a lot of Katy's presence lingering in the form of photos, clothes, and feminine decor, but there wasn't a single trace of the dead woman. The walls, still shiny in places, had been freshly painted a dark navy, the shoe rack was full of men's brogues and boat shoes, all men's, and on the coffee table was a stack of books about making money and magazines about the stock market and cryptocurrency. Sure, maybe Katy liked that stuff, too, but the area was far from feminine.

"How about a drink?" Daniel offered. "We'll sit in the sunroom. The rest of the house had just been repainted."

"I can smell that," Gabriel replied. "What caused the change?"

"I guess seeing Heather's offer to help me. It felt like being offered a ladder when stuck in a well. A fresh start. So I decided to make it one by redecorating."

"Fair enough. Nice color."

"Yeah, I never was much of a fan of pastels. Hopefully, once I'm exonerated, I can get someone in to retile everything, too."

"Yeah," Gabriel said. "For sure."

An awkward silence descended as Gabriel's discomfort grew. He hadn't known that Daniel was expecting a guaranteed exoneration, and that applied an extra helping of pressure to the situation. On the one hand, it might stop him from hiding potential closet skeletons if he thought they were on the same team, but on the other, there was a lot of potential disappointment to be had, especially if he was innocent. Gabriel didn't like Daniel thus far, but it was painful to see a broken man resurrected and knowing that you might have to break him all over again.

"So, where's Heather?" Daniel asked.

"In London," Gabriel responded, "On vacation."

Daniel pursed his lips. "With Julius?"

Gabriel felt like Daniel might be the kind of person who could see through lies, so he coughed out a, "Yes," which only caused Daniel's expression to darken more.

"So, this is all on you?"

"No. I mean, I'll be doing most of the legwork, but I'll call her to discuss and..." He trailed off, as Daniel was clearly no longer listening.

Then, he plastered on a brilliant smile. "Well, good for her. She always works too hard. How about that drink?"

"Yeah, um … coffee would be awesome."

"Coming right up."

—

Daniel left Gabriel on his own in the sunroom for quite an extended period of time, giving Gabriel nothing better to do than scroll through the photos Heather had sent and seethe with jealousy. Julius's house was, of course, insane, and ironically, it was sunny in famously bleak and drizzly London, while Seattle was the epitome of gray.

Finally, Daniel joined him, holding two overtly complicated-looking coffees in tall glass mugs. He waited eagerly for Gabriel to take a sip before touching his own. Gabriel obliged but was relieved he didn't need to fake his reaction. It was delicious. Clearly, Daniel had a lot of time on his hands, and this was one thing he'd chosen to master.

"Wow, it's great. Is that chili and dark chocolate?"

"Yep. I'm trying out a lot of subtle palettes at the moment."

It wasn't exactly subtle, but it was tasty, so, needing caffeine, Gabriel took another sip before firing his first question. "So, Katy. When did you meet her?"

"You already know this," Daniel said bluntly. "I'm sure Heather has been seething about it since December. And rightfully so."

"For the sake of my records."

"So it's going to be like this, is it?" Daniel sighed. "May 2018."

"And how did you meet?"

Daniel raised an eyebrow. "I thought you were supposed to be interrogating other people?"

"I can't have any blind spots," Gabriel retorted.

Daniel lifted a hand apologetically. "Of course. Sorry, I'm a little defensive around the police, considering."

"Understood."

"So, I actually met Katy while rock climbing. Not on an actual cliff, mind you. The gym variety. I've always had a thing for sporty, fit women."

This struck Gabriel as odd. Heather was fit, incredibly so, but she was not sporty, and she avoided the gym at all costs. So what had drawn Daniel to her back when they first met?

"She was fitter than most," Daniel continued. "But sweeter than apple pie and enthusiastic about everything. I guess that comes with being young and successful. She was just so optimistic, which was a breath of fresh air. And between you and me, I've always been a sucker for redheads."

"So, she was everything your wife wasn't?" Gabriel asked, a little accusatory.

Daniel shrugged. "Heather was an outlier, but honestly, I'm not as picky as that made me sound. It was just that Katy ticked all of my boxes instead of eighty percent of them."

"So it was a match made in heaven?"

"It was. Though, I sweetened the deal by offering to take her picture. She was only a semi-pro model at the time."

"And when did you start the affair?" Gabriel asked neutrally, pretending as if he didn't care that this man had dared to cheat on his best friend.

"May 2018. Day one."

"Wow," Gabriel said, judgmentally this time, unable to control his tone.

Daniel chuckled and threw his hands up. "Hey, I'm not saying it was the right thing to do, but it's what we did. The chemistry was just crazy; I'd never felt anything like it other than when I first met Heather. And by that point, everything between me and Heather was completely burnt out. You can revive a droopy or thirsty plant, but a blackened one? Nope. And that's what Heather and I were. We weren't just thirsty; we were dead. And all of a sudden, here was someone that made me feel alive."

"Do you ever have any regrets?"

Daniel nodded. "Oh yeah. Plenty. Mainly that I didn't tell Heather on day one. Six months was too long to pretend I still loved her, and she felt it. I know she did. But she was already so fragile and drinking way too much. I guess I was scared to tip her over the edge. And I was scared to see the hurt. So, in the end, I did the cowardly thing and slunk off in the middle of the night. I justified it a thousand ways, but really, I was an asshole, and I wanted to be with the love of my life instead of my wife."

"I appreciate the honesty," Gabriel replied, the transparency endearing him somewhat to the man but not enough. He had to remind himself about what Julius had said, that Daniel could charm the paint off of a boat.

"And your engagement. When did that happen?"

"I proposed maybe two weeks after I left Heather. We were planning to get married in 2022, but she wanted a huge wedding, so we delayed it to 2024 to save up. Buying a house together was expensive enough, so I was happy to wait. Well, maybe happy is the wrong word. I would've married her down at the judge's office on a Tuesday. But I knew she'd never be happy with that."

Gabriel looked into Daniel's eyes, scrutinizing. "You really loved her, huh?"

"I did."

"Good relationship?"

"Always."

"Good sex?"

Daniel smirked. "Daily."

"Arguments?"

44

"Never."

"And the day she died?" Gabriel asked.

"Exactly how I told it. I went for a jog at 2 p.m. on Sunday, July 2nd. I stopped to grab lunch for both of us at Subway. The workers—Paul and June, I think—testified to that. I ordered two Italian meatball subs as usual. It took extra long because they were out of black olives, and that was Katy's favorite topping on anything. Their restock guy arrived at 2:45 p.m., and I texted Katy around 2:30 to say why I was going to be late. She didn't reply, which wasn't unusual. She had a lot of hobbies— yoga, baking, embroidery, writing poetry, you name it, she did it. She worked long hours as a model, so on the weekends, she packed everything in and was occupied from dawn till dusk. Honestly, she wasn't much of a texter, either. She was hard to get ahold of, to be honest, but I liked that she wasn't clingy. I like that about Heather, too. Then I jogged back with the sandwiches, got home at 3:22 p.m., and found the door unlocked and slightly ajar. There was no mud, footprints, or anything broken, but the open door was weird. It had a latch, so it locks automatically if you pull it shut, which I could've sworn I did."

"No Ring doorbell to back this up?"

"Believe it or not, the HOA banned them. They thought cameras might make possible homebuyers wary about the crime rates."

"And none of them saw anything?"

"Apparently not."

"That's—"

"Weird? Yeah, it is if you don't live here. I guess that's why everyone thinks it's me because surely, they would've noticed an altercation or a stranger in the area, but I don't have nosy neighbors. Everyone here is young with kids. They're way too busy to be spying from behind the curtains."

"And if she let the killer in peacefully, then there'd be nothing to pull focus."

Daniel nodded. "Exactly. Which is why I think she did let them in. If they had a key and entered without permission, surely she would have screamed."

"Unless they snuck up on her. She could've thought they were you," Gabriel said, but upon noticing Daniel's visible discomfort, he kept the conversation moving. "So, what happened when you entered? If you're okay to continue."

"I'm fine. I've told this story so many times it feels like nothing. It's the theorizing that gets to me. That feels fresh, you know? It's not just a rehash."

"I get it," Gabriel sympathized, hearing how constricted the other man's voice had become.

"Anyway. I had a bad feeling, which only got worse when she didn't respond. So, I made my way to the downstairs bedroom with 911 on speed dial in one hand and a walking stick in the other." He paused to laugh bitterly. "As if I could've taken him. I'm a big guy, but I've never thrown a punch. But yeah, the downstairs bedroom. I don't know why I went there. I think I was hoping that she was just taking a nap. It's usually a guest room, but we used it during summer heatwaves because it stayed cool, even in the day." Daniel inhaled sharply. "I found her unconscious in bed with her wrists bound and her neck bruised. I was in denial that she was dead and called an ambulance instead of the cops. Eventually, they got someone down here to pronounce her dead and then came the cops to arrest me. Despite being in shock, they interrogated me for hours, then they released me, yada, yada, yada, and now we're here."

"We are. Is there anything else I should know?" Gabriel asked as his phone buzzed. He apologetically checked it; Betty was asking him to come over. "Crap," he muttered.

"Girlfriend?" Daniel asked.

"Yeah."

Daniel chuckled. "Well, I think that's everything. So, you head on home to your girl. If I think of anything, I'll call you." Daniel held out his hand, waiting for something Gabriel realized was a card after an embarrassingly long pause.

"Here you go."

"Thanks. And I recommend you talk to Katy's sister, Suzie Graham, her best friend, Lola Price, and her ex-boyfriend, Shane Gibson. Just pretend to be a journalist. They're all fame-whores, but hate the cops."

"Good to know."

"I'll send you the first two's numbers, but Shane is up to you, my friend. The guy is a mess and hard to track down, so good luck."

"Was he still in contact with Katy?" Gabriel asked, a little confused.

"I'm sure of it," Daniel replied coldly.

Gabriel frowned. "Wait, do you think Katy was having an affair with her ex?"

Daniel's face betrayed nothing as he slowly stood. "All I'm saying is that her girlfriends might know a lot more than I do." He reached for their mugs and opened up the sunroom door. "I'll be seeing you soon, Mr. Silva."

CHAPTER SEVEN

THE DETECTIVE

AFTER A LOT OF RESEARCH AND ANOTHER EXCESSIVE sleep, Heather was finally feeling fresh. Earrings on, hair down, and dressed in a funky abstract jumpsuit and yellow high-heels, Heather was confident that she looked the part of a millennial journalist. She had initially opted for all black or a skirted pantsuit, but Julius was adamant that that wouldn't go down well amongst the hip Londoners and young people living on tips. She needed to look professional yet funky, intelligent yet relatable, and as far away from narc as possible.

Julius was also in disguise as Heather's loyal assistant. So he'd softened his usually chic, attention-grabbing look for something softer: a gray sweater, black jeans, and beat-up dad-style sneakers. Heather was somewhat jealous. She hated being the center of attention, but as she tucked her middle-parted locks behind her ears, she had to admit she liked the look, even if she didn't look like herself. It was undoubtedly an improvement on the last time she'd gone undercover.

Instead of filling her pockets, she'd also donned a large tote bag from a cute, eco-centric boutique to put her belongings in. It was made of hemp and covered in a mushroom print that conflicted with that of her outfit, but upon seeking reassurance, Julius reassured her that people in their twenties didn't care so much about clashing. Fashion sins were out; fashion fun was in.

For some reason, she trusted him, even though he was older than she was, and as she pushed open the door to The Thistle & Pig and looked around at the Sunday evening clientele, she realized he was right. She'd never seen so many novelty earrings or funky socks. There were plenty of nondescript old geezers, too, and a couple of pasty, Royal-looking young men wearing suits, but generally speaking, everyone looked just as fun as she did.

She approached the bar with a smile, and a young woman with dark hair twisted into what Heather believed were called 'space buns' greeted her enthusiastically. "Hi, what can I get you?" The young woman paused, looking her up and down. "Ooh. Cute jumpsuit, where'd you get it?"

"Oh, a vintage store down that way," Heather replied, pointing abstractly. "I love your earrings. Are they little wine bottles?"

"Sure are. Made them myself," the girl replied proudly.

"They're great."

"Are you American?" the girl asked, wonder in her eyes.

"We both are," Heather replied, beckoning Julius over. To Heather's surprise, the girl hardly gave him a second glance. Today, all eyes were on her.

"Tourists?"

"Not exactly. I'm actually here on business."

"Here as in the pub or London?"

"A bit of both. I'm a true crime journalist," Heather said, feeling a little dirty. She knew there were plenty of amazing journalists out there. Unfortunately, she had also met more than her fair share of vultures.

"Oh, cool," the girl replied with genuine enthusiasm, which was a relief until her face fell. "Wait, are you here about Lilly?"

"You knew her?"

"She was my best mate. Name's Poppy," the girl said, sticking out a hand.

"Ah, I've read your witness testimony," Heather replied, shaking. "Do Liam and Greg still work here by any chance?"

"They do. If you hang about, we can take fifteen and have a chat with you. The trainees need to find their legs anyway. Why not today? Bottle of red sound okay?"

"Sounds perfect."

"My type of woman," Poppy enthused. "Take a seat at that reserved booth; that's our spot. We'll all be out in a minute." She paused, shaking her head, jewelry swinging. "You know, it's mental; not one person has tried to write a story on her murder. Not properly, anyway." Poppy was starting to babble, and Heather could practically hear the adrenaline coursing through her veins as her hand began to shake.

"Well, at least I'm here now," Heather said kindly, "No rush."

"That was easy," Julius muttered as Poppy flew through the staff door.

"I guess if my best friend had been murdered and no one seemed to care, I'd be happy to talk too," Heather said, leading the way to the large corner booth. "I hope they won't be too disappointed when there's no story."

"Well, maybe there will be. I have contacts. I'm sure somebody could write something based on your notes."

That eased Heather's twisting, guilt-ridden guts, and she nodded as she sat. "Yeah, good idea. Even if I don't solve it, she should—"

"You will," Julius said, sliding in beside her. He didn't even have the chance to further inflate her ego before three people emerged, holding a bottle of red and five glasses. Poppy looked over to the three nervous young employees standing at the bar and gave them a thumbs-up before plopping herself down.

Still running on nervous energy, she filled all the glasses and slid them around the table with skill as her co-workers sat down. As they made themselves comfortable, Heather took a minute to get a good look at each of them.

Poppy was clearly young, early to mid-twenties, with a doll-like face complete with rosebud lips and big, round, pale blue eyes. She had at least six piercings on each ear and a nose ring. Her top was low cut, and Heather could see her sternum and collarbone clearly due to her lack of body fat. Two of her fingernails were stained yellow from smoking. People smoked a lot in the UK, Heather had noticed. There were smoking areas everywhere. It seemed to be dying out in America aside from in poorer rural areas, but even among the wealthy here, cigarettes were all the rage.

Liam—who had a cigarette tucked behind his ear just like Jonno—was probably the same age but seemed a little bit older due to the bags under his eyes and the lines on his forehead. He also possessed the style of an old punk with his DIY tattoos, buzzcut, and obscure band t-shirt with holes and tatters all through it. He didn't smile or look up as he reached for his drink and grunted a hello.

Greg, the manager, was clearly the oldest of the three and definitely the least edgy. He had long brown hair, wire-rimmed glasses, and a goatee that seemed accidental due to the patchiness on either side. He reminded Heather of videos of Woodstock attendees, and the marijuana smell and patchwork poncho did nothing to dissuade this impression. He, unlike Liam, smiled wide and shook hands with enthusiasm.

"Nice to meet you, everyone. My name is Heather Singh, and I'm a journalist with the New York Times," Heather announced as everyone nodded in reverence. Clearly, that newspaper had made it across the ocean in the same way the BBC and all of its excellent programming had made its way to them. "And this is my assistant, Julian." No need for a last name there, she'd decided. Nobody was going to Google the assistant.

"And you're looking into Lilly's death?" Greg asked, wide-eyed, eager.

"I am. The case caught my attention when I was last in England, and I remembered her the other week, for whatever reason, and was disappointed to see the case had gone cold. My boss needed a story, an interesting one, and I thought, perfect. I get to kill the bee in my bonnet and maybe bring this poor woman some justice. Or, at the very least, apply pressure to the police to reopen the case."

Poppy made a sound somewhere between a sob and a sigh. "Sorry," she squeaked, hand over her mouth. "I just thought everyone had forgotten about her."

"Except us," Liam added, his voice deeper than expected, and he glanced up at Heather momentarily before staring back into his glass.

"So, Heather, how long have you been looking into the case?" Greg asked. "I saw you in here with Helen Slater yesterday."

"Only a day or so," Heather admitted, although it was a lie. "I've managed to get my hands on a lot of the reports, but all that official stuff doesn't paint much of a picture. So, I thought it best to start here, at her place of work, with her friends."

"Quite right," Poppy said, sounding posher than she was for a second in her faux indignance. "We were the ones that knew her best, and I think the cops only spoke to us once!"

"So, what can you tell me?" Heather asked, rummaging for her notepad and recorder. "Do you mind?"

Knock yourself out was the general consensus, and then the information began. Poppy took the lead, Greg input plenty, and Liam added bits and pieces. All of it was valuable, regardless of quantity or enthusiasm.

Their story matched Helen's to a tee, which was a promising start. Lilly had been jumpier than usual. She'd rushed out at 1 a.m. after an unpleasant encounter with Barry and had left officially at 2 a.m. with a bottle of wine. They, like Helen, had no idea what the man had said to her but had quickly barred Barry, and Liam had offered to walk her home at the end of the night while the others cleaned. Poppy had witnessed this and could attest to this rejection.

Then came the new information, the kind of knowledge lesser cops struggled to get their hands on, and if they did, they overlooked it. Yet, to Heather, the devil was in the details. Not only did Lilly rarely drink, but she'd hardly drunk for weeks. It was giving her 'hangxiety' apparently, and considering her father had been a raging alcoholic—something she blamed for her mother's rapid deterioration—and the drunks that surrounded her, she'd started to consider booze as poison. Still, no one thought much of it, as it had been a bad night, and everyone needed to blow off steam now and again.

Before Heather could ask questions, everyone jumped on top of each other to volunteer further information. Despite mostly being perturbed by her creepy admirers at the bar, Lilly was known to be somewhat promiscuous and a little naive when it came to men. She often had much older boyfriends, many of whom pretended to be photographers or model scouts and claimed they could make her famous. That's what she wanted: fame, money, comfort. The ability to buy her own place and put her mum in a great assisted living facility. No one said this with any judgment, but the concern was apparent. Apparently, there were too many boyfriends to count, and none of the group could name any of them. Lilly would regale her friends with stories of dining at The Ritz, but other than that, the details—names specifically—were kept private.

Then, as everyone finished their first glass of red, a shadier side to the story appeared. They seemed hesitant to discuss it until Poppy finally spat it out; Lilly was an escort. Full service, not the legal kind. She worked for an agency owned by a madam named Vicky Chapman. Lilly was paid well, they begrudgingly admitted, and seemed happy with her work. She was even considering quitting bartending altogether and was interested in becoming part of a brothel. Considering Lilly was only 18, this deeply concerned her friends, but their worries fell on deaf ears. It was obvious that she cared little for her safety so long as she was financially comfortable. Heather asked for more information, but once again, they didn't know the names of any of the men, though she was certainly in high demand.

"She was out with them three nights a week," Poppy said. "We didn't tell the police because we didn't want her name to be dragged through the mud. Didn't want people blaming her for what happened. In retrospect, that was a big mistake. It was probably one of them that did it."

"Did anyone know about all of this besides you, the clients, and the madam?" Heather inquired.

"I don't think so," Poppy replied. "Though the designer goods might've given it away."

"I get why she did it," Liam muttered. "She knew all these blokes were obsessed with her. Why not capitalize on it?"

"You know manic pixie dream girls?" Poppy asked. "Like from the movies."

Heather nodded. "Yeah, like *500 Days of Summer*. That sort of thing."

Poppy nodded back as she drained another glass of wine and puffed on her vape. "Yeah. She was that, but in real life. If you ask me, it was a curse. I have enough creeps looking my way, but she had it ten times worse and went between loving it and hating it. Everybody loved her. I've never seen anything like it. Even Liam had eyes for her, didn't you?"

Liam stiffened but spoke, "Yeah, 'spose I did. Ages ago. We were only mates, though."

"They really were," Poppy insisted, realizing she might've misspoken and revealed too much. Unfortunately, it was too late for Liam. His body language and proximity to the victim alone had landed him on Heather's list, and adding a crush into the mix underlined his name. Sure, he was nowhere near as suspicious as Barry Watts, but she hadn't flown thousands of miles to overlook valid possibilities.

"I'm sure," Heather said regardless, doing her best to reassure everyone. "Now, I know you have to get back to work, but before you go, do any of you recognize this man?"

Heather retrieved a slightly crumpled photo of Daniel from her tote and passed it around the table. The three inspected it closely—looking at it together and separately—before passing it back.

"Don't think so," Greg said.

"Nah," Liam added.

"No, I don't recognize him," Poppy said. "But it was so busy that night. As you might've read, we could barely list any patrons. Maybe try asking the vendors instead. Eyes like hawks, that lot. I had a stalker once, and one of them jumped over their own counter to give him a bollocking."

Heather smirked. "Will do. Now, here's my number if you think of anything else. And thank you so much for speaking with me. I'll have my assistant drop off some release forms later in the week."

Pleasantries and thanks were exchanged, and the trio returned to work while Heather and Julius continued to sip their drinks, side-eyeing each other and trying to keep their excitement under wraps. It was an enthusiastic, informative start, and though Heather could see why it was a tricky case to solve—considering seemingly every man in London wanted Lilly—it still felt like a long jump in the right direction.

CHAPTER EIGHT

THE PARTNER

"**A**NOTHER JOURNALIST," SUZIE GRIPED, MORE TO Lola than to Gabriel. "I think I've lost count of how many I've spoken to. This country seems to be obsessed with death."

"No kidding," Lola said, putting her foot up on a park bench to tie her shoelaces.

This had been going on for a while. As it turned out, the women he'd been instructed to speak with were also best friends, which made things somewhat easier and much more difficult. Apparently, they, along with Katy, had been the unbreakable trio. As a result of this closeness and the fact that they were over being interviewed, they answered his questions by talking to each other. Despite happily inviting him along on their walk through Kerry Park and grabbing him a coffee, it was as if he didn't exist.

For example, he'd opened with, "How well did you know Katy?"

And Lola—a vegan chef from LA—had addressed Suzie and asked, "How well didn't we know her?"

The pair had laughed and gone on to explain that they knew her inside and out. There were no secrets between them. It was a slightly frustrating line of answering, but ultimately, it got the job done.

"So, what makes your story different?" Suzie—a chiropractor for animals—asked. "There's already been so many."

"Well, I've read them, and they all say the same thing. There's no detail. No one talks about who Katy was. They talk about the crime, about the investigation, and then they tack on a picture of her and Daniel and call it a day. I want to write something deeper. I want this to be an in-depth cover story. I want this to go viral. I want people to know who Katy Graham was and not just how her story ended. I want to keep her story going."

Gabriel had been listening to a lot of Second Deaths—Crime Time's competitor and sister podcast—and hoped it wasn't too transparent. Clearly, it wasn't because the women cast looks at each other that could only be translated as approving.

"Now, Daniel has told me a lot," Gabriel added, doing his best to sound like somebody else. "But you knew her longer."

"A lot longer," Suzie said. "I'm her older sister."

"And we met in kindergarten," Lola added before nodding at Suzie to take the lead.

"I'm a writer," Suzie added. "As a hobby, but I'm pretty good. I'll send you everything I know about her and everything I think is worth mentioning, but for today's sake, I'll give you the rundown. Katy was an outgoing tomboy. If there was a sport, she played it. If there was an afterschool club, she was in it. If there was a Girl Scouts badge, she had it. If there was somebody needing a friend, she extended a hand. She had a huge friendship group. One we could barely dream of."

"We're introverts," Lola explained, dreamily flipping her beach-blonde locks over her shoulder.

"And homebodies," Suzie agreed. "We're pajama girls. But Katy was up and at 'em. She had so many hobbies I lost track. And she was an incredible model, as well as a very beloved vet tech."

"And she volunteered at the animal shelter."

"She sounds great," Gabriel said, typing as fast as he could on his phone, unable to write with a pen while walking.

"She was perfect," Suzie corrected gently, a faraway look in her eye. "When we all lived together in LA, we had so many rescue animals. Then, she came up here to visit our grandparents, met Daniel, and the rest is history. I followed her up here."

"And I followed them both," Lola laughed. "I love it. Not as much without her, though."

Suzie shook her head. "No. But it's too expensive to move back. So I guess we're stuck here with her ghost, which isn't so bad. I'd hate for her to be lonely. We talk to her sometimes, you know. Have you heard of dowsing?"

"Yeah, my mom is into that sort of thing," Gabriel replied, but not wanting to lose focus, he asked, "Are you close to Daniel?"

"No," the women replied in sync, casting furtive glances at each other.

"And don't think we haven't tried," Suzie clarified, looking at Gabriel for the first time. "Me and my family. But Daniel is controlling. He likes to have things all to himself."

"He's jealous," Lola said, a little colder than Suzie, not trying so hard to play nice. "He was jealous of us. Of her ex-boyfriends. Even of her AA group. Which is ridiculous." She also looked at Gabriel, waiting for him to agree.

He nodded hastily. "That does sound extreme. So, Katy was in AA?"

"Yeah. When did she get sober?" Suzie asked Lola.

"2017," Lola confirmed. "A year before she met Daniel. She'd just broken up with Shane—"

"Finally," Suzie groaned, tightening her ginger ponytail, her nose scrunched as if she'd smelled dog crap.

"Would you say she was vulnerable when she met Daniel?" Gabriel questioned.

"Oh yeah," Lola said. "She was really broken and was just getting out there again when he scooped her up. She didn't even know he was married and was devastated when she told us. We told her to dump his ass, but she of course she didn't."

Suzie pursed her lips. "And she must've told him what we said because he was always prickly after that."

"I hate to ask, but do you think his jealousy was ever founded?"

The women shook their hair, their matching earrings jangling.

"No," Lola said. "Never."

"She would never cheat," Suzie clarified. "Never, ever. She was a true romantic. And she loved him to death, even if we didn't."

Gabriel continued to type, his fingers cramping. "And their relationship, aside from the jealousy, did it seem good to you?"

The girls hummed, looking at each other again before Lola spoke. "Well, he certainly doesn't compare to our partners."

"In what way?"

"Well, my boyfriend loves my family," Suzie began. "He's friendly. He posts about me on social media. He incorporated Lola's husband and my disabled younger brother into his friendship group and takes them on fishing trips three times a year."

"Yeah," Lola continued. "My husband loves everyone, and he doesn't hide me away. He's a feminist. He lets me speak my mind."

"And Daniel isn't like that?" The silence answered Gabriel's question, so he asked another. "Do your husbands like Daniel?"

More silence followed until Lola finally spoke. "I feel like Daniel wanted a diminutive housewife. He wants control. You've met him. I'm sure you can see the effect he has on people and how he uses it to his advantage."

"I can see that," Gabriel admitted, telling the truth but also saying what they wanted to hear. He hesitated but pushed the conversation further. "Do you think he was abusive?"

"Not that we know," Suzie said in a way that didn't sound like a yes or a no. "She was certainly reserved toward the end.

And when we did see them together occasionally during the holidays, they seemed tense and awkward. But, I suppose, a difficult relationship does not a murderer make."

"So, you don't think he did it?" Gabriel inquired, surprised, considering their disdain.

"I really don't know. He's certainly on my list, but I highly recommend you speak to her ex-boyfriend, Shane. If it wasn't some random home intruder, he's my next best guess. Not that I know where he is. Haven't seen or heard from him since they broke up."

"Thank you, I'll look into that."

"Well, it's time for hot yoga, so we have to leave you," Suzie said, perking back up. "But I like you, and I believe you can tell this story. We will be in touch. What's your e-mail."

He blinked. "Matiassilva37 at gmail."

"Great, we'll see you around, Matiás. I have a lot more to tell you about my sister and some pictures that you can use that don't include that awful husband of yours. I am the executor of her estate, after all. Let me know, and I'll schedule a Zoom with my parents, too."

"Awesome," Gabriel enthused. "Thank you so much for your time."

The women left him as they'd joined him, pretending he didn't exist, but he didn't mind. Caffeine and knowledge coursed through his veins, and though it curdled in his empty stomach, he felt like maybe he could do this after all.

CHAPTER NINE

THE DETECTIVE

THE NIGHT AIR BLEW GENTLY THROUGH THE GAP IN THE double-hung office windows as Heather and Julius scoffed down slices of wood-fired pizza and pinned photos to the corkboard. Despite the time of year, it was lukewarm outside—a definite fluke considering their location—and Heather was content in her favorite sweatshirt, basketball shorts, and tube socks. With her hair in a ponytail, she looked and felt like herself again and was able to slip back into detective mode and let Heather Singh rest for the day.

Julius, who wearing a similar outfit, stood shoulder to shoulder with her, a slice of pepperoni in one hand and a picture of Liam Butler in the other. "Where does this one go?" he asked.

"Top left."

"Are they in any particular order?"

"Yes, but not in a way I can explain," Heather laughed. "It's sort of a gut feeling. I look at them, and then I know where they have to go. There's not really a reason, but if they're in the wrong place, it bugs the hell out of me. Victims are normally central but not always."

"I think I understand. It's the same with me and my tools. There's no real reason for my favorite scalpel to be on the far right with the blade facing inward, but it has to be, or else my skin crawls."

"Good to know that I'm not alone in my neuroticism."

"You certainly are not. There are millions of us. We have meetings. You should come."

Heather snorted and pinned Barry Watts' mugshot on the bottom right of the board. "I'll pencil it in."

"It's fascinating to watch you work."

"Huh. I never thought about the fact that you wouldn't have seen my side of an investigation."

"I only ever see the inside of a laboratory and a courtroom. The rest is a mystery to me."

"Have you ever been to a crime scene?" Heather asked.

"Only once," Julius replied, polishing his spectacles. "A long time ago. I find it's better if I don't. If I see the scene, I might come to my own conclusions and fail to remain neutral when writing the autopsy report. I might miss things because I'm so focused on proving the investigators' theory or because I saw the bloodied pipe and not the vial of poison."

Heather's eyes widened. "I never thought about that before. Has that ever happened to you?"

"Luckily not, but it happens all the time."

"And your job, all the bodies..." Heather trailed off. "Sorry. I've always wanted to ask."

"It can be harrowing," he admitted. "But it's easier to compartmentalize in a clinical condition. It seems less real."

Heather nodded. "This part feels the same way. Like I'm playing some messed-up game. It's only when I'm onsite and see it, smell it, and taste the copper in the air that it all sinks in. Even then, it probably doesn't hit me hard enough."

"You're not as cold as you think," Julius replied warmly.

"Maybe not anymore," Heather said, a little bitterly, sad smile flitting across her face. "I thought it would be the opposite, like a healing scar, but it's more like having a bum hip. It just gets more painful the older I get. I think there's something wrong with me."

"Maybe you're not burying it all as deeply as you used to. It's easier for ghosts to climb out of shallow graves."

"Yeah, you're right. It makes me want to quit sometimes."

"What about right now?"

Heather shook her head. "No. Despite Daniel, this whole cold case thing is easier. Without a body to look at, it's not as painful, and without weeping loved ones, a race against the clock, or the media in my face, I can actually take my time and concentrate."

"You sound like you prefer it."

"I don't know. Maybe I'm just burnt out on the alternative. Not that it matters. I'll be back to usual soon enough. Not much use for a cold case detective in Glenville."

"Yeah, I guess not," Julius replied, watching with intrigue as Heather pinned the last photo and began to pace.

"This helps me think," she explained.

Julius smirked, sat on the reclinable day bed, and reached for another slice of pizza. "Are you ready to tell me what you're thinking?"

Heather glanced at the board and nodded. "So, here we have three suspects, which would normally be great, but there's clearly a hell of lot more players to put on the board."

"Half of the men in London, apparently," Julius mumbled, covering his full mouth.

"Yup. But let's focus on what we do have. So, there's Liam Butler. He had a crush on her and left at the same time as she did. He could have followed her when she said she wanted to walk alone."

"But why kill her?"

"Rejection is the obvious motive. As you might have noticed, men don't take too kindly to being turned down. Hey, maybe he followed her, and she emasculated him somehow. She was likely drunk, and maybe he pushed her too far. Maybe he leaned in for a kiss and got slapped. Lots of things could have happened, and it's important not to overlook the innocent ones. I've made that mistake before. He looks fit, too. Lithe. Not that he needed to be strong, considering how small she was, but he would've needed to be fast. Her high school report said she exceeded in track, and she wore sneakers and comfortable clothing every day to work. She'd be able to move if it came down to it."

"The wine might've slowed her down, especially if she wasn't a heavy drinker."

Heather turned and smiled at him. "Did Gabriel coach you?"

Julius pulled an innocent expression. "I don't know what you mean."

"Oh yeah? He didn't mention anything rhyming with schmevil's schmadvocate?"

"Considering those aren't rhymes—"

Heather waved him off. "Anyway, it's a good point. If she was drunk, she would've been easier to attack. However, I have a feeling she shared it with someone else, which would probably have made her buzzed rather than drunk unless she was on medication."

"Do you have her toxicology report?" Julius asked.

"Only the prelim, as it turns out, which isn't very thorough and was made by a different forensic pathologist. Dr. Watkins—"

"Jonno wants to meet us tomorrow now that you've gotten the okay from Helen," Julius interrupted.

"Great," Heather exhaled before continuing to wear a groove into the floorboards.

"Maybe she was drugged," Julius suggested.

"Maybe, but that would be tricky considering they were drinking from the bottle. I guess we'll find out tomorrow. But for now, let's move on to Barry Watts."

"I know one shouldn't judge a book by its cover, but..." Julius trailed off, gesturing at the mugshot with grimace.

"It's tempting, I know," Heather acknowledged, looking at the seedy-looking figure. "And in this case, it's warranted."

Barry Watts was a bad man. Everyone in the area seemed to know it, too. There were plenty of reports about him being a general nuisance and a fair few arrests, too, including but not limited to intimidation, drunk and disorderly conduct, and spousal abuse. None had ever landed him in prison, but he was certainly well acquainted with the drunk tank.

And Julius was right that he looked 'bad.' He was the kind of man somebody might cross the road to avoid, especially on a dark night. He had heavily receded but long, oily hair that he combed over and wore in a low ponytail, which might've been okay on its own, but when combined with saggy but beady eyes, sallow skin, a horseshoe mustache, and patchy stubble, it looked downright creepy. His wrinkly but muscular and oddly bronzed body was covered in blurry blue tattoos, likely hand-made and designed to make him look tougher during his years spent in basements as an illegal bare-knuckle boxer. He'd retired a while back, but Heather still wouldn't want to mess with him.

Julius's look of disgust furthered as Heather told him all about Barry Watts. "I think I like the book's inside even less than the cover."

"Yeah, me too. And combined with Helen's conviction, he's my focus for now. That is if I can find him. Nobody knows where he lives anymore, but he's definitely alive according to these CCTV photos." She picked up a wad of printed-out stills before slapping them back on the table.

"So he's your number one?"

"So to speak."

"And then it's Daniel?"

Heather hesitated and sighed. "Yeah. I mean, as much as I hate to admit it, that's why we're here. It feels positive that nobody recognized him. We'd been there earlier that day, but he people-watched while I went up to the bar. I'm sure they would've remembered his face if he'd gone back in alone. Everyone remembers Daniel."

"They did say they were swamped."

"And he could've waited around outside, I know. Maybe he actually was jogging and spotted her walking home. Who knows?" Heather paused and threw up her hands. "And talk about fit and fast dudes. Daniel is a marathon runner."

Julius hummed and furrowed his brow. "How long was he gone for?"

"Two hours, I think. I was half-asleep, but I vaguely remember him coming and going."

"Do you remember the time?"

"No," Heather admitted. "Had I known how important it would end up being..." She groaned. "I was half asleep and jet lagged, and it was nearly seven years ago, but I'm still beating myself up."

"Did he seem in distress when he got back? Or bloodied?"

"I heard him get in, but I didn't look up. He told me he was going to take a shower, as he always did after jogging, and I went back to sleep."

"All three men are physically fit," Julius noted. "Which doesn't mean much unless we know for sure that she tried to run," he added, sounding a little embarrassed.

Heather swiveled to him. "There are no stupid suggestions," she affirmed. "And you're right that physicality matters and not just when it comes to fitness. For example, if one of them was missing a finger or a foot..."

"We'd see it in the bruising or footprints," Julius finished. "Okay, so what's next?"

"Well, no one knows where Barry is. So, I say let's start by speaking to Jonno, and then I want to talk to Vicky Chapman."

"The madam?"

Heather nodded. "Lilly's friends conveniently excluded the fact that Lilly was a sex worker when talking to Helen, which means it's an unexplored avenue and a particularly pertinent one. Nobody gets murdered more than sex workers."

"Do you think she'll speak to a journalist?"

"No, which is why she isn't going to speak to one. She's going to be speaking to an escort looking to join her agency."

Julius cringed. "Isn't that a bit dangerous?"

Heather shrugged. "It's pretty typical vice work for female officers. You can uncover a lot by dipping your toe into the world's oldest profession."

"I don't want to sound prudish or misogynistic," Julius began, cleaning his already spotless glasses, "But I have seen way too many bodies of young women who had been sex trafficked, shot by pimps, strangled by johns, for this to not make me uneasy. It's not shameful what they do, but it is dangerous."

Heather wandered over to him, pulled up a chair, and leaned forward. "You're right. It is. And you don't sound like an asshole. This is clearly a sore subject for you. But this is high-class stuff. I'm not going to get abducted, I promise. It'll just be an interview in the daytime, in a public place. And that's only if I can score the meetup in the first place."

"I know, and I'll never tell you what to do—"

"No, you won't," Heather teased before patting him on the knee and standing.

"I'm a bit of a coward, I'm afraid," Julius said, looking up. "Me in my little laboratory. I suppose it's hard for me to understand."

There was something about the look in his eyes, or maybe the smell of the room, the adrenaline of a new case, the softness of her clothes, the co-habitation, that felt intimate, desirable, and something in her imagined a different, actually brave woman, swooping in and making a move—a hand on a cheek, sitting on a lap, intertwining in one way or another.

Buzz.

Her phone made an awful sound again on the metal desk, and she broke the tension by holding up her cell phone and smiling apologetically.

"It's Gabriel," she said. "We said we'd call and catch up."

"Well, don't let me interrupt," Julius said. "I have dishes to do anyway."

As he moved past, empty pizza box in hand, Heather reached out and squeezed his arm appreciatively, and he winked before leaving the room.

She sat on the daybed, plucked her glass of wine from the cool windowsill, and answered the still-ringing phone, not keen to reiterate all that had already been said but excited and terrified to find out what Gabriel had discovered.

"Hey, Buster," she said.

"Hey," Gabriel croaked.

"Are you okay?" she asked, putting him on loudspeaker on the wooden table next to the daybed.

"Yeah, just been all over the place today. Lots of talking."

"What have you found?"

Heather repeated what she'd just gone through with Julius with no less enthusiasm, and Gabriel responded with one-word replies and hummed in all the right spots before saying, "Well, it seems we've had an equally productive day."

"Oh yeah?" Heather asked, leaning back against the propped-up seat, her eyelids growing heavy once again.

"Yeah. I found out Katy has an ex. Shane Gibson. Apparently, the guy was an asshole. Even more so than Daniel."

"You think Daniel's an asshole?" Heather questioned, surprised by the statement.

"Duh. He cheated on you."

"Yeah, I know. It's just surprising because everyone always loves him despite the stuff he does."

"I guess I've heard enough to see through the facade." Gabriel paused. "Weird question, but when you were together, was he super jealous, controlling, and argumentative? Did he stop you from seeing your family and friends?"

Heather blinked rapidly, trying to remember everything she'd just been asked. Eventually, it came to her. "No. He was flawed, but not like that. Maybe he was a little jealous, but he hid it well. To this day, my parents think we should get back together. They still have our wedding photos on the walls. And as far as friends go... Well, all of my friends were his friends first, so I wouldn't have seen them without him anyway. Maybe it would've been different if I had a 'BFF' that disapproved or something."

"Yeah, it seems like he turned the toxicity up a notch when he was with Katy. I spoke to her sister Suzie and best friend Lola. They said they barely saw her outside of Christmas and Thanksgiving, and even then, he was there, and it was tense."

"I think, if I'd given him an inch, he would've taken a mile," Heather admitted, though she hated to do so. It was easier to do all of this—traveling the world—for a good person and not just because she needed to know either way. "You said she had an asshole ex?"

"Yep. And she was a recovering alcoholic."

"Whew. Younger than me, too?"

"1994."

Heather pawed at her mouth and nodded. "She would've been vulnerable, and sometimes, men who feel emasculated seek out vulnerable women to mold into subservient partners. And I certainly emasculated him."

"I'm sure he deserved it. Do you know how they met?" Gabriel asked.

"Do I need to?"

"Well, I guess—"

"I'm kidding," she interrupted, though she decidedly wasn't. "How did they meet?"

"At some rock-climbing thing, but what was weird was that he lied. He overheard that she was a model and said he was a photographer."

Heather's blood ran cold, and she stood abruptly, splashed wine onto leather, and moved out into the dimly lit hall, looking around for Julius. "Can you repeat that?" she asked.

"Yeah, Katy was an amateur model, and he pretended to be a photographer."

"Yeah, okay," Heather panted, moving to the top of the stairwell and seeing Julius at the bottom.

"What's wrong?" both men asked.

"Lilly Arnold also wanted to be a model. Apparently sketchy, fake photographers picked her up all the time."

"Oh," Gabriel said, voice low and grave. "Do you think Daniel could've been one of those guys?"

"I do now," Heather laughed hysterically as she lowered herself to the top step.

"Well, that's definitely creepy," Gabriel admitted as Julius padded up the stairs. "But don't panic. I'm going to try to get in touch with her ex soon and go to her AA group, and hopefully, it'll turn out that Daniel is just kind of an asshole and not a murderer."

"Okay."

"You sound exhausted. Do you want me to go?"

"I don't want you to, but..."

"You need to crash. All good. I'll call you when you know more."

"Thank you. Good work."

They said their goodbyes as Julius sat beside her on the stairs. Once again, shoulder to shoulder, she asked, "What if it really was Daniel who killed both of them?"

"Then it was him," Julius replied, wrapping an arm around her. "And you'll be the one who caught him despite him being your ex-husband."

"What if I looked the other way because I loved him?"

"Well, did you?"

"I don't think so, but..." Heather trailed off, chewing her lip.

"You have a saying about 'what ifs,' do you not?"

"I do."

"Want to go bury this one?"

"Not yet. Not when it could be the truth."

Julius squeezed her. "How about having a cup of tea in the garden instead? You can pick out a plot for when it's time to dig the grave."

"Okay," Heather replied, and though it took at least five minutes to move, eventually they did, and she had to admit that the smell of Earl Grey mixed with petrichor helped alleviate the knots in her guts enough for her to sleep soundly when the time came.

CHAPTER TEN

THE DETECTIVE

HEATHER HAD CONTACTED MONARCH BUTTERFLY Companions—Vicky Chapman's escort service—early in the morning but, expecting no immediate reply, had changed into her Journalist Singh outfit and gone to wake Julius. He was already awake and in the garden in his now usual spot. As it turned out, he was a very early-morning person and an eager one at that. He'd already exercised and eaten by the time she boiled the electric kettle. She hoped that his raring-to-go attitude would wear off on her soon, but as of yet, early on a Tuesday morning, all she could feel was jealousy. Though she'd convinced herself she'd fought it off, jet lag was still kicking her ass, and while she gulped water in the corner of the ring, he was ready for the next round, humming as he sipped his to-go coffee.

"Musical, are you?" she asked, grumpy and groggy, as a black cab pulled up outside of Farfalla House.

"Piano. Mum sang, though, when she was young. She does again now, if less tunefully. Still nice to hear, though."

Heather's irritation softened. "How is your mum?"

"Up and down. I feel bad leaving her for so long, considering she's not well enough for phone calls. Every time I go away or miss a visit, I just await 'that call' from her home. It seems that people always die when you're furthest away."

"I guess Death is not known for his kindness."

"You'd be surprised. When I was in medical school, he sometimes seemed like the most loving creature in the building. Though, sometimes, definitely not. I think old mum is just fighting him off for my sake. Which, I suppose, makes me the asshole in this circumstance."

"You're a lucky man to have a mum who'll battle the bloody reaper himself for you," the taxi driver chimed in. "If you don't mind my saying."

Julius smiled. "I don't."

"I think my mam would've fed me to him if it would've scored a winning lotto ticket." The taxi driver chuckled. "You two sound American; mind if I ask what you're doing here?"

"Honeymoon," both said in sync and then looked at each other and laughed. It wasn't rehearsed nor discussed, but it seemed a fitting lie. It also sounded too natural, making Heather feel as if she was standing on some sort of unstable precipice, and the ground was sliding beneath her feet whether she liked it or not.

They arrived at Jonno's office, which was not dissimilar to Julius's forensic center, except in size. In fact, it was significantly smaller, with only five parking spots in the cramped lot. This made sense when Julius explained there were many private practices of its nature scattered around London, and the police didn't rely on one behemoth as they did in Seattle. Jonno's place was apparently bigger than most of its kind because he was not only the best but also in good standing with those who ran New Scotland Yard.

As the GPS announced their destination and they veered to the side of the road, the taxi driver seemed somewhat confused. He squinted at the sign, then at them, and Heather could practically read his thoughts: what would honeymooners want with such a place?

Seeing his expression, Julius quickly explained, "The man who works here is an old friend."

"Ah, of course," the cabby said, rubbing his shiny bald head. "Couldn't make it to the wedding?"

"It was only a small affair."

"That's funny. You two strike me as the big wedding type. I mean, look at you."

Heather did look—at herself in the rearview mirror and at Julius—and realized they did appear more elegant than usual. She supposed it was London and their alter ego rubbing off on them, and she laughed and explained they were much more modest than they looked.

The cabby didn't seem convinced but bid them farewell after being generously tipped, and once he was a speck in the distance, Julius chuckled. "You know, Jonno actually was at my wedding. And it was not a small affair."

"Oh yeah?" Heather asked, sometimes forgetting that they were both divorcees.

"Sixty-four attendees," Julius said, shaking his head.

"Try over two hundred," Heather replied, no less repulsed. "He paid, at least, despite the tradition. My parents could never have afforded it."

"Me and Chrissy split it and left our parents out of it to make it less stressful. Not that it worked."

"It goes by so fast," Heather agreed. "I barely had a second to breathe, let alone have fun."

"If I ever get the opportunity again, I'll elope."

Heather laughed and nodded. "Oh, God, yeah. All I need is a decent beach, a thrift store dress, my parents, my dogs, and Gabriel as my male of honor."

"Exactly. Who needs the stress at our age? A big wedding would probably give me a coronary."

Heather rolled her eyes. "While you're definitely too healthy for that, I agree. All the planning? Ugh. Give me a cheap and cheerful wedding and a two-week honeymoon abroad any day."

Julius smiled as he pressed the buzzer, and Heather felt comforted by the warmth of the sun but also the imagery in her head. They'd talked about moving to a farm together before, but this was different. Despite trying not to, as she pictured herself barefoot in a white sundress, walking across the sand, the only person she could picture waiting for her was him. It was ridiculous. She knew it was too early for any of that, too unrealistic even, but she allowed herself to daydream. Working the job that she did, her mind rarely received such blissful reprieve.

Jonno opened the door without replying to the speaker, wearing a red and white striped t-shirt and looking much more like a disheveled artist than a medical professional. Cigarette tucked behind his ear, he hugged Julius and, to Heather's surprise, turned on her, too. It was backbreaking, but she was pleasantly surprised by his sea salt and sandalwood aroma.

"Friends," he rasped, "Come on in."

They followed him up a flight of concrete stairs to a narrow, windowless door that was held open by a wedge of rubber. Inside was a chaotic office—which was clearly where Jonathan organized his files rather than practiced his work—and he sat at a desk before gesturing to two uncomfortable-looking plastic chairs.

Heather and Julius lowered themselves into the seats, and Jonathan opened the large folder before him and began to rummage, flicking to sectors marked by neon tabs. He looked up at Heather. "Obviously, I'll give you copies of all of this, but I thought you might want to hear my opinions first."

"I do," she enthused. "It's always valuable to hear what lies beyond the notes."

"Exactly," Jonno beamed, his teeth a little yellow but all intact. "I'm not great at notes, but I'm bloody wonderful in a courtroom."

"He is," Julius agreed. "His testimony has put many a man behind bars."

"Not to say that I'm not thorough in what I write, but you know. Paperwork and all that. It's a drag."

Heather nodded. "So, what didn't I find out in the preliminary report?"

"Well, loads, to be honest. The prelim wasn't done by myself, for starters. It was done by some bloke who, frankly, I think is a bit of an idiot. Not to mention a massive git."

"Did he test her blood?"

"He did, and he was right about that. No drugs, but 0.11% BAC."

"Is that high?"

"I'd put that at about five drinks considering her weight and what she was drinking."

"So, not the entire bottle."

"Not in my opinion," Jonno confirmed. "Though it's hard to say. Now, this fella was also right about her weight, height, and the manual strangulation being the cause of death. What he failed to mention, however, was that whoever strangled her tried to revive her with chest compressions, fracturing her 3rd and 4th ribs, her manubrium, and her sternum."

"He tried to bring her back?" Heather asked, raising her brows.

"Seems that way."

"How do you know the strangulation happened first?"

"Well, to put it in layman's terms—no offense—it was clear that the body wasn't healing itself. It's a little bit like if somebody dies before they're stabbed, then there's less blood than there should be, right?"

"Right," Heather agreed.

"The body works miraculously quickly, and when it's alive, it's also pretty hardy. The severity of the breakages, in this case, implies that doing so was easy because of a lack of resistance in the musculature or otherwise. I mean, there's a lot more I can say, and it's all in the report, but trust me, if he was trying to bring her back, he was doing so once he'd already done her in."

"I believe you."

Jonno eyed her with amusement, his eyelids uneven. "Got the sixth sense, do you?"

"What do you mean?" Heather asked, similarly mirthful, his cheeky, youthful demeanor wearing off on her.

"Well, I meet a lot of stuffed shirts—detectives mostly—and some of them believe me because they're thick or trying to shut me up. But you actually know that I'm telling the truth. I can tell."

"I—" Heather started. "I've never had someone call me out on that before."

"Oh, I see it alright. It's called a gut feeling. I can tell if a supposed suicide victim was actually murdered before I dig in. Julius here has it, too. It's why I agreed to train him up."

"Not like either of you," Julius clarified. "Mine's all learned rather than anything preternatural. But yes, I suppose I get a feeling, and I'm normally right."

"Get or have, tomato-tomahto. Whatever it is, it makes us the best." Jonno moved to a window, slid it open with great effort, and lit up. Heather thought he really must been the best to allow this kind of conduct. "So, what do you make of that? The attempted revival."

"That it was an impulsive killing," Heather replied. "That they regretted what they'd done."

Jonno leered. "I know you don't think the killer is a they or a she."

"I don't. But I have to allow for all avenues."

"Heard that one before. I get it, but for our purposes..."

"It was a man," Heather said, allowing her gut to speak in the presence of a kindred spirit.

Jonno nodded, blowing smoke out of his nostrils and sucking it in through his mouth. "Now, this next piece of information is something the first guy also missed. Lilly Arnold was pregnant. Six to eight weeks by my measurements. Harder to tell post-mortem."

Heather's mouth fell open, and she swallowed saliva before speaking. "Did you test for DNA?"

"Always. But no cigar. So early on in gestation, it's tricky, and if the dad isn't on our records, we're screwed. But as far as I'm aware, pregnancy is a pretty good motive. She is probably the one-hundredth pregnant victim that's seen the inside of my lab."

"So, she gets pregnant, tells the father, says she wants to keep it, or that she doesn't, he flies into a rage, kills her, and then regrets what he did," Heather murmured, jotting it all down.

"That would be my guess," Jonno agreed. "If you can find out who was screwing her—sorry to be crass—get them to send DNA my way. I still have the fetal tissue preserved in the fridge downstairs. I get an inkling about when I need to hold onto stuff that the cops tell me to chuck."

"Will do," Heather said, looking up and noticing a sudden severity take hold of the older man's face.

"Now, there's more. This was not just a murder but a rape. Likely done before she died on account of the state of severe muscular spasticity we found her in. Once again, I hate to be crass, but the bloke would've had to be slanging a knob the size of my pinky finger post-mortem, if you get my drift."

"I do," Heather said with a grimace. Jonno may have been crass, despite apologizing for it, but she appreciated the honesty and, to a degree, the vividity of his descriptions. Detective work was no place for squeamishness.

"I don't have much to back this up, but I reckon he killed her at the same time as he was assaulting her. Erotic asphyxiation gone wrong, maybe?" Jonno shrugged. "No clue, but it would explain the attempt at revival."

"I doubt it was something she partook in consensually. She never had bruises on her neck in her pre-death photos," Heather said, thinking back to all the pictures she'd seen of Lilly while alive.

"She did wear a lot of makeup, even on her neck," Jonno countered. "But you're right. The bruising was all fresh, so it's hard to say. However, from the groinal injuries, I would agree that this wasn't consensual. But that's not to say it was a random attacker."

"It almost never is."

"Exactly right," Jonno said sadly. "First case I trained Julius on, back in—fuck me—2002, was a woman who'd been raped brutally by her husband. He stayed out of a cell for a long time because the idiots who arrested him couldn't believe a husband could do that to his wife."

"That's awful," Heather said.

"It was," Jonno replied gravely. "Poor Julius nearly quit over that. They just wouldn't listen to us."

"I did," Julius admitted.

"Anything else?" Heather asked, her stomach churning thinking about Katy and Daniel and just how possible it was that he had been abusing her in a similar manner behind doors.

"Yeah, one more thing before I have to get back to slicing. Now, this came from the first guy, so you'll have to take his word for it. But her hoop earrings were missing—that I'm sure you know already—but so were her underwear, bra, socks, and shoes. He put her dress back on neatly, but all that was under it was gone."

"He removed her makeup and cut her nails too," Heather said.

"He did. Weirder still was the hair."

"The hair?" Heather asked, bile rising.

"He'd cut a lock. Quite a chunk, actually. Round the back under the top layer so no one would notice."

"He wanted a trophy. Or something to remember her by, if the resuscitation theory is correct."

"Either way, you're looking at one sick bastard. And one that made her suffer for a while. 2 till 4:30? I mean, that's not just murder. That's torture."

"Yeah," Heather said quietly, trying and failing not to picture Daniel carrying out every second of it and feeling profound relief when the two men began to catch up and moved on from the subject and onto ridiculous tales from their youth. Though the imagery remained, at least it was lighter, her images of Daniel obscured by immature pranks. It only lasted half an hour, but she took all that she could get.

CHAPTER ELEVEN

THE DETECTIVE

AS THEY SAT IN THE BACK OF ANOTHER BLACK CAB, wads of photocopies in hand, Heather received a reply from Vicky Chapman with the date, time, and location of their approved meeting. So, instead of going home, Heather asked the driver to take them to wherever the best clothing stores were.

"Sloane Street, please," Julius chimed in.

The driver obliged, and soon enough, there they were, on Sloane Street, surrounded by every single high fashion brand that Heather had heard of and many that she hadn't. It was amazing and a little daunting, considering she hadn't bought clothing from anywhere more exciting than Old Navy since she left Seattle.

Fortunately, Julius seemed the opposite of daunted, and despite being hesitant about Heather's plan, he lit up as they joined the mob of shoppers on the sidewalk. He looked from side to side, on either side of the street, and when something caught his eye, he grabbed Heather's shoulders, turned her toward a door, and ushered her inside. She just managed to catch sight of the sign before entering—Bottega Veneta. From the name alone, she knew it was out of her price range but pretended as if she belonged when the attendant greeted them.

The woman and Julius conferred and plucked dresses from the rails and held them up against Heather before bringing them to the dressing room. There, she was left alone with a selection of six while Julius waited for her on a couch with a glass of champagne. As she got changed, she noticed the price tag on one of the five chic garments and did a double take. Though once she had the first one on—a structured black dress with a low v-neckline—she understood the cost. It fit her like a glove and flattered her body shape in a way it had never been flattered before.

"Wow," was all she could say.

It was a far cry from what she'd seen her colleagues wear back in Seattle while working undercover. They'd worn leopard print, neon, body con, fishnets, platform heels, and colorful wigs. That's because they were talking to girls who worked on the city's sidewalks. The woman Heather was going to be, Rebecca Wilkes, may have started there, but now she was occupying upscale hotel lobbies and the bedrooms of penthouses. The sexuality was subtle rather than brazen, and though Heather would've done anything to find out what happened to Lilly, she was relieved. What was even more reassuring was the discovery that prostitution was technically legal in the UK.

Heather tried on the rest of the dresses and decided on the first one. It was chic and glamorous, but it was also simple enough to be professional.

She emerged, and Julius beamed at her, his eyes crinkling behind his glasses. "Is this the one?" he asked.

"I really like it," Heather admitted, turning and examining herself in the mirror. "But it's a small fortune. Maybe we should go to Zara or something instead."

Julius shook his head. "Don't worry about the money."

"Julius."

"You need to look convincing, right?"

"Yeah, but this is ridiculous," Heather whisper-yelled.

"Consider it a souvenir. Now, pick out some shoes, a bag, and a jacket."

"I feel like you're *Pretty Woman*-ing me."

"You don't need my help with that."

Heather snorted. "Charmer."

"Go on, we don't have all day. If it makes you feel any better, I'm using my inheritance money rather than my income."

"It doesn't," she replied, but begrudgingly made her way to the shelves and selected a pair of black pumps with a gold knot heel, a matching gold 'mini sardine bag,' and then she grabbed the cheapest black blazer she could find.

Opting to wear the outfit out, the sales assistant enthusiastically packed the clothes and shoes Heather had been wearing while Julius paid and refused to tell Heather the total. After some compliments from the employees, they returned to Sloane Street, and Heather felt as if she truly belonged in her new garbs.

"What time is the meeting?" Julius asked, trying and failing to sound as if he was uninterested in the whole affair, and Heather realized that the retail therapy was more for his sake than hers.

"Two hours."

"So you have time for a blowout and a trip to the makeup counter, I guess."

"Yeah, I guess," she said hesitantly. "Are you okay?"

"Slightly paranoid about you getting sex trafficked."

"It's in a public place. You can come with me if you want and sit at another table."

He nodded. "Perfect. I could do with a coffee and some lunch."

Heather patted him on the shoulder condescendingly. "You'll be okay."

"I'm sure I'll survive," he laughed. "I'm not trying to be protective. It's just a sore subject. My cousin *was* an escort."

Heather thought to ask more, but the emphasis on 'was' told her all she needed to know. "I'm sorry."

"Me too." He cleared his throat and looked at her fondly. "Come on, let's go. That mane of yours isn't going to tame itself."

Despite her muscular legs, Heather felt much like baby Bambi as she tottered into the extremely expensive-looking hotel bar. Still, she was glad to be wearing what she was, considering the strict dress code on the front door. She was sure she could've found something cheaper that would fit the bill but surrounded by Chanel and Louboutins, it was better to be safe than sorry.

Julius wasn't far behind, entering a couple of minutes after Heather and, pretending as if he didn't see her, made his way to the bar. Like her, he also blended perfectly amongst the wealthy patrons in his new getup. He looked good, she thought, and seemed happier, too, confirming her theory about him shopping when anxious.

Heather looked around for the woman she'd seen on the website and, fortunately, spotted her quickly. Vicky waved to confirm the identification and waved Heather over to the two-seater table by the bright windows. Despite trying not to break an ankle, Heather kept her face composed and strode toward the woman. Somehow, Rebecca Wilkes, escort extraordinaire, took hold of Heather Bishop's body and guided her elegantly across the room, clicking her heels against the floor in time to the lounge music beat. She was cool, she was calm, and she was collected.

She sat opposite Vicky and crossed her legs before holding out her hand. "Lovely to meet you," she said, affecting a somewhat English accent.

"You too, Rebecca. Stunning dress."

"Thank you. I like yours too."

Vicky scoffed. "This old thing? It's out of season. But I'm not the one that needs to attract attention. In fact, it's better if I don't," Vicky laughed a smoker's laugh.

"Still, it suits you."

"Flattery. That'll get you everywhere with me. Fancy a glass?" Vicky asked, gesturing to the bottle of white on ice. Heather internally cringed. The whole trip was starting to shape into a booze fest, and her body was beginning to pay the price. Still, it didn't seem like saying no was an option, so she nodded politely.

"Here you go," Vicky said, pouring a generous portion. The woman didn't sound posh like Heather had expected, and up close, she didn't look that posh either. Rich, maybe, but not classy. Her fake tan, makeup, and filler were a bit much. As was the wrinkled cleavage. Yet there was something attractive about her. She possessed a confidence most didn't and was certainly commanding.

"Thank you," Heather said, doing her best to mimic her dad's accent. That part of the disguise wasn't something she hadn't considered until she walked in.

Her attempt didn't fool Vicky. "American, originally?"

"Yeah, I've been back and forth," Heather admitted, easing up on the lilt. "Mum's in New York, Dad's in Yorkshire. I've been in London for a year now. Initially, I was interning at Dad's friend's startup, but you know how those things go."

"So you decided to look for something a little more lucrative?"

"Yes. And reliable."

"And you've serviced gentlemen before?"

Heather nodded. "Eleven. Not many, I know. I've only been working in this field for six months."

"Self-managed?"

"Yes."

"Looking for bigger pockets and gentler hands."

"The former more than the latter."

Vicky grinned. "Well, darling, I've taken on less experienced girls than yourself and much less pretty ones, I might add. Not to mention, you seem confident. The men might like wallflowers, but I don't."

"Sounds like you're offering me the gig," Heather retorted, putting her cocky charm to work.

Vicky narrowed her eyes, amused. "How old are you?"

"Twenty-nine," Heather lied, shaving five years off of her real age.

"Sorry, did you say twenty-five?"

"No—" Heather caught herself. "I mean, yes."

"Perfect. Don't worry, you can pass. Beautiful skin. Indian?"

"Yes."

"Well, most blokes like them white or east Asian, but I have a few that are less picky. So long as you're young." She clicked her fingers in the air, and a waiter came running. "I'd like the salmon, and my friend Rebecca here would like the salad." The waiter nodded and hustled off, and Vicky fixed Heather with an apologetic look. "Sorry, but you girls need to stay thin. That's another rule. Personally, I like the look of a girl with some meat on her bones, but our plus-sized quota is filled. Tone down the weightlifting, too. They'll be intimidated by those arms of yours."

"Will do," Heather said obediently.

"Good girl. Now, have some wine and tell me about yourself. And please, for the love of God, tell me you can hold your drink. Clients expect you to drink with them, but you must never get drunk. Three units at max, and never seem more than flirtatiously tipsy."

Heather took a sip. "I can hold my drink. Do you have anyone for me?"

"I do. This evening, in fact. Raymond Doyle. I was going to set him up with Trish, but they haven't been clicking. In fact, he hasn't clicked with anyone since his favorite died."

"Died?" Heather asked, pretending to be shocked while simultaneously feeling as if she'd hit the jackpot.

"Oh, don't worry, dear. Nothing to do with being a Monarch girl. Her name was Lilly. Went by Lilah professionally. She was only with us for seven months, but she was one of my best girls. Fiery little thing. Scared of nothing. A master conversationalist." Vicky sighed. "She was murdered nearly seven years ago, and though Raymond continues to use our services, nobody, as of yet, has been able to satisfy him. He doesn't even finish, poor bugger. I'm hoping you might change that, and if you do, I'll let you keep the entire payment."

"Perfect. I'll see what I can do," Heather replied, faux-modest.

"Tonight at eight, then? I'll have a car pick you up."

"Sure." Heather wrote down her address on a napkin and slid it across.

Vicky looked her up and down as she pocketed the address. "Wear that outfit. It's gorgeous, and Raymond loves black. And please be careful between clients. We lose too many girls in this industry. No more hotels, you hear me? Or I'll drop you. I can't take the heartache."

"Of course. I plan to be loyal to Monarchs." Heather paused to sip her drink. "Do that many die?" Heather asked, probing. "Was Lilly murdered?"

Vicky looked scathingly at Heather for the first time. "Of course she was. Have you never seen a true crime documentary before? Jack the Ripper. Peter Sutcliffe. Gary Ridgway."

"Yeah, of course, sorry."

Vicky waved her off, and it was clear Heather could push the conversation no further. "Now, let me get you up to speed on Raymond. You will call him Sir. You will sit with your legs crossed. You will let him order for you. You will call going to the bathroom powdering your nose. You will laugh at his jokes. You will speak when spoken to. And you will wear a blonde wig. We will provide that. Do you know how to apply a lace front?"

Heather nodded, remembering her trip to Texas to interview Clarence Dixon Jr.'s wife.

"Good girl. He will also pay upfront. So, when he asks you to go upstairs, you go. He always pays for the entire night, which runs out at 8 a.m. You give him what he wants until then." She paused, smirking. "Luckily for you, he's not one for stamina."

"Understood."

"I'm excited to work with you, Rebecca. Truly. This might be the start of a wonderful relationship."

Vicky raised her glass and they clinked before moving on to small talk. Heather tried not to zone out but couldn't help it. She was already in too deep. She knew this because there was no way in hell she wasn't going on a date with Raymond Doyle.

CHAPTER TWELVE

THE PARTNER

ACCORDING TO THE SLIGHTLY GRUMPY PASTOR, THE AA meeting was in a church basement with an exterior entrance around the side of the building. Gabriel yawned as he walked around the side and spotted the group of attendees; it was just before 6 a.m. on a Tuesday morning, and he was momentarily surprised by the turnout, considering the sun had barely risen. That was until he realized that the rest of them were here for more legitimate reasons than snooping. They needed this, even if they had to wake up early and go before work started. That's also what he was planning to do. He'd woken up at 4:30 a.m. to be here, and with any luck, he'd be back in Glenville before starting at the station at 9. Then he'd get that damn bike thief paperwork done, and no one would be any the wiser.

He, being ten minutes early—just in case he couldn't find the location—hadn't expected anyone else to be here yet. However, he seemed to be the last one to arrive. Everyone was eager, chomping at the bit. It felt like they were camping out for a trendy new videogame or iPhone. It wasn't what he'd expected. He imagined that going to AA was kind of like going to school: unpleasant but necessary. Perhaps even compulsory. Instead, people were smiling and chatting as they smoked cigarettes and drank their coffee. The people themselves also weren't what he'd expected. He'd anticipated burly old truckers, retired barflies, war casualties, and divorced businessmen. There were admittedly a few who fit that bill, but mostly everyone was young and didn't fit into his idea of alcoholics. There was a middle-aged woman with rosy cheeks who looked like she'd been ripped from a children's book, a slightly nervous-looking goth girl who looked no older than nineteen, a grandma with her hair in curlers, a young surfer dude, and what Gabriel could only describe as an archetypal D&D nerd.

If he hadn't already been feeling guilty about this plan, he would've been consumed with it by now. These were real people who had struggled and were still struggling. This was a safe place, and he was intruding on it. He was an infiltrator. A snake in a chicken coop.

It's not like I'm going to tell anyone about what they say, he tried to reason with himself as he made eye contact with the fedora-wearing nerd and smiled. *I just want to find out if anyone knew Katy.*

The man smiled back, approached, and as he held out his hand, all of Gabriel's attempts at rationalizing his actions felt pathetic. Not that he was going to leave. Daniel had jealousy issues about this group, and neither he nor Suzie nor Lola thought of mentioning it to the cops. It felt important. He was going to stay. He was just going to have to own up to being an asshole to himself instead of pretending otherwise.

"Toby," the guy said. "And you are?"

"Matías."

"You new to the program?"

"I've been before, once or twice, years ago. Didn't stick," Gabriel replied, trying to at least lie believably.

Toby looked at him sympathetically. "Hey, don't beat yourself up. You're here. It's a new day. That's the point of all of this. That we keep getting back on the horse."

"How long have you been sober?"

"Six months," Toby said proudly, his pink, round face lighting up. "I get my chip today."

"Congrats, man. That's awesome."

"And yourself? If you don't mind me asking."

Gabriel hesitated but, for whatever reason, ended up answering truthfully. "About seven hours. Had a beer at 11 before crashing."

"Hey, you can still pick up a white chip for rejoining. And hopefully, next time I see you, you'll be picking up that 24-hour chip."

The idea of walking out of there with a chip was agonizing. Gabriel didn't know that they gave you one just for showing up. Toby must've noticed because he furrowed his brow. "Hey, you okay, bud?"

"Do I have to take a chip?"

"Not planning on staying sober?"

"I—"

Toby threw his hands up and lowered his voice. "Hey man, no judgment. It's cool to be sober curious, too. Some people are more old-fashioned about it, so I'd keep that to yourself. But you can just say you already have a white chip. No problem." Toby patted Gabriel's shoulder with a sweaty hand. "Seriously, man, it's cool. Just keep it on the down-low. And I hope I'll see you at the next one. I know you're not ready yet, but seriously, it's going to change your life when you can commit." Toby craned his neck, looking past Gabriel. "The big man's here. Time to go in. Good luck, buddy."

Toby approached the graying man in the yellow and black flannel shirt and began to babble enthusiastically about his six-month achievement as they descended the stairs toward the heavy basement door. Gabriel liked Toby, and the concept of being sober curious made him feel like less of an imposter. He didn't know that was a thing before now, but honestly, he was curious about sobriety or at least cutting back. He'd been drinking too much as of late. A lot more than people knew.

It had started around the time he'd shot Dennis Burke in the forehead, which seemed an understandable catalyst. At first, he had some control because he'd only drink with Heather, and she as got herself together, and reduced her intake, so did he. Beau, being sober, was also a good influence. Unfortunately, a harmless beer in the garage while he strummed his guitar or listened to music had turned into a six-pack several nights a week, and he was beginning to feel the effects of that in fatigue and lethargy.

He hoped that maybe he'd garner something meaningful beyond the case as he descended the stairs. Suddenly extremely nervous as he entered the room, he waited for the others to take their seats and grabbed a cup of water before joining the circle. The room smelled like an ashtray. It seemed most of these people were smokers. He supposed that was the replacement addiction—something to kick further down the line. It was something he also needed to give the boot eventually.

"Good morning everyone. We are glad you are all here. Especially newcomers," the tired-looking man in flannel said, glancing in Gabriel's direction. "In keeping with our singleness of purpose and our Third Tradition, which states that 'The only requirement for AA membership is a desire to stop drinking,' we ask that all who participate confine their discussion to their problems with alcohol. Alcoholics Anonymous is a fellowship of men and women and others who share their experience, strength, and hope with each other that they may solve their common problem and help others to recover from alcoholism. There are no dues or fees for AA membership; we are self-supporting through our own contributions. AA is not allied with any sect, denomination, politics, organization, or institution; does not wish to engage in any controversy; neither endorses nor opposes any causes. Our primary purpose is to stay sober and help other alcoholics to achieve sobriety." He softened, his well-memorized monologue at an end, and gave a small wave. "My name is Harold, and I'm an alcoholic."

"Hi, Harold," the rest responded.

"I have been sober for twenty-three years and have been running sessions at this church for the past thirteen. Now, who wants to speak first? Toby?"

Toby nodded. "Hi, I'm Toby. I'm an alcoholic."

"Hi Toby," the crowd, including Gabriel, responded.

"And today, I am six months sober."

Toby began to wax poetic about his journey while Harold excused himself to get something. When he returned, he approached a pulpit and asked that everyone turn and watch as Toby accepted his blue token. They did so with bated breath, and Toby walked toward Harold, looking as happy as a man on his wedding day. And when he turned back, token in hand, there were tears in his eyes.

They then sat back down, and Harold began to read from the 'Big Book' before looking for somebody else to speak. Fortunately, or maybe purposefully, he did not pick Gabriel. The young man was trying to shrink into himself and stare at the ground, and it seemed that Harold was a merciful leader.

"Elijah, how about you?" Harold asked.

"Um, yeah, sure. Hi, I'm Elijah, and I'm an alcoholic," the young surfer dude said, tucking his chin-length, highlighted blonde, salt-waved hair behind his ears, revealing small silver hoops. He drummed on his bare, tan knees, sticking out of his cargo shorts as everyone chimed back at him. "And I'm," he paused, voice trembling, "24 hours sober."

"Well done for coming back," Harold said. "Would you like to talk about what happened?"

Elijah nodded jerkily. "I, um... I reached six months, as some of you know. Then eight. It seemed like I'd make a year. And then Katy died. I fell off the wagon as soon as I heard the news, and then I climbed back on in October. Then, two weeks ago, I had to put my dog down, got home, and saw her face on the news and snapped. Went on a six-day whiskey bender, then settled down to the usual six pack a day, and now I'm here."

Everyone murmured their 'well done's and 'good for you's, and Elijah sat back in his seat, bobbing his knee, holding back tears as he looked up at the ceiling light. He looked so young and so old all at once. His dark brown eyes, angelic hair, and glowing skin gave him the youthful look of a surfwear model, but there were lines there, too, and bags and scars. The kind of scars people got from fighting or being a punching bag.

After the session, Gabriel hurried through the doors first, hoping to catch Elijah on the outside. He was clearly very close to Katy, perhaps even romantically. It was vital that Gabriel found out all he could. So, he waited with two cigarettes and a lighter, and when Elijah eventually emerged, he introduced himself, using his brother's name, and offered a smoke.

Elijah took it happily. "Thanks, man, I need this."

"No kidding. Sounds like you've had a rough time."

"Little bit," Elijah said wearily.

"I'm sorry to hear about your friend Katy."

"Thank you," Elijah said, quieter that time. "She was five years sober and never once slipped up. The best sponsor I could've asked for."

"Was she a heavy drinker before that?"

Elijah hesitated. "Enough to bring her here."

"Were you two friends outside of here?"

"Yeah. Of course. We saw each other probably twice a week. Texted a lot."

"What happened to her, if you don't mind my asking?"

Elijah shifted. Clearly, he did mind but was struggling to be rude. This whole thing seemed to hinge on politeness. "She was murdered."

Gabriel widened his eyes. "Shit. That's awful. Do you know who did it? Boyfriend?"

"Listen, man," Elijah said, "It's still unsolved, I'll say that much, but let's not talk about Katy when she's not around to consent to it. What is said in AA stays in AA. You know the drill."

"Sorry. Didn't mean any offense. Just being nosy. You hear the word murder and—"

"It's all good, brother," Elijah interrupted, extinguishing his half-smoked cigarette. "Catch you at the next one?"

Despite the faux pas, Elijah looked hopeful, and Gabriel nodded, unsure if it was a lie. "Yeah, I'll try."

"That's the spirit. Have a good day, man."

Elijah threw his cigarette into the trash and strode away, seemingly cheerful, all of his baggage dumped in the church basement. Gabriel, on the other hand, felt the opposite of light. He felt guilty, embarrassed, and painfully curious all at the same time and hoped that infiltrating this group wouldn't have to become a regular thing.

Even more frustratingly, he realized he hadn't caught Elijah's last name, and looking at stony-faced Harold, he knew that no one who knew it would give it to him either. All he could do for now was return to Glenville and hope that one day, with enough effort, Elijah would open up to him.

CHAPTER THIRTEEN

THE DETECTIVE

HEATHER'S WIG WAS ITCHY. IT WAS HUMAN HAIR, VERY expensive, and professionally laid by a very nice lady at the hair salon. Yet, it was still uncomfortable, and her real hair—tightly braided into cornrows to minimize the volume—tugged at her aching scalp. She also definitely did not suit being blonde. She'd seen other girls with her complexion pull it off, but she was not one of them. She felt washed out and weird and hoped that Raymond Doyle didn't care about things like undertones and palettes and simply saw blonde hair and liked what he saw.

"How are you going to leave?" Julius asked as they waited outside for the car to arrive. "Before you take it to the next level?"

"I don't know. I'll pretend I'm sick or something, run out, and hail a cab."

"What about his money?"

"Monarchs offers full refunds. I checked the website."

"Good. No broken kneecaps for you."

"Fingers crossed."

"I'm going to follow you over," Julius suddenly announced. "I did some research. There's a nice bar next to the restaurant. Text me SOS if I need to come save you."

Heather rolled her eyes but gave his hand a squeeze. She knew what a cruel thing trauma could be. "I won't need you to come save me. It's dinner in a public restaurant. What's the worst he can do?"

"Drug you. Have his henchmen drag you upstairs. Take—"

"Rhetorical question."

"But one with a lot of real answers."

"He's just a businessman," Heather said. "I think."

"A businessman who was obsessed with a now deceased eighteen-year-old prostitute."

Heather frowned. "It does sound bad when you say it like that. According to his social media, he's in his late forties. But I guess I wouldn't bother going if he didn't sound suspicious. He could be our guy."

"I don't know if I'm hoping that he is or isn't," Julius replied, releasing her hand as the shiny black sedan pulled up.

It had tinted windows, which made her nervous, and yet it was precisely what she'd pictured. "Me neither. See you later," she said as the driver emerged and opened the door for her.

Julius nodded, watching with an almost pained expression as she entered the car, and the door slammed shut behind her. He remained rooted to the spot as she left, but she didn't watch him for long. She was Rebecca now. She didn't know that man on the sidewalk. She knew Vicky, and soon she'd know Raymond. She was an escort and a good one. She was going to be charming. She was going to be elegant. She was going to be funny. She was going to find out everything she could about Lilly Arnold.

Heather stepped into the bustling, chic restaurant with its low lights and rumbling conversation. There must've been at least a hundred people there, and she estimated that the room itself was likely around two thousand square feet. There were plenty of witnesses, but it was horribly overwhelming to a woman who'd spent the past five years in dive bars and dinky Italian restaurants. However, to Rebecca, it was comforting and glorious, and she, not Heather, approached the hostess station with a smile.

"I'm looking for Raymond Doyle," Heather said in her half-English accent.

The hostess, who looked more like a model, replied with a smile and a thick French accent. "He's right there, in the middle. Best seat in the house. He's wearing the maroon suit," she added, clearly used to directing women in Mr. Doyle's direction.

"Thank you," Heather replied.

"Someone will be over in a moment to take your drinks order."

Thanking the woman once again, Heather began to walk, swaying her hips to and fro and flicking her ribcage-length locks over her shoulder. She was Rebecca Wilkes, the most desirable woman in the room. She was Heather Singh, journalist extraordinaire. Best of all, she was Heather Bishop, homicide detective. She had been through much worse things than a classy dinner. Then, Raymond looked up at her, and her heart skipped a beat. She nearly faltered, fumbled, and fell, but at the last second, she gave him her best coy, seductive smile and finished the journey to the table.

Raymond rose once she was near enough and towered above her, an absolute mountain of a man. Not only was he tall, he was also wide, and his neck was thicker than most men's thighs. He was definitely overweight; his British bulldog cheeks and the rolls at the back of his head make that clear, but he was also strong like a bear, and no amount of blubber could hide that musculature.

As she was trying to figure out how much his custom suits must cost, she held out her hand to shake, and he flipped it and kissed her knuckles. "Enchanted," he rumbled, his voice cavernous and lined with brown liquor and cigars.

"Pleasure," Heather replied and sat gratefully as he pulled out her chair.

"An American?" Raymond roared. "How exotic. Indian too?"

"Yes."

"Mm. Beautiful. Though it must be hard work keeping your hair that color."

Heather smiled. "A little. But it's worth it. No?"

"Oh, it is. You know what they say about blondes. And I'm nothing if not a fun lover."

Heather laughed politely. "I myself am a lover of fun."

Raymond looked at her, his expression somewhere between fondness and salivation. "Drink?" he asked, clicking his fingers at a nearby waiter in the same manner as Vicky had. She wondered if this was just a thing rich people did or if it was still considered rude amongst the one percent.

"Yes, please," she cooed, doing her best to make her voice sound like velvet.

"What'll it be?"

"Surprise me," Heather requested, fixing Raymond in his small gray eyes.

Raymond turned to the waiter. "Surprise us both. And don't cheap out on me. This is an expensive woman."

How expensive? Heather wondered. "So, tell me about yourself, Raymond," Heather requested, having ascertained that Raymond liked his women strong and assertive and was a little submissive in the bedroom. She also knew that all powerful men liked to talk about themselves.

"You are a breath of fresh air, love," Raymond laughed. "Talking with younger girls is about as invigorating as pulling teeth most of the time. And sure, the older ones are chatty, but in the wrong way. Feels like having a conversation with my mum after a parent-teacher evening."

"Well, I promise you I haven't got a mumsy bone in my body."

"Not yet," Raymond corrected her. "It'll happen to you too, eventually. Time. The ruiner of women. Men get to stay young forever. Boys with their toys. But you, you have to be responsible." He shook his head. "It's a shame, really. Word of advice. Get the implant. Or an IUD. Seeing you turn into some idiot's housewife would be like stripping the paint off a Ferrari. Or worse, swapping it out for a bloody people mover."

"I'll bear that in mind," Heather said, struggling to retain her flirtatiousness considering the topic at hand. So, she decided to circle back to talking about him. "So, are you from London?"

"No. I'm from up North originally. Yorkshire. I moved down here in the nineties, though, when my boxing career took off. I made some good investments. Retired young. Now, I live off the proceeds."

"You were a boxer?" Heather asked dreamily.

"Oh yeah. Way before your time. But I was pretty good. Set a few UK heavyweight records."

"Wow," Heather responded, leaning forward and perching her chin on her palm.

Before she could continue to question, a bottle of red and two glasses were delivered to their table, along with what looked like tumblers filled with scotch.

"Mmm," she said, even though she was actually repulsed by the idea of drinking that much liquor alongside a full-bodied Merlot. Still, she knew that it would ease any tension between them, and from the smell of his breath, Heather figured Raymond was already halfway to drunk.

"Mortlach," he said, reaching for the glass. "Twenty Years."

"Single malt whiskey?" Heather asked, putting her knowledge to the test. At her worst, she'd drank anything and everything and didn't care too much for labels, but in recent years— drinking for pleasure rather than a burning necessity—she'd begun to refine her palette.

"Indeed," Raymond confirmed. "Do you drink scotch?"

"It's the best whiskey, don't you think?" she asked, even though she was definitely a bourbon girl. Her dogs' names— Turkey, Fireball, and Beam—were a testament to that.

"Most women don't drink scotch," Raymond replied. "I'm glad to have a drinking buddy for once."

"I'm not most women," Heather replied coyly, masterfully hiding her self-disgust.

"No, you're not. My favorite girl wasn't either. She was young, but fuck me, she was a firecracker. Wicked sense of humor. A real dirty birdy. And she could hold her liquor despite being a waif. Too much makeup, in my opinion, but it didn't stop my dick getting hard," Raymond laughed. "You, on the other hand, are more of a classic beauty. I feel like I can't just bend you over in an alleyway. Or maybe I can."

"You can do whatever you want after dinner," Heather replied. "And another round of these."

"Well then, drink up."

Drinks were certainly drunk, conversation was had, a delicious meal was eaten, and all in all, it wasn't as bad as Heather had anticipated. Raymond wholly bought her schtick, and while she didn't like the man, he wasn't hard to converse with when she was pretending to be someone else. The booze certainly helped as lubrication, and it was only when Raymond began to slur that she summoned the courage to ask, "What happened to your favorite girl? Did she quit?"

Raymond frowned, his bald, shiny bowling ball head reddened from the drink. "Murdered," he spat.

Heather gasped. "Really?"

"Really. That's why you have to be a good girl. Don't just go screwing any chappy who makes you laugh. There's a lot of sickos out there. Stick with me, and you'll be fine."

"I plan to," Heather simpered. "Do you know who did it? Was it another client of hers?"

Raymond glowered. "Let's not, love."

Heather blushed and lowered her gaze. "Of course. My apologies."

"You're alright, love. How about you make it up to me by coming up to my room?"

"Your room?" Heather asked. "Here?"

"Yup. The golden suites. Only three of 'em. And I always get the best one."

"You know," Heather started, "I'm suddenly not feeling very well."

Raymond, who had previously been swaying in his seat, became very still and focused in on her like a stalking predator. "You haven't gotten cold feet, have you? Because I'm sorry to say you're in the wrong line of work if you think 'dessert' is optional. You're not a normal woman. This isn't really a date. This is a business transaction. So far, it's been a successful one. Don't ruin it."

"I don't intend to. I just don't want you to have me when I'm not at my best," Heather said, maintaining eye contact while extracting her phone from her purse.

"A little drunk, are we?"

"Just a bit. And technically, it's not allowed," she replied, using her muscle memory to open her messages, click the top one, type a bunch of letters, and send them to Julius.

"Well, I won't tell if you won't. Drunk sex is my favorite kind," Raymond slathered, and Heather wondered if all clients were so uncouth or if he got away with more for being so wealthy.

The front door to the restaurant opened with a bang, and Julius appeared in the doorway, wild-eyed and rain-soaked. He charged forward, masterfully dodging servers, as everyone in the restaurant watched on, concerned. When Raymond realized Julius was heading for them, he stood—a good half a head taller than Julius and probably a hundred and fifty pounds heavier.

Heather worried for her friend, but he kept his distance as he yelled out, "Seriously, Becky?"

Raymond looked down at her. "You know this man?"

"She should. I'm her husband," Julius replied indignantly.

Heather blinked, surprised by the direction this was taking, but she looked at Raymond and nodded. "He is."

"Who the hell is this guy, Becks?" Julius asked, really delivering on his acting skills. "Is this where you always go when you say you're going out with friends? To see him?"

"Honey, I'm sorry," Heather said, standing as Raymond sat.

"We can talk about it in the car," Julius growled, turning his back on her. Then, realizing she wasn't following, turned his head. "Now, or you'll be hearing from my lawyer in the morning."

"I—" Heather hesitated, looking at Raymond.

Raymond shook his head, less angry than expected. "You go. I'm very sorry, Mr. Wilkes."

"Yeah, yeah," Julius said. "Screw both of you."

Raymond looked at Heather sorrowfully as she moved toward Julius. His expression said, what a shame. She was a caged bird, after all, and not one he could happily screw either. Perhaps he had a conscience after all.

CHAPTER FOURTEEN

THE PARTNER

AFTER A LONG, DULL, BUT SOMEHOW STRESSFUL DAY at work, Gabriel decided to head to Sherwoods to take the edge off, which felt somewhat ironic considering where he'd spent his morning. Still, despite his experience at AA—and the fact that Betty and his best friends were unavailable—he was undeterred from his mission to consume a well-earned, frosty beer.

Before he'd headed out the door, his parents had guilt-tripped him about going out again and had tempted him with fajitas, free beers, and a movie night. Unfortunately for them, he was not beguiled by their offerings because he knew that—

while delicious—it was all a trap. The moving-out conversation had begun to crop up recently, and thus, Gabriel was avoiding spending too long with them, even taking to eating dinner in his bedroom or the garage under the guise of studying.

He just hoped they could hold their horses for long enough for him and Betty to get serious. She already had her own adorable, two-bedroom apartment above the fishing supplies and tackle shop that only cost eight hundred dollars a month. A dream come true, considering the state of the economy. All he had to do was stay in her good books and duck his parents. They were the traditional kind and likely would disapprove of his plan, and Gabriel had no intention of escalating passive aggressiveness to full-blown arguments.

After sending a text to Betty, pouting about how much he missed her, he entered Sherwood's. He'd expected to be empty, like how it used to be on Tuesday nights, only to find it absolutely jam-packed. The seating had been moved to make room for square dancing, and there was a new special fried chicken sandwich on the board. The room smelled amazing, but Gabriel wouldn't stick around to taste Amber's latest masterpiece. He had no desire to spend his night standing, packed like a sweat sardine, so he left without ordering anything.

Still not wanting to go home, Gabriel looked up his other options. It seemed that almost everywhere, including Sludge, was closed on Tuesdays, leaving him with only one option— Molly Malone's.

Molly Malones was a 'traditional' Irish pub that most of his co-workers frequented. Despite the makeover, most of them still regarded Sherwood's as a bit of a dive, and Molly Malone's was within walking distance of most of their houses and the station. Gabriel himself had only been two times before and remembered very little about it, including its exact location.

Still, it wasn't hard to find, and as he looked up at the swinging, wooden sign depicting the 17th Century fishwife and hawker, he wondered if this was how the pubs in Ireland actually looked. Having never been abroad, he was unable to judge, but he liked to think so. He could also do with a European getaway.

Peering through the tiny, sunken window, he saw that it was mostly empty and entered the rustic, stone building through the heavy, wooden door. It was quiet inside; the quiet ballad emanating from the jukebox, crackling fireplace, mild conversation, and clinking of glasses were all that could be heard. It was a pleasant change from his usual venues, and the candles and dark wood interior made it feel exceptionally cozy.

He ordered an on-tap beer, sold in pints here, thanked the surly bartender, and sat in a booth, comfortable alone. As he sipped, he looked around at the framed photos of C-list celebrities who'd stopped by for a drink decades ago. Just as he scooted closer to one to read the plaque beneath, recognition struck him. Two voices from across the room. Of course, this was not surprising, as his co-workers came here almost every day. However, only one of these voices belonged to a police officer; the other he knew from somewhere else.

Cautiously, trying to be subtle, he turned around, looked over the back of the booth, and spotted Amanda Dinkley and none other than Crime Time's very own Brittany Hart. They were sitting at a table in the corner that wobbled and clunked against the flagstone floor. He couldn't make out what they were saying, but whatever it was, Amanda wasn't being quiet about it, and her pinker-than-usual cheeks and slumped body language implied that she was already beyond buzzed.

She leaned in to whisper something, and Brittany raised her perfect eyebrows high. It was then that Gabriel realized, without a doubt, that Amanda was their rat. They'd known that there was one in their midst for quite some time, Tina included. How else did Brittany always get the scoop on all local cases before the media did? Sure, none of the leaked information was classified, so no federal offenses were being committed, but it was still shady and unprofessional. Not to mention frustrating and downright unhelpful when sensitive, grieving parents were involved, like in the Violet Kennedy case.

A cat with a rat in his sights, all Gabriel had to do now was choose a plan of attack, and soon enough, it came to him. He was going to wait for Amanda to take a smoke break and leave Brittany behind. Amanda was a pack-a-day smoker, so it wouldn't take long, and while he didn't know for sure that Brittany wasn't a smoker, he was confident that she would deem the habit too smelly and unhealthy to partake in.

Sure enough, Amanda stood, pack in hand, and excused herself while Brittany stayed rooted to the spot. After a brief wait, Gabriel made his move and exited through the narrow backdoor, half-drunk beer in hand. The smoking area/beer garden was a small, fence-surrounded deck with a couple of picnic benches, a TV screen playing tonight's basketball game, and a heat lamp. It was similarly cozy on the inside but was half as pleasant and twice as stinky.

Gabriel started and waved at Amanda as if he hadn't known she was there. "Hi," he enthused with fake surprise.

Amanda's shock was genuine, but she eagerly waved him over as it wore off. "Hey, Gabe. What brings you over here? Have you finally realized this is the superior bar?"

"Square dancing night at Sherwood's."

"Aw, I love square dancing," Amanda pouted as if he'd insulted her personally.

"Of course you do," he jabbed.

"Yeah, because I'm fun, and you're not." She glugged from her pint glass, leaving a foam mustache behind that filled Gabriel with irrational rage. "Maybe I'll have to give that place a shot after all."

"They also have karaoke."

"Wow. They've upped their game. Still, there's no beating Molly's. Feels like home here."

"It is pretty comfy," Gabriel admitted. "Brittany come here much?"

Amanda chuckled. "Now and again. Prissy bitch barely even drinks. Watching her size zero figure, apparently. She likes hanging out with me, though, so I manage to coax her into shots now and again."

Gabriel doubted that the perfect princess, Miss America, cheerleader champion, and ice queen, Brittany Hart, enjoyed Amanda's company. Poor Amanda just couldn't see that she was being used. It was her own fault, and Gabriel loathed a blabbermouth, but he still felt some pity for his colleague.

"Oh, yeah?" he asked. "What do you talk about? She seems a bit, I don't know, boring," he said, making it sound as if Amanda was the one who was too cool for Brittany rather than the other way around.

Amanda laughed loudly. "She is kind of boring. But she can be fun, too, once she settles in. We talk about crime stuff mostly: my job, her job, the cases she's looking into. That sort of thing."

"What's she looking into right now?"

"Well," Amanda began, puffing out her chest, "I just gave her a good lead. That Daniel Palmer, Katy Graham case. She thinks it could be the next series."

Gabriel's blood ran cold. He'd been expecting this, banking on it even, but hearing it out loud made him realize how much he didn't want that to happen. "Oh yeah?" he asked weakly.

"Don't worry, I gave you credit."

"Thanks. Appreciate it."

"Anytime, bud."

"You know," Gabriel said, leaning forward conspiratorially, "I've actually been doing some more digging. I used Heather's contacts in Seattle and asked some questions. Apparently, there's a suspect that never made the papers."

"Oh yeah?" Amanda asked, moving closer, her breath hot on Gabriel's face.

"Oh yeah. A guy named Steve Adamski. Apparently, Katy was having an affair with him, but he didn't know she was married."

"Interesting," Amanda said before loudly slurping her drink. "That would give him and the husband motive."

"Exactly. Now, you're not going to find this information anywhere—top-secret stuff. But I'll tell you what I know. I can trust you to keep this between us, right?"

"Of course," Amanda insisted, lighting up another smoke.

"Okay, so Steve is 34 years old. He works as a plumber and lives in the suburb—Violet Fields—nearest to Katy and Daniel's. They lived in Lavender Meadow. These suburbs are only fifteen minutes away and separated by a park."

"Okay," Amanda said slowly.

"I think they met because he serviced her house, and she used his job as an excuse to have him over. He pulls up in his van, and the neighbors think nothing of it. And obviously, whoever killed Katy, she let in voluntarily, which makes me think he stopped by while Daniel was out jogging. Maybe she thought it was a booty call, but he was there to confront her."

"Things got heated," Amanda murmured. "Took a nasty turn."

"Exactly."

"Anything else?"

"They questioned him, but there was no evidence, and supposedly, his partner said he was at work at the time."

"Close friends always lie."

"Exactly. Unreliable alibi. He also passed a polygraph but—"

"Those are also unreliable," Amanda said, beaming, glad to sound competent.

"Exactly."

"Wow. Maybe we can solve this case together."

Gabriel chuckled. "Yeah, if we weren't so busy."

"Yeah," Amanda replied, looking glum and then looking past him through the glass door. "I think Brit is getting antsy; I better get back, but thanks for the tea."

"Anytime," Gabriel said, satisfied. "See you later."

"Yeah, man. Come join us, and I'll buy you a drink."

Gabriel smiled and offered up a feeble, 'Maybe.' He had no intention of further fraternizing with Amanda. He'd done what he'd set out to do and planted the necessary seeds to expose her as the snake she was. All he had to do now was wait and listen to Crime Time for Steve Adamski—a fictional man—to make an appearance.

CHAPTER FIFTEEN

THE DETECTIVE

WITH HIS HAND STILL WRAPPED TIGHTLY AROUND her wrist, Julius dragged Heather out of sight, around a corner, and across the road. Only then, standing in the protective darkness of surrounding park trees, did he drop the act.

"Sorry," he panted. "That was a little melodramatic."

Heather, a little tipsy, began to laugh. "You're quite the actor. I should call The Academy and let them know. Can CCTV footage be up for nomination?"

"I was hardly acting, to be honest. I was lying, sure, but the anger was real."

"My hero," Heather teased, batting her lashes.

Julius snorted derisively. "The man was an ogre. He looked like he wanted to eat you."

"Oh yeah. He was a real piece of crap, that's for sure," Heather agreed, blocking Vicky's number before the woman inevitably started blowing up her phone. She glanced up and saw that Julius still wasn't laughing. "Hey, I'm okay. It's all good. This is hardly an undercover horror story."

"I'm sure it isn't. Which is why I won't say it's too dangerous or something equally ignorant or condescending. I know you can handle yourself. I just don't like seeing you do so. Not like that anyway. Having to put up with his slavering."

"Well, at least it's over for now. Let's head back to the house and unwind. I need to get these damn shoes off. Did you eat at the bar? I'm sure we could grab something from around here before we call a taxi." Heather stopped babbling and looked up at Julius when he didn't answer a single question.

He sighed. "We can't go home, not yet."

"What do you mean?" Heather asked, scratching at the lace portion of her wig.

"I know where Barry Watts is. Jonno just called me with a tip. There's a not-so-legal speakeasy that he likes to attend, and apparently, Barry Watts has made it his new regular. He's there tonight. It might be a good opportunity to observe him in the wild."

"And I have to wear this?" Heather asked, knowing she was focusing on the wrong thing but unable to think about much more than her poor feet.

"The dress code calls for cocktail attire," Julius said, pulling a tie out of his pocket and popping his shirt collar up.

Heather laughed. "Do you always have that on you?"

"I like to be prepared," he said, with a shrug, as he wrapped one piece around the other.

"Alright, James Bond. Let's do this."

Julius smirked, tightening the knot. "That's the spirit. Though, if anyone in this partnership is a 007, it's you."

"I suppose that makes you Honey Ryder."

"I suppose it would," Julius said, offering his arm to alleviate Heather's hobble. "But tonight, we're Mr. and Mrs. Wilkes.

We're a passionate couple who have a complicated relationship. You know that I'm screwing my interns, and I know that you enjoy the company of rich older men. Yet our love-hate relationship is just too piquant to abandon."

"Are we wealthy?"

"Disgustingly. But we're also new money. Flashy and over the top. Sports cars, designer goods, and shady practices. That's why we belong in an upscale speakeasy. It's got everything people like us want: sex, drugs, and attention. Are you ready?" he asked, hailing a taxi with his free arm.

Heather flashed the same sultry smile at him that she had at Raymond Doyle. "Do your worst, Mr. Wilkes."

—

"Are you sure you've got the right address?" Heather asked as they entered a dingy alleyway that she wouldn't have noticed had it not been pointed out to her, let alone looked twice at. Weirder still, there was no music. No rumbling bass, no oontz-oontz, no boisterous DJ. She considered that maybe it wasn't *that* sort of venue, but there was no gentle lounge, classical, or acoustic either. Nor were there any people talking or loitering outside. She and Julius were completely alone.

Julius didn't say anything, just nodded toward the dark part of the alley where the streetlights no longer reached. Heather squinted, and as they continued their approach, she spotted a smooth metal door at the end.

Subtly looking around as if they might be being watched and recorded, Julius said, in a posh English accent, "Of course I have, darling. I've been here before, you know?"

Heather played along, realizing surveillance was likely, and put her hands on her hips. "And you didn't think to bring me?" she whined, unusually nasally. Despite her dad being a Londoner, she knew she wasn't going to be able to pull a convincing local accent out of the hat, so instead, she traveled to LA. The local toff and his loud American wife. A duo as old as time.

"Well, you've been a bad girl as of late. I didn't think you deserved a treat."

"What I deserve is a Nobel Peace Prize for putting up with your crap."

Julius smirked as he knocked on the door. A metal peephole slid open, and a voice from inside, gruff and thickly accented, said, "Password."

"Crowing cockerel," Julius replied confidently to the set of sunken eyes on the other side.

A loud clunk sounded, and the entire door slid open, revealing an enormous bouncer on the other side. Heather thought the man was Raymond for a split second, but upon double take, she noticed he was much younger and definitely not Caucasian. He was, however, equally large and shiny-headed.

Without speaking, the man unceremoniously patted them down and waved them toward another door, which was guarded by a similarly large man. The other man pulled it open for them, unleashing the music on the other side.

"Welcome to The Catacombs," he said flatly.

As they passed, they thanked him, and the door shut behind them, heavy and thick. Heather swore she heard it lock behind her, which, while not exactly fire-safe, was the least of their concerns for now. The stairs were wet and made of concrete, the music humming and trancelike, and feeling as if her kidneys were about to be stolen, she and Julius descended into London's underbelly.

As they pushed through a swing-door at the bottom, she found herself pleasantly surprised. The place was stylish, with black and white diamond tiled floors, gold gilding, and a plethora of fake tropical plants. A dance floor took up half the room, and the other half was adorned with tables and booths. The bartenders were dressed in black suits with bowties. The female bartenders wore short, form-fitting skirts, thin black stockings, and high heels.

At first glance, it seemed to be precisely the same as any other upscale nightclub, but soon enough, her cop brain picked up on the exchanges of powder-filled baggies and telltale signs of cocaine use amongst the patrons. Despite this, it didn't seem dangerous exactly. In fact, it was a little disappointing. It was her first foray into a 'semi-legal speakeasy,' and she was being greeted with pleasantries, and the scent of heritage rose.

Maintaining their cover, they remained interwoven until they reached the bar, where they parted to thumb through the leather-bound menus. This turned out to be the most shocking part about the place thus far. Duck liver, caviar, lobster, truffles, and quail eggs covered the 'bar snacks' page, and though she had yet to master the conversion rate, she knew that twenty-five pounds for a house red was steep. Playing the part, Heather loudly refused to split the bill, causing her classier husband to exasperatedly inform her that at this type of venue, one paid at the end.

Sitting at the only available table, Julius loudly told her to "Pretend like you belong, dear," and, "It's rude to stare; has anybody ever told you that?"

Heather gawked definitely, the ploy working to her benefit; she didn't have to be subtle so long as everyone could hear their faux tiff. Thus, she stared around to her heart's content.

The first thing she noticed was how many sex workers were present. In fact, they seemed to make up roughly sixty percent of the female population and 90 percent of the ones under forty. They sat alone at the bars or two-seater tables and waited to be approached, leaving Heather to wonder if there were also rooms here for that sort of thing. A door swinging open on the upstairs balcony in the shape of a love heart soon answered her query.

"What is Jonno doing hanging out in a place like this?" she asked quietly.

Julius shrugged. "He's always been a bit rebellious. He was a punk in the seventies and eighties. Then, he became a pot-smoking hippy. Now, I guess he's rebelling in a different way. I think he enjoys spending money in a way that the police won't approve of. Not that being here is strictly illegal, but it must give him a thrill."

"It's giving me heart palpitations."

"Well, if it helps, I've found him. Barry, I mean. Three o'clock."

Slowly, Heather turned and watched as Barry Watts emerged from an unmarked door on the left side of the dance floor. He was just as greasy as he was in his mugshot, except today, he was dressed in a three-piece pinstriped suit instead of a gray prison tracksuit. He moved like Jagger across the corner of the dance floor, stopping intermittently for handshakes and back pats before moving to the bar. Heather hated to admit it, but he had something about him—a charisma she hadn't been expecting.

"Okay. Now what?" Julius asked. "How do we get close to him?"

"We?"

"Okay, fine. How are you going to get close to him?"

"Better question is how am I going to ask him questions without sounding like a cop?"

"Become Heather Singh. The journalist."

Heather looked at Julius, eyebrow cocked. "You really think he's going to like journalists any better?"

"Maybe we just sit and watch for today, then. See what we can learn about him and his behavior. We could follow him home even, and see if he does anything suspicious." He was becoming more flustered as he spoke, way out of his comfort zone and depth.

Heather shook her head. "We won't get anywhere being overly cautious."

"Is blowing your cover straight out of the gate any better?"

Heather fiddled with her wig and had a lightbulb lit up upon seeing the blonde wrapped around her finger. "How about I put my outfit to good use? If you get my drift."

Julius side-eyed Barry with disgust. "If you really think that's the best method."

"Better than a cop or a journalist. I'll play young and dumb." Before Julius could protest, she stood and raised her voice. "I have not 'had enough'! I can get another drink if I want to!" His look of shock was genuine, and she swallowed her amusement as she stormed toward the bar, half-drunk glass in hand.

She neared, and roughly four feet away from both Barry and the bar, she pretended to trip. She flew forward, sloshing booze, but despite the dramatic display, Barry—seemingly oblivious due to the combination of drugs, drink, and music—moved out of her way, drink in hand.

Distracted by him doing so, Heather's slow-motion vision suddenly sped up, and she realized that she was no longer pretending to fall. She collided with the bar, which was at least better than the floor, smashing her glass against the surface. In between profusely apologizing to and thanking the staff, she watched him walk away and disappear back into the mysterious room.

Luckily, the staff were understanding, but she burned all over with humiliation as they and the patrons failed to muffle their laughter. Her plan had been to knock into him, hopefully spilling his drink in the process so that she could buy him a new one. She'd then complain about her husband and how she wanted to make him jealous with a powerful alpha male. Unfortunately, this was not the type of plan that she could try again. However, a small cut on her finger gave her a new idea, and she veered toward the bathrooms that were also on the left side of the dancefloor.

She entered the ladies room, cleaned her finger with a paper towel offered to her by a brusque woman—who charged her several pound coins for a spritz of perfume—and then exited shortly after. However, instead of returning to her seat, where Julius was watching intently, she very casually veered into the mysterious door.

She got as far as placing her palm flat on the dark green wood when another enormous bouncer stopped her in her tracks, his meaty sausage fingers gripping her bare shoulder.

"Ahem. Where do you think you're going?" he asked.

"Oh, is that not the smoking area?" she responded, beaming at him. "Silly me. I just saw a man go through here holding a pack of cigarettes."

"Smoking area is that way, ma'am," the man said, turning her and letting go before gesturing to a glass door on the other side of the room that led to some sort of conservatory.

"Silly me!" she laughed, slapping her forehead gently. Then, having another idea, she changed her posture, sticking her chest out and letting her arm fall to her side. She looked up at the man with dark, eyeliner-rimmed eyes and tilted her head toward the door. "What's in there, anyhow? Something fun, I'll bet."

113

The man looked down disapprovingly and didn't answer, and after a few moments of awkward silence, Heather admitted defeat and shuffled back to her seat in shame. She sat across from Julius, who looked mortified on her behalf and took a large swig of her replenished drink.

"I guess we're going with your plan tonight," she said.

Julius nodded, seemingly relieved that her attempts would go no further. After that, it turned into a reasonably pleasant night. They had some crudites, drank a little bit more wine, and talked about London. Then the clock struck midnight, the lights lowered, and the music was turned up. Things were getting rowdy, and there was still no sign of Barry Watts. Initially undeterred, they swapped to water and tried to make small talk over the din. Then 1 a.m. came and went, followed by 2, 3, and eventually 4. Then, last call was announced, the lights came up, and the bouncers began to remove people in small groups.

Julius paid the bill with a bouncer looming behind him, and their attempt to wait for Barry in the alleyway was soon thwarted. "We have to find out what's behind that door," Heather croaked, beyond exhausted, leaning on Julius as she limped toward the road. "I have a bad feeling about it. Talking to that bouncer tied my guts into knots."

"You think it's worse than what's behind the heart-shaped one?"

"Way worse than an orgy, yes. And he has power here. We may have made it inside, but we're just plebs compared to him. Do you think Jonno could—"

"Jonno is a bit of a coward, I'm afraid," Julius interrupted. "But he might be able to get us behind that door if I find the right key to his combination, so to speak." He paused. "We'll speak to Barry. One way or another."

Heather nodded, eyes watering as she yawned and waved for a cab. She was worn out, frustrated, and not entirely hopeful. Yet, all was not lost. Her tumultuous night had been valuable in more ways than one. She had a new suspect to add to the list and a secret to be unveiled. She just hoped she wouldn't need to keep wearing a wig to uncover it.

CHAPTER SIXTEEN

THE PARTNER

SITTING ON THE GRUNGY COUCH—WHICH HAD BEEN 'rescued' by Gabriel and his bandmates from a curb in Otter Point—in his parent's garage, Gabriel cracked a beer and nestled beneath a blanket that still smelled like cats despite not having owned one in years. Then, he eagerly clicked on the newest episode of Crime Time and sat back with a sigh.

While the Wi-Fi took its sweet time and the theme music and lengthy ads played, he scrolled on his laptop that was precariously perched on the arm of the couch. Katy's file was on the screen. He wasn't a corkboard man. He was all digital. And what he'd put together on Katy, Daniel, and those that surrounded them thus far was starting to shape into something meaty. He may not have had Heather's intuition, but he kicked her ass in report writing and file management.

"Welcome to Season 6 of Crime Time," Brittany eventually said, rambling on and on about yet another 'life-changing' meal kit. This one's gimmick was low-calorie, high-protein for gym junkies. Gabriel thought the dishes sounded disgusting. What was with all the green beans? Where was the seasoning? Where was the joy? Gabriel enjoyed hitting the weights, but you would have to pry paprika and garlic powder out of his cold, dead hands.

He was getting distracted and forced himself to focus as Brittany continued. "This season, we're covering yet another Washington State case," she announced. "It's a little bit niche, but some of you might have heard of it—the murder of Seattle supermodel in the making, Katy Graham. You guys, this poor girl. I'll post a picture of her on Instagram, but wow, she was so beautiful, and only twenty-nine."

Brittany wasn't exactly eloquent, but she was engaging, and Gabriel knew from her enthusiasm that she'd taken the bait: hook, line, and sinker.

"So, I'm calling this season 'The Hunt for the Lavender Meadows Strangler' because that's what we're going to do as a team. We're going to solve a real-life unsolved murder together! There will be a tipline you can call and an email address you can write to if you know anything at all. Locals will get priority, so include your zip code at the start of your messages. Seriously, I think we can do this. I've received some really juicy information."

Clearly thinking this was going to be her Golden State Killer, Brittany could barely contain herself. He knew it was partly an act—just like ghost hunters who scream when nothing is happening to rile up the audience—but he could tell she was really into this, and it gave him some twisted pleasure to know he'd been the one to dupe her.

"So, let's get into it," Brittany said. "Katy Graham was murdered in her home in the newly built Lavender Meadows suburb of Seattle on Sunday, July 2nd, 2023—"

"Boring!" Gabriel yelled aloud as Brittany recited all of what he already knew. She was discovered by her fiancé, Daniel Palmer, at 3:22 pm in their downstairs bedroom. Her wrists had been bound with her phone charger to the headboard, and she'd been strangled to death. He'd been gone for one hour and twenty-two minutes, and the door was unlocked, meaning that Katy had let her killer inside.

"Now, I know what you're thinking, ladies. It's always the romantic partner. Her fiancé could've easily unlocked the door himself and said he'd found it open. No one could prove otherwise. Cameras weren't allowed in their HOA."

Gabriel furrowed his brow. She'd already been digging. Talking to the neighbors, most likely. That made him uneasy.

"There was also no mud, footprints, or evidence that anyone had been inside," Brittany continued. "But there was no evidence pointing to the opposite either. That is to say, a lack of evidence isn't exactly proof of anything. The killer could've worn gloves. They could've taken their shoes off. It was also a dry day. No mud so long as you stick to the streets and sidewalks. And most people don't realize that most materials don't hold fingerprints. So what I'm trying to say is there's equal evidence to say that Daniel did it as there is to say that he didn't. Which, I suppose, is why, after a brief bout of questioning, he was let free." She paused and laughed. "I know, I know. It seems so obvious. It's got to be him, right? But I promise you that I'm not being obtuse for the sake of the show. I genuinely think there's more to this than meets the eye, and I don't want to lose scope by focusing too much on Daniel."

"Here we go," Gabriel said, leaning forward.

"So, let's talk about another suspect. Steve Adamski."

"Whoo!" Gabriel cheered and clapped. He had her and Amanda in his trap.

"A man whose name never left the police reports and made it to the media. Until now, thanks to my very trustworthy anonymous resource. Okay, so Steve. Steve is a plumber who lives in the same suburban area on the Seattle city outskirts. You might know it as 'The Garden' because each block of new builds is named after a flower. Steve lived in Violet Fields, a two-minute drive away from Katy and Daniel's house, which would give him plenty of time to commit this crime, even if he traveled on foot. Now, why is Steve suspicious? Well, according to my source, he'd been having an affair with Katy for several months at the time of her death. They'd met because he was their plumber, and Katy had always preferred a man who worked with his hands—"

Gabriel laughed. Amanda had even added details. This was perfect.

"And they used his job as an excuse to hook up while Daniel was at work. Now, they never brought Steve in for questioning, which I thought was weird. What's even weirder is I couldn't find a Steve Adamski, so I think he might've changed his name or moved away. I'm leaning toward the former because I found several plumbers in the area; one is named Steve, and two have Polish surnames. I'm going to have to do some more digging and get back to you on that. But I think this is a promising lead."

Gabriel hummed. He was going to have to confront her before she started dragging innocent plumbers into this, but he figured he had just enough time for one more prank before that was necessary. As Brittany started in on Katy's life and background, Gabriel texted Betty and told her that there was a change of plans for their Wednesday night date—they were going to Molly Malone's.

—

"So, why Molly's?" Betty asked as they pulled up. She'd been distracted before that, talking about the new grill at work and how it had changed her life. She hardly seemed to remember where they were until she saw the wooden sign blowing in the wind.

Gabriel shrugged and parked. "Sherwood's was slammed the other night, so I came here instead. I liked the atmosphere and heard that they do really good fish and chips. Since Heather is out of the country, I figured a little culinary travel might be fun for us."

Betty smiled. "That does sound fun. I don't think I've had real fish and chips since I went with my family to Cornwall back in… oh God, 2005." She kissed him on the cheek before hopping out of the car, and stage one of his plan—keeping his girlfriend happy—was in full swing.

He joined her on the sidewalk, took her hand, and spun her. The skirt of her pink gingham dress flared out as she tottered around in her pink platform pumps, and she jumped up and down eagerly. "This place is so cute," she squealed, looking in through the windows. "The candles! The photos! And the fireplace! Oh, we should go to Ireland this summer. Rent a little cottage surrounded by a field of those hairy cows."

"I thought those were Scottish?"

"They're a Celtic breed," she corrected, the superior know-it-all. "But let's go to Scotland too!"

Gabriel smiled and wrapped an arm around her, glad she was already making plans for the future and even happier that she could be her quirky, excitable self around him. She'd tamped it down at first, more cool and collected than childish or silly. Now, she was both, and he loved all of her moods—even the slightly grumpy, post-night shift ones. Even then, she was still like felt like sunshine to him, warm and nurturing.

However, he was sorry to say that Molly Malone's might be as close as they get to Ireland until he finished his degree or got promoted, and neither was visible on the horizon.

As he pushed open the door, she noticed the street sign and whispered. "Oh, they do trivia nights on Thursdays. We have to do that. I am the queen of random knowledge."

"Well, that's funny because I'm something of a king, my lady," he joked, holding the door open for her. "We're going to destroy these old geezers," he whispered in her ear as she brushed past, and she giggled.

He joined her, letting the door close of its own accord, and they trailed up to the bar, where the bartender—a woman in her sixties with short gray hair—eyed them with exhaustion.

"Pitcher, please," Betty requested.

"Of what?" the surly woman asked.

As Brittany asked what they had, and the bartender began to list absolutely every option in a droning monotone, Gabriel looked around. To his relief, Amanda was there, nursing a glass of something brown and creamy with Lee Pearson and Patrick Reeves. He noticed the numerous empty glasses beside her and raised his eyebrows. It was barely seven o'clock, but crazier still was that she didn't seem particularly inebriated. The woman was like a tank. In another life, she would've been a great circus addition as a strongwoman. She could even bench Gabriel, as he was unfortunately aware, thanks to their last work Christmas party.

Brittany hopped toward him, pitcher in one hand and two glasses in the other. "Speaking of strong women," he accidentally said aloud.

"What?" Brittany asked him, half-laughing.

Gabriel flushed. "Oh, my friend Amanda is here. She's like stupidly strong."

"Oh, the one with the short hair and fun t-shirt?"

Gabriel laughed, not sure if a 'fun t-shirt' was an insult or not. "Yeah, that's her."

"She's going outside. Do you want to hang out with her? I'm not that hungry yet. Kitchen's open for another hour and a half."

Stage two—talk to Amanda—was going to come easier than expected, it seemed, and Gabriel nodded. "Yeah. Pitchers are for sharing, after all."

"Exactly! And I've hardly met any of your friends," Brittany said, charging toward the back door with purpose, leaving Gabriel to jog after her, his hands empty and outstretched.

Outside, they honed in on Amanda, and Gabriel, distracted by his master plan, suddenly remembered Amanda's very vocal dislike of Betty as his girlfriend sat opposite his colleague. Fortunately, Amanda lit up and raised her glass.

"Gabe!" Amanda roared. "And Little Miss Thing!"

Gabriel cautiously joined Betty at the table as his girlfriend placed the pitcher in the middle of the table. "Help yourself," she said. "Any friend of Gabe's is a friend of mine."

Amanda looked genuinely touched and drained her drink to make way for beer. "Thank you kindly, ma'am," Amanda said, affecting a fake southern accent.

Gabriel considered that maybe she was drunker than he thought and hoped she'd be able to remember what he was about to tell her in the morning. "Hi, Amanda," he said, pulling out his pack of smokes.

"Back again?" she asked.

"I thought we'd try the fish and chips for date night."

"Good choice. The tartar sauce is sublime," Amanda responded, nodding but not looking at him. Instead, she was staring openly at Brittany, a glazed look of fascination on her face like one might pull when quietly examining a beautiful bird in their backyard. "How do you get those lashes on?" she asked, running a finger over the top of her bare eyelid.

"Oh, it's just a lot of practice. I sucked maybe the first one thousand times. The trick is to try putting them on other people first. It's easier to see what you're doing. Then, you move on to yourself. The big, thick ones are easier, too. Those natural floppy ones are near impossible."

"I don't think I could ever do it," Amanda admitted. "No makeup skills for me. Mom was a tomboy, so I'm a tomboy. Sometimes, I think I'd look nice all done up in a dress, but when I put one on, I look like a bridge troll."

Amanda laughed self-deprecatingly, and Gabriel could hear Betty's sensitive heart break. She began to hype the other woman up and hit her with all sorts of advice regarding her face shape, body type, complexion, and so on. A lot of it went in one ear and out the other, but when he heard her say, "You'd definitely suit being a strawberry blonde," Gabriel looked at Amanda and realized she was right. Then, it was their time to hype Betty up.

Getting on like a house on fire, Gabriel decided to strike when the first lull arrived. "Hey, you know the Katy Graham case?" he asked nonchalantly.

"Yeah?" Amanda responded, eyes wide. She was now both giddy and drunk, which was perfect. He just hoped she had easy access to Brittany as soon as possible.

"Well, I found out something else. Apparently, Katy was a long-time member of a BDSM club in Seattle. Which might explain the tied wrists and choking."

Amanda gasped, putting a hand to her mouth before slowly lowering it. "Do you think it could've been erotic asphyxiation gone wrong with a club member?"

Gabriel nodded solemnly. "I do."

"Or maybe it was Steve, and she asked him to do it, but because he wasn't experienced, he went too far."

Gabriel shrugged. "Your guess is as good as mine. She used a pseudonym on the scene. Copperhead. I've only ever seen it written down, mind you. You won't find it anywhere online."

"Wow, because of her ginger hair," Amanda said, eyes glassy. "What was the club called?"

"The Castle," Gabriel lied, finding it scarily easy to do so after a beer and a half. "But don't bother contacting them. I already pushed way too far."

"Of course not. But that's fascinating."

Though Amanda continued to enthuse, and they went back and forth on the conjured theories, Gabriel steadily felt Betty tense beside him, and not wanting to fail part one of tonight's mission, he suggested, "Should we go order?"

"Yeah, sounds good," Betty said, her tone a little clipped. "So nice to meet you, Amanda."

"Same to you, Betsy," Amanda slurred, having drunk most of the beer.

Inside, after ordering, they sat in a booth, and Betty seemed unusually terse despite Gabriel's ploys to keep the happy mood going. Eventually, he asked, "Is something wrong?"

Betty looked at him, her eyes unusually sad. "You lied to her," she whispered.

Gabriel froze but decided not to deny it. "How could you tell?"

"I just could. Your voice changed. Why did you lie to her about the BDSM club or whatever? And who's Katy Graham?"

Gabriel felt he had no choice but to come clean. He couldn't lie to Betty. Amanda, sure—she was screwing over the police department and fraternizing with the enemy—but not Betty. So, he told her about his investigation, Heather's investigation, Heather's relationship with Daniel, Amanda being a rat, and how he was trying to catch her red-handed. It was a long-winded spiel, and the food arrived halfway through, and though he demolished his own portion, Betty merely picked at hers.

"That sounds dangerous," she said once he wrapped up the final details. "For you and Heather. I mean, Daniel might be a murderer, and you're just hanging out at his house, sneaking around, pretending to be a journalist, and going behind your boss's back. What if you find out that he did do it, and he kills you?"

"Just pretend I'm a private investigator. People less qualified than me look into homicides all the time. Look at Brittany Hart, for example."

"I get that, and I get why you're doing this. Heather is your best friend. And I get why you're mad at Amanda. But pretending to be her friend to trick her just seems so mean. Why not just confront her? She'd probably tell you the truth."

"I needed to know for sure."

"You said you already knew for sure this morning. Why keep going? Not to mention saying that stuff about a dead woman is pretty messed up."

Gabriel groaned, the guilt finally hitting him. "I know. Ugh. I guess because I'm still mad at her. She got us in a lot of trouble during the Violet Kennedy case. Now, I want her to get into trouble. But I should've never said any of that."

"No, you shouldn't have. And need I remind you that an eye for an eye, and the whole world goes blind," Betty muttered, looking down at her plate.

Gabriel threw up her hands. "You're right. I'll stop. Not the case but with Amanda. And if it makes you feel any better, we'll join that tracking app we talked about. That way, you can see where I am when I'm looking into Daniel."

Betty nodded, a little deflated but clearly working hard to better her own mood. She took a big bite of fish and smiled wide. "This *is* really good."

"Yeah, it is."

They ate quietly after that, and though the tension had largely dissipated, some discomfort remained. And when the night was over, Gabriel dropped Betty off at her place without asking to come in, and when she didn't ask, he drove away, feeling like the biggest jerk in the world.

CHAPTER SEVENTEEN

THE DETECTIVE

A FTER STRIKING OUT INFORMATION-WISE WITH THE other food trucks, Heather—dressed in her colorful journalist getup—waited in the long line leading to Ambrosia Kebabs. When she reached the front and the swarthy man running the truck apologized, she turned on the charm, displaying saint-like patience to win him over from the jump. Then, she, of course, ordered a small portion of food—as she had from the other trucks—and as he prepared it, she dropped the journalist bombshell.

The man paused, looking down at her with an unreadable expression. She readied herself to be denied service or be told to 'piss off,' but instead, enthusiasm, starting in the mouth, spread across his features.

"A food blogger?" he asked, grinning, his Greek accent thick. "I can make something special for you. Something better than chips."

"Sorry," Heather replied sheepishly, shaking her head. "I'm in the true crime business, actually."

The man raised his eyebrows. "True crime, huh? My wife likes that stuff. It's not for me. I have to plug my ears walking through the living room." He laughed loudly but then stopped abruptly. "Why are you telling me this?" he asked, looking behind Heather nervously as the line continued to grow. He waved apologetically at his would-be patrons.

"Does the name Lilly Arnold ring a bell?"

His face fell and he sighed. "It does," he said gravely. "I watched her walk home every night. She often bought dinner from me."

"And you saw her the night she was killed?"

"I did. Poor girl. I think she had something on her mind. The others," he said, gesturing to the other trucks with a tilt of the head, "Didn't seem to notice. But I did. She didn't look at me. Didn't wave or smile. She seemed inebriated already and was holding a bottle of wine in hand and applying some lipstick. I'd never seen that before. I called out, but as she turned into the woods, I saw that she was wearing headphones. You know, the little bud-type ones."

"Did you see anyone follow her?"

"Not exactly. If I had and could identify them, I would've told the police. The problem was so many people headed in the same direction. Some on the path, some through the trees."

"Does this man look familiar?" Heather asked, handing over the photo of Daniel that she'd passed around The Thistle & Pig.

The man nodded repeatedly, tapping at the photo with his finger. "Oh, I saw him. Hard to forget that face. Or his voice. Booming. American. I first noticed him because he was wearing jogging gear, and yet he was only walking. Then, he ordered two kebabs even though he was alone and headed off that way. It was not quite the same way Lilly went, but it was close. There's a clearing next to the one she was found in that's full of picnic benches."

"Did he come back before you closed?"

"He did not. But most people only go one way through Hyde Park."

"What about Lilly? Was it normal that she didn't reappear?"

"No. It was not. Nothing about her behavior was normal."

"Were you concerned at the time?"

The man frowned. "Yes. And I should have called somebody. I know that now. But I managed to convince myself that she'd taken another route home or was hanging out with friends. I didn't want to be a busybody. I have been deeply ashamed of myself for this."

"Don't be. Someone wanted her dead. Saving her that night would only have delayed things. Besides, she was already dead by the time you closed up shop." None of these things were true: Heather wasn't one hundred percent sure the murder was premeditated, even though it seemed likely; Lilly might still be alive today; she died about forty minutes after the owner of Ambrosia Kebabs headed home. However, he didn't need to know that.

The man sighed and handed over Heather's fries. "London is not the same as it used to be."

Heather took the food and glanced behind her at the now ridiculously long line. "Thank you so much for your time. I'll let you get back to work."

"I wish you luck," he said. "In solving this, or whatever it is that you're doing. Food is on the house."

"That's very kind but not necessary," Heather replied, hanging over a fifty-pound note. "Thanks again." She left before the man could protest, allowing the queue to keep moving, and rejoined Julius, who was snacking on a spring roll from a different stand.

"Are you okay?" Julius asked, noticing Heather's professional neutrality falter as she turned.

"He saw Daniel," she said, suddenly feeling dizzy. "He saw him that night. In jogging clothes."

"So it was definitely him."

Heather nodded. "And he ordered two kebabs."

Julius's mouth fell open. "You think he was going to meet her, don't you?"

"I don't know. It could be a coincidence. Maybe he was meeting somebody else. Maybe he was just really hungry. Maybe he was meeting her. Maybe they exchanged numbers while I was in the bathroom or something. Maybe he pretended to be a photographer like he did with Katy Graham."

"I have to admit the double kebabs are suspicious. I mean, look at those portions," Julius said, watching with amazement as somebody tore into their lunch on a nearby picnic bench. It was about the same size as their head. "I mean, I could handle the one. But not two. And I like my food."

"Yeah," Heather said, feeling her heart palpitate, and her hand trembled as she brought a hot, salty fry to her lips. "And he went in the same direction as she did."

"And he didn't come back."

Heather grimaced even though the food was delicious. "What if I'm just going after Raymond and Barry because I can't face the truth?"

"All the more reason to go after them. Then you'll know for sure. Process of elimination."

"Yeah, I guess so." She chewed fiercely, thinking hard. "The jogging thing is weird, too. He was also jogging when Katy died. That feels like something."

"What kind of something?"

"Well, he's used it as a sort of alibi. A reason for him to be out of the house for a brief period of time. He wears the outfit and gets sweaty, and maybe it convinces the police. It probably wouldn't hold up in court, but it's something."

Julius nodded. "Like the front door being open. It creates doubt."

"Exactly. And it would also allow him to run in a public place without seeming suspicious or scaring people. He could use it to get close. And the clothes and shoes would aid his pursuit."

"So you think it's him?"

"I didn't say that, but it's pretty damn compelling." Heather grimaced, a little disgusted with what she was about to suggest. "What if it's a fantasy thing? You know how serial killers have rituals? What if jogging is part of his 'ritual'?"

Instead of replying, Julius hesitated and said, "I know you're sick of drinking, but—"

"Oh, please. Let's go to the pub. I need a glass of wine stat."

"Lead the way."

They finished their small portions as they walked, and as they ate the scraps over a bin, Heather spotted Poppy and froze, half of a chewed chip tumbling from her lips. The young woman was standing in exactly the same position as Lilly had been in the background of Heather and Daniel's vacation photo, and for the first time, Heather realized something—Lilly and Poppy were nearly identical.

"Plan C," she muttered, charging ahead. Before Julius could catch up to her and ask her what she was talking about, she'd darted across the road and made eye contact with Poppy. "Hey!" she called out, jogging toward the girl who reciprocated her friendly expression.

"Hi, Heather," Poppy said. "You alright?"

"Yeah. Good, thanks. Mind if I bum a smoke?" she asked, again trying to seem more cool than cop. "I dropped my pack earlier."

"Yeah, sure," Poppy said, handing over a brown pack of rolling tobacco, papers, and a tube of filters. Heather didn't know how to roll, and hoping Julius would, handed the supplies over to him. To her relief, he got going, and Heather smiled bashfully.

"Sorry. American."

Poppy chuckled. "No, you're alright. You're not alone. Even over here. I spend half my nights out rolling for mates." Poppy paused, scrutinizing Heather. "You look like you've got a bee buzzing around in your bonnet."

"Yeah. I do. I need your help," Heather responded breathlessly.

"Oh yeah?" Poppy asked, trying to seem indifferent but clearly excited at the prospect of helping an investigative journalist.

"Yeah. Basically, there's this suspect, Barry Watts—"

"Oh, I know him," Poppy glowered. "Massive creep."

"Yeah. Well, we got into this speakeasy bar, and we found him there, but he kept disappearing behind this guarded door. I want to know what's behind it."

"Uh-huh," Poppy said slowly, the concept not yet clicking.

"And I think that with a little 'makeover,' you could be the spit of Lilly."

"And then he'd let me in?"

Heather shrugged. "Worth a shot, don't you think?"

Poppy nodded slowly, taking a drag, as Julius handed Heather a cigarette and popped another one in his mouth for good measure. As it turned out, being undercover was full of bad habits.

"Alright, I can do that," Poppy said. "I was thinking of going blonde anyway. I never did because people said we looked like twins. But now, what's the harm? I can pop in some hoops and darken my makeup. Done."

"Can you do it by tomorrow night? I'll pay for you to go to a salon. And don't cheap out. I'd hate for you to fry your hair."

Poppy laughed. "Nah, no need for that. I've got a bleach kit at my house. If it falls out after it falls out."

Heather rolled her eyes and counted out one hundred pounds while puffing free-handed. "Here," she said, handing over the cash. "The club is called The Catacombs. Meet us there at seven. The address is—"

Poppy held her hand up. "Oh, I know where The Catacombs is. Everyone does. Just very few of us actually get to go inside." She smiled wickedly and narrowed her eyes. "We're going to catch this bastard. I feel it. There's something different about you."

"I really hope you're right."

"I'm almost never wrong," Poppy said with a wink.

"That I believe."

"You better," Poppy said, stepping forward, suddenly close enough to hug, and Heather understood why the girl had never looked in Julius's—nor any other man's—direction. "Drinks are on me, sweet. Head on in. I'll be there in a sec to join you. I'm dying for a pint after today's lunch rush."

Heather and Julius filtered in through the exiting mob, and though her partner seemed unhappy about the contents of Plan C, he didn't say anything. Heather knew that he agreed that it was a good idea, even if it was a dangerous one, and with any luck, they'd have Barry—if guilty—in handcuffs by the end of the week. No harm and a little foul.

CHAPTER EIGHTEEN

THE DETECTIVE

AFTER TWO MIMOSAS AND A DELICIOUS HALLOUMI wrap, Heather felt oddly confident and relaxed as they walked through Hyde Park despite the unsettling revelations about Daniel. Maybe it was because she had something more pressing and hopeful to focus on—the infiltration of The Catacombs. Poppy was perfect. She was going to get into that room. They were going to find out what Barry's deal was, one way or the other. So long as they didn't let Helen catch wind of their plan, it was all going to go swimmingly. Heather was sure of it.

"I'm on coffee for the next few days," Julius grumbled.

"Too much hooch?"

He nodded, pinching the bridge of his nose. "I forgot how much English city dwellers drink versus American ones. Rural towns are probably a toss-up, but nobody drinks in Seattle. If you have more than three cocktails at a party, I've heard they throw you into rehab."

Heather laughed. "It is pretty full-on over here."

"Maybe we should come back for a proper holiday someday," Julius suggested. "Without all the interviews, meetings, and dates, we'd probably manage to stay mostly sober."

"That sounds awesome," Heather laughed. "I'm getting too old for this crap. Give me historical buildings and double-decker bus tours over a couple of rounds at a pub any day."

"That could be arranged. Madam Tussauds then the Black Tower. A bus tour during the day and a ghost tour at night. The changing of the guards. Harrods. The museums." Julius shook his head. "We're missing out on all the cliches!"

"And yet," Heather replied, gesturing around. "I'm still loving it."

"I'm glad, because I'm serious about coming back."

Heather didn't respond. Instead, she stopped and narrowed her eyes, trying to extend her not-so-great vision into the middle distance.

"Heather?"

"Is that Liam?" she asked.

Julius paused, copying her stance and following her gaze. He benefited from wearing glasses and nodded, "I think it is."

Sure enough, Liam—dressed in all black, including an oversized, road-worn leather jacket—stumbled out of a bush and onto the path ahead. People gave him a wide berth, and he laughed loudly and lunged at an elderly, wealthy-looking couple like a reactive dog on a chain. He was laughing so hard that he, clearly drunk and unbalanced, fell back unceremoniously and returned to the thorny-looking bushes.

Heather tutted and strode toward the young man, and when she reached him, she moved into his line of sight, blocking the sun, her hands on her hips. He looked up at her, eyes unfocused, head wobbly, and then he smiled.

"Heather Singh," he slurred, confirming his inebriation, "And that guy!" Julius and Heather extended their hands, offering Liam help, but he gently slapped them away, still chuckling to himself. "Nah, I'm pretty cozy down here."

"You're laying in a gorse bush drunk out of your mind, and it's not even six," Julius replied, trying to sound firm but clearly amused.

Liam looked up at him and stuck out his arms. "Alright. Help me up then."

They heaved Liam to his feet and held onto his upper arms on either side, worried he might fall again. "You good?" Heather asked.

Liam twisted toward her and leaned in close enough that she could smell the beer on his breath. "I want to talk to you," he hissed. "Poppy said you were at the pub, so I wandered over from my mate's place. Didn't realize how drunk I was until I got going. Tried to go for a piss by that tree and tripped over my trousers."

"Well, you found me," Heather said. "Impressive considering the state you're in."

"Well, I really need to talk to you. So can we have a chat? Alone."

Julius's face said no, but Heather's mouth said yes, and she told him to wait behind while she followed Liam, who was already lumbering through the trees of Hyde Park.

The further they ventured, the more nervous she became. At first, she was confused as to why she felt that way. She'd undoubtedly put herself in stranger, riskier scenarios to garner information. Then she realized that she wasn't Heather Bishop right now. She was Heather Singh, an unarmed journalist. Sure, she still had her muscles and training, but she felt naked without her weapon. Luckily, she didn't think Liam wanted to harm her, not yet, despite the fact he was muttering to himself and leading them far off the beaten path. If he was a killer, she wasn't the target. If he was a killer, he was a remorseful one.

Eventually, they came to a clearing, and though the route was unorthodox and long-winded, Heather recognized it instantly. She'd been here once already. It was where Lilly Arnold had been killed.

Her eyes on the back of Liam's neck, she asked, "This is where she died, isn't it?" as if she didn't already know.

Liam nodded and wandered slowly, stumbling over the picnic bench and sat, waiting and watching, for Heather to join him. She did, and as they sat face to face, she felt as if she was sitting in an interrogation room at the cold metal table and that Liam, his hands clasped together, was shackled to it.

"So," Heather began, a little nervous without her usual uniform and identity.

"I know who you are," Liam interrupted.

Heather's stomach did a flip that would earn it a spot in the Olympics. "I've told you who I am, Liam."

He looked at her, some deeply buried sobriety shining through. "They did a good job. Whoever you work for. You've got a profile and a couple of AI-generated articles that make you look passable. But I can spot a fake. So, I did a little digging. Heather Bishop, you have had quite an illustrious career."

"I suppose I have."

"I'd like to help you keep your streak."

"Okay," Heather said slowly, pulling out her notebook.

"I lied to the police before, but I'm not going to lie to you."

"What did you lie about?" Heather asked, opening the leather binding.

"Well, it's more that I kept my mouth shut. I don't get along well with cops. You'd understand if you also had half of your family locked up." He stared down at scarred knuckles.

"I'm sure I would."

"But I like you. You seem honest. Aside from the whole pretending to be a journalist thing." He looked up from his hands and into Heather's eyes and chuckled. "Don't worry. I'm not here to confess. I'd have done that long ago if I was guilty. No, the reason I'm here is to help you find the killer and to do so, you need my side of the story."

"Do I?"

"You do. And you might decide it was me who did it once I tell it. But if that's what it takes to find justice, lock me up and throw away the key. But I'm telling you, I would have never hurt her. Never."

"Okay," Heather said, strangely affected by the intensity of his gaze. "Tell me everything."

Liam met Poppy in late 2016 when she'd been hired on as a server at the Thistle & Pig. She'd turned eighteen the month before. He himself was freshly nineteen, which caused him to ask if she was also a Scorpio. She was, and on their smoke break, they bonded over reading their daily horoscope. They even had the same app, and it told them to expect blossoming friendships and embrace fresh starts. Though he didn't say it aloud, he suspected the friendship it talked about would be theirs, and the entire experience felt a lot like kismet.

Soon enough, it seemed that the stars were right, and the pair became almost inseparable—at work anyway. For reasons initially unknown, they never became quite as tight as Lilly was to additional newcomer Poppy. It didn't take long for Liam to realize why Lilly so often shot him down for outside-of-work hangouts despite getting on so well during their shift. It wasn't that she didn't like him; it was that there was no romance between the girls despite Poppy playing for the other team. There was, however, something bubbling beneath the surface of his relationship with Lilly. Something that prevented hanging out one-on-one.

Then came the work party. It happened in 2017, about a month and a half before Lilly was murdered. It was the first party they'd ever been to together. Greg was hosting at his beautiful detached home in an upscale suburb. Thanks to his wife's position as CFO at a big tech firm, they had plenty of bedrooms, a pool, and a sound system, and they even hired caterers and bartenders. It was all the staff could talk about for weeks in the run-up, and it did not disappoint.

The party was already raging by the time Liam had arrived, and though he wasn't a big drinker at the time—though he admitted to being in the danger zone nowadays—he took every shot offered to him. So did Lilly. The drunker they got, the cozier they became, and despite Poppy trying to maintain order, she failed to prevent the inevitable. At first, it was a kiss, then making out, then a skinny dip in the pool, and by the point they headed to one of the bedrooms, neither could be reined in. Not that anyone cared much by that point. They were all focused on their own goals of getting laid or blacking out. They fell asleep in each other's arms, and in the morning, when Liam woke, Lilly was gone.

At work, they didn't mention what had happened, and fortunately, neither did anyone else. Liam had feebly attempted to broach the subject on a few occasions in the hopes of pursuing a relationship, but it was clear from her shift in demeanor that it was only ever going to be a one-night stand.

That then led them to the night she was murdered roughly six weeks later. Earlier that day, she'd told Liam that she needed to talk to him and to meet him at the very park bench that he and Heather sat at now. She also said to him that she didn't want anyone to know, so they devised a plan to make it clear they were heading home separately. He would ask if he wanted company, she would loudly say no, and then he was to follow her no earlier than fifteen minutes later. He did as he was told and found her looking up at the stars and drinking from a bottle of red.

He had high hopes that this was the moment that she confessed her feelings and that they'd go home together, but when he sat down and she passed the bottle, her eyes red-rimmed, he knew it was not to be. It took her a while, but eventually, she spat out—

"That she was pregnant," Heather said. "And it was yours."

Liam sniffed and rubbed his nose with the back of his hand. "Yeah. She'd slept with a few other people in that time period—clients mostly—but without being crass, there were things that led her to believe it was mine, not theirs. Vasectomies, johnnies, you get the picture."

"And how did you feel about that?"

Liam rubbed his velvety head. "I don't know. Shocked, I guess. But I also loved her—or at least, I really liked her."

"So you wanted her to keep it in hopes you'd be together?" Heather asked.

"No, it wasn't like that. She was one of my best mates and my best workmate. I wanted to support her. I told her that whatever she did, I'd support her. I'd go with her to the clinic if she wanted; if she wanted to keep it, I'd co-parent. I even said I'd take the kid full-time if she needed me to. I had a pretty cushy flat and didn't have to look after my mum like she did. My dad pays most of my bills, and my mum would love it if I had a kid. They're both retired too and would be happy to turn their home into a daycare." Liam sighed. "I just didn't want her to feel stuck. You know? I wanted her to know that there was an endless list of options, none of which ended in her life being ruined."

"That's kind of you," Heather said, meaning it but unable to keep the suspicion out of her voice.

"I know, I know," Liam replied. "I was here the night she died, and she told me she was pregnant. I know how that looks. I do. That's why I've never told anybody about that night. Thought I'd be locked up for good. But it's been over six years, and it haunts me every day. So, whatever happens, I'm glad I told you."

"I suppose it helps that I can't arrest you. Though, once I tell Metropolitan about this, I can't make any promises that they'll feel the same. For your sake, I hope I find somebody more suspicious in the meantime."

Liam nodded. "Still. At least I have a few days of peace while you make your case."

Heather hummed. "So, what happened next? What did she say?"

"A lot of crying. From both of us, if I'm honest. Then we kept drinking, and even though she didn't say for sure, she kept going on about this being her last drink for nine months. So, maybe my suggestion sounded appealing. I don't know. Maybe she was just drunk. Still, we laughed about it. She moaned about not being able to eat brie anymore or smoke. She worried about whether it would be okay too, after months of messing about with all sorts of stuff, but I told her everything would be alright."

"And then?" Heather asked, waiting for some sort of sick punchline.

"Then I checked my watch and saw it was after 4 a.m. and suggested we head home. She said she wanted to sit and think on her own for a while and got her headphones out to listen to some music. I tried to talk her out of it, but it did seem like she needed to sit, think, stargaze, and enjoy maybe her last drink for a while. Hyde Park is safe as houses, really, so I gave her a hug and left." Liam began to choke up at the end, and Heather retrieved a tissue from her pocket. He turned it down, though she wished he hadn't when his nose began to run.

"Do you remember what time exactly?"

"Four twenty-four."

"And did you see anyone as you were leaving? She died shortly after, as I'm sure you're aware."

"No. Even the vendors had closed up shop by then. Totally empty."

"And can anyone vouch for you getting home?"

"My mate Tommy was crashing on the couch. He heard me get in just after half past."

"Great. I mean, friends aren't exactly reliable witnesses, but it does help your case. Heather paused. "Should it come to it, would you be willing to submit DNA to see if you're a match to the fetal tissue?"

"Of course. Whatever you need."

"Thank you, Liam. Now, go home and sleep this off. And please, for your sake, don't wake up and run."

"Don't worry. I'm not a coward."

Heather stood and looked at him, a slight smile on her face. "Yeah, I can tell."

CHAPTER NINETEEN

THE PARTNER

USING ONE OF HIS ALLOCATED DAYS OFF FOR STUDENT work, Gabriel once again decided to head to Seattle. What he planned to do there, he wasn't exactly sure, and he hoped the inspiration would come to him. He supposed there were a lot of options. He could try AA again. He could see Daniel. He could try to track down Katy's ex-boyfriend, Shane Gibson. He could reach out to Suzie and Lola for a longer sit-down discussion. All he knew was that it was the place to be today, so he headed up early, before his parents woke, in hopes of doing as much sleuthing as humanly possible. He was new to this—investigating a homicide alone—and though he felt adrift without Heather, he was also motivated to prove himself in her absence.

When he arrived, however, his endless possibilities felt like tangled balls of yarn, and not knowing where to pull or pluck, he headed deeper into the city and parked when he saw a spot. He wasn't familiar enough with Seattle to know where he was exactly, but it was a bougie shopping district, which gave him an idea. It was clear that he'd upset Betty the other night, so why not shop for a gift while he tried to make sense of his thoughts?

Feeling a little more settled, he wandered into the nearest boutique, hoping he wouldn't have to leave in shame upon seeing the prices. Fortunately, it wasn't quite that steep, but it was still over budget, so he wandered to the clearance rack and began to flip through. Zoned out, he stared blankly at each garment, and when he came to, he realized he not only didn't know what size she wore but that he was also looking at jeans, which she never wore. He pulled away, hoping for better luck among the marked-down accessories.

As he swiveled, he knocked into a woman who was standing silently in the middle of the aisle, looking equally spaced out. She jumped out of her skin upon collision and stepped backward into the opposite rack, apologizing profusely as she knocked overpriced t-shirts to the ground. Gabriel repeated after her and offered a hand, which she accepted.

"Are you okay?" he asked.

She nodded before laughing, though the fear lingered on her face. "Yeah, sorry. Just having a weird day."

The way she said it made him realize he was not the one who had shaken her. "Weird, how?" he questioned before elaborating. "Sorry, police officer. I see someone looking upset, and I have to ask."

The woman chewed her lip. "Do you ever feel like you're being followed?"

"Only when I'm actually being followed."

"Yeah, me too. Which is the problem. I think someone is following me. It happens every time I go jogging in my neighborhood."

He frowned. "Have you filed a report?"

"No, because I haven't actually seen anyone. I don't think anyone would take me seriously."

"I'm sure they would. I mean, I don't work for the Seattle PD, but I've heard good things."

"I don't know. It would be hard to arrest a ghost," she said.

"Do you think it is a ghost?" Gabriel asked, genuinely curious.

"No. I don't know. I think I might be losing it. I came out here for some retail therapy and find myself jumping at everything."

"Maybe you should go get some rest," Gabriel suggested. "Take a day off work."

The woman sighed. "Yeah. You're probably right."

"And maybe try taking a different route when you go jogging. See if that helps."

"God, you know I've been so zoned out lately I didn't even think of that. I'll try the park. Much prettier anyway."

Gabriel smiled. "Good idea. Have a nice day..."

"Hannah Roy," she replied. "Thank you. You too."

After Hannah left, Gabriel stayed rooted to the spot for a moment before catching sight of a leopard print bag. He gravitated toward it, but his interaction with Hannah was bugging him. Maybe it was because she looked so much like Heather—brown skin, black hair in a ponytail—but mostly, it was because of how scared she was. He should've pushed harder to convince her to file a report, even accompanied her to the station, but looking around, it seemed she was already gone. All he could do now was hope that his advice would keep her safe. Admittedly, she did seem exhausted. Maybe she was seeing or feeling things that weren't there. At least that was better than a stalker.

As he took the bag from its hook and inspected it, someone spoke behind him, this time causing him to jump. It was a man's voice. "Didn't take you for a leopard print guy," he said. Gabriel looked over his shoulder to see Elijah from Katy's AA group.

"It's for my girlfriend," Gabriel explained.

Elijah chuckled. "I figured. Nice choice. Sorry to spook you. I just wanted to ask if I'll see you at the meeting later this week?"

"Probably not. I, um, fell off the wagon," Gabriel improvised, feeling once again like he'd overstepped by going in the first place and unsure if he could hack a second go. That one-week chip would feel so wrong.

"Damn, been there." Elijah looked at his watch. "Want to go grab a coffee? Talk about it. I could give you some tips. I'm not quite sponsor material, but hey, I'm doing okay."

Gabriel felt like the universe was putting his day in order for him, and he keenly accepted. After buying the bag and throwing it into his car, he followed Elijah into a nice, hipster-type coffee shop, the type with a fake grass wall, pop culture nicknames for the specials, and an array of conflict-free, vegan, organic, non-GMO breakfast and lunch foods.

Needing a wakeup, Gabriel ordered his usual black coffee, while Elijah ordered something complicated Gabriel had never heard of before and an acai bowl.

They sat by the window, a little way away from the rest of the patrons, and Elijah fixed Gabriel with a somewhat conde-scending—though probably unintentionally so—smile. "So, what's your poison?" he asked.

"Beer," Gabriel replied, telling the truth.

Elijah nodded. "That's a common one, especially for men. You have a few after work, a few watching the game, and a few on the weekend at the barbeque. It doesn't feel harmful. You're not drinking a bottle of Jack alone on the couch each night. You might not even be hungover. But your body feels bad, you say stupid stuff, and soon enough, a few means a six-pack or more. The problem with beer, in particular, is the lack of stigma and the fact it takes a fair few to get really drunk."

"Yeah," Gabriel replied quietly.

"Hey, no shame in it. I'm a vodka guy, personally, which can get really messy. But it's all the same poison. Do you drink alone or with friends?"

"Both. More alone."

"That's where it gets dangerous for a lot of people. What about your triggers? For me, I can't go out dancing anymore. Clubs and bars are a big no. But if I'm at home alone, I'm okay."

"For me, it's relaxing in my garage, and then I lose track, and before I know it, another six-pack is gone."

"Do you want to quit again?"

"Maybe." This was turning into an honest discussion, and Gabriel was becoming uncomfortable. So he changed tact. "If I did, should I find a sponsor who drank beer, too? Like, did Katy drink vodka?"

"Nah, she was a wine drinker. And like you, she was a glass at the end of a stressful day person, which quickly turned into her being a bottle at the end of the day person. Just if you keep going, watch out for that; monitor yourself. I've seen moderation work for some people." Elijah paused. "Sorry for snapping at you the other day. She's just a sore subject."

"Were you two, like, an item?"

Elijah widened his eyes. "God, no. No, that's not allowed. Well, it's very looked down upon. All relationships are in the first year, but especially within your AA group. Or in AA as a whole. Also, I'm gay."

"Sorry, my bad. You just seemed really upset, and I wondered."

"I get it, but she was just a good friend. Maybe it's the way she died, but it's still really affecting me."

"That makes sense."

Elijah narrowed his eyes. "You seem really interested in Katy. Is there something else going on? Are you a cop?"

Gabriel laughed and hoped it sounded believable. "No. I'm not a cop. Just nosy."

"Alright. I believe you. Now, not to be rude—"

"Hey, I've already been rude enough for the both of us."

Elijah smirked. "My Tinder date is showing up early, and you got coffee to go, so..."

"Oh. Right!" Gabriel said, the implication clicking, and he stood hastily, grabbing his cup and thanking Elijah for his time. Elijah shooed him fondly out the door, calling after him about seeing him next week. That wasn't going to happen. In fact, Gabriel was unlikely to ever see Elijah again, but if nothing else, the man had some good advice. It was time to stock the fridge with sparkling water as well as beers.

Coffee in hand, Gabriel wandered back to his car, deciding that his next step would be tracking down Shane Gibson, Katy's ex, but immediately lost his train of thought when he saw someone leaning up against his car. A very blonde and preppy someone. She waved, one of those waggling finger gestures that he normally only saw in *Mean Girls*-esque movies. He scowled back as he approached.

"Brittany," he said once in earshot. "Get off of my car."

"Nice to see you too, Gabriel."

"Are you following me?" he asked. "What the hell are you doing here?"

"Actually, I was here to buy myself a little treat after a frustrating morning, but then I saw this shitbox and decided to wait for you to emerge from whatever dive you've been sitting around in."

"What do you want?"

She smiled, wide and white. "I know what you've been doing."

He shrugged and moved to open his door. "I don't know what you're talking about."

"Amanda. You've been feeding her false information about the Katy Graham case."

"Doesn't ring a bell," Gabriel retorted.

"And then I asked myself, why would he do that, other than to screw with me? Then it clicked. You're investigating this case too, and you're pissing on your territory."

"Yeah, sure." He opened his door, but Brittany closed it. "What the hell?"

"We could work together, you know. I've actually found a lot of dirt on Daniel from sources far better than Amanda."

"They didn't make it to your podcast, I noticed."

"Hey, I can't blow my load at the start. Haven't you heard of foreplay? I know Amanda isn't the most trustworthy person, but it was an interesting enough tidbit to lure people in, so I didn't really care if it was true or not. They won't be disappointed if it's a dead end. Not when I drop what I've got."

"Okay, tell me then. I'm an officer of the law. You have to tell me."

Brittany scoffed. "You're an officer of the law in Glenville. You don't have any jurisdiction here."

Gabriel smirked. "I knew it. You're bluffing."

"There's no way to know for sure, I guess, but I assure you I'm not. But I guess you'll just have to find that out when I solve this first."

"Yeah, good luck with that."

"Oh, it's you who needs luck. As does Heather, because believe you me, I am not leaving her out of this. Glenville's beloved detective married to a murderer. How juicy is that?"

"Brittany, please don't," Gabriel said, looking in her mascara-framed eyes, his heart suddenly pounding.

"Oh, I won't. Not yet. I need something juicy for my finale. I guess you better hurry up before I get there." She tightened her ponytail. "I might be further dissuaded if we were partners in this."

"I'm not teaming up with you, Brittany. This is a homicide investigation."

"Suit yourself. See you around, Gabriel. Oh, and nice purse," she sneered, glancing into his car before striding away to a store that was definitely out of his budget.

Gabriel stood for a moment, a glitching robot, stuttering and fuming, before getting into his car and gripping his steering wheel tight. She was right about one thing: he did have to solve this case before her. If he didn't, he'd not only risk exposing Heather but also look incompetent in the process.

Shane Gibson, here I come, he thought, veering out onto the busy street.

CHAPTER TWENTY

THE DETECTIVE

U NABLE TO SEE THROUGH THE CAB'S WINDOWS DUE TO the torrential weather and unsure if they had arrived, Heather leaned into the middle seat and peered through the windshield. A sturdy wiper brushed a thick layer of water aside, and a very blonde young woman appeared in the headlights, standing beside The Catacombs' alleyway entrance. The woman, sheltering from the rain beneath a slender overhang, exhaled smoke and adjusted a strap of her teensy cobalt blue dress. Heather's heart skipped a beat. She knew it was impossible, but for a split, illogical second, she was convinced that she was staring at the ghost of Lilly Arnold.

When she realized she was actually staring at Poppy Smith, she was no less shocked. Post-peroxide and glammed up, the young woman really was the spit of her dead best friend. Sure, there were differences to be had, but the similarities outweighed them tenfold. They were the same height and build, their faces were short and heart-shaped, their eyes big, blue and round, and with the new blonde do, they could've been sisters if not twins.

Heather shook off the jarringly uncanny moment, exited the car, and jogged toward Poppy with a smile while using her hands as a poor excuse for an umbrella. Poppy called out, and the two embraced excitedly, bobbing up and down on the balls of their feet and swaying side to side. Heather glanced around. Nobody even looked in their direction. As far as all the onlookers were concerned, they were merely friends going for a drink. They certainly were not an undercover detective and a bartender-turned-amateur spy, because why on Earth would they be?

"Polly!" Heather exclaimed, using the name they'd agreed upon via text. "How are you?"

Considering Poppy was new to this and that she was the one who really mattered tonight, they'd decided to keep her moniker close to the truth. That way, slip-ups could be blamed on a twisted tongue or may go entirely unnoticed. Similarly, Heather had ditched Rebecca and returned to the far easier surname alteration.

"I'm lovely," Poppy replied, employing a much posher accent and waving at Julius over Heather's shoulder. "It is so nice to see you two. It's been ages. How was your honeymoon?"

Nice improv, Heather thought, as a group of people walked past and turned into the alleyway. Heather affected her over-the-top American accent and replied with, "Well, the French are as snooty as ever, and I think I've gained ten pounds from all the bread, cheese, and wine, but I'll tell you, they don't call it the city of love for no reason."

"Wow," Poppy said dreamily as Julius led them down the alleyway. "You know I went once in high school. Just a day trip to Boulogne. We made crepes and had a picnic on the beach."

A day trip to France, Heather considered with envy, able to tell that the story was true. Due to the sheer magnitude of

America, it would be challenging to have a day trip to another state, let alone another country.

"The South is the best part," Julius added as they joined the short queue. "We're thinking of buying a second home there. Maybe in Avignon."

One of the men in front of them nodded approvingly, and Heather noticed Poppy straighten, gaining confidence. People believed them. They belonged here. Polly wasn't a bartender. She was a socialite. She was a nepotism baby. She was a millionaire in waiting.

Heather, too, felt solid, unshaken, as she recited the password, and the door slid open for them. She whipped off her coat in a way she hoped was elegant and approached the coat check as the bouncer muttered an emotionless, "Welcome back."

"Thank you!" Heather chirped as she grabbed her ticket and strode toward door number two, which was already wide open and awaiting them.

Heather reached for Poppy and pulled her close before linking her arm. Stepping in sync in towering heels, they descended the stairs with Julius pulling up the rear. Jazz music grew louder as they traversed further underground, as did all the voices below, and Heather noticed Poppy's eyes widen in the corner of her peripheral vision. The world below was in sight now, and Heather murmured, "I know, right?"

"This is—"

"Yeah."

They emerged into the opulent room, and the live music seemed to surge upon their arrival. The live band was an improvement on the monotonous, obnoxious dance music, and Heather thought, on another day, she might enjoy being here. She unhooked Poppy's arm, angled herself toward her companion, and watched as the amazement drained away, leaving nothing but boredom behind. So great was her vitriol that Heather half expected her to roll her eyes and scoff, and it took her a perplexed moment to realize that Poppy was acting. Although Poppy was excited to be here, Polly had seen it all before.

They moved to a booth near the band so that they wouldn't be overheard, and Heather leaned forward as they all sat next to each other on hard wooden chairs. "Okay, so you remember the plan?"

Poppy nodded. "Find Barry. Flirt with Barry. Make it clear that I want to spend time with Barry in hopes that he'll take me behind the door."

"And if he does?"

"I tell him I have to say goodbye to my friends, and you and I powder our noses."

"I'll place a camera and microphone on you, and the recordings will be sent live to our phones. We'll monitor you for your safety and with any luck—"

"He'll say or do something incriminating."

"You got it." Heather paused, trying to read Poppy's inscrutable posture and expression. "Are you okay?"

Poppy's mouth curled at the corner before blasé Polly took the wheel once more. "I'm ready to catch this bastard. I know it's him."

"Let's hope so."

"You don't sound sure. Why don't you sound sure?"

"I..." Heather trailed off, faltering, not wanting to give Poppy cold feet but unable to lie when asking so much of her.

"Well, who else could it be?"

"Remember that guy I showed you a photo of?"

"Yeah. The tall, handsome black guy. The one that none of us recognized."

Heather nodded. "Well, somebody did recognize him. One of the vendors. He was there at the same time as Lilly and headed in the same direction after buying two kebabs."

"Kebabs from Ambrosia's?"

"That's the one."

"Oh, well, he wasn't going to see Lilly then," Poppy replied matter-of-factly, her smile indicating relief.

"How do you figure?" Heather said, not wanting to kill her buzz but knowing there was no way to be 100% sure. Not yet, at least.

"Lilly was a strict vegetarian, and the only vegetarian thing on the menu at Ambrosia's are the chips."

"Huh," Heather said, absorbing some of the relief being exuded. It didn't necessarily mean much. Daniel could still be a killer. He could've still killed Katy, for one thing. He could've also not known that Lilly was a vegetarian. They might not have talked much before if they had indeed decided to meet for a late-night tryst. They might not have talked at all, and he'd followed her, thinking his forward proposition might go down better with food. Still, it felt like good news, and Heather wasn't one to look a gift horse in the mouth.

"There he is," Poppy hissed, tilting her head toward the bar.

Sure enough, Barry Watts had emerged from the mysterious room and was ordering a drink at the bar. His long, wiry hair was pulled into a low ponytail and swung between his bony shoulder blades, as shiny as ever. Heather wondered if he ever showered or if the oiliness came in a bottle. It was hard to say. His nails were dirty, but his clothes were clean. His mustache was well groomed, but his neck was covered in stubble. He also seemed to care about what he wore, even if it wasn't to Heather's taste. Today, his outfit consisted of a crisp white t-shirt, a button-up vest, tight skinny jeans, and wooden beaded jewelry. He looked like a burnt-out rockstar, still living large on his one-hit wonder from the eighties.

"I'm going in," Poppy said. "Wish me luck."

Heather didn't even have time to do so before the young woman was striding across the room in dangerously tall heels. She seemed as uncomfortable in them as Heather was, but she made it work for her. Probably because, in such a figure-hugging dress, nobody in the room was looking at her feet.

"I need a drink," Julius said, waving over a wandering server. "Double Macallan on the rocks, please," he informed the young man.

"Maker's Mark for me, please," Heather added. She didn't really like to partake on the job, but this situation and her nerves called for a heavy-duty remedy.

"Right away, Madam," the server said, memorizing their order without a pen or pad. He strode away in his perfectly tailored suit, and as the crowd parted for him, Poppy and Barry came into view.

Julius groaned. "I can hardly look."

Heather, on the other hand, could look and took every opportunity to do so. Despite being unable to hear anything,

149

Poppy's success was apparent, and her technique was impeccable. She'd leaned over the bar, pretending to umm and ahh about what she wanted; all the while, the shark watched his prey's behind waggle. His eyes wandered up and down, and slowly but surely, he ambled over and seemingly ordered for her before sticking his hand out. Poppy accepted enthusiastically, any disgust she might've felt buried so deep that Heather believed every bat of her glued-on lashes.

Then came the drinks—some sort of shot and chaser followed by a glass of champagne—and instead of returning to his room, he sat down at the bar, and she joined him. She laughed on command, tossed her hair back, touched him frequently on the arm and shoulder, and was attentive and doe-eyed when he spoke. Barry was obviously besotted. Or perhaps hungry was the more accurate word.

Heather's 'ick' was overwhelming, but stronger still was her sense of pride. She thought it must be akin to watching one's kid shine in an otherwise dire—and in this case disgusting—school play. It would've been difficult enough to convincingly fancy Barry Watts as a straight woman, but Poppy didn't even like men, no matter how handsome. Acting might just be the young woman's calling, and Heather supposed being nice to a variety of rude pubgoers had given her plenty of training.

A server reached out and topped up their glasses of champagne, and at the same time, a different server placed Heather and Julius's drinks on the table. Heather hastily pretended that she wasn't staring as she thanked the man, and when she had the opportunity to return to rubbernecking, she saw that the two had risen from their seats. Poppy pointed at Heather—who once again averted her gaze—and came running over as Barry lowered himself once more, clearly willing to wait.

"Ready to powder your nose?" Poppy asked breathlessly.

"Of course," Heather replied, grabbing her tiny bag, which was, unbeknownst to Barry, full of equipment.

She glanced at him as they passed, and the man smiled and wriggled his fingers, clearly none the wiser. This was women's business. Something foreign to him. If he thought about it at all, he probably imagined them hyping each other up to spend the night with their respective powerful men while sharing lipstick. He struck Heather as the type of man who didn't consider women smart enough to be devious. It was rare, but on occasion, misogyny worked in Heather's favor.

The bathroom attendant made Heather nervous. The woman's eyes were watchful. Yet, as a pair of women ahead of them in the queue entered a stall together, it was clear that she didn't care half as much as her expression implied. Poppy and Heather entered the large disabled stall without eliciting so much as a look, and on the other side, they quickly got down to business, not wanting to push their luck.

Poppy pulled her dress down and stood before Heather in her underwear. Her bra matched her dress, and her underwear matched her bra. Both were sheer and clearly a pricy set, and Heather wondered how far she was willing to go with Barry. Most women only wore lingerie like this if they were planning to be seen in it. However, she kept her worries private and told herself that Poppy was merely in character, down to the fine details.

Nerves steadied from her sip of bourbon, Heather attached wires, a tiny camera, and a microphone to Poppy's pale and, fortunately, bone-dry skin. The microphone sat under one of her thick dress straps—which would muffle the sound but was better than nothing—and the camera was stuck to her sternum so that it could peer out through the underbust cut-out. It was tiny, and once Poppy swung her gemstone-laden necklace back around, the silver speck blended in amongst the gems. Nobody could see it if they weren't looking, but upon checking the feed on her phone, Heather could see everything clearly, including herself. She gave a thumbs up, and Poppy returned the gesture. It was go time.

⟶

Barry was waiting for Poppy by the mysterious door as the pair exited the bathroom. Poppy blew a farewell kiss at Heather and ran toward him, and Heather offered him a polite wave before walking through the mostly empty dance floor. Her coy expression melted away when she looked at Julius, and her eyes drifted toward her drink. She moved toward it with as much enthusiasm as Poppy had to Barry and sat down hard before bringing it to her lips. She heard the door open and shut from across the room, deceptively thick and heavy.

Julius had already ordered a second round—singles this time, mercifully for Heather's tolerance—and his phone was lying face up on the table with the screen on and brightness low. He glanced at it absentmindedly between sips and idle, false chatter, though his drumming fingers indicated he was far from relaxed.

"What can you see?" Heather hissed after her spiel about remodeling their bathroom.

"See for yourself," Julius replied, voice low, disgust on his lips.

Heather opened her own phone and, pretending as if she was texting or doom-scrolling, opened up the feed again. The room behind the door was dark, lit by dim wall sconces, and painted a deep plum color. Despite this, she could see everything, and she didn't like what she saw.

A group of nine men sat around a large green felt-topped table, most of them smoking cigars or thin, dark cigarettes. One of them was sitting at the head of the table and dressed like the servers, shuffling cards and stacking chips. *The dealer*, she realized. This was a private poker game.

This in and of itself didn't bother her; she liked poker herself so long as it was legal. It was the men who were making her skin crawl. She may have been a believer in 'don't judge a book by its cover,' but her twisting stomach told her she had a legitimate reason to be concerned. Like Barry, they all toed the line between sleazy and swanky, and though they came in various shapes, sizes, and styles, their lust for the women in the room was as obvious as their abundant wealth.

"Polly, come 'ere," Barry cooed. His accent—South London, Heather identified—was thick as expected, and the pitch was appropriately squeaky for someone who looked so much like a rat. Poppy did as she was told, and Heather felt jarred by the first-person POV, as if she was the one in the room, moving forward against her will. Guilt arose. If she felt queasy just watching, how must Poppy feel? When the young woman was close enough, Barry scooched his chair back from the table and patted his lap. "This here is my new lucky charm, lads. Look how she shines."

Heather grimaced as heads turned and then froze as they stared into her eyes through the screen. For a horrible moment, she thought they were looking at the camera, but then she remembered its placement and realized their eyes were latched onto something worse. Heather and Julius exchanged unsettled glances and took deep swigs from their glasses, trying and failing to look away as the group assaulted their spy with their eyes.

"Right, gentlemen. Shall we begin?" the dealer asked.

The men responded in the affirmative, and as they pulled their eyes away from Poppy's cleavage, the screen went black.

"What the—" Heather began, frantically tapping and pressing buttons. Her phone hadn't died, but the feed definitely had.

"Yours too?" Julius asked.

Before Heather could respond—though her answer was obvious—a voice called out over the speakers. "Welcome to Old Timey Tuesdays! You all know what that means. We're winding back the clock to when this bar was built. No more Wi-Fi. No more phones. It's time to talk and dance like it's the good old days."

"Crap, crap, crap," Heather hissed, hastily swapping to data, but of course, there were no bars in the windowless underground speakeasy.

"Does the camera have an internal storage?" Julius questioned, tapping away on his much better phone but still coming up empty-handed.

"No," Heather groaned. "I couldn't find a nano spy camera that wasn't Wi-Fi-based. I should've looked harder."

"So we're blind?"

"Looks that way."

"Crap," Julius agreed, pulling at his beard.

"God," Heather groaned, burying her head in her hands. "She's stuck in there, and we have no way of reaching her."

"Hey, it's okay," Julius said, reaching out and telling her with his eyes to cut the dramatics in case they were being watched.

"She'll be out to grab another drink soon. We can talk to her then."

"Yeah. You're right," Heather replied begrudgingly, bouncing her knee and chewing her lip. She reached for her glass angrily after shoving her phone back into her bag, took a big sip, and looked at Julius. "Let's talk like it's the good old days. Goddamn Old Timey Tuesdays."

—

After only forty-five minutes, Poppy emerged from the room and headed straight toward Heather and Julius. At first, from a distance, Heather thought she looked happy and was temporarily relieved until their proximity allowed her to see the girl's harrowed dead eyes.

"Just getting some more drinks," she said, waving around Barry's credit card.

"Are you okay?"

She looked from side to side, then leaned forward, hands on the table. "Did you see that shit?" she whispered.

Heather tensed. "The line disconnected when they turned off the Wi-Fi."

"Seriously?"

"I'm so sorry, Poppy."

"No, it's not your fault. It's just... Ugh. Do you think my testimony alone is good enough?"

"In court? Probably not. But tell me anyway. Every piece of evidence helps."

"They're not betting with money," Poppy said gravely. "They're betting with *stuff*."

"Stuff?" Heather asked, the word usually loaded.

"Yeah, like girl's stuff. They call themselves the Conquerors Club. They're betting with used underwear, bras, jewelry, shoes. That sort of thing. It's all stuff they've nicked from the women they've screwed. They're like a bunch of pervy collectors. All the items have a story, and various aspects make the items worth more points. Like, for example, one of them screwed a seventy-year-old Nepalese woman in Thailand. The rarity makes it a big-ticket item. Sex workers win or lose you points depending on how much it cost to sleep with them."

"Jesus," Julius coughed, half-strangled by repulsion.

"Couldn't they lie?" Heather asked, knowing she was focusing on the wrong thing, but the whole concept was mind-boggling.

"Nah, they have some weird truth pact, and there's this massive bloke who used to work as an interrogator sat in the corner. He's got a suitcase. Wouldn't be surprised if there's a lie detector in there... or torture devices."

"What did Barry have to offer?"

"Lots of stuff," Poppy replied, and Heather watched her flat hands curl into fists. "I think... I think I saw Lilly's hoop earrings. The ones that were taken the night she was killed."

"Did he say how he got them?"

Poppy nodded, her skin blanched. "He said they were from an eighteen-year-old."

"If they were Lilly's, wouldn't he have gambled them away already?" Julius asked.

"It seems this 'club' is pretty new. Another guy put a dress on the table that he scored back in 2015 in Ibiza."

"Don't go back in," Heather urged. "Let's leave now before it's your dress on the table."

"I can't," Poppy argued weakly. "I need to know more."

"There's no point without cameras."

"He won't invite me back if I ghost him now. So, if you want that video proof..."

Heather groaned; it was a good point. "Fine. But we'll wait for you, and if it gets even weirder, run. We all want to know what happened to Lilly, but it's not worth ending up in the same position as her."

"I've got pepper spray in my bag," Poppy said, attempting to be reassuring. Heather wished she had a gun instead. "I'm all good. I promise. There are other girls in there, too. They come and go as they please."

"Okay," Heather replied, unable to believe what she was agreeing to. Not that she really was *agreeing*. Poppy had made up her mind, and Heather was merely supporting her from the sidelines. Still, it made her feel sick. Poppy had initially been an interloper, but now she felt more like bait.

Poppy hugged them both—either for morale or to keep up her cover, Heather wasn't sure—and toddled back to the bar to order another round. Heather looked at Julius, his knuckles white and lips pursed. He only parted them to sip, and the next hour continued in anxious silence.

After that hour passed, Poppy emerged again, but this time, she didn't approach. Heather wondered if she'd been reprimanded, and when she re-entered, Heather decided to spark conversation, if only to help pass the time. Most of what was said went in one ear and out of the other, and her eyes never strayed far from the door or the bar.

Another hour passed, then another, and Poppy emerged periodically to reassure them from afar. Then, finally, she ran over to them, her eyes sparkling once more. Poppy had told Barry that she needed her beauty sleep and was free to go. Apparently, it was time for the men to be alone anyway. It was all over, and the three of them—inebriated and shaken—made a hasty departure up the stairs long before closing time.

In the alley, Heather said, "I'm surprised he let you go."

Poppy shrugged. "I told him I'm a virgin and that he'd have to work for it. He seemed to like that and invited me to come back any time. Apparently, he's there every weeknight."

'Well, that's something, I guess," Heather said, hailing a taxi.

Poppy did the same, summoning a second vehicle. When Heather looked confused, Poppy explained. "My mate texted me. She's having a little get-together at her flat. I fancy letting off some steam."

"I'll bet," Heather said. "Stay safe," she added as Poppy got into the car. "And let me know how much the ride costs. I'll send you the money."

She wasn't sure if Poppy heard her over the persistent rain, but at least she was going somewhere safe.

"All's well that ends well," Julius said groggily.

Heather agreed. Despite the disaster, and thanks in entirety to Poppy, they could try again. All they needed was a better camera. Then they'd have the evidence they needed to send Barry to prison, get justice for Lilly, and, with any luck, put the entirety of the Conquerors Club behind bars. If their 'conquests' were anything akin to Lilly, there was a lot more justice to be had.

CHAPTER TWENTY-ONE

THE PARTNER

"SHANE GIBSON," GABRIEL MUTTERED TO HIMSELF, sitting in his car in a local park, staring at his phone.

I need to change providers, he thought, frustrated as his device struggled and repeatedly failed to provide search results. He could have gone home or stayed within city limits instead of pushing the boundaries of what was considered Seattle, but he wanted to keep his distance from Brittany, and there was too much of interest in the city to abandon ship so soon.

Eventually, the results came pouring in, and as they did, Gabriel's brows raised higher and higher until he could practically feel them tickling his hairline. He'd garnered from Suzie and Lola's tone of voice that Shane was a bad guy, but as it turned out, their information was only the tip of the iceberg. The man had been arrested for every petty crime Gabriel could think of and several not so petty. Then, seven months ago, he'd finally crossed the line separating him and the worst of the worst. Second-degree murder. Fifteen years in prison. Possibility of parole in ten.

Reading the article and staring at the somehow both muscular and emaciated man with his mullet, wispy mustache, and neck tattoo, Gabriel couldn't help but wonder whether this man had also gotten away with first-degree. Katy had been killed only a month before Shane had headed to the slammer. Timeline-wise, it worked.

The murder of Jordan Phillips had been a brawl gone wrong. Shane and Jordan had gotten into a fight outside a bar—that Shane, of course, had started—not far from where Gabriel was parked. Shane had hit the man—a firefighter and a father of two—so hard that he'd collapsed. Typically, this wouldn't result in death, but Jordan had hit his head on a USPS drop box on the way down and died upon impact. The official cause of death was a broken neck, but the damage to his skull and jaw didn't help Shane's case as there was no proof that that damage hadn't been caused by his fist.

Katy's name was mentioned in the article right down the bottom. Apparently, like Daniel, Shane had also been brought in for questioning and had been released due to lack of evidence and a feeble alibi provided by his roommate Isaiah Nash. Gabriel obviously didn't know the ins and outs of the scenario, but he couldn't wrap his head around why the cops had let either one of them go so easily. Typically, an unlocked door and a roommate weren't enough to escape the sharp hook of the law. Did the police know something? Was there another suspect or an incompetent investigator? Did they know that Shane did it, but it was easier to lock him up for something else?

Gabriel didn't know, but Shane intrigued him, and he decided he'd speak with Isaiah Nash after 'catching up' with Suzie and Lola. They'd withheld a lot of information, and he wanted to know why. Specifically, he wanted to know why

159

they wouldn't mention that Katy's ex-boyfriend was in prison for murder.

Gabriel returned to the search results page and blinked rapidly at the title of the link. He clicked on it and was no less shocked. It could've easily been missed, considering it was on Facebook rather than an accredited news site, but he was so glad he'd found it. It was a warning to the people of Seattle. Shane Gibson had escaped from prison two weeks ago today. It seemed that the prison and police wanted to keep this hush-hush and out of the media so as to avoid panic, but the more he looked, the more panic and wanted posters he found.

After a morning of floundering, Gabriel finally had a clear goal in sight—find Shane Gibson and bring him to justice, regardless of whether he killed Katy. Hopefully, in doing so, he could ally himself with the Seattle PD and obtain the more secretive information he craved—if there was any. It was possible, likely even, that this was a slapdash job because the Seattle PD had bigger fish to fry. Fine by him; he had plenty of space on the grill.

After trying and failing to get ahold of anyone of interest—it was after all work hours on a Tuesday—Gabriel headed back home to get some actual studying done. He hated doing so but tried to reassure himself that everyone—Daniel, Suzie, Lola—would reply eventually and that he was only an hour away should he need to head back.

Upon arrival, he snuck into his home through the garage roller door so his parents wouldn't ask him where he'd been. Then, he sat down hard on the couch and reached for the textbook at the top of the pile. He opened it and stared at the page, but his eyes kept blurring, and his brain failed to absorb any information. His mind was in other places, and he'd been losing interest in his studies for a while. He was, of course, eternally grateful that Jason Fleming had paid for his course but often worried that his debt was the only thing keeping him going.

Still, he couldn't force the impossible, so he swapped his book for a laptop and started hammering away at the keys, padding out his report to send Heather's way. She had enough on her mind without reading a bunch of nonsense, so he made sure to run it all through a grammar checker and spent eons choosing a font, spacing, and font size. He was procrastinating, and he knew it, but at least he was doing *something*.

He was so focused that he barely registered the front door slamming shut or a car roaring to life. It was only when he noticed how dark the room had become that something felt amiss. As hard as he tried to ignore it as he finished linking all the necessary articles, his chest tightened, and his heart panged. Eventually, the sensations became unpleasant enough that he felt compelled to check his phone. It had been on silent, and there were not only two calendar notifications but also half a dozen missed calls. Two were from Betty, and four were from his parents.

"Shit!" he yelped, remembering the dinner plans that he had made in order to introduce his parents and his girlfriend for the first time.

The dinner was at a Tapas place in Hallington called La Cocina Pequeña at 6 pm. It was already 5:44, and it took half an hour to get there. He was already going to be late, and he was still wearing sweatpants and hadn't showered. He figured there was no time for the latter as he threw the garage door open and ran upstairs. He pulled on the nicest shirt and pants within his reach, doused himself in cologne, and ran back down the stairs, nearly killing himself in the process when he missed a step and stumbled. Luckily, his mom hadn't polished the banister in a few weeks, and he maintained his grip, keeping him upright and, more importantly, alive.

However, he didn't learn his lesson and jumped the last few steps, feeling his shins and knees cry out in agony and shock as he landed. He ignored their wailing as he ran outside to his car. Luckily, Betty's present was already in the back, and hoping that would smooth things over, at least on her end, he revved his engine and reversed chaotically over the front lawn and into the road.

He didn't speed on the way to Hallington. He was a police officer, after all, but he overtook often and drove the limit like it was his job, and somehow, he made it to his destination in record time. He was still late, but only by fifteen minutes.

He started to feel like luck was on his side when a parking spot appeared directly beside the restaurant, but the anxiety returned when he saw Betty and his parents' cars parked beside each other. Still, all three had ignored his texts, so he assumed they must be getting along like a house on fire.

Unfortunately, upon walking in, his hopes were soon dashed by the waitress, who pointed him in the right direction. His three loved ones were sitting in a corner booth at the far end of the restaurant, and though they picked at bread and olives, none of them were looking at each other. The restaurant was busy and noisy, yet somehow, their silence cut through the din and rang in his ears.

Awkwardly, Gabriel shambled over, offering an apologetic wave and noting that he was underdressed in comparison. He felt sweat forming in the pits of his shirt, and by the time all three were staring at him, he felt metaphorically and literally drenched by his nerves. They were clearly furious.

He sat down beside Betty and moved in for a peck but was met with her cheek. He laughed it off, his ears turning red, and reached for some bread. This turned out to be the wrong move, and everyone watched with disdain as he silently worked through his oversized mouthful of dry Pan de payés. He then reached for his father's glass of water and tried to wash it down. He failed to do so, and mouth still full—though tactfully covering the obscenity with his hand—he mumbled, "I'm sorry. I got distracted with studying and forgot what day it was."

"That's not like you," his mother, Luisa, said, squinting disapprovingly.

"This section is hard," Gabriel replied indignantly.

"What's it about?" Betty asked sharply, clearly equally unconvinced by his excuse.

"Um, weapon-carrying laws for agents," he replied, lying poorly. In all honesty, he couldn't remember a single thing from that textbook.

"Huh," Betty replied dryly. "I didn't realize a criminology textbook would include the FBI handbook."

She had him there, and he considered whether he should own up or keep digging his hole. The shovel was already in the soil, so he kept going. "It doesn't, but I went on a Google rabbit hole. I guess I just got excited about my future career." He nudged her with his elbow and offered his most charming smile. She leaned away. Whatever he was doing wasn't working, so he changed tactics and ventured into the likely already well-trodden small-talk territory. "What's everyone ordering? Unless you've already filled up on bread." He laughed as if he'd told a good joke and was met with stony expressions.

"Aren't you going to introduce us?" Betty asked, looking at him expectantly.

Gabriel figured they would've done that already and then figured he was an idiot in the same breath. He imagined himself in a reversed scenario and how awkward it would be to meet Betty's parents without her around. "Of course," he said hastily but enthusiastically. "Mom, Dad, this is Betty Barber, my girlfriend. And Betty, these are my parents, Luisa and Martin Silva."

As predicted, they knew this already, but they greeted each other across the table and shook hands. To Gabriel, it seemed like everyone was willing to start over, and for that, he was deeply relieved. Then, his mother turned toward him and said, "So, Betty here was just telling us about how she doesn't go to church."

Crap, Gabriel thought. If he'd been here, that conversation would've never gotten going. Betty was a staunch atheist, and his parents were the complete opposite. He can only imagine the unpleasant passive-aggressive small talk that had been occurring. Not that his parents were particularly old-fashioned, but he could read his mother's expression and thus her mind. She was imagining a future filled with pot-smoking hippies, polyamory, communes, and non-baptized bastard children.

"Mom, come on," he said, half-begging. "No politics or religion at the dinner table." Gabriel laughed again, nervously this time. "Let's order drinks."

"We've already ordered everything," Betty retorted.

"Right, let me take a look at the menu."

"*Oh no*," she clarified, her voice higher than usual. "Your mom ordered for you."

"I always order for him," Luisa responded. "I know what he likes."

"Mom," Gabriel replied as sternly as he could muster. "I know you know what I like, but I can order for myself. And Betty knows what I like too."

"You've only been together a month," Luisa protested while Martin pretended to be highly absorbed in the fascinating reading material that the menu provided.

Gabriel saw this for what it was. It was a pissing contest. A woman with her baby, her youngest son, the last one to fly the nest, and another woman in a new serious relationship, unwilling to bend to the matriarch. Nor should she, Gabriel acknowledged, though it would've made things easier.

"I'm sure I'll love the food," Gabriel said, trying to keep the peace. "Now, how's everyone's day been?"

After that, the small talk became more pleasant, and when food filled mouths, the silence was even more so. By the end of it, after everyone had had at least one drink and Luisa had had three, things were completely copacetic. Betty even got a hug when his parents left; better still, they footed the bill and invited her for a Sunday dinner, which Gabriel hoped would be a little less awkward. Baby steps, he thought. They may not have clicked, but they'd grow to like each other, and then, one day, everyone would be best friends.

Outside, Gabriel wrapped his arm around Betty, and they waved as his parents drove away. When they were out of sight, he reattempted a kiss but was once again met with her soft cheek.

"I'm sorry," he said earnestly, standing in front of her and rubbing her upper arm. "I'm an asshole."

"I just..." Betty trailed off and sighed. "Between this and the Amanda thing, I think I just need to think."

"About what?"

"Us. I need someone reliable. Somebody who doesn't lie. You know I've dated a lot of assholes, and I know you're not an asshole, and I still like you a lot, but..."

"I've let you down."

"A little bit, yeah." Then she shook her head. "I don't know. Maybe I'm being unfair."

"I don't think you're being unfair," he said softly. "If you need space, I'm happy to give it to you. Better to nip it in the bud if this isn't right for you."

Betty sighed again and then laughed sadly. "God, I hate that you're being so respectful, and I'm still not happy."

"What would you rather me do?"

"Fight for me. Ugh. I don't know. Maybe that's just a hangover from all my toxic relationships."

"I'm sorry."

"I am, too," she whispered, staring at her shoes. "I'll contact you before dinner on Sunday. I don't want to leave your parents in the lurch." She stepped forward, wrapped her arms around his neck, and exhaled into his ear. "Take care of yourself. I don't know what you're involved with, but it seems to be taking its toll."

"I'll be fine."

"You better be."

She pulled away, and Gabriel looked at her, trying and failing to smile. "Have a good week," he said.

Betty sighed, looking on the verge of tears. "I probably won't," she said before walking away.

Gabriel thought that this, right now, was the moment to fight. He could make a big romantic gesture, run after her, and give her the bag he'd picked out. However, this wasn't a movie, and she wanted something different, something healthy. She was used to toxicity, and though she still craved that, he decided to listen to the rational part of her. The part that wanted space. So, he stood, rooted to the spot, and let that space grow, and grow, and grow, until she disappeared into the night.

CHAPTER TWENTY-TWO

THE PARTNER

"IF UNDEREXAGGERATION WAS AN ART FORM, YOU TWO would be world famous," Gabriel said, addressing Suzie Graham and Lola Price via video call. It was a bold opening statement, but it felt warranted.

The women looked at each other, their lids heavy and expressions dreamy. Whatever they were on, Gabriel wanted some. He was feeling pent-up and jittery. Unfortunately, the answer was probably herbal tea, meditation, and chakra alignment, all of which he was decidedly uninterested in.

"What are you talking about?" Suzie drawled, admiring her nails instead of looking at the screen.

"You told me Shane was a jerk," Gabriel began.

"And he was," Lola croaked, her sinuses clogged by a cold. She reached for a mug of steaming tea and sniffled before looking at Gabriel expectantly.

"*Yeah*," Gabriel replied, the 'no shit' implied but unsaid. "I get that. But you failed to mention that he recently escaped prison after serving only six and a half months of his fifteen-year sentence."

"What?" was all Lola could muster, wide-eyed and alert, a tissue pressed against her leaking nose. Suzie, on the other hand, was silent, but Gabriel had her attention at last.

"Yeah. He killed a guy in a fight and pled guilty for second-degree murder."

"And he broke out?" Suzie asked, placing shaking fingertips on her lips.

Gabriel looked at her skeptically. "Yeah. And they still haven't found him. You really didn't know about this?"

"No, we didn't stay in touch," Suzie replied curtly. "I'm sure you can imagine why."

"Once Katy finally left him, we thought he was out of our lives forever," Lola added. "And we were so relieved. She bore the brunt of his temper, but he harassed us too. Especially when she stayed with either of us. I used to have to call the cops to make him leave."

"So he was abusive?" Gabriel asked.

"Yes," Lola admitted. "And when Katy left him and met Daniel, he encouraged everyone to get a restraining order and offered to pay for all the legalities, so we did."

"He still sent anonymous letters, though," Suzie said. "Threatening us, our husbands, calling us all sorts of awful things. We got cameras installed."

"I ended up moving to a suburb on the other side of the city," Lola whispered as if Shane might be listening.

"Jesus. Why didn't you tell me any of this?"

"Because we don't like to think about him," Suzie snapped. "We've spent a lot of time, effort, and money to not think about him. That's why I told you to track him down yourself. I didn't, and don't, want any part of it. The last time I saw him was awful. He was rolling around on my front lawn, drunk and crying, holding a gun, telling us that he'd commit suicide if Katy didn't come out and speak to him. She wasn't even there!"

"Do you think if he showed up at Katy's home while Daniel was out saying he was going to kill himself, she'd let him in?" Gabriel questioned, a theory arising in his head.

"I have given that more consideration than is likely healthy," Suzie confessed. "And I think the answer is yes. She always felt she could control his temper and get through to the 'good guy' beneath all the trouble."

"Like those Florida nutjobs who own 'pet' tigers and bears," Lola grumbled. "They could lose an arm and still feel like they're somehow in control."

"Did he ever hurt her? Physically, I mean."

Lola nodded. "She underplayed it, but we saw the bruises. If she was wearing a scarf on a hot day or a muumuu at the beach, we knew."

"Do you think he killed her?"

Suzie sighed. "I don't know what I think. As I've said, I don't like Daniel either. I think it could have been either one of them, and probably for the same reasons."

"Which are?"

"Control. Possessiveness. Both of them were paranoid, jealous men. Shane just made it more obvious. The police officers we spoke with didn't tell us much, but I think they suspected Shane more because of his erratic behavior. I wouldn't be surprised if they were tailing him, just waiting for a reason to lock him up because if they couldn't get him for her murder."

"I'm of the same opinion," Gabriel replied. "So, unfortunately, you two knew Shane pretty well."

"As well as anyone can know a man like that, I suppose," Suzie answered.

"Do you have any idea of where he might be hiding?"

"No," Lola said quickly, her tone sharp. "And if I were you, I wouldn't go looking for him. When we recommended you speak with him, we didn't know about any of this. We didn't even know he was in jail at all. I thought that maybe you could've met him in a public place and listened to him wax poetic about Katy and cry into his beer, but this is different. This is dangerous."

"We're not going to talk him out of this," Suzie said to Lola while scrutinizing Gabriel. "Are we?"

"No, you're not," Gabriel stated.

Lola pursed her lips, and Suzie sighed before saying, "Then I'd start by talking to his roommate, Izzy."

"Isaiah Nash?"

"Yeah. He goes by Izzy and lives in a dump just outside of the Flower Gardens Development."

"By Buttercup Dreams," Lola added. "The section to the left of Violet Fields. The developers tried to buy him and Shane out, but they wouldn't sell. There's a cul de sac with a roundabout you can park at. Then, follow the dirt path a little ways into the woods. You'll spot it."

"Will Izzy talk to me?"

"Izzy's nice," Suzie confirmed, her eyes filled with sadness. "But he's terrified of Shane, so he might be hesitant."

"We used to call him his boyfriend because that's how Shane treated him," Lola murmured. "He tracked his location and had the poor kid cooking and cleaning for him."

"Why did he stick around?" Gabriel asked, dumbfounded.

"Because Shane got him hooked on crack, and so long as he behaved, his supply never ran dry," Suzie sighed.

"I think he also knew that if he left and Shane found him, he wouldn't just cry on the lawn and beg him to come back," Lola said before dragging a finger across her throat.

Gabriel frowned. "Jesus."

"So you can talk to him," Suzie continued. "But be careful not to put either of you in harm's way."

"And whatever he tells you, we don't want to know," Lola insisted. "Tell the cops instead. I'm not getting dragged into this shit again."

"Of course," Gabriel replied, and noting the women's agitation, he drew the conversation to a close. He had things to do anyway, and they'd told him all they needed to know. "Well, thank you for your time and the information."

"You're welcome," Suzie said, looking relieved that it was all over. "But you didn't hear any of it from us. I don't want to see my name in any newspapers, got it?"

"Got it."

"Goodbye, Matías, and good luck."

After the events of last night, Gabriel had called in sick as soon as he'd woken up. It wasn't exactly a lie. His heartbreak was making him nauseous. It was, however, dishonest, as his reason for taking time off had nothing to do with Betty. He knew he'd be speaking to Lola and Suzie in the morning due to their late-night texts. He was just lucky that work had hit a lull, and they were, for the first time in months, over-manned. Now, he just had to cross his fingers and toes so no one saw him heading toward Seattle. That was a conversation with Tina that was best avoided.

He arrived at Buttercup Dreams at around 3 pm and noted that it seemed like the five-sectioned suburban paradise's affordable sector. He also noticed that much like with Steve Adamski, his fictional suspect, it couldn't have been a particularly far walk to reach Lavender Meadow where Daniel, and once Katy, lived. Shane, too, would've had the ability to enter the house consensually. Rename Steve Adamski to Shane Gibson and replace plumber with manipulator, and there was a compelling theory to be had, though it had originally been nothing more than fiction.

As Suzie and Lola had said, the house was easy to find after a short trek up a narrow path. It looked at least seventy years older than the rest of the buildings, and Mother Nature had begun to eat it long ago. It was lopsided, sinking into the damp soil. Half of the windows were boarded up, shingles were missing, and ivy consumed the walls. However, in contrast, the lawn was mown, immaculate ornaments covered the bright green grass, the mailbox was brand new and covered in painted ladybugs, and the windows that weren't broken were polished to perfection. The house itself may have been disintegrating, but whoever occupied it was clearly proud of what they had left.

Gabriel walked over stepping stones and knocked on the front door. His rapping was very quickly—almost abruptly—

answered by a very skinny, pale man with a short red bowl cut, borderline invisible eyebrows, and an abundance of freckles.

"Can I help you?" he asked, his voice faint, airy, and so weak it seemed as if the wind might prevent it from reaching its destination.

"Hi. I'm a journalist. Matías Silva," Gabriel said, holding out his hand and feeling a little stupid for continuing to use his brother's name as a pseudonym and feeling stupider still when Izzy left him hanging. He cleared his throat. "I work for The Seattle Times, and I'm writing a piece on the Katy Graham homicide. An exposé if you will."

"Oh," Izzy whispered. "Katy."

"I know you were Shane Gibson's roommate at the time at the time of her death."

"I still am, I suppose," Izzy responded. "His stuff is still in his room."

"Would you mind answering some questions about him? I doubt anyone knows him better than you do."

Izzy looked around the clearing nervously as if Shane might suddenly spring up from the bushes. Then, he nodded and opened the door wider. "Quickly," he hissed, ushering Gabriel in before slamming the door shut.

Gabriel watched in horror as Izzy slid five bolts across and then turned a key. All the locks were brand new. "New security measures?" he asked.

Izzy nodded as he shuffled into the living room, wearing what seemed to be oversized children's pajamas in a pirate print. "I thought I had fifteen years," Izzy whispered as he lowered himself into an old leather armchair and crossed his legs. "Or at least a decade. Instead, I've gotten a lousy six and a half months. Long enough to get off the hard stuff and start mowing lawns for cash again, but not nearly long enough to get enough money together to get out of here. I was going to head overseas. Or at least to a different state. But I'll never be able to now. Not until they catch him."

"So he hasn't come 'home' yet?" Gabriel questioned. Izzy hesitated. "It's okay. This is off the record. Shane will never find out about this meeting. But I need to know more so that I can find him and send him back to prison."

Izzy nodded shakily. "I don't know where he is if that's what you're wondering. And I haven't seen him since the cops came. But my lawn ornaments keep breaking. It could be the local teens, but I have a feeling it's him taunting me. He always loved to do that."

"No cameras?"

"Not yet. I've ordered a Ring doorbell." Izzy shifted. "Where did you park?"

"A couple of minutes away. I didn't want to draw attention to you."

"Smart."

"Am I making you nervous?"

"I—" Izzy faltered, then nodded.

"I'll make this quick then. All I want to know is what really happened the night Katy Graham was murdered. You gave the cops an alibi and said he'd been here all night, but I have a feeling—"

"I lied," Izzy admitted, much more quickly than Gabriel expected. "He was out when she died. He said he was going to the bar—The Grotto, where he killed that poor man—and when he wasn't back by 2 pm, I called them and asked for him. I wanted to know what he wanted for dinner because I was heading to the grocery store, but they told me he wasn't there. Then I tried to call him directly, but his phone was off. I was so worried. He hadn't been himself lately. Just as I was about to call the local hospital, he showed up."

"What time was this?"

"Nearly 4. I'll never forget the look on his face. He was white as a sheet. He wouldn't speak to me either, but he wasn't angry. It was almost as if I was a ghost. I followed him around the house until he slammed the bathroom door in my face. He showered for over forty minutes and didn't look much better when he came out. He wouldn't even eat what I'd made for him, and it was his favorite—steak and roast potatoes. Instead, he went straight for the whiskey, and when I worked up the nerve to ask him if something had happened, he told me to never ask again, or he'd break my jaw. At first, I thought that maybe he just got the shit scared out of him by the guy he bought drugs from. He owed him money, and they were threatening him."

"Do you know who his supplier was?"

"God, no," Izzy laughed weakly. "He didn't tell me much about anything. I was like a 1950s housewife. Drunk, high, and neglected. Hell, maybe that is where he was, but there was something about the way he told me to shut up that seemed different. He looked like he wanted to hurt me."

Gabriel must've looked surprised because Izzy continued with, "He never hurt me. In fact, he was kinder to me than anyone else. I just knew what he was capable of." He sighed. "So when Katy turned up dead, and the cops came around, I lied on impulse. I regret that every day, but I couldn't help myself. I wanted him gone but was terrified of telling the truth. I even managed to pass the polygraph test. I don't know how. I think maybe I convinced myself that I *was* telling the truth. And between that and whatever he said to them, he was free as a bird. Until he killed that man, that is."

"Do you know what he told them?"

"No. I didn't ask. I sometimes think that maybe he snitched on his supplier in exchange for them leaving him alone." Izzy paused to take a shuddering breath. "I was so relieved that he was gone, though I pretended not to be when we said our good-byes. Once I was alone, I threw myself a little party. I bought a bottle of champagne and a cake. He never let me drink alcohol when he was home. Said I got behind on chores when I did."

"And did you get clean the same day?"

Izzy shook his head. "It took two weeks to use up the rest of my supply. Then I got help. Local drug services helped me through it. Six months clean as of yesterday."

"Congratulations. Seriously."

"Thank you," Izzy murmured with a smile.

"And you don't have any idea where he is now?"

"If I did, he'd already be back behind bars. I've come too far to lie for him again. And if you knew what's good for you, you wouldn't be looking for him either."

Gabriel ignored the warning. "When I find him, and he's back in handcuffs, would you be willing to take the stand and testify against him? I have contacts at the Seattle PD. I could put in a very good word for you."

"I don't care if they lock me up and throw away the key for lying," Izzy said. "As long as I'm far away from him and sober. So, yeah. I'll testify against him if you can guarantee my safety."

"Well, with your help, he'll be in a high-security prison for the rest of his life."

Izzy smiled and sunk deeper into his seat. "That sounds like Heaven."

"Agreed. Now, I have one final question. Do you think he murdered Katy Graham?"

"Yes," Izzy said without hesitation.

"Then you need to take this," Gabriel said, pulling all the cash out of his wallet. He rarely used it cash, so he'd amounted quite a fund. Roughly six hundred dollars. He handed it all over to Izzy without hesitation. "Get somewhere safe. A hotel. Somewhere he doesn't know. I've heard he tracks your movements."

"I smashed that phone. Got a burner."

"Good. But it's not enough. Promise me you'll get out of town until we catch him."

"Okay."

"Great. Here's my personal number. Call me if you need anything or hear anything." Gabriel handed over his personal card, and Izzy squinted at it.

"I thought your name was Matías?"

"I lied. I'm a cop. I'm investigating this case."

"Well, I'm hardly one to judge," Izzy said with a shrug, placing the card on the coffee table. "In a way, it makes me feel a bit better. To know that an officer has my back."

Gabriel offered a small smile as he stood. "Seriously, though. Get out of here until this blows over. He'll be back behind bars soon enough."

Izzy laughed sadly but didn't say anything.

"I'll find him."

"If he doesn't find you first."

CHAPTER TWENTY-THREE

THE DETECTIVE

HEATHER'S PHONE BUZZED LOUDLY ON THE SIDE TABLE, stirring her from sleep. She reached hazily for the phone as it continued to ring and turned to extend her reach. In doing so, she caught sight of the alarm clock and groaned. She'd overslept again, albeit not to the same extreme. It was 9:44 in the morning: reasonable for a holiday but not for investigating a case on the verge of a breakthrough.

She flopped back onto her back and pressed answer without checking the number because what was the point? Everyone in London was an unknown contact.

"Hello, Heather speaking," she said, avoiding her surname because of the variety she'd acquired.

"Heather?" a young man replied, his surroundings noisy.

Heather had been expecting Jonno, Helen, or Poppy to call, so it took her a few brow-furrowed seconds to recalibrate. "Liam?" she asked, finally placing the voice.

"Yeah." He sounded anxious and breathy. He wasn't exactly a chatterbox, but he seemed particularly tight-lipped, and Heather pictured a serious expression on his face. She wondered if he was calling about their conversation in the park and whether he had more to admit to.

"Can I help you with something, Liam?" Heather asked, adopting a formal, almost police dispatch-type tone as she sat up in bed.

"Yeah. Sorry. Weird morning." He paused to um and ah, seemingly unable to spit out what he needed to say until it finally worked its way out with a bang. "Poppy hasn't shown up for work today, and I can't get ahold of her. She was with you last night, right?"

"Wait, what?" Heather choked out, her muscles tensed as if the phone in her hands was electrocuting her. "I mean, yeah, she was with us until around 1 am, but she went to her friend's house afterward."

"Do you know which friend?"

"No idea. But she said they were having a get-together, and she was already pretty drunk. She's probably just hungover."

"Yeah," Liam exhaled. "You're probably right."

"It doesn't sound like I am."

"I don't know. Poppy never misses work. Never. Hungover or otherwise. She never lets her phone die either."

"Well, last night was pretty crazy," Heather said, a pit in her stomach forming as she thought back to last night. Could she remember the taxi driver's license plate? What the man looked like? No, was the answer, but maybe it would come to her in time with enough coffee and needling.

"She probably went to Lindsey's, so I'll call her and see what's up," Liam said.

"Good idea."

"I'll call you back in a min."

Liam hung up, and Heather hauled herself out of bed and got dressed, feeling as if she might need to head out of the door at any moment. She pulled a garish thrift-store sweater over her head and examined her exhausted countenance. Surely, Poppy had merely overslept. Or maybe she'd gotten her days mixed up and was out for a hair of the dog brunch. Like most people, she probably rarely went all out on Wednesday nights, and doing so had thrown off her body clock. And despite what Liam had said to the contrary, her phone probably was dead. Heather knew hers always ended up that way if she crashed at somebody else's house.

Heather made her way downstairs, phone clutched in her clammy hand, and wandered toward the kitchen, where she could hear the electric kettle rumbling as it boiled. Julius was leaning against the counter as she entered, scrolling on his phone, likely reading some sort of article, and when he eventually looked up, his relaxed expression instantly turned into one of concern.

"Are you okay? You look like you've seen a ghost. Which is admittedly possible considering this house's history."

Heather shook her head. "No ghosts. Not yet, anyway."

"Hungover?"

"Yes. But that's not the problem. Liam just called and said Poppy didn't show up for work today."

Julius frowned and scratched at his beard. "Wasn't she going to her friend's house to keep the party going?"

"Yeah, she did. We saw her get into the taxi."

Julius squinted. "It's a bit of a blur, to be honest."

"She did," Heather confirmed. "I'm sure of it. Liam's going to call someone named Lindsey and get back to me. I'm sure it's fine."

"I'm sure you're right," Julius said, sounding decidedly more convinced than Heather. "Speaking of hangovers. Coffee?"

"Yes, please," Heather groaned, suddenly acutely aware of the headache brewing in her temples. The noise caught in her throat as her phone began to ring again, and she rushed to answer it. "Hello?" she asked, heart in her throat, stomach in knots, pushing the offered mug of coffee back toward Julius's chest.

"Heather!" chirped a decidedly feminine, American voice.

"Who is this?" Heather questioned with a frown. She hadn't been expecting either aspect and was once again struggling with early morning, hungover recalibration.

"Oh, come on. You know who this is. This voice is famous."

"Brittany."

"Bingo."

"What the hell do you want?"

"I want to know what you're doing in London."

"I'm on vacation," Heather answered flatly.

"Come on, Heather," Brittany chided.

"Isn't this costing you like a dollar per minute?" Heather asked, changing the subject.

"I can afford it."

"Well, I can't," Heather retorted and moved to hang up, pulling her phone from her ear.

"Wait!" Brittany yelled, unusually desperate. Heather put the phone back. "It doesn't cost you anything. I promise. It's all on me."

"I'm busy."

"Please. Five minutes."

"Okay," Heather said slowly, deeply confused by the manic, pleading energy emanating from the speaker. "What do you want?"

"I want to know what you're doing in London."

"We already did this. I'm on vacation."

"No, you're not. There's no way you'd assign Gabriel your ex-husband's case if you didn't have something equally important to do."

"How did you—"

"It's my job. Anyway, we may not see eye to eye, but I know a driven woman when I see one. You're not the vacationing type. Neither am I."

"Surprising," Heather responded dryly. "I always took you for a spring break sort of girl."

"Please. I'm a dark tourist at best. If I'm in Daytona, it's because I'm researching Robert Hayes or Aileen Wuornos."

"Well, maybe I just really needed a break."

"Cut the crap."

Heather laughed in shock. "Why would I tell you anything, Brittany?"

"Because I have dirt on you. Because I can tell everyone in town about Daniel. Because I can tell your boss what you and Gabriel are really up to."

Heather snorted. "Oh, so you're blackmailing me? That's smart."

"No, I—" Brittany groaned. "I want to work with you. I have sources. So many sources. Hundreds of thousands of people listen to my podcast. Thousands of them write to me. Hundreds of them know stuff. People like Katy. They go to grocery stores, hairdressers, gyms, bars, and gas stations. People see and hear stuff. And I have turned up a lot of dirt about the men in her life, especially your ex-husband. Dirt that I will put in my podcast if you don't help me."

"You'll do that anyway."

"Maybe. But I want us to solve this together. We can help each other."

"Brittany, if you have legitimate information, you need to tell me. Not only am I cop, but this is personal."

"Not until you tell me what you're doing in London."

Heather sucked her teeth and resisted name-calling. "You're so full of it. You just want something juicy to tell your listeners."

"So you admit that you're doing something juicy?" Brittany asked.

"Seriously?"

"Sorry," Brittany said, sheepish for the first time ever. "I really do want to work together."

"Then why don't you go first?" Heather questioned. "Maybe I can give you a hint in exchange for some decent information."

Brittany didn't reply.

Heather smirked. "Yeah. I thought so. You're bluffing."

"Gabriel said the same thing."

"Yeah, because he's not an idiot."

"You two are going to be the idiots when I solve this before you."

"If you solve anything before I do, I'll retire," Heather retorted.

"I look forward to it. I really—"

179

Heather's phone lit up, announcing she had an incoming call, and she took it without saying goodbye, shaking her head angrily as she greeted Liam. "Hey, Liam. What did Lindsey say?"

"Well, Lindsey was the one who contacted Poppy, but Poppy never showed."

"Wait, what?" Heather asked, turning her phone onto speaker mode and placing it on the wooden countertop.

Liam's voice echoed around the conservatory-style room. "She didn't make it to Lindsey's house. The girls couldn't get ahold of her either. They figured she just decided to go home and were too drunk to think anything of it. When they woke up this morning, they started to panic."

"Have they called the police?" Heather asked.

"Yeah. They're going down to the station to file a missing person's report."

"They're not going to find her," Heather murmured.

Julius looked at her inquisitively, and Liam spoke for him. "What do you mean?"

"I think Barry Watts took her after meeting her last night. Maybe the taxi driver worked for him. I don't know. But the problem is, nobody knows where Barry lives. And if we spook him, we'll never find out."

"So, what are you going to do?" Liam asked. "Poppy told me a bit about your plan and stuff."

"We're going to go back," Heather said confidently. "My friend Julius is going to enter the poker game—"

"The what?"

Heather ignored Liam, addressing Julius. "He's going pretend to be a new member of the Conquerers Club, and using my belongings, he's going to enter a game and record all of those sick freaks. Then we're going to send the footage to the police; they'll raid the venue, make arrests, and Barry will have to talk."

"What if he's already killed her by then?" Liam asked, voice breaking. "Or what if he refuses to talk? Wouldn't it be better to tail him back to his place so we know where it is?"

"He'll talk," Heather said, staring out into the garden. "He's a bragger. I can tell. Once he knows he's going to prison, we won't be able to shut him up."

"I should come too," Liam said. "Poppy's one of my best mates. Lilly was, too. She was pregnant with my kid, for fuck's sake."

"And that's exactly why you can't come," Heather said gently. "You'll take one look at Barry and want to break his face."

Liam sighed and stayed quiet for a while, continually making noises like he wanted to start a sentence but couldn't find the opening word. Eventually, he said, "Yeah. You're right. I would. But keep me in the loop."

"Of course."

"Should I tell Lindsey and the girls to hold their horses?"

"Tell them you've already spoken with the police, and they said to come back tomorrow. They'll be pissed, but it buys us some time and stops Barry from getting jumpy. We need him to come out tonight whether we follow him or not."

"Okay. I trust you," Liam said. "I—shit—I have to get back to work. I don't know how I'll—"

"It's going to be okay," Heather said firmly.

"Okay. I, uh, I have to go," Liam panted, clearly on the edge of having an anxiety attack as customers flooded into the building. Then he hung up without ceremony, and Julius pushed the mug of coffee back toward Heather.

"We'll need to find a better camera," he suggested.

"Yep," Heather said, eyes glazing over.

"And I'll need to join this club."

"Yep."

"I'm sure Jonno can help with that. He has contacts. I wonder what the requirements for entry are?" Heather looked at him, bemused, and he nodded. "Right. Of course."

Money.

CHAPTER TWENTY-FOUR

THE PARTNER

GABRIEL HAD FALLEN ASLEEP IN THE GARAGE AFTER one too many beers. Neither of his parents had bothered to wake him. He considered that maybe they were still pissed at him for dinner the previous night, or perhaps they'd become adjusted to going to bed before him. Either way, they'd left him to his nightmares that often arose from a lack of sleep hygiene. Not that he could blame them. He was an adult, and it had been months since he'd yelled out in his sleep, thanks to the nightly routine advice provided by his new therapist, Dr. Plemmons. They probably thought he never had them anymore. He nearly didn't.

When he did, they were usually about shooting Dennis Burke in the forehead with poor, pregnant Alice Warren pinned beneath the feral monster. Specifically, he focused on the light leaving the other man's eyes, the bloody hole oozing viscera, and how the wiry body had gone limp as if it had never had any strength at all. He also dreamed about how it had felt when Heather hugged him and how the moment of platonic intimacy had caused him to make a move on her later. That part, more than the rest, often caused him to wake sweaty and anxious. It didn't make much sense to him, considering he had killed a man, but who was he to question his nervous system?

When he wasn't dreaming about that, he dreamed very boring dreams. They weren't nonsensical, nor did they have plotlines. They hardly even pulled from his day-to-day life. Most often, he was a Whitetail deer, chewing on grass in a meadow by the lake or running through the forest unabated. Maybe this had a dark, underlying meaning he'd discover should he open a dream interpretation book. Perhaps it meant that he felt like prey. Yet, he had no intention of looking that deeply into the matter. Sometimes, things were best left alone, especially if they brought you peace.

Tonight on the couch, however, he did not face Dennis Burke in that cabin, nor did he have hooves and fur. No, tonight he dreamed about Suzie Graham, Lola Price, and Izzy Nash. He dreamed about them peacefully sleeping in their beds while Shane Gibson snuck in like a reaper to take them in their sleep. However, he did not use a scythe, nor guide them peacefully into the afterlife. No, he put his hypertrophic knuckles, calloused palms, and muscular fingers around their slender throats and squeezed so hard that no sound came out nor breath went in. He killed them all, one by one, going from one house to another under the protection of nightfall, and Gabriel could not scream or move to stop him. Then, the monster arrived at a fourth building, and when Gabriel recognized Betty's apartment steps, he awoke, panting and drenched in sweat.

As if he wasn't already disorientated enough, his phone began to ring at full volume, and he rushed to answer it, unable to bear the awful noise. "Hello?" he murmured.

"Is this Gabriel Silva?" asked a deep, male voice that Gabriel didn't recognize.

"Speaking," Gabriel replied without thinking.

"Ah, good. I found your card on my friend's coffee table and hoped you might be able to tell me what you were doing in my home."

Gabriel squeaked; he couldn't help it. Those sturdy hands were reaching out from his phone screen and wrapping themselves around his throat. "Is he—"

"He's asleep. Doesn't even know I was there. I've been coming and going for the past two weeks. Keeping an eye on him. Glad to see he's kicked the habit, but that might complicate our relationship."

"Shane," Gabriel said, although he already knew to whom he was speaking.

"Very good, Gabriel," Shane cooed in a breathy, nasally twang. "Now, let's try again. What the hell were you doing in my home?"

"As far as I'm aware, it's Izzy's home," Gabriel retorted, their distance giving him some confidence. "His name is on the deed. Not yours."

"And is your name on your parents' house's deed?" Shane countered.

A chill began to permeate Gabriel's skin, and it wasn't just the night air and the uninsulated garage. "How did you—"

"Just a guess. You sound young, Gabriel. My point is a home is a home, regardless of the legalities."

"I was asking about Katy. I'm trying to figure out who killed her," Gabriel admitted, not cognizant enough to lie and knocked off kilter by Shane's enunciated manner of speech and pronunciation. It wasn't like Gabriel hadn't met well-spoken hillbillies before. He was surrounded by them. It just wasn't what he'd expected.

"But you don't work for the Seattle PD, do you, Gabriel? So what are you? Some kind of vigilante? Do you go around at night beating the tar out of criminals in a balaclava?"

"The case interests me."

"It interests me too. Have any findings you'd like to share?"

"Not especially."

"Do you think it was me?" Shane asked gleefully.

"Well, you're nothing if not suspicious."

"And that's enough for you to point the finger at me, is it?"

"I think we both know there's more to it than that," Gabriel replied. "You're surprisingly well-spoken."

"You're deflecting."

"Humor me."

"I suppose I could say the same about you," Shane said. "I was expecting you to oink."

"Funny," Gabriel retorted dryly.

"I went to U-Dub. English. First in my family to go above a GED. But I suppose you're more interested in my extracurricular activities."

"I suppose I am. Why deal drugs if you have a bachelor's degree?"

Shane laughed again. "There's a lot more money in drugs than literature."

A sad but true fact, Gabriel supposed. "And assault, vandalism, and murder? Did those make you any money?"

"An unfortunate side effect to drugs is they make you do stupid shit."

"Are you high right now?" Gabriel asked.

"No," Shane said, defensive for the first time. It was clearly a sore spot. "Why?"

"Because calling me is pretty stupid."

Shane's laugh rattled in his throat. "Why? Are you tracing the call?"

"I have your number."

"Oh, this phone is going down a storm drain in T-minus five minutes. I'm staring at it right now. No, they'll never catch me. The pigs. Neither will you. But I respect what you're trying to do, which is why I want to tell you that you're pointed in the wrong direction. I didn't kill Katy."

"Do you know who did?"

"Not for sure. If I did, he'd be dead. But if I was a gambling man—which I am—I'd put all I have on Daniel Palmer. He wanted her all to himself, forever. Now he's got her ashes sitting on his fireplace. Oh yeah, I've paid him a visit too. A few times, actually, before he tightened security. You'd be surprised how easy it is to break into the average house nowadays."

"If he killed her and you've been in his house, surely you would've seen or heard something suspicious," Gabriel replied, only growing more dubious of Shane despite his attempts to change Gabriel's mind.

"He's careful, unlike me," Shane chuckled. "If I'd killed Katy, you'd know about it."

"Don't be so sure that I don't. Her family and friends say you were abusive. That there were bruises, guns, threats. They all took out restraining orders."

"Katy liked it rough," Shane replied, and Gabriel could hear the shrug in his voice. "That's why she invited me over whenever Daniel went away on business trips. He couldn't satisfy a woman like that."

Gabriel rolled his eyes. "Sure. What about the rest of it?"

"Don't you think it's interesting that they only got the restraining orders once Daniel came on the scene? Don't you think that's because he wanted me out? Surely, if they were that scared of me, they and their equally powerful husbands would've already pulled the trigger? No, they went along with it because Daniel needled away at them. Then he offered to pay, and they thought, why not? They didn't like him either. I'm sure they've told you that."

"They don't like either of you. I'm in agreeance. But I still want to hear what you have to say, and I don't think you've said it yet."

"I haven't. Katy and I were in love. I mean crazy love. The kind where the whirlwind never stops. But her parents and family are rich. Generationally so. The Graham name matters around these parts. One of them—an uncle, I think—built this goddamn suburb."

This. He was still in The Flowers Development. He was probably still in Buttercup Dreams. Gabriel—hoping he didn't sound too distracted—reached for his laptop and pulled up the tips webpage for the Seattle PD.

Shane cleared his voice, aware of his slip-up. Gabriel heard heavy boots on the ground. He was moving. "Anyway. Katy was close to her family. She loved both of us equally, but they hated me. She couldn't choose, so she started to drink, and I hated it. She wasn't like Izzy, who kept it together. She was messy, violent, and bitter. After a couple of incidents, her family and friends distanced themselves, and I made the mistake of getting her to sober up for a couple of days. During that week, she realized that she couldn't bear the isolation, so she left. I was devastated, obviously, and a drunk myself at the time, I behaved in a way I'm ashamed of. They were right to distance themselves, but I would have never hurt her. Every time I showed up, it was to give apology letters and gifts. I know now that if I'd given her some space, maybe she would've come back to me."

"And then she met Daniel," Gabriel said, his voice a little vacant as he typed in and sent off his location tip.

"Then she met Daniel and ruined both of our lives."

And that was precisely why Gabriel couldn't trust Shane. He hated Daniel too much. He blamed him for everything— stealing his girl, sending him off the deep end, and probably going to prison—and he wanted Daniel to pay. More than that, he struck Gabriel as the kind of guy with the attitude of 'If I can't have her, neither of us can' and if 'I have to rot in prison, he should too.' All of this was wrapped up in jealousy and vengeance, which meant Gabriel needed to take more than a grain of salt while listening to him.

"Well, Gabriel, it's been great getting to know you," Shane said, a little out of breath, the distinctive sound of a nylon jacket brushing against branches muffling his words. "But I'll be in touch. I want to see you put Daniel behind bars. Maybe I'll wear a disguise and show up in person."

"I'm sure I'll see you in the courtroom one way or another."

"Here's hoping."

The line went dead, and Gabriel was left reeling. It was Shane; it had to be, and he spent the next three hours refreshing the search results for his name and Izzy's, hoping something would crop up for the former and praying the latter remained unmentioned. In the end, nothing arose for either, and Gabriel fell back asleep in the sticky, clammy cold of the garage, ready to be haunted by two new faces—Shane's and Daniel's.

CHAPTER TWENTY-FIVE

THE DETECTIVE

"**D**O YOU THINK THEY'D LET A WOMAN JOIN THE club?" Heather asked, addressing Julius's profile as he made a final adjustment to his shirt-button-slash-nano-cam. They'd had to go to a tailor to get a shirt with identical buttons made. Luckily, Jonno's friends didn't ask questions. Nor did Jonno when Julius said he wanted to play poker at The Catacombs. And when Heather asked him if he knew what went on in that room, Jonno had replied, 'No, but my gut is telling me that's for the best.'

"I've already paid for my seat," Julius said assertively. "I'm doing this. And you're going to wait outside in the rental car."

"But you've never been undercover before," Heather protested, adjusting her heavy laptop bag.

"I've met enough sleazebags to play the part. Do you think I have enough to gamble with?"

Heather began to list the items she'd provided—now safely tucked away in Julius's leather satchel—and held up a finger for each one. "My favorite bra," she grumbled.

"You said it had to look worn."

"Yeah, I know. Three pairs of underwear of varying sexiness. The earrings I used to wear every day before you gave me these ones. A pair of tights with a small tear. Hair ties, with hair attached. A bracelet. An unwashed undershirt. Socks—cute ones. Is that it?"

"A lock of hair," Julius answered with a frown.

"I hope we get this stuff back. Not that I can reattach the hair, but I really do love that bra."

"Well, I'll do my best to not lose."

"Save the bra for last if you do."

Julius chuckled and dropped his hands to his sides. "I'm sure the police will give it back to you if we succeed."

"We will," Heather said, finally unlocking the nondescript, mid-priced silver rental. "We have to."

While Julius entered the building wearing the spy camera—complete with microphone, internal storage, and 24-hour battery life—Heather clambered into the back seat and opened her laptop. She had parked around the corner between cars that must belong to the apartment building residents so as to not attract suspicion, but she wished she could've opted for tinted windows. With every person that walked past, she found herself swiveling, turning the screen away from their uninterested gaze. These sorts of stakeouts and undercover missions made her paranoid. It had been a very long time since she'd been roped into one, and it was the first time she'd elected to do one of her own free will. Yet, she knew she didn't have a choice. This was their last resort.

Despite the comfort of the modern sedan, she couldn't help but miss her 1977 Ford Granada that was wasting away in her garage back in Glenville, and she briefly wondered how much it would cost to transport it to London and then how much it would be to change it to a left-hand drive. Probably way too much. Realistically, she'd have to sell. Then she wondered why she was wondering at all, but before she could figure it out, Julius's feed appeared on her screen.

He was descending the stairs for the third time. The quality of the camera was surprisingly good, but the microphone was better. She could hear his shoes on the concrete steps, the steady breaths exhaled through his nose, and his heart beating. The latter sounded like the bassline for an up-tempo jazz song. He was nervous. Far more so than he had appeared. That was a good thing. It meant he could control his anxiety visibly. Of course, she knew this about him already. His surgical hands never shook. She just hoped his poker face was half as steady.

First, he made his way to the bar and waited patiently to be served, and Heather found herself wishing for a fast-forward button. Trying to stave off frustration and nerves, she tuned into the fine details of the ambient sound. The conversations primarily. The bartenders were complaining about overcrowding and spoke disparagingly about a man named Bruno, whom Heather could only assume was the head bouncer and in charge of population control. The couple to his left were clearly on a first date, and though the lust was apparent, every opinion stated seemed like a misstep. Their politics didn't align even remotely, and Heather doubted there would be a second date. In juxtaposition, the elderly gay couple to his right were completely simpatico. They spoke in sync. They ordered drinks for each other. They made Heather feel something akin to yearning. A desire to have what they had.

"Thank you," Julius said as a young bartender slid his martini across the bar. It looked perfect, like something out of a magazine, and Julius's satisfied sip confirmed this. As he took another, his heartbeat slowed momentarily, but when he turned to face his destination, it spiked once more.

Still, he made his way without hesitation, greeted the bouncer politely, and said, "I'm on the list. Julian Andrews."

The bouncer made a crack about Mary Poppins while patting Julius down, which Heather mostly missed due to Julius's faux but convincing laughter. The door opened, Heather inhaled sharply, and the room was revealed in HD.

Barry was already seated, and a different young blonde sat on his lap. She didn't look much like Poppy or Lilly—her eyes were dark brown, her face dotted with beauty spots, and her lips artificially plumped—but Heather knew what her fate would be if this didn't go accordingly. Sick to her stomach, she wondered how many other blondes had come before and since Lilly Arnold and where they'd all ended up. Hopefully alive. It was possible that Lilly was the only one who was six feet under. Maybe she rejected his advances, and his ego couldn't bear the refusal. However, from what she knew of killers, this was improbable, and Heather tried not to cling to comforting unlikelihoods.

"Ah, you must be Julian," a man said, and Julius swiveled to face him. He was narrow, emaciated, covered in tattoos, his ears pierced with diamonds. His suit had cufflinks to match. Heather didn't doubt that they were real. They shone even brighter than his shock-white hair.

Julius stuck out a hand. "I am. Nice to meet you..."

"Paul Sugar."

A name, Heather realized, lighting up and sitting up straight. They needed names. As if reading her mind, Julius traveled around the table and introduced himself to every man in the room. Including Barry, who fortunately stated his real name. After all, why wouldn't he?

Julius then tactfully chose a seat opposite Barry to keep the camera focused on their suspect and again reached for his martini.

"So what is it you do, Julian?" Barry asked, sounding somehow lecherous despite his apparent heterosexuality.

"I am a plastic surgeon," Julius replied with an air of smugness.

The men around him guffawed with delight. Getting to look at breasts professionally was clearly an enviable position with this crowd. It was a clever improvisation on Julius's part.

"Do you get to feel them? Before and after? The titties, I mean," a man called 'Kev' slavered.

"I do. And I must say, I enjoy my job greatly," Julius replied coyly, and Heather could picture a self-satisfied look on his face that she didn't enjoy. This was men's locker room talk, something she had never been privy to. On one hand, it was sociologically and anthropologically fascinating, and on the other, absolutely disgusting. At least she knew that Julius disliked it as much as she did.

"I bet you do," Paul howled. "And the arses, tell us about the arses."

Julius regaled them as best he could, leaving out the gory medical details and instead describing the results of a Brazilian butt lift and the aesthetic pleasures derived from performing them. The men took this as an opportunity to begin debating breasts and butts when they were interrupted by a late arriver.

Julius turned, and Heather already knew she was in for a shock when his heart practically exploded. There he was, standing in a doorway that was almost too small for him. Raymond Doyle.

"Gentlemen!" he exclaimed. "Are we ready to begin?"

"Indeed," said the dealer as Raymond sat beside Barry and shook the man's hand.

Then Raymond turned to face Julius, and his face turned from jolly to glowering. "Haven't we met?" he asked.

"Yes," Julius replied sheepishly. "I caught you on a date with my wife." The room went silent, and Julius hastily continued. "She admitted everything to me afterward. We're separating."

"Well, I'm sorry—" Raymond began, blustering. The fact Julius was in this room, part of the club, and male, had started him off on a baseline of respect, it seemed, despite their awkward history.

"No, I should apologize. I had no idea that she was..." Julius trailed off. "You did nothing wrong. I, too, enjoy the company of escorts. Though, don't tell her that. I'd hate for her to get anything more in the divorce."

Raymond surveyed him for a moment before bursting into a deep belly laugh. "Well, maybe you can hire her for her services one day."

Julius laughed back. "Oh, she's not worth the money. I promise you that."

Heather tried not to be offended. *It's just a character,* she told herself, though her hackles refused to flatten.

"No harm, no foul then," Raymond said, sticking out his hand to shake. Julius took it. "Raymond Doyle."

"Julian Andrews."

"Wonderful to meet you, Mr. Andrews. Glad that you're joining us. And if now that you're one of us, I'm sure we can find you a wife of higher quality."

"Yes," Paul agreed enthusiastically. "No need for whores. You can sleep with them, but you don't marry them. My wife has plenty of hot, single friends of fine breeding. Virgins mostly."

Raymond nodded. "Yes. You marry the virgin and screw the whore on the side. It's a tale as old as time."

Julius raised his glass. "To virgins and whores."

Everyone joined him, laughing and clinking. Eventually, the dealer's voice rose above the din, informing them that the game was about to begin, and everyone became very serious. They sipped their drinks in silence as the cards were dealt, the chips were stacked, and the first items with which they were betting hit the center of the table.

Julius started with underwear, inventing a story about a nanny he'd been sleeping with. Joining Heather's green briefs were a variety of other items, including Paul's conquest stockings. Then, it was Barry's turn, and Heather realized that Julius was holding his breath. The man, who was once again wearing a full three-piece suit, placed a padded, leopard print bra on the table and spoke of an exotic dancer he'd brought back to his place. Supposedly, she liked him so much he didn't have to pay. Heather doubted that but thought back to the previous night when Poppy stripped down her underwear. Her bra had been unpadded, sheer, and blue.

Then Raymond—whose eyes were oddly bloodshot—put that very same bra on the table, and Heather gasped. She covered her mouth as he opened his to speak and turned up the volume. "From a darling little creature I met last night," Raymond said. "Her taxi driver had dropped her off in the wrong spot, so I offered her a lift. Then, I made her a deal she couldn't refuse."

The men cheered again, and Julius, none the wiser for not having seen Poppy in her underwear, picked up his cards. He had no idea that the mission had pivoted. That Poppy's abductor, and likely Lilly's killer, was not Barry after all but the man that Heather had gone on a date with. Raymond Doyle.

Julius's first hand was bad. A seven, a three, and a ten. One of the diamonds, one of the hearts, one of the clubs. Still, he played it for all it was worth and bluffed as well as he'd lied. His next hand was better, and though he still didn't win, he made it to the river without folding.

More items were added, hours passed, drinks were ordered, and in the final game, Raymond placed a pair of shoes on the table that Heather recognized instantly. Lilly's dirty white sneakers. Apparently, he'd been holding them back for a special occasion, but when he refused to elaborate, he was forced to add a sexier item to the stack.

They had him. She didn't even care when another one of her personal items was scooped up by Raymond because soon enough, they'd be back in the washing machine, Poppy would be found, and he would be behind bars. They had him. The killer. At long last. And by the grace of the universe, it wasn't Daniel.

CHAPTER TWENTY-SIX

THE DETECTIVE

THOUGH HE STUCK AROUND FOR A JIGGER OF WHISKEY and a cigar during the interim, Julius didn't stick around for round two—much to Heather's relief. Instead, he excused himself from the despicable group under the guise of having to 'babysit' his kids early in the morning for the sake of winning the custody battle. No one tried to persuade him to stay. Instead, they were sympathetic toward their newfound friend, Julian Andrews. It seemed he was not the only one to have his ex-wife try and take the kids.

As he left the room, the dealer called for everyone to return to the table, and everyone hunkered down for the next hand.

This gave Heather plenty of time to enact phase two, and as Julius joined her in the car, she threw her arms around him and squeezed. Tired, tipsy, confused, and surprised by the gesture, he hesitated before chuckling and returning her affection in equal measure.

Heather reluctantly peeled herself away and placed her palms on his cheeks with a gentle clapping sound. "You did it," she laughed. "You got him."

"Good," Julius exhaled. "That was exhausting."

"You did great."

"Worth it to see Barry behind bars."

Heather removed her hands and shook her head. "Not Barry. Raymond. He had Poppy's bra and Lilly's shoes."

Julius's eyes widened. "Jesus. I was paying so much attention to Barry that I didn't even notice. Thank God he decided to sit where he did."

"And thank God I had you to intervene on our 'date,'" Heather grimaced.

Clearly not wanting to even think about that, Julius asked, "What do we do now?"

—

Shortly after getting off the phone with a simultaneously disbelieving, angry, stressed, and overjoyed Helen, blue and red lights filled the street, and sirens rang loudly in chorus as four squad cars and a riot van sped toward The Catacombs. It was happening. There was no back exit. Raymond was trapped.

Heather and Julius exited the car and rounded the corner to the commotion before moving forward to settle into their front-row positions for the show. After showing their IDs to the cops who were setting up barricades, they were allowed to pass and loiter by the alleyway entrance, and they peered into it Scooby Doo-style as a group of armor-clad officers banged on the door.

"This is a raid! Open up!" one woman yelled.

The bouncer didn't hesitate to open the door and stepped aside to let them through without protest. Heather hoped the innocent workers wouldn't be in trouble, but her worries shrank and slunk to the back of her mind as Paul Sugar appeared at the top of the stairs in handcuffs. One by one, the rest followed, and finally, Raymond appeared, escorted by men who were almost equally enormous. He huffed and protested, his suit fit to burst as his chest heaved, but then he saw Heather and Julius and became very still. She offered a coy smile—the same one she'd given him on their date—and watched smugly as the penny dropped inside his cavernous skull.

To her surprise, as he walked past, too close for comfort, he paused to tip his head in respect before facing the front with tranquil stillness. He was a gamesman through and through, and the biggest game of his life was at an end. He knew he had been bested. He knew in looking at them that there was no getting out of this. All he could do now was be a gracious loser and bow before the winners.

"Congratulations," Helen said from behind them, causing Heather to whirl around.

"Thanks," Heather said, her voice hoarse. It had been a long week.

"I think you just solved half of my rape cases. Not to mention the Ribbon Killer case. I've fudged some paperwork to make it look like I'd hired you to go undercover, just in case. I trust the truth will stay between us. Come by later to sign off on that, won't you?"

"Sure."

Helen nodded, looking past Heather and at the bags upon bags of evidence. "Great. His home is being raided as we speak. With any luck, we'll find Poppy Smith unharmed."

"Is there anything we can do?"

"I think you've done quite enough, don't you?" Helen asked, meeting Heather's gaze for the first time. Her tone was cold, but a small smile played upon her lips. "Go home. I'll call you when we find Poppy."

Heather and Julius waited impatiently at Farfalla House for an update. Heather had somewhat naively hoped that she'd be allowed to attend the interrogation, but of course, she couldn't. She had no jurisdiction here and, as Helen had implied, had already massively overstepped her boundaries. So, despite their hard work, the only thing that they could do was wait. Julius ordered Chinese food—satay king prawn for him and Szechuan pork for her—from a nearby twenty-four-hour restaurant, and despite Heather's stomach's voracious growls, she could barely manage three mouthfuls.

After a terse, silent dinner, they sat outside in the garden, their only light source a small candle and the distant kitchen lamp. The moon was black, almost completely new, and yet the koi still seemed to glow as they danced around the pond. Heather focused on them as she indulged in an oversized glass of wine, while Julius opted to watch the trees blowing in the wind as he sobered up with an espresso.

"I'm sorry for calling you a whore," Julius said after an impossibly long yet comfortable period of silence.

Heather barked a laugh. "That's okay. You were just saying what they wanted to hear. You're quite the actor, in fact."

"I feel like I should wash my mouth out with soap."

"Please don't do that," Heather said softly, turning on her chair to face him. They were closer than she'd thought they were, and something in her—spurred on by adrenaline—moved her hand to his beard and her face toward his. Just as she closed her eyes and heard his lips part, her phone rang.

She retracted abruptly and whispered an apology as she answered, her face crimson even in the dark. "Hello?" she asked.

"Detective Bishop," Helen said. "I have your update."

Heather checked her watch and saw that three hours had passed. It was about time. She gave the go-ahead, placed her phone on the table, and pressed the speaker button.

"We found Poppy Smith in Raymond's basement. She has been beaten fairly severely but is conscious and has reassured us that no sexual misconduct has occurred."

To her and Julius's surprise, Heather burst into tears and clapped a hand to her mouth as she curled in on herself. Julius rubbed her back as sobs wracked her body, and though she willed them to stop, it seemed they were here to stay. She'd been burying her worry and guilt for the sake of the case, but to find out that Poppy was not only alive but had not suffered any form of sexual violence was more than she could've ever hoped for.

"Is she okay?" Julius asked in her stead as he continued to comfort.

"She's in surprisingly good spirits," Helen said fondly. "She cracked jokes the entire way to the hospital. And aside from a few bruises, she's physically fine. We will, of course, pay for counseling for as long as she needs it. We don't leave heroes in the lurch." Helen paused. "I am cross, to say the least, that you got her involved in something so dangerous, but perhaps I've been playing it too safe. After all, thanks to Poppy, yourself, and Julius, Raymond Doyle will never hurt a woman again."

"You got the confession?" Heather sniffled, more tears pouring out. She'd given up on trying to tamp the flood. The relief it brought was too satisfying.

"We did," Helen said kindly, detecting the tears over the phone. "He folded immediately when we told him we'd found Poppy in his basement. He knew he wasn't getting out of it."

"And Lilly?"

"He owned up to that shortly after. Apparently, he'd over-stepped her boundaries during their last 'encounter,' and she'd 'ghosted' him. Unfortunately for her, Mr. Doyle is not the type of man who takes kindly to being avoided, nor does he take no for an answer. Though I'm sure you found that out yourself on your little date."

"Sorry," Heather whispered.

"No apologies necessary, Detective. Anyway, her avoidance triggered an obsession in Mr. Doyle. He went so far as to hire a PI to stalk her, and the said PI informed him that she was in the park that night. So, he rounded up all the gifts he'd bought for her, bought some flowers, and headed over, hoping to win her back. He was intending to ask her to be his sugar baby so that she'd stop sleeping with other men and hoped to move her into the guesthouse on his property."

"But when he got there, she was talking to Liam," Heather said, sadness replacing relief. She knew how this story ended.

"Yes. Upon hearing that she was pregnant with someone else's child and intending to keep it, he, as he puts it, flew into a blind rage. When Liam left, he confronted her and begged her to abort. He said he could give her everything she wanted, even children, but she grew frightened, which only angered him further. Then, she became defiant. She told him she was keeping her baby. That she was going to take out a restraining order. That he'd never be able to touch her again. He lunged. She used pepper spray. It didn't stop him. And before he knew it, he'd killed her."

"God," Heather muttered.

"I know," Helen sighed. "Then—in what he calls a state of insanity—he had an idea. He wanted her to look forever young, like an angel. So he used his gifts of makeup and nail polish to take away all of the parts of her that made him sad, including what he'd done. The ribbon was from the bouquet of flowers he'd bought for her. He used it to hide the bruising."

"Wow," was all Heather could say, picturing the scene in her head in unpleasant vividity.

"Now, he claims that he hasn't killed any other women, but we're going to press him on that."

"Do you think he was going to kill Poppy?"

"He says he had no intention of doing so. He wanted her as more of a pet, so to speak. He reminded her of Lilly. According to her, he even called her Lilly. I suppose it comforted him to pretend he hadn't done what he'd done and that they could be together forever."

Heather swallowed back spit and bile. The concept was revolting, and she owed Poppy a colossal apology. "Do you think he'll get a life sentence?"

"Hard to say, but I hope so. I'll be visiting Poppy in the morning should you want to join me. I can bring your things. We won't hold them as evidence. It'll only confuse our investigators."

"Thank you."

"No, thank you, Heather," Helen replied sternly. "I didn't think you or Julius had it in you, but you have stopped a monster. I can put your name—"

"You take it," Heather said. "Seriously. You deserve it. You laid the groundwork. You arrested him. I don't want the applause."

"Well, then, I have to thank you again. I think you just made me the most powerful female police officer in London."

"Use it for good," Heather teased.

"I intend to. And Heather?"

"Yeah."

"Write the story anyway. If anyone deserves to tell it, it's you, and I have plenty of friends at the Guardian and the BBC who would be interested in what you have to say."

"I'll try my best."

"Well, considering what I've seen so far, you don't even have to try. Now, get some rest. I'll see you tomorrow."

The call ended, and Heather fell forward onto the table, half sobbing, half laughing. She looked at Julius and saw that he was doing the same, and she wrapped herself around him once more. This time, however, she didn't break away, and when she was half asleep, she allowed him to scoop her up and carry her to bed.

CHAPTER TWENTY-SEVEN

THE DETECTIVE

UPON ENTERING POPPY'S ROOM, HEATHER REALIZED that her decision to avoid buying flowers had been the right one. Not only did Poppy likely now know where the ribbon around Lilly's neck had come from, but her room was already covered in flowers. Bouquets ranging from holdable to enormous occupied every surface, and balloons took up the entirety of the ceiling. Much to the medical professionals' apparent irritation as they swatted, ducked, and weaved to get across the room. It seemed bordering on a health hazard at this point.

Poppy laughed when she saw Heather looking. "I know," she said. "I feel like I've died. A wreath of lilies? Seriously, nana? That's in bad taste on at least two counts."

Heather chuckled. "Yeah, maybe not the tactful option."

"So what have you brought for me then?" Poppy asked, folding her arms and sticking her nose in the air.

Julius pulled his arms from behind his back to reveal a McDonald's Happy Meal and a portion of mozzarella sticks. "We thought this might be better than flowers," he said, dodging a drifting balloon.

"Oh, you absolute legends!" Poppy exclaimed, uncrossing her arms and reaching out with grabby toddler hands. They were soon filled with food, and her mouth followed suit. "The shit they serve in hospitals, I'll tell you," Poppy said between bites, shaking her head. "Even the jelly pots are depressing. Tell me how something neon green that wobbles can be so sad?"

"You seem... okay," Heather stated slowly, looking her up and down.

"I'm fine. Great even. We caught the killer! I can actually live my life now." Poppy paused, staring at a limp French fry. "I can let her go. She's been living in my head, you know. Lilly, that is. Talking to me. Crying. Begging. It's weird; ever since this morning, she's barely there. I reckon I'll say goodbye later." Poppy's voice cracked, but she quickly plastered on a smile. "It's going to be hard, being alone, but I reckon she's got better digs waiting for her than this noggin."

Heather stepped forward. "I want to apologize, I should have never—"

"Don't do that," Poppy instructed firmly. "Don't you dare. I knew what I was signing up for, and I'm glad I did it. I'm glad of every second. This black eye will fade, but the photos they took of it to use in court won't. You helped me figure out what I was supposed to do to help her. So don't you be sorry."

"Well, don't thank me either."

"I can agree to that," Poppy said with a wink. "But I can think it. I can use my telepathic powers to tell you." Poppy put a forefinger to each temple and stared intensely. To her credit, Heather felt what she was transmitting, whether she liked it or not. "And good job, Julian. Didn't take Mr. Silent over here for much of an actor, but it seems you had everyone convinced."

"It's Julius," Julius replied. "And thank you. I'm thinking of taking up a new career in the West End."

"Don't push your luck," Poppy teased. "So I'm guessing your name isn't really Heather Singh either."

Heather shook her head. "No. My name is Heather, but my last name is Bishop. I'm a cop. He's a forensic pathologist."

Poppy leaned back, smiling to herself. "Yeah. I know. Liam is such a shite liar. Nice job on the Paper Doll Case. I read about that back in the day. You know, if this was the olden times, they'd make you a saint. St. Bishop. Hah. Patron of abused women and girls. I bet you'd hate that."

"I would," Heather chuckled.

"Too modest."

"I agree," Julius said, nudging Heather. Heather, smiling, slapped his elbow away.

Poppy raised her brows. "Oh, I see. We have a power couple on our hands."

Heather didn't protest but changed the subject. "Have you ever considered a job in law enforcement? You'd be good at it. I don't know if London has a vice squad, but—"

"Nah. I love The Thistle & Pig. They're my family. I even love serving all those creepy old bastards. You'd have to pry it out of my cold, dead hands for me to quit. I'll be there till I'm 100."

"I don't doubt it."

"Come by the pub before you leave, yeah? I'll be back tomorrow."

"Seriously?"

"Yeah. They've promised me all the tips. Plus, it won't be the first time the patrons have seen me black and blue," Poppy joked, putting her fists up.

"We'll be there," Heather replied, laughing as much today as she had cried last night.

Poppy looked thoughtful and turned her gaze to the window. "I hate to ask, but it's been bugging me. That guy in the photo, you know him, right? Is he—"

Whatever Poppy was going to ask was interrupted by Helen click-clacking into the room, holding an exceptionally splendid bouquet of flowers and an evidence bag full of Heather's belongings. They all turned to look at her, and Heather laughed again—joined by the others—as Helen stared around.

"Bugger," she hissed.

"Just pop them by the bed," Poppy said. "Thank you. These are the nicest ones yet."

"I should hope so," Helen replied, placing the bouquet and tossing the bag to Heather. "They cost a fortune. They're not just some petrol station pick-up."

Poppy snorted. "You don't mince words, do you, Helen?" Poppy nodded at Helen while keeping her eyes on Heather. "We're best mates now, her and me."

Helen pursed her lips, but a smile escaped regardless. "I must admit that Miss Smith is rather charming."

"That's what they all say, love," Poppy slurred, evidently sleepy. They must've given her a couple of painkillers, Heather realized and watched as she scooched down, surrounded by flowers and fast food, and closed her eyes. "Be back in a minute," she muttered.

"Well, speaking of not mincing words," Helen said, addressing Heather while looking at Poppy fondly. "I have something to offer you. A job."

"Oh yeah?" Heather asked, surprised, considering the stunts she'd pulled.

"Yes. As the lead cold case detective of Scotland Yard. Our previous lead just retired, and I can't think of anyone that would fill his boots better."

Heather hesitated. "I mean, it sounds great. I love London."

"But?" Helen asked, looking at her sharply.

"But I'm an American."

"Your father is English, no? And your mother is a triple citizen. India, Britain, and America."

"Yeah. You've done your research."

"Of course I have. And the way I see it, you're an Englishwoman with a funny accent. Not to mention, getting you a visa would be a piece of cake. Especially for me."

"Well, that's something," Heather admitted, her mind going a mile a minute. "But my home is in Glenville."

"Glenville," Helen repeated, a sour expression taking hold. "Yes, I've researched that too. Far be it from me to belittle a small town. I'm from Malvern, after all. Yes, I know you haven't heard of it. That's my point. I love the countryside. But you belong in a metropolitan area. More specifically, your skills do. To put it bluntly, Heather, we need you."

"I don't know."

"I will triple your current salary. You'll never see a dead body in the flesh again. You'll have a company car and phone and want for nothing."

"I kind of like wanting for things."

"Then I'll pay you minimum wage. Whatever suits you." Helen's tone remained formal, but Heather saw that same desperation as she had at the start of the case.

"I'm sorry, but the answer is no."

Helen sighed, grinding her teeth. "Well, feel free to get in touch should you change your mind."

"Will do. And thank you."

"And Julius," Helen said, holding out her hand to shake. "Good work."

Julius took it. "Same to you."

"You were absolutely repugnant in that footage. Color me impressed. You've always been too sweet for your own good."

"I'm more of a savory man nowadays."

"Well, let's hope Heather doesn't have a sweet tooth."

"I don't," Heather quipped affectionately before blushing.

Poppy began to snore, halting the conversation, and the three filtered out into the hallway. "Think about my offer, Heather. And I'm sure Jonno would be happy to have you back, Julius," Helen said before striding away without goodbye. She'd reached her limit of soppiness, it seemed.

Heather looked to Julius, ready to laugh, but he had a grave expression on his face. "What?" she asked.

"Nothing," he said, shaking it off. "Now, what are we to do for your last days in London?"

Heather smirked. "Reckon we could find a horse and carriage or double-decker bus?"

"I'm sure that can be arranged."

CHAPTER TWENTY-EIGHT

THE DETECTIVE

HEATHER AND JULIUS SPENT THE DAY DOING EXACTLY what she'd always wanted to do in London—tourist stuff. And being particularly interested in the macabre aspects of history, they started the day with a Jack the Ripper tour, which led to a very heated lunch debate over the famous serial killer's identity. Heather believed his real identity to be that of Walter Sickert, the painter of prostitutes, while Julius firmly thought it was Aaron Kosminski, the Polish barber.

The debate became so passionate that, at a certain point, they both just stopped and laughed. Somehow, they were both still at work, even on their holiday. After a little more pushing and shoving, they met in the middle by agreeing that Prince Albert Victor was undoubtedly the most entertaining suspect.

Then, to continue the horrors, they headed to the Tower of London, where Heather found herself falling in love with the ravens and spent a good half an hour talking to their handlers. Julius was more interested in the armor, but each humored the other, and they ended up spending a good five hours there before moving on to Madame Tussauds.

Despite the Madame's grisly origins of sculpting the beheaded of the French Revolution, there wasn't much darkness to be found there, and though the artistic abilities of the sculptors did impress Heather, the experience mostly reminded her of how little she knew about pop culture. Then they reached the Chamber of Horrors, and she perked up, realizing she could flex her knowledge muscles.

"I thought you didn't like true crime," Julius mused, listening to her speak with impeccably patient listening skills.

"I do, and I don't," Heather replied with a shrug. "I don't like it when it's supposed to be entertaining, but I find it fascinating, and I think it's important to be educated. The old stuff is easier, too. I guess there are several degrees of separation there that stop it from being painful." She paused, looking around at the displays. "I guess this is 'entertaining,' but hey, I'm on holiday."

"I agree," Julius said, looking at the Kray twins. "It might be in poor taste at times, but maybe it's best that we don't look away from monsters. Lest they grow stronger in the shadows," he said, adopting a spooky, ghost tour guide-esque cadence and wriggling his fingers.

"You're right," Heather said. "If we look away, they just get bigger," she replied, pointing at the genuine historical artifacts taken from serial killer John Christie's home after his arrest. His was a case that had always interested her, mainly because she never wanted to do as poor of a job as those investigators had. They let Christie keep killing while they sent a poor, traumatized man to his death. That's why she'd done everything she had done in the past week. She refused to send Daniel or anyone else away for something they hadn't done.

After thoroughly examining that room and being bored by pop stars and celebrities, they moved on to yet another tourist attraction—the London Eye. Heather thought, as they reclined at the top and looked out over London, that it might be her favorite of them all. She loved heights, and this was a particularly impressive one. She thought it was how a bird must feel and even envied the trash-picking overweight pigeons for their daily view.

"I'm going to miss it," she said. "London."

"Me too," Julius said. "But I'm sure we'll be back. After all, Farfalla House will always be waiting for us."

"Ugh, don't remind me. I already miss that kitchen, and we haven't even left yet."

Julius shifted, tilted toward her, and it seemed like he wanted to say more. Heather waited, and eventually, he said, "I've booked dinner for us tonight at one of my favorite Italian restaurants. My father was a sous chef there when he was young."

Heather ignored the fact that that was definitely not what he was going to say and smiled at him fondly. "That sounds amazing. I didn't know your dad was a chef."

"He wasn't always. He got bored easily. But he was always a good cook. He taught me most of what I know."

"I guess that dress is going to get one more spin before I go back to Glenville, and it never sees the light of day again."

"And the heels?"

Heather sighed. "Unfortunately, a dress like that deserves heels. I think my feet are adjusting, though. You should see my blisters."

Julius snorted. "I think I'm good."

"What about my bunions?"

"You don't have—"

"Callouses?"

"Heather."

"Carbuncles?"

Julius laughed and groaned. "I'm nauseous enough as is, thank you."

"Oh, so you hate my feet. I get it," Heather harrumphed jokingly, looking away.

Julius reached for her hand. "I could never hate any part of you. Even your disgusting feet."

"Thanks. I like you too."

"Yeah. Yeah."

The restaurant was named L'Arte del Gusto, and considering the swan-shaped napkins, the rich teal walls, the dark wooden furnishings, and the oil paintings on the walls, it was also very expensive and probably very exclusive. Apparently, Jonno had poured some money into it when it was struggling during COVID. Maybe it was an investment, but more likely, it was a kindness to Julius. Either way, the man seemingly had his finger in every pie in the city. Heather thought that it must be exhausting to know so many people, but in a way, she envied it. He was important. He would never be forgotten. His life was always exciting. She bet that retirement didn't terrify him either, as it did her.

A young man who could've been Julius's brother showed them to a table—and considering the stories about his father, he could've been—and they sat opposite each other, smirking as thick, silky napkins were laid across their laps. There were also roses on the table and a bottle of champagne on ice. It felt deeply romantic, like a romcom proposal dinner, and oddly, Heather found herself becoming a little put off by the formality. It wasn't that she didn't have romantic feelings for Julius. This trip had made it clear that she did. She was dreading his return to Seattle and her return to Glenville, where their one-hour distance and busy schedules would inevitably keep them apart. Especially as they weren't actually together. When would they next see each other? Days? Weeks? Months? Whatever it was, it was too much. Still, this also felt like too much, but she tried to shift out of her discomfort and started up some small talk.

"So, what do you—" she started just as Julius also began a sentence. They chuckled awkwardly. "You go," she said.

"No, you," he replied.

"Alright. What is your favorite Italian dish?" she asked. "I'd like to try it, whatever it is."

"Pasta con le sarde."

"Oh, what does that have in it?"

"Sardines and—" he stopped, likely because of Heather's involuntary grimace.

"Sorry," she said, flushing. "Not a sardine gal."

"What about prawns?"

"Are they the same as shrimp?"

"Yes."

"I love prawns," Heather enthused, looking at the menu, which was almost impenetrably Italian. "What to have. What to have."

"You know what I want," Julius said abruptly. "Ambrosia Kebabs."

Heather looked up at him. "But this restaurant—"

"Is too uptight for a celebratory meal," Julius finished. He grabbed the bottle of champagne, put one hundred pounds on the table, and stood, extending his hand.

"Are you sure?"

He thrust his hand a few inches further forward, and she grasped it before standing. Giggling like teenagers, they fled the restaurant and ran across the road. "Do you even know where you're going?" she asked, her ankles nearly rolling as they traversed various terrain that her shoes were absolutely not adequate for. A week ago, she would've already twisted one. Maybe she really was adjusting.

"It's an adventure," Julius replied, pulling her forward, looking ten years younger in the lamplight.

An adventure it certainly was, and as they approached grass, Heather removed her heels to run barefoot through the park, not caring about germs or dirt. Then, as if guided by the north star, they saw it, the wide pathway that led to and from The Thistle & Pig and the food trucks that lined it. Mercifully, Ambrosia's was still open, and they approached at full speed, thankful for the lack of queue. They looked up at the kind man who'd told Heather so much, and before they could greet him, he held his arms out wide with excitement.

"Ah, you're back!" he exclaimed.

"We are, and we'd like to try those lamb kebabs," Heather replied.

"Champagne?" the man asked, thick eyebrows waggling. "Celebrating, are we?"

"We solved the Lilly Arnold case," Heather said.

The man lit up, raising his brows and eradicating wrinkles. "My God. Did you really?"

"We did. Well, she did," Julius explained.

"In which case, dinner is on the house," the man said firmly.

"No need for that," Julius replied, handing a wad of cash over. "*Efcharistó.*"

"And to you, my boy," the man replied before beginning to count. He moved to the till, but Heather stopped him by talking.

"What's your name?" Heather asked.

"Konstantinos," he said as he got to work on their food. "I tell you, I think you've made my entire year."

"Well, you're definitely about to make our night," Heather responded kindly before handing over another wad of cash and piling it on top of Julius's.

"No, no. This is too much money," Konstantinos protested. "The kebabs are only cheap."

"No," Heather insisted. "No change. Please. Go home. Be with your family. I see that photo of your wife and kids back there."

"Are you serious?" Konstantinos asked, a cheeky smile on his lips but a furrow in his brow.

"We are," Julius said firmly.

"Really?"

"Yes!" Heather laughed.

"Oh my—" Konstantinos said, shaking his head. "Thank you, thank you, thank you!"

"Please just consider it payment for your information and all that you do to help keep your community safe.

Konstantinos nodded and pretended to zip his lips before putting the money in the till and getting to work. His silence didn't last long, and the three of them enthusiastically chit-chatted as he cooked. They learned his family's names and how long he'd lived in London, and he and Julius had a humorous argument about whose food was better: Greece's or Italy's? Then the food was done, and Konstantinos closed his shutter after one more mutual thanks and a wave.

"Where do we go now?" Julius asked.

"Lilly's bench," Heather replied automatically. "It feels like the right thing to do for some reason."

—

It really was the right thing to do. The clearing no longer felt haunted; the metal picnic bench was surprisingly comfortable, and there seemed to be twice as many stars as usual. She supposed they had more opportunity to shine, considering the new moon.

She was staring up at them as Julius uncorked the bottle with a bang. She flinched and tilted her chin back down just as he pressed the bottle's lip to her own. She drank messily, fizzy liquid pouring down her chin. It was delicious, and her mouth tingled pleasurably from the bubbles.

"You good?"

She nodded, mouth full, and made the mistake of laughing and smelled champagne in her nostrils. Everything was funny on a day this sweet. Julius looked at her, eyes twinkling as he took a swig.

Somehow, she swallowed her oversized mouthful, wiped away the excess, and said, "I don't want this to be over."

"Maybe it doesn't have to be," Julius said softly.

"What do you mean?"

He hesitated. "I know that you said no to Helen's offer."

"Uh-huh."

"But I know how much you enjoy working cold cases, and I can see how much you're thriving being in a city again. I know Glenville is important to you, but—"

"But you think I should accept Helen's offer and move all the way to London?" Heather asked skeptically, brow arched.

"Maybe. I don't know. I think you should think about it."

"I think I'm too old to start again, you know? From scratch."

"You're only thirty-three," Julius reminded her kindly. "I know it doesn't feel that way, considering everything you've been through."

"I like Glenville."

"And you don't think you'd regret staying there for the next seventy years?"

"That's generous."

"Heather."

Heather sighed. "Yeah. Maybe. But that town needs me."

"It seems to be doing okay in your absence. No disasters as far as I can tell."

"That's because Gabriel and Tina are good at their jobs."

Julius looked at her as if to say, 'Now you're getting it.'

"Alright, alright," Heather muttered, digging into her monster-sized kebab, which soon ceased her grumbling.

"I'll drop it," Julius said, putting the bottle in the middle of the table. "I just wanted to put my two cents in."

"What do you think Daniel was doing in the park that day with two kebabs?" Heather asked, abruptly remembering.

Julius lowered his brows. "Certainly not eating both of them. I doubt I'll get through half of it."

"Exactly." Heather chewed her lip in thought. "I guess he was cheating on me even back then." She shrugged, her expression lifting. "But better a cheater than a killer."

"True. I'm sorry that he was so awful to you, though."

"It's fine. It was a long time ago," Heather said, and for once, she believed her words. "And I'm not going to let him ruin tonight."

"Cheers to that," Julius said, taking a swig before passing the bottle to Heather.

Heather placed her lips on the slightly wet green glass. It felt akin to a kiss, and she thought that would be nice, kissing Julius. She hoped it would happen soon, but tonight, she was content with the bottle.

CHAPTER TWENTY-NINE

THE PARTNER

GABRIEL ENDED HIS EVENING CALL WITH A HIGHLY enthusiastic, slightly drunk Heather with a smile on his face. She'd solved the case and in less than a week at that. Raymond Doyle, the murderer of poor Lilly Arnold, would likely be safely tucked away in a prison cell for the rest of his life, never to touch a woman again. Similarly, the other members of this disgusting Conquerors Club were also facing jail time for assault, theft, illegal gambling, and a host of various offenses most of them had racked up as individuals.

It was a big win all around, and fortunately, Gabriel had some good news of his own. Well, good-adjacent. Shane Gibson was still on the run and breaking into people's houses, but after mentally processing their call, Gabriel was about ninety-five percent sure that he was Katy's killer. Now, all he had to do was get him back behind bars and Izzy on the stand.

This news, of course, only bettered Heather's already elated mood, and she promised to help him as soon as she returned to Glenville. When that would be, she wasn't exactly sure, likely at the start of next week. That was, 'Unless you need me now?'

Though it had sounded as if she really would come back to Glenville at the drop of a hat, he could tell that she didn't want to. So, he told her what she wanted to hear. That he was fine on his own. That he was in the process of convincing Izzy to go to the Seattle PD. That they'd likely use Izzy, or at least his home, as bait to catch Shane. That they'd get him to wear a wire or plant hidden cameras. That they'd arrest him in a similar manner to Raymond Doyle. That this would all be out of his hands and over soon.

Putting it in such a matter-of-fact manner felt a little anti-climatic, especially considering what Heather had just pulled off, but he'd had more than enough of lying, sneaking around, putting himself in risky situations, and neglecting his girlfriend. In fact, he was relieved that it was nearly over. And all that really mattered in the end was knowing who did it and giving Heather closure. His boyhood desire to be an action hero was secondary to all of that.

Heather had left the call because Julius wanted to watch a movie before they went to bed. She sounded so happy and content. He wished the feeling was mutual because when she was gone, he felt paranoia creeping in. He was irrationally worried that Shane was going to break in and kill his entire family. And he was rationally worried that he might kill Izzy or another innocent person before the police managed to round him up. And when Gabriel felt paranoid or worried, he wanted to be proactive. Which meant that despite it being close to midnight, he no longer wanted to be in bed. He wanted to be planning, researching, and doing anything but lying in the dark and listening to his own thoughts.

"Maybe I could pretend to be Izzy," he muttered as he climbed out of bed. "I could cover myself with a blanket and lay on the couch. Then, when Shane comes in, I'll arrest him at gunpoint." He paused and yawned. "Am I even allowed to do that?"

He didn't know. He was going to have to do some research. So, he trudged downstairs, toward the icy garage, still in a baggy t-shirt and boxers, where his laptop was located.

Knock. Knock. Knock.

The sound of knuckles rapping against the front door caused Gabriel to freeze. Through the stained glass, he could clearly see a figure. Surely, Shane hadn't come all the way to Glenville as a wanted man. Surely, Gabriel wasn't worth killing when there was an entire squad of officers out looking for him. Surely, getting here would be close to impossible—Glenville and Seattle weren't exactly within walking distance.

The porch light turned on, and the vague silhouette took shape. Gabriel exhaled, lightheaded from holding his breath. The person on the other side of the door definitely wasn't Shane, nor were they male. Not unless a drag queen with a bee-hive hairdo had come a-knocking. Considering the hairdo, he also knew precisely which woman was standing there—Betty.

He jogged down the stairs and opened the door quietly. "Betty?" he asked, confused. "What are you doing here?"

Betty, who was all done up in leopard print and black, stumbled a little on the porch step. "I was at a party down the road and wanted to talk to you."

"Okay, we can talk. Just be quiet."

Betty pressed a finger to her lips to show that she understood and stooped to slip off her heels before following Gabriel into the house. They were both completely silent, their footsteps muffled by the orange carpet, but they didn't really need to be. Gabriel's parents could sleep through anything and always had the fan going full blast, no matter the time of year.

He opened the door to the garage and held it open for Betty, who curtsied in thanks before stepping through the threshold. They turned on a lamp each, casting just enough light in the room to see where to sit and each other. Gabriel was embarrassed about the mess but decided not to mention it, just in case she was too drunk to notice.

"I'm sorry," Betty said unexpectedly as she threw herself down on the couch. "And I owe your mom a big apology."

"For what?" Gabriel asked, sitting beside her with his back against the arm.

"For the whole dinner thing. Your mom made a kind of bitchy comment about my clothes, and I noticed she was wearing a cross, so I said something to upset her on purpose. It was edgy and stupid, but I was feeling defensive and cornered, and to be honest, I was mad that you weren't there to defend me."

"Which is why it's me who should be apologizing."

Betty waved him off. "You already did that. Now it's my turn."

"Okay."

"So just stay quiet."

Gabriel smirked. "I can do that."

"Alright," she said, inhaling and exhaling. "I really like you. Which I think makes me nervous, like I'm waiting for the other shoe to drop. I'm thirty years old, and nobody has ever treated me this nicely before. All of my relationships have been horrible from start to finish. I guess that makes it hard for me to trust people, and to be honest, I think I'm looking for problems to prove my theory right."

"Your theory?"

"That I'm unlovable. Or doomed. I don't know."

"Betty, you're not—"

"I know. Logically anyway. And this is great. And I know you'd never hurt me on purpose. But the whole thing scares me to death, and not just because I have to be vulnerable and trust you, but also because of what you do. I don't want to fall in love with somebody who could get shot or killed, or God knows what. Your job is dangerous. What you're doing is even more dangerous. And you want to join the FBI? I mean, Jesus, Gabriel, I'd feel more relaxed dating a deep-sea fisherman. And I know that you'll always be worrying about me, too."

"I will," he admitted. "I'm worrying about you right now. Were you seriously just going to walk home drunk on your own at night?"

"I was. And I probably will again." She laughed a little sadly. "I think we're destined to scare the shit out of each other forever. And I'm not sure if that's a good thing or not."

"I'd rather be terrified than alone."

"Would you?" Betty asked earnestly, looking at him with wet eyes.

"Better to have lived and lost than not lived at all," he said. "Not to mention, the likelihood of tragedy is tiny. I work in Glenville, not New York. We've had an interesting couple of years, but come on, it's Glenville."

"The same Glenville where you were captured by a terrorist?"

"Yeah, but—"

"The same Glenville where the cocaine-addicted mayor crashed his plane into the laundromat?"

"Yes."

"The same Glenville where you've apprehended two serial killers?"

"Okay. I get it. But I lived, didn't I?"

Betty laughed. "You did."

"But I can compromise. No more secret, solo investigations. No more lying. No more being an idiot. I promise. I'll be sensible," he said, holding out his pinky finger.

"And I'll get that tracking app so you can keep an eye on me," she replied, linking his finger with hers.

"Deal," he said and squeezed before releasing. "So... Are we still on a break?"

"No. Not unless you want us to be."

"Definitely not."

Betty leaned in for a kiss, and Gabriel met her in the middle. A kiss turned into a hot and heavy makeout session, with Betty pulling him on top of her, but before things could escalate, Gabriel pulled away. She looked confused and flustered and reached for him again. He intercepted her hands, holding them in his own and kissing her knuckles.

"I've got a present for you. I was going to give it to you after dinner, but..."

Betty retreated and clapped her hands together. "What is it? Should I close my eyes?"

"Yeah, close your eyes," Gabriel said, scooching from the couch and rummaging in a pile of coats and blankets in the corner. He pulled out the leopard print handbag and approached. "Hold out your hands."

"Okay," Betty said, giddy, bouncing, unable to stop smiling.

He placed the bag in her hands, and she opened her eyes and immediately gasped in delight. "Oh my God. I love it. It goes with my outfit!" She held it to her dress and leaped around before tackling Gabriel with great gusto. He didn't even have the heart to tell her to stop yelling.

Making out resumed, and as Betty began to reach for the zip at the back of her dress, Gabriel's phone rang. Recently, it felt like that's all it did, and he had half a mind to throw his phone down a storm drain, too. He hoped it would stop, but when he didn't, he pulled away, planking above her.

"Sorry," he groaned. "I have to take it. Just, you know, with everything going on."

"Yeah, of course," Betty said, rolling out from under him and hitting the dirty rug with a giggle. She readjusted her dress as she wandered to the mini fridge to grab a beer and bent over seductively as she retrieved it. Gabriel groaned again, reached for his phone, and answered the call.

Before he could say hello, Suzie asked, "Matías? Are you there?"

"I'm here. What's wrong?"

"I don't know why, but I had this weird feeling. I guess I was worried about Izzy after you called earlier and told me that Shane had contacted you. So I got some officers to do a wellness check, and they found him beaten half to death."

Gabriel coughed, choking on his own saliva. "Is he going to be okay?"

Betty stopped wiggling and dancing and looked at him with concern. "What's—" she began, but Gabriel held up his hand before mouthing an apology.

"Yeah," Suzie answered. "He's at the hospital now in stable condition. He won't speak to the cops, though. He seems absolutely terrified. I think you should call them and tell them what you know. I know you want to do this story, but—"

"Screw the story," Gabriel said, feeling guilty for maintaining the lie. "I'll call them. I should've done that earlier when Shane called me. Shit. Shit. Shit. I'm sorry."

"Me and Lola are skipping town," she added. "I think he's on a rampage. A woman has gone missing from Lavender Meadow."

"Wait, seriously?" Gabriel asked, his worst nightmares coming true. He silently asked for a beer, and Betty came to his aid quickly, even going as far as to crack it open for him.

"Yeah, she's been missing since yesterday morning. Hannah Roy. She's my nephew's kindergarten teacher."

"Wait. What?" Gabriel asked, placing the cold can to his forehead, hoping to numb the erupting stress migraine.

"Do you know her?" Suzie questioned.

"Yeah. I met her a few days ago. She seemed really scared. Thought someone was watching her, or following her, or something."

"She was last seen heading into the little park at the center of the suburbs. I have a feeling that's where Shane has been hiding. There's an old maintenance building that nobody has used since the new one was built earlier this year. It's waiting for demolition. I didn't even think about it until now."

"Did you tell the police?"

"Yeah, of course, but I haven't heard back from them."

"Okay, okay." He stammered, not sure of what to say. The pain in his head was making his teeth ache. "Well, don't let me keep you. Get out of town, and I'll tell the police everything."

"I'm already on my way," she replied, and it was then that he could hear the distant hum of a car engine.

"Okay. It's going to be okay. They're going to find him."

"I really hope you're right," Suzie sniffled. "Stay safe."

"You too."

Then she was gone, and Gabriel looked at Betty, his mouth ajar, his body limp. "I..."

"Are you okay?" she asked.

"Yeah," he nodded, folding forward. "But I think I'm going to be in a lot of trouble tomorrow."

CHAPTER THIRTY

THE DETECTIVE

HEATHER WOKE IN BED AND FELT AN UNUSUAL WARMTH. She rolled over and found Julius asleep beside her, fully clothed. Nothing had happened between them. Nothing sexual, anyway. Profound, perhaps. The night before, as they walked back to Farfalla House, they'd dove deep into their childhoods, hopes, dreams, and embarrassing secrets, and they'd realized that despite being exhausted, they weren't ready to sever the conversation. So, once they were inside, they changed into their pajamas and clambered into the four-poster bed.

There, they'd lit the bedside candle in its Dickensian holder and told stories of before they'd met by firelight with cups of tea in hand. Heather—wearing a nightgown and in bed with a man who looked as if he'd been plucked from 19th Century Italy—had felt like she was in some sort of historical romance. And despite the lack of kissing or touching, it was probably the most intimate moment of her entire life. Even once the candle was blown out and the witching hour approached, they continued to talk until their voices were hoarse. By the end of it, they were borderline delirious, like two kids at a sleepover, asking ridiculous questions like 'What does a baby pigeon look like?' or 'Which name came first? The fruit orange, or the color orange?' Heather couldn't even remember falling asleep, but apparently she had, and a great sleep it had been.

Julius looked beautiful when he slept, she thought. It was actually a little disgusting how good he looked. Heather knew the same could not be said about her if the photos her parents and Gabriel had taken were anything to go off of. She snored, for one thing, and always laid on her back with her mouth ajar. Thus, she was glad she was the first to wake so that she could stare at the Greco-Roman masterpiece rather than forcing him to bear witness to her particularly noisy corpse.

Subconsciously, he must've known he was being watched and stirred awake, big brown eyes blinking blearily. "Morning," he mumbled.

"I want to stay in London for another week," Heather stated, sitting up and peering down at him. "I have enough paid time saved up."

He blinked rapidly. "Really?"

"Really."

"I'm going to have to get an itinerary together and—"

Heather interrupted him. "Worry about that tomorrow. Let's just have a lazy day today. It's sunny. We can have a picnic in the backyard and paint along to Bob Ross. Whatever, so long as it's relaxing, I'm down. Planning can wait."

"I thought Glenville needed you," Julius teased.

Heather rolled your eyes. "As you said. I think Gabriel has it handled. I've worked hard since I was eighteen. I have been on two holidays since I became a detective. I deserve this. And I don't want to go."

"Good. I don't want to go either. Now, would you like to start your day with more sleep or French toast?"

"Let's go with both," Heather said, collapsing back onto the mattress and burrowing down deeper beneath the heavy duvet.

"Excellent," Julius whispered, almost nose to nose with Heather.

This was the moment, she thought. This was where she finally moved in. God knows he never would. He was too respectful. Too fearful of her trauma and grief. If anyone was going to initiate the first time, it would have to be her. She knew he'd stop when she wanted to. She knew she didn't have to do anything she didn't wish to do. However, she knew she wanted to kiss him. She wanted it. Badly. She, too, could tell that he was waiting for it, peaceably, unmoving, an unmissable target.

It was then that her phone rang, because, of course, it did. When did it not? Grumbling, she moved to decline before seeing it was Gabriel and reluctantly answered, hoping that whatever he had to say was good or, at the very least, brief.

"Hey, Heather," he panted. "I know we called last night for you."

"Uh-huh."

"And I told you Shane Gibson contacted me."

"Yup," Heather said, propping herself up on an elbow.

"Yeah, well, he beat his roommate half to death shortly after."

"Jesus," Heather said, moving from elbow resting back to sitting. "Have they caught him?"

"Not yet. And there's something worse. Another woman has gone missing from the area. Weirdly, I bumped into her a few days ago, and she said she thought someone was watching her. Hannah Roy. They can't find her anywhere."

"Have you talked to the police?"

"I'm just about to call them and tell them everything I know. Which means I'll also have to come clean to Tina."

"Yeah," Heather said slowly. "Yeah, I guess you will."

"I think... I think I need your help."

"Okay," Heather stated, emotionless. It was an automatic response, and she kicked herself for it even though she knew it was the right thing to say.

"Really?" he asked in disbelief.

"Yeah. I mean, I'm not sure what I can do beyond ironing everything out with Tina, but if you need me, consider me already on my way."

"Are you sure?"

"I'm sure. This is my job, and even though it's your case, I gave it to you. I should help you see it through."

"Thank you. Seriously. You're the best."

"Yeah, I know," she grumbled. "I'll text you when I'm boarding."

"Will do."

"Bye, Gabe."

Heather hung up and looked at the already dejected Julius. "Duty calls?" he inquired glumly.

"Yeah. I think Shane Gibson is on a killing spree, and we're going to have to come clean to Tina and probably the Seattle PD." She pinched the bridge of her nose. "Jesus. What a mess."

"Right. Okay. It's okay. Let me look at plane tickets," Julius said, suddenly wide awake and reaching for his glasses and phone.

Heather reached out and put a hand on his upper arm. "You don't have to come if you don't want to."

"Well, it would be pointless staying here without you," he countered as if it were a fact. "We can come back in the summer."

"Ugh. Say that again," Heather said, faux-lusty, leaning toward him.

He tilted his face toward her and lowered his voice. "We can come back to London in the summer and have picnics in the park. I'll take you to all of my favorite National Trust historic properties. We can rent a canal boat."

"Ugh, stop. It's too much," Heather joked, moving away.

"How about that French toast before we pack?"

"Sounds heavenly," she replied, knowing those slices of egg-dunked toast would be the last slices of heaven she'd see for a while.

CHAPTER THIRTY-ONE

THE DETECTIVE

TINA WAS STARING AT HEATHER IN A WAY THAT HEATHER hadn't been stared at for a long time, like she was a young student caught copying someone else's pop quiz answers or a daughter who'd accidentally left the front door open and let the cat out again. She didn't like it. It made her feel small and decidedly stupid. Which, Heather supposed, was the point. She had taken the blame for all of what Gabriel had done, and while they hadn't done anything illegal, lying to Tina this way felt like a crime. Not because she was mad—though she was— but because her hurt was evident.

"Well," she said at long last. "You did the right thing by turning all your information over to the Seattle PD."

"Wait, how did you know about that?" Gabriel asked.

Tina turned her stern gaze to him. "Because they contacted me shortly after you did. Believe it or not, but Sheriffs and Sergeants talk to each other, especially when their employees go rogue."

"You didn't say anything this morning."

"I assumed you were waiting on Detective Bishop here to rescue you. I was willing to wait. And you're in luck. The Seattle PD is pleased with your work rather than annoyed about your amateur hour investigation. Your information about Izzy having lied about Shane's alibi will certainly help them put Shane in front of a jury. And once Shane is in custody, maybe Izzy will feel brave enough to speak up."

"Have they found him yet?" Heather inquired, watching Gabriel clench and unclench his fists. She should've never put him in this situation despite his apparently invaluable information and reports.

"Not yet, but they have found him, so to speak. Thanks again to your information. They put nanny cams in the old maintenance building as well as Isaiah's, Lola's, and Suzie's homes. Additionally, the number he provided when calling you was helpful. It couldn't be used to track him, but it was traced back to where he purchased it, and apparently, due to safety regulations, there's only one drain in that area big enough to throw a flip phone down. They found evidence of squatting in the suburban houses that were up for sale on that adjoining street. He had also clearly been hiding out in the maintenance building. They found supplies and blood there, but as of yet, don't know who the latter belongs to."

Tina sighed. "What I'm trying to say is your writeup is good, and you managed to dig up just enough information to put him away. I mean, considering he broke out of prison and nearly beat a second man to death, I doubt, even without being convicted of the murder of Katy Graham, that he'll even see the outside of a prison again. But still, you have done the Seattle PD a great service, and they intend to reach out to give their thanks." Tina's voice was cold, her information clipped. She sounded like a computer being forced to read a transcript. It was making Heather's palms sweat.

"That's great," Gabriel said enthusiastically.

"I suppose all's well that ends well," Tina said sourly. "But did you ever consider—either of you—that asking for permission might've made all of this easier? I mean, they're going to have to jump through loophole after loophole to have your findings hold up in court. They'll probably have to hire you as a consultant and backdate the paperwork."

"They would've never agreed to let him investigate the Katy Graham case," Heather said. "And neither would you. I've worked for both Seattle and Glenville, and I know that you're equally stubborn. You wouldn't want the pain of transferring him to them, and they wouldn't take him. And as far as I'm aware, it's not a crime to investigate from an armchair. People do it all the time. Look at the Golden State Killer, for example."

"Maybe not. But impersonating a journalist? Really guys? It's shady at best."

"In the sake of fairness," Heather muttered, resisting a yawn after her nearly ten-hour flight and abrupt change in time zone, "I feel I should come clean about what I've been doing."

"Oh, I already know," Tina retorted snarkily. "You told me where you were going to be staying, so as soon as I saw Raymond Doyle, the *Hyde Park* Ribbon Killer, pop up on the news, I knew you had something to do with it. I like to think I know you fairly well, Heather, and you don't jet-set for the fun of it. Congratulations, by the way. I'm sure Scotland Yard is happy with you. Unless you also went behind their backs, that is."

"I had permission. For most of it anyway."

Tina hummed disapprovingly. "Well, I'm willing to let this all go. Thanks to the pair of you, two dangerous killers are facing life in prison. I'm willing to call that a win. Especially as I realize there's a personal aspect at play for you, Heather, regarding your husband, Daniel Palmer. I'm sure this must be quite a relief for you."

Heather stammered. "H-How did you know?"

Tina rolled her eyes. "Please. It's on your damn background check. Previous legal names. Marital status. I didn't get this job by being bad at what I do."

"Of course not," Heather said, face burning.

"Which is why I would have helped you if you had come to me."

"I'm sorry. Really, Sheriff."

"It won't happen again," Gabriel insisted.

"No, it won't, Mr. Silva. Above board from now on. I know you're destined to become some sort of bigshot, but you're not above the law. Or me. And Heather, I know you'll do this again. So, no false promises, but just try not to drag my officers into it."

"Understood," Heather said. "And this was a rare circumstance. Now that I'm sure of Daniel's innocence, I'd like to put that part of my life behind me and start again."

"Good. And you'll be able to soon enough, but in the meantime, a week's suspension for both of you. Paid, of course, I'm not a monster. Seattle is taking over the case now. It's time to let go and get some rest. Consider it an extension of your vacation. Then you're on desk duty until I require your 'skills' in the field."

Heather thought that, ultimately, Tina was being more than fair. She could've fired them for what they'd pulled. Heather supposed they were just lucky that their work had done more good than harm, and she was telling the truth when she said it would never happen again. She didn't enjoy being sneaky, even if it was for the greater good.

"Now, leave me alone to finish sorting out your messes," Tina requested. "And leave your guns, badges, and IDs on the table."

They did as they were told, thanked their boss, and slunk away with their tails between their legs, Gabriel's more than Heather's. "I guess I can kiss a promotion goodbye," Gabriel lamented.

Heather shook her head as she held the door open for him and tried to ignore their coworkers' burning gazes and gossiping whispers. "I actually think the opposite. You proved how good you are at what you do, even on your own. Imagine how great you could be with an entire team."

"Yeah, I guess." Gabriel groaned. "This week has been..."

"Yeah, I know the feeling. Though at least I got to have one fun day in London."

"How's the jet lag?"

"Crappy."

"Is Julius in Seattle?"

"Yep," Heather responded, clipped. "No idea when I'll next be able to see him."

"I'm sorry for dragging you back. That probably could've been a phone call."

Heather smirked. "Yeah. It probably could have. But hey, if you hadn't dragged me back here, I might've never left."

"It was that good, huh?"

"I enjoyed myself when I wasn't working a homicide case, yeah," Heather said mildly, majorly underexaggerating.

"And you and Julius?"

Heather smiled. "We're getting there. How about you and Betty?"

Gabriel shrugged. "We're getting there too."

"Want to talk about it?" Heather offered with a frown. His 'getting there' sounded like a step backward rather than forward.

Gabriel laughed. "Honestly? Not really. I think I've talked myself half to death this week. My tongue is barely holding on."

"How about a drink then? A little alcohol to help it heal."

"Yes, please. You know I haven't been to Sherwood's since you left. I miss it."

"Yeah, me too," Heather replied, spotting the bar from afar and crossing the empty road with Gabriel in tow. "Drinks are on me. Consider it an apology for dragging you into my bullshit."

"Unnecessary, but I'll take it," Gabriel laughed. "God, this feels almost like deja vu. But in a good way. It hasn't been the same without you. Promise me you'll never leave again."

Heather chuckled weakly. "Yeah."

That was something she couldn't promise. Not yet. She wanted to be in too many places at once. She wanted to be here, a small-town detective, Gabriel's best friend, Tina's difficult but shining star. She also wanted to be in Seattle, resuming her old position, popping into the forensic center on lunch breaks to hang out with Julius. She also wanted to be in London, a powerful, respected cold case detective who got lunch from food trucks in Hyde Park, went to the pub, and relaxed in Farfalla House. All of them seemed like good, viable options, and she knew she would have to pick one soon. However, today, she was going to leave the decision-making until the jet lag was over.

She smiled at Gabriel and slung an arm around his neck. "Nice work, Buster."

"Yeah, yeah. I'll be happy when they actually lock Shane up."

"They will."

He gave a small, dejected nod, and she knew exactly what he was feeling. It was hard to be benched at the end of a case. It was hard to take a backseat in your own car. It was hard to let go. Yet, sometimes, the only way to move forward was to change lanes, and that's just what she and Gabriel were going to have to do. Sometimes, you just had to take the win and let someone else step up to the plate.

CHAPTER THIRTY-TWO

THE DETECTIVE

"SO, IT'S DEFINITELY SHANE," HEATHER STATED after polishing off the contents of her beer. The statement-slash-unspoken-question was abrupt, and Gabriel's expression reflected this. For the past couple of hours, they'd run through a variety of random topics, none of which had to do with work. Topics like Gabriel's disaster dinner, Heather's date with Julius, what they'd been watching on TV, Gabriel's feelings about AA, Heather's trip to the Tower of London, and her newfound affinity for ravens. They also decided that as soon as the Katy Graham case was wrapped, they'd be sober for a month together.

"Yeah. Why? You don't think so?" Gabriel asked, his expression turning from surprise to discomfort.

"No, I don't mean it like that. He definitely makes sense. I mean, why else beat Izzy half to death? He's trying to intimidate witnesses and you."

"But?"

"I don't know. Were there any other suspects or anything I should know about?"

"Not really. I thought it was Daniel, then I thought it was Shane, and back and forth, back and forth, until Shane made it obvious. I talked to this guy, Elijah, who attended AA with Katy. He cried a lot in the session, which seemed weird, and apparently, Daniel thought something was going on between them, but in the end, he just turned out to be her sponsee. And he's gay, so Daniel was definitely wrong." Gabriel paused, staring at the bottom of his glass. "Are you still worried about Daniel?"

"Do I have any reason to be?" Heather asked, trying to sound blasé. She'd been angling for reassurance and definitely didn't intend to lessen Gabriel's confidence in his findings.

"I mean, I guess he feasibly could've killed her, but considering he definitely didn't kill Lilly Arnold and isn't a serial killer, him killing his wife-to-be seems a little out of character. Especially when he never showed any signs of psychopathy when you two were together."

"Beyond being a narcissistic cheater."

"Yeah, beyond that."

"And taking Hannah Roy when he's this close to freedom would be crazy. Shane has nothing to lose."

Gabriel nodded. "So just a dick then."

Heather smirked. "Yeah. Just a dick."

"Another round?"

"Yeah, one more, but then I'm heading home to spend some quality time with the dogs."

"Yeah, sounds good. My parents want me to have dinner with them anyway. What are you having?" Gabriel asked, standing, turning, and nearly walking smack into Brittany Hart. "What the—" he began as he fell back down onto his seat.

Heather wasn't sure how long she'd been looming there at the end of the booth, but she didn't like the idea of her listening in. "Brittany," she said, smiling wryly. "How much was the phone bill in the end?"

"Affordable for me," Brittany retorted.

It was then that Heather really looked at her, and she drew the curve of her smile into a tight line. Brittany looked *off*. She was wearing thick rectangular glasses and was makeup-free for the first time ever, but that wasn't what was throwing Heather off. Nor was it the low ponytail, baby blue tracksuit, or pristine white sneakers in place of her usual glam. It was her body language. She looked tense and a little manic, reminding Heather of a chihuahua about to bite or vomit.

"I heard you two have been suspended," Brittany continued. "That's a shame, considering you still haven't caught the killer."

"Shane will be apprehended soon enough due to Officer Silva's hard work," Heather replied, hoping that would be enough to shut Brittany down and up. She wasn't in the mood to engage in whatever this was. She was having a good time with her friend. She'd just solved an enormous case. She didn't need this.

"It isn't Shane," Brittany said, not smugly, but matter of fact.

"Okay, who is it then?" Heather inquired dryly, staring at her empty glass sourly. "Daniel, I assume?"

"Wouldn't you like to know? But I'm not going to tell either of you anything," Brittany said. "You blew your chance. I just wanted to let you know that you're wrong, and I'm going to solve this myself."

"Yeah? Good luck with that. The Seattle PD have even less patience for know-it-all amateurs than I do." It came out crueler than Heather intended, and she looked at Brittany to check for a reaction and found none. Just a hint of smugness and telltale signs of a lack of sleep.

"You're going to regret not listening to me," she said. She was becoming somewhat of a broken record.

"Yeah, you've said that already," Gabriel grumbled, saying aloud what Heather was thinking. "And you know, maybe we'd listen too, if you actually gave us something to listen to. All you've said so far is a bunch of cryptic crap. If you have so much information, why don't you go first? Then we might tell you about our cases."

"But you won't because you don't have anything," Heather added. "You just want us to give you free content for your podcast."

"It's flopping, isn't it?" Gabriel asked, pretending to pout sympathetically. "The new series. That's why you're doing... this?" He gestured at her generally.

Brittany took shot after shot without flinching, and with each insult, the corners of her mouth began to curl upwards. "It might've had a rocky start, thanks to you," she said. "But what I have in store is going to put me on the map. I'm going to win awards for this. Maybe even get a medal."

"It's all about fame with you, isn't it?" Heather questioned. "See, that's exactly why we don't trust you. You're shady, Brittany, and you only care about what's sensational rather than what's true."

"Maybe you should go write for the Weekly World News," Gabriel said wryly. "That seems like a job you could excel at."

Heather wanted to say more but bit her tongue. At this point, it was starting to feel a little bit like bullying, but it was so tempting when Brittany was taunting them and refusing to move or leave them alone. It was as if she wanted this. Then Heather got a bad feeling.

"You're not wearing a wire, are you?" Heather asked, imagining their words being taken out of context and posted on the podcast as Brittany 'solved the case' against all odds.

To Heather and Gabriel's shock, Brittany lifted her sweatshirt up high, revealing an almost see-through white undershirt. There was blatantly no recording equipment. However, when she lowered it again, she looked angry for the first time, likely because she hadn't thought of it first. Then she hauled her yellow backpack from her shoulders, unzipped it, and revealed turned off recording equipment.

"So, is there something else we can help you with?" Heather inquired.

Brittany shrugged nonchalantly, a happy grin on her face. "Just wanted to tell you that you've missed the boat, so to speak, and while I'm pulling into port, you two are headed straight for a desert island."

"Aye, aye, captain," Gabriel said, monotone. "Now, if you don't mind."

Brittany stood there for a minute, all of her playful braggart energy draining away until all that was left was a very tired husk. She looked at Gabriel, then at Heather, and her eyes asked, 'You're seriously not going to ask me about what I know?' Heather shook her head in answer to the silent question, and Brittany whipped her body to the left, her ponytail fanning out behind her, and stormed toward the front entrance.

"Jesus. I really need that drink now," Gabriel laughed.

Heather snorted. "No kidding. Good job on not giving her what she wanted. The best thing to do with attention seekers is to starve them of it."

Gabriel stood. "I wonder who she's going to point the finger at."

"Hopefully not Daniel. The last thing he needs is another half-assed media exposé. Not when he's so close to freedom."

"Well, he can always take her to court for slander and defamation. But honestly, I don't think she has anything or anyone. She has no idea how to wrap this series up. She'll probably make somebody up."

"She definitely seems to be grasping at straws," Heather agreed.

"That's why she needs our 'scoops'. She can't afford to lose fans and sponsors. Literally. She's living above her means, considering her podcast isn't even in the top forty US-based crime podcasts."

"Seriously?" Heather asked, genuinely surprised.

"Seriously."

"Huh. I always thought she was more famous than that."

"Because she pretends that she is. Fake it till you make it, you know? I mean, she's definitely got fans, but she needs something to take her to the next level."

Heather nodded slowly, staring at the front door as it swayed in the breeze. "I just hope she doesn't do anything too stupid. Defamation trials can be a bitch."

"Hey, it's her funeral."

Heather looked at him and sighed. "Let's hope not."

CHAPTER THIRTY-THREE

THE DETECTIVE

IN THE END, THE PAIR'S SUSPENSION DIDN'T QUITE STRETCH an entire week, and by the following Tuesday, Heather and Gabriel were back at their desks, sifting through the stacks of paperwork. After the events in London, Heather found that she relatively enjoyed desk duty as it allowed her to pop earbuds in, nestle next to the radiator, sip coffee, and occasionally tinker with the article Helen had asked her to write. In fact, it was borderline luxurious compared to the alternate option of highway patrol.

The energy in the precinct was, as expected, strange, but it wasn't negative either. In fact, it seemed that most people were glad of their return, and both received their fair share of awe-struck congratulations regarding the Ribbon Killer and Shane Gibson. Despite Tina's best attempts at containment, word had traveled through her office walls like gamma radiation.

Gabriel, in particular, saw a spike in popularity. Especially considering that Shane had finally been apprehended on Monday morning and was being held without bail while await-ing trial. His name might not have made the papers, but their co-workers knew the truth and revered him as some sort of local James Bond. He had stopped a great evil and solved a mur-der all on his own while undercover. A murder that—thanks to Amanda—everyone in the precinct seemed to have become wildly invested in, though if they had come across Heather's association with Daniel, nobody mentioned it.

It was only when Amanda made a nervous beeline toward her oasis halfway through the day that Heather's patience was tested. Gabriel had told her all about Amanda's drunken blabbermouth, and though Heather was doing her best to be copacetic with the woman and certainly had no intentions of confronting her, she definitely needed more space while she processed the predicament.

Heather then watched in shock and awe as Amanda—somehow brazen and sheepish all at once—pulled up a roller chair to the opposite side of the desk and moved Heather's work to one side to make way for her elbows.

"Can we help you?" Gabriel laughed in disbelief, gliding from his adjacent desk to join Heather at hers.

Amanda tried and failed to answer the question and instead looked between the pair, her mouth opening and closing like a goldfish. They looked at each other, confused and bemused, before looking back at her.

"Please spit it out," Gabriel begged. "Or none of us are get-ting out of here at six."

"I..." Amanda began before trailing off, her eyes glassy and staring past the pair toward an ugly painting of a deer behind them. "It's silly," she finished.

"Okay. Silly is fine," Heather said slowly. "But can you please tell us what's wrong so that we can all get back to work? I can feel Tina's eyes on the back of my head." She was trying to be kind, not condescending, but she could tell she had missed the mark by Gabriel's poorly muffled chuckling. Not that Amanda seemed to notice. The woman was on a different planet. "Have we done something to upset you?"

"No, not at all," Amanda insisted, suddenly sharpening. "I mean, I know the stuff you told me was made up," she said, addressing Gabriel. "But I deserved it. You knew there was a rat problem at work, and you set a trap that I walked right into. I admit it; I'm the leak," she announced as if they didn't already know. "I have been telling Brittany things. When I drink, I can't help it."

Maybe don't drink, Heather thought but didn't say. "Well, I'm glad you've admitted it. You know you could get in a lot of trouble for that. Especially with Tina."

"I know," Amanda whimpered. "Are you going to tell her?"

"We'll think about it," Gabriel answered.

"I believe in second chances," Heather added. "But never again. Seriously."

"I won't," Amanda promised. "I doubt Brittany will ever take me seriously again anyway. Not after all the lies I told her. That's actually who I want to talk about," Amanda added before taking a shuddering breath.

Heather narrowly resisted rolling her eyes. The melo-drama—or perhaps genuine emotion, it was hard to tell—was killing her. "Please tell me you're not about to pass on a message from her. Because, honestly, I've had it up to here with Brittany Hart." Heather scrutinized Amanda. "And please tell me you haven't told her about London. I know that all of you know about that."

"No!" Amanda insisted, meeting Heather's gaze. "I just told you... I couldn't—"

"Alright, what is it then?" Heather snapped.

"She uploads full episodes on Mondays," Amanda explained.

"Uh-huh."

"This was supposed to be a big one. She kept talking about it on the Friday mini-sode. She was saying she was going to blow the lid off of the Katy Graham case and that she expected us to tune in on Monday for the big reveal. She was really building it up, teasing the audience. A real cliffhanger, you know? And then come Monday, nothing. No episode. No update on her Twitter explaining the delay. Nothing. I waited and waited and refreshed my feed, and still nothing. Then I did the same today, but there just isn't a new episode."

Gabriel snorted. "Yeah, because she doesn't have anything to say. The media beat her to it after Shane was arrested, and we've given her absolutely nothing. Anything that she does know is already public information or made up."

"Yeah, that makes sense," Amanda muttered, nodding. "Probably just embarrassed."

"Are you upset about the podcast or worried about her?" Heather asked.

"Worried about her!" Amanda insisted with enough force to attract nearby attention. "This isn't like her."

"Well, if you two are such close friends, why don't you text her?" Gabriel inquired.

Amanda rolled her eyes and sunk down low in shame. "Because we're not really friends. You know that. I hoped we could be if I gave her information, but I know she was just using me."

"Yeah, because she *is* a user," Heather said, managing to sound genuinely kind this time.

"I know. It's just... I sucked in high school, but I always wanted to be one of the cool pretty girls. So having one of them give me the time of day and seem genuinely interested in me made me feel cool and pretty."

Heather chewed her lip. Amanda may have been annoying, but she hated Brittany for making her feel this way. She knew what it was like to be unpopular in high school. However, mercifully, she didn't feel the need to be popular now, considering most of those mean girls had peaked at seventeen. Sadly, the same clearly couldn't be said for Amanda.

"You need some real friends," Heather told her softly.

"And I have them," Amanda replied. "But this was different. She made me feel special."

"You get how gross that is, right?" Gabriel asked, seemingly concerned. "Of her, not you."

"Yeah. I guess," Amanda said dejectedly.

"Just ignore her and stop listening to that stupid podcast," Heather advised.

"Yeah, I will. I just want to know if she's okay."

"She's fine," Heather insisted. "She's just throwing a tantrum because she put all of her eggs into the wrong basket. And after spreading misinformation, her listeners are probably dropping like flies. Especially when there are actually good podcasts out there." Amanda shifted uncomfortably. She still wasn't appeased. Heather sighed. "What do you want from us?"

"I thought that maybe we could do a wellness check on Brittany. Just to put my mind at ease. Maybe you could talk to Tina."

Heather looked at Gabriel and could tell they were of the same mind about this—they just wanted it to be over. "Fine," Heather agreed, at last. "We'll stop by her place after work."

"Really?" Amanda asked, lighting up. "Hey, maybe we can go to Molly Malone's afterward. Dinner and drinks on me."

Once again, Gabriel and Heather cast furtive looks at each other before looking at Amanda. "Take an accident report from my pile, and we've got a deal," Heather replied.

"Really?" Amanda asked again.

"Yeah," Heather said wearily. "I miss London, and I figure Molly's is the closest I'm going to get to Europe for a while."

"You won't regret it," Amanda enthused. "I can drive us. And I'll drop you both off. I can even pick you up in the morning to grab your cars. I'll be a sober driver."

It was a fair deal, and combined with Brittany's failure and Amanda's promise to never blab again, Heather was begrudgingly excited about the scenario. It felt like almost all of their problems had been crossed off the list now that Shane was behind bars. And once the police located Hannah Roy's body and got their confession, the whole debacle would be over at last. The olive branch being extended was more than Amanda likely deserved, but Heather was in a generous sort of mood considering.

"Alright, back to work," Heather said softly. "And take this report. We'll meet you outside at five, and I'll talk to Tina and relay my personal concern about Brittany's well-being so we can get permission. Hell, I'll even ask for a warrant, just in case."

"Thanks, Heather, you're the best," Amanda said cheerily, standing up with vigor. "I'm sure you're right about Brittany, and I'm really looking forward to hanging out tonight."

Heather shooed the woman affectionately, too tired to be sardonic or sarcastic, and looked to Gabriel as she scampered away. Luckily, he didn't seem annoyed that Heather had agreed to dinner plans on his behalf. He'd been in a stellar mood since the news had broken yesterday and maintained a skip in his step even on his way to the broken coffee machine.

"I'll invite Betty," he said, drifting back to his desk, his eyes bloodshot from staring. "She and Amanda really clicked last time."

"Good idea," Heather replied. "I need all the buffer I can get."

"Oh, Betty has patience in spades and the conversation skills to match. I don't think she's ever hated anyone."

"I'm jealous," Heather admitted. "Because Brittany Hart is getting on my last nerve."

"Well, hey. We won't have to think about her much longer if the podcast is dead in the water."

"That's exactly what I'm thinking," Heather said, a weak smile flickering across her features as she popped her earbuds back in and hunkered down to finish off yet another vandalism report.

CHAPTER THIRTY-FOUR

THE DETECTIVE

As promised, Heather asked for Tina's permission to do a wellness check on Brittany Hart. Surprisingly, Tina not only told her to knock herself out but also seemed a lot more concerned than either Heather or Gabriel, and though they didn't legally need a warrant to enter the home while conducting a welfare check, she got to work on the extra paperwork right away.

"Do you think something's wrong?" Heather asked. "Because you and Amanda seem a lot more concerned about Brittany than we are."

"I don't think there's anything wrong," Tina clarified before reaching out to touch the wood-paneled walls for luck. "It's just that Brittany has been loitering as of late. At the station. At Molly Malone's. At my house. You name it. Ever since I suspended the pair of you, she's been my shadow. She's been asking questions. Questions I, of course, didn't answer. But when you mentioned her just now, I realized I hadn't seen her since Sunday night."

"I think she's freaking out about her podcast. Nobody seems to want to give her the juicy details of either case. Shane getting arrested probably put the last nail in the coffin for her grand finale. Who's going to tune into a show about a case that's been solved?"

"I'm sure you're right. But just in case."

"Yeah, of course. Just in case."

—

At Tina's insistence, Heather, Gabriel, and Amanda packed into the latter's tiny, two-door car at 4 p.m. and headed toward Brittany's house. Heather had no idea where the young woman lived until they pulled up at one of the fancier sections of the Glenville suburbs, near but not on the lake. Brittany's house looked exactly like she did. It was all-American, complete with a pristine flag protruding from the gabled roof. The wood paneling was painted baby blue, the windowsills and door were white, and the lawn was a lush green thanks to the sprinkler system. Most beautiful of all was the abundance of flowers, neatly organized into tidy wooden raised beds. Not a thing seemed out of place. Except for the fact that she didn't have a garage, and there was no car in the driveway.

"She's not here," Heather stated, looking at the dark windows.

"Maybe that's what they want you to think," Amanda whispered as she botched her attempt at parallel parking. "Maybe they dumped her car in the lake."

"Who's they?" Heather asked.

"I don't know. She's a famous podcaster. She probably has a lot of enemies."

"I'm sure she'd like to think so," Heather retorted, definitely imagining Brittany having quippy, winnable arguments in the mirror with her so-called haters. Then she caught sight of Amanda chewing her cheek and sighed. "No one has dumped her or her car in the lake. She's probably just up in Seattle harassing all the people Gabriel spoke to. Hanging outside of the hospital, trying to bribe nurses about Izzy. That sort of thing."

"How can you be so sure?"

"Want to go find out?

"If she's not home, we won't be able to tell either way."

Heather gritted her teeth. She wanted to ask, 'Amanda, are you familiar with breaking and entering, crime scenes, or signs of foul play? Are you a cop or somebody who just wandered into the precinct one day in a Halloween costume?' But of course, she didn't. Amanda was just worried about her 'friend' and wasn't thinking straight.

Before Heather could actually respond, Amanda nodded. "Right. They would have had to break in. Stupid."

"You're not stupid," Heather said, exiting the car and pulling her seat forward for Gabriel to scramble out of the backseat trap. "Let's go check it out."

Amanda hesitated for a moment and then followed them up the walkway. As expected, nothing seemed amiss. There were no broken windows, the front door was locked, the mailbox was empty, and upon peering through one of the front windows, Heather saw an anally perfect living space.

"Look," Heather said, beckoning Amanda over to a different window. "I guess this is her office. Look how perfect this is. Even the chair is tucked in. I promise you, she's probably at a spa right now in Seattle. Maybe she's visiting her parents. Who knows. But she's not here, and I guarantee that nobody took her either."

"Yeah, I guess you're..." Amanda's voice faded away, and she pulled her spare brows together. "What's that?"

"What's what?"

"On the desk."

Gabriel joined them, pressed his forehead to the glass, and used his hands to block the reflection. "Looks like an envelope," he said. "I think there's something written on it."

Heather pushed the pair out of the way and copied his stance. Sure enough, on the spotless white desk, next to the pastel yellow keyboard, was a manila envelope. There was something written on it in perfect loopy handwriting. Heather's name.

The day went from sunny to sinister in an instant, and though Heather was sure it was because of the sunset, she was suddenly very cold and uneasy. "Let's see if we can get in through the back without breaking anything," Heather said, voice low. "I don't want to freak out the neighbors."

"What did it say?" Amanda asked.

Heather didn't answer her and jumped the white picket fence into the backyard, leaving the others to chase after her. She approached the glass sliding door and found that it was unlocked. Heather was unsurprised by this as she slid it ajar. Considering there was an envelope with her name on it in plain view, Brittany had clearly been anticipating her arrival. Or was this a trap, and Amanda was right about Brittany's enemies? Either way, Heather entered the building without hesitation and looked around. Aside from an empty wine glass by the sink and a takeout bag sticking out of the trashcan, the kitchen was as spotless as the rest of the building.

Nobody jumped out from the shadows; no alarms went off, and no bombs began to tick. It wasn't a trap, at least not of the typical variety. Then Heather had an unpleasant thought. What if Brittany, distraught about her podcast, embarrassed about her investigation, and worried about the future, had gone so far as to end her life?

As Gabriel and Amanda joined Heather in the building, Heather took off and began throwing open doors as she passed them. Each time she did so, she braced herself for a blood-filled bathtub, flies buzzing around a bed, or a rope secured to one of the beams. Fortunately, beyond the gleaming, magazine-ready interiors, none of the rooms contained anything strange.

A little abashed by her outburst, Heather slunk back into the kitchen and was met with a pair of stunned faces. "She's not here," Heather clarified breathlessly. "Sorry, I just got this really bad feeling."

Amanda shook her head fervently. "No. I get it. There's something spooky going on, isn't there?"

"I... I don't know," Heather said honestly.

"I'm with Amanda. This is weird. It's like somebody walking over your grave," Gabriel said. "That's what my mom calls it. You know, when you shiver randomly."

"More like we're walking over *somebody's* grave," Heather muttered, looking around at the shadowy interior.

"This is for you," Gabriel said, stepping forward and holding out the envelope. "I grabbed it while you were running around upstairs. Don't worry, we didn't open it."

Heather could tell. The sticky edge was still sealed shut with Brittany's saliva. Gabriel spoke again, but his voice, along with the birds in the trees, the wind whistling through the open door, and Amanda's heavy breathing, was all just white noise as she moved to the breakfast nook in the corner.

She sat and began to rip the lip open carefully, noticing for the first time just how heavy the folder was. Once it was open, she turned it upside down and caught the contents in her hand before laying it out in a stack on the table. The wad of pages had been stapled twice on the left-hand side, turning it into a book. Sections were marked with Post-it notes. Whatever this was, it wasn't a suicide note. Heather was sure of that as soon as she flipped open the blank cover page and saw a photo, not of Brittany, but of an Indian woman about Heather's age.

"Is this Hannah Roy?" Heather asked Gabriel.

"Yeah," he answered, sitting beside her.

Heather turned to the next page and found a handwritten letter addressed to her. It read: *Hello Heather. Don't worry. If you're reading this, I'm not dead. Or, maybe I am. Who knows. However, I'm not expecting to be. I'm on a secret mission of my own. I know where Hannah Roy is, and I intend to find her. Considering that neither Glenville nor Seattle's Police Departments have listened to me, I figure it's my only option.*

You know, I really expected better of you. You're a rule breaker. You listen to your gut. And yet you laughed me out of the room. However, as I'm writing this, I realize I made a mistake. I should've just told you everything I knew. Tried to convince you. So, I'm telling you now to give you a respectful head start. Just remember, I'm the one who's solved the case, so don't even think of taking credit. Not that you'll want to, considering who killed Hannah Roy. I advise you to keep reading and come to your own conclusions. If you're as good of a detective as everyone thinks, it shouldn't be hard. I'll be back on Tuesday, and if I'm not, turn this folder over to the FBI. Maybe they'll listen to me. XOXO. Brittany Hart.

"What did it say?" Gabriel questioned, keeping his distance and not reading over her shoulder.

"She says this is all of her evidence and that she's gone to find Hannah Roy. I think she's implying Daniel..." Heather's words failed her.

"Wait, Daniel. Isn't that your husband?" Amanda asked. "Is that why you've been—"

"Not the time, Amanda," Gabriel snapped. "Go wait outside."

Amanda did as she was told with haste and shut the door behind her. Once she was gone, Heather folded the letter around the back and found a black and white screenshot from a forum of a website she'd never seen before. It was so basic it could've been from the late nineties if the date didn't indicate otherwise, and the title had clearly been made with word art. The browser looked weird, too. There was a circular purple logo that was solid on one half and layered on the other like an onion. Heather leaned in and then turned the page toward Gabriel.

"Tor," he said.

"Tor?"

"Yeah, that's the browser you use if you want to get onto the dark web," he answered. "I've been doing my research, you know, for joining the FBI."

"Right."

The website was called The Butcher's Lounge, which might've ordinarily been a little silly, but considering they were talking about murder and murderers, it made Heather's blood run cold. The logo made it worse—a mean-looking anthropomorphized pig in a butcher's apron wielding a knife. There was so much to take in, but she decided to get to the meat of it. The title of the forum thread was, 'It's getting worse,' and it was created by user runrabbitrun on November 2nd, 2022.

The post read: *Hello. Long time lurker. First time poster. I, like many of you, though not all of you, have never killed. I've certainly daydreamed about it. I've pleasured myself over it. I've thought about it when sleeping with women. The sex, in particular, keeps it under control. It scratches an itch as long as it's rough. I met this amazing woman about a decade ago now, and she made me better for a time. I thought about hurting her, but I was never worried I'd do anything. Then I met somebody new, and it's not the same. I think about hurting her all the time, and I am worried I'll go through with what I want. And that's exactly the problem: it's no longer a dark fantasy or a desire; it's a need and a want. I barely want to be talked out of it, but I'm holding on to the last dregs of my humanity. Any advice for doing so? Should I engage in the roleplay pages on this website? Has anyone found that helpful? This is my last resort.*

"Shane?" Gabriel asked.

"You think?" Heather questioned, re-reading the post. She didn't know as much about Shane as Gabriel, but she knew the timeline was all wrong.

"I guess not," Gabriel admitted. "Brittany said it wasn't him. This has to be somebody else."

"Unless she's trying to lead us away from Shane so she can take all the glory."

"I mean, that's definitely possible."

"Hard to say when it's anonymous," Heather murmured, feeling her pulse in her fingertips.

She continued to read. The replies were full of a range of advice. Some of it seemed helpful—starving the desire and therapy for violence-based OCD—and some of it encouraged roleplay, BDSM dungeons, and other 'peaceful' solutions. Then there was a reply from somebody called 'skullcrusher' who simply said, "KILL HER," in all caps. He was heavily downvoted, at least. Runrabbitrun replied that he appreciated the advice and would try to indulge in some roleplay to release this energy.

She flipped to page 2 and found herself staring at the same website but a different thread. It was from several months later—May 7th, 2023—and was titled, 'I'm going to do it.'

I'm going to do it, runrabbitrun said. *I don't think I have any choice in the matter.*

That was all it said. There were a lot of replies this time. Some tried to start roleplaying and were subsequently told off by admins. Some identified non-killers gave helpful advice. Some actual killers elaborated, telling him how terrible prison was. Most of them seemed to think he should break up with this woman and distance himself from women in general. They advised him to commit a non-violent crime that would send him to a men's prison briefly or to get himself put into psychiatric hold.

The freaks—those who killed but had never been caught and loved what they did—encouraged him to give in to his urges and gave advice on butchering and burying. Then they all started to argue, and Heather couldn't tell if half of them were making stuff up or not or if this forum had any rules at all. Surely, the posters *had* to be full of it. They were fetishists and edgelords. Yet, Heather's gut told her that was not the case and that a few, including runrabbitrun, were telling the truth.

Heather flipped the page. She froze. *I love my fiancée, but I'm going to kill her.* That was the title. June 29th, 2023. Gabriel sucked his teeth, and Heather's head began to spin, her vision blackening around the edges.

"Lots of people kill their fiancées," Gabriel suggested.

Heather didn't respond and turned the page. *I did it. I killed her.* July 3rd, 2023. The day after Katy died. Heather was hardly surprised. She knew this had all been leading to that conclusion.

Most of the reactions were ones of sympathy, and they suggested a more appropriate website to move to now that runrabbitrun had graduated beyond their help. There was, of course, another screenshot of this website with the same username and a post titled, *I want to do it again.*

Heather closed the book. She got the picture. "This has to be..." she trailed off, gesturing vaguely at the stack of paper.

"Bullshit?" Gabriel asked. "I mean. Yeah. It could be."

"Do you think that we need to—" Heather retched, doubling over, nausea coming out of nowhere. She put her hand over her mouth and ran to the sink before releasing. Nothing came out, but she gagged again and again.

"I think we need to pay Daniel a visit," Gabriel said. "And then we need to hand this over to the Seattle PD."

"Or the FBI," Heather whispered, too quiet for Gabriel to hear. It was getting dark, and Brittany wasn't back yet. Heather whimpered, every expletive running through her mind. She resisted a scream, knuckles white. Gabriel gave her a minute and heard him pack everything back into the manila envelope.

"It's probably just a coincidence," he said. "There are no names. Or locations. Runrabbitrun could be in England or Australia, or God knows where. People murder people all the time. It's probably just a coincidence."

Heather nodded, but the problem was that try as she might, she didn't believe in coincidences.

CHAPTER THIRTY-FIVE

THE DETECTIVE

"HEY, HEATHER," DANIEL SAID, OPENING THE DOOR and upon catching sight of Gabriel, stuck out his hand. "Gabriel! Nice to see you again, man."

"You too," Gabriel said, taking the outstretched hand with a smile.

After a hearty shake, Daniel dropped his hand and shoved it back into the pocket of his hoodie. He wore an amused look, obviously confused as to why the pair were on his doorstep after dark, after six, still dressed in the uniform, and why they had shown up unannounced. He did not, however, seem nervous or hostile, as Heather had anticipated. In fact, the only thing remotely *off* about him was that he was dressed in jogging gear, but even this was not that strange. While Heather was solely a morning runner, Daniel would often go out after dark. Male privilege, she supposed.

"Sorry, are you heading out?" Heather asked, simpering as if she was a total idiot and pointing at his lycra getup.

"I was," he said slowly. "With Shane back in custody, I'm starting to dip my toe into the outside world. It's easier to do so at night without anyone around to stare at me." He paused and laughed. "Sorry, but can I ask what you're doing here?"

"Oh right," Heather said, smacking her forehead with her palm. "We were in the area—"

"Visiting the Seattle PD," Gabriel interrupted.

"Exactly. And we thought we'd stop by and see how you're feeling about everything and if you have any questions about the case or our conclusions."

To her surprise, Daniel stepped back and smiled broad and bright. "Come in, come in. I'd love to talk about the case."

"Great," Heather chirped, squeezing past him. I'm sorry. We should've contacted you sooner. It's been a crazy couple of weeks."

"Please don't apologize. My ex-fiancée's killer is heading back to prison. What more could I ask for? Now, come through to the living room. I've finally finished redecorating."

Gabriel had mentioned in passing that Daniel had recently repainted, but the actuality of the matter took Heather aback. Daniel had not merely changed the colors of the walls but eradicated any sign that Katy had ever lived there. Gone were the floral throws, the pastel cushions, and the mint-colored couches, replaced by navy, charcoal, and leather. Gone were the dried flowers, the porcelain figures, and the potpourri, replaced by fishing trophies, framed sports memorabilia, and a magazine rack. Even the framed photos of her or them together had been replaced by pictures of Daniel's parents and friends. It was understandable to want a fresh start, but Heather still found the extremity of the transformation jarring.

"It looks good," she said, her memory of what it looked like before fading fast.

"It's okay," Daniel said with a shrug, pretending to be modest, though his eyes sparkled as he admired their surroundings. "Just a lick of paint and a couple of nails in the wall. You know me. I'm not exactly DIY savvy. You were always the one with the good eye."

"What about Katy's eye?"

He chuckled. "If I'm honest, our eyes never really got along. But decorating made her happy, so I let her do her thing. It was sad, really, taking it all down, but I can't live in her dreamland forever."

"That's understandable," Heather replied, lowering herself onto the cold, stiff couch.

"Drinks?" Daniel asked. "I've been saving a bottle of champagne for the official ruling, but I can always get another."

"I could go for some champagne," Gabriel answered, plopping himself down in an armchair.

"Yeah, go on then," Heather encouraged, smiling up at Daniel and hoping that he couldn't see through the facade as she reclined in his living room.

"You're not in a rush?" he asked.

"Nah, the PD told us to swing by today or tomorrow. We can always try again tomorrow," Gabriel replied nonchalantly.

"Yeah, they just need a couple of signatures," Heather added.

"Great," Daniel exclaimed, clapping his hands together. "Let me pour you a glass and take you on a house tour. Then, if you like, I can put some snacks together, and we can have another around the firepit outside."

"Sounds awesome."

Daniel smiled broadly. "I'll just be a second."

He seemed very excited to have company, and Heather wondered when he'd last entertained anyone in this manner. Surely, his family and friends had visited at some point during the last eight and a half months. Or maybe not. Perhaps they hadn't wanted to risk the media exposure, or perhaps his lawyer advised against visitors to drive a depressed, self-isolated narrative. The general public could be very judgmental when it came to grief, and being photographed enjoying yourself was a definite no-no. Regardless, his loneliness was apparent. So much so that she briefly forgot why they were there and pitied her ex-husband.

She felt Gabriel watching her as she stared at the hallway that led to the kitchen and heard Daniel rooting around in the fridge and cupboards. She didn't meet his gaze and kept smiling as if she wanted to be here and was enjoying her evening. She couldn't risk breaking character when everything was going so well. They needed to go on that house tour.

Bang.

The champagne bottle went off like a gun as the cork was removed, and though Heather and Gabriel flinched, they readjusted the moment Daniel walked into the room. He, like they, was still smiling, holding the base of the bottle in one hand and three flute stems between the fingers of his other. Heather waited patiently for him to pour as he babbled about the year, notes, and location. It was actually from Champagne in France. Most weren't, apparently.

Once the drink was in her hand, she raised it high. "Cheers," she said, reaching out to clink glasses. The others met her in the middle over the central coffee table, and they all sipped and murmured appreciatively. Then, Heather cleared her throat. "So, before we continue to enjoy this evening, do you have any questions for us?"

Daniel pulled at his chin thoughtfully. "Where did they find him?"

"A real estate agent found him in the basement of one of the houses in Peony Crescent."

"The newest development," Daniel acknowledged, nodding. "They've been empty for a while due to some sort of sewage issue."

"It seems he was passing himself off as a construction worker. He'd grown quite the beard during his near-seven months in prison and shaved his mullet off, and because the prison failed to mention this, nobody recognized him. He bought a hi-vis jacket and stole ID from some drunk guy at the bar."

"Smart," Daniel said. "Surprisingly smart." He frowned. "To think he's just been wandering around in broad daylight all this time."

"I wonder why he stuck around."

"I suppose because he had unfinished work to do. I'm sure you're aware Hannah Roy is missing."

Heather nodded. "We are. Has she lived here long?"

"A few years now. I'd sometimes pass her on my own morning runs before Katy died. It wouldn't surprise me if Shane had gotten fixated on her. I saw the way the local men stared at her." Daniel paused to sip. "Do you think he'll get life in prison?"

"If he's found guilty, yes. Which is likely considering he beat his ex-roommate and the case's key witness half to death."

"Poor Izzy," Daniel said, shaking his head. "He should've gotten a restraining order like the rest of us."

"At least he's free now," Heather said.

This—the back and forth, the pretending—wasn't as hard as Heather had expected. She supposed it helped that, for the most part, she wasn't lying. Shane was going to prison, and he probably would spend the rest of his life there for breaking out and what he'd done to Izzy. It was also possible that he killed Hannah Roy and stashed her body in one of the endless houses. And if he had access to building supplies, it was also possible that she was encased in cement somewhere. The question was, in the trial of Shane Gibson, would Katy Graham be on the docket, and should she be?

"As am I," Daniel added with a contented exhale. "You know, once it's over—the trial, that is—I'll have to take you all out to dinner. Julius, too. It's been so long since I've been to a restaurant. Do you remember Boogie's?"

"How could I forget?" she laughed and looked at Gabriel to explain. "It's where we went on our first date."

"Don't forget trivia nights. Every first Saturday of the month."

"We were the Arnold Palmers," Heather snorted.

"And Palmer Springs."

Heather laughed loudly. "God. What stupid names. Didn't have anything to do with trivia. And we always lost."

"Hey! We won once."

"Yeah, because it was empty!"

They smiled at each other, and Heather could see the man she married glimmer in this stranger's eyes. She had loved him once, and for the briefest of seconds, she remembered how it

257

felt to love him. However, she wasn't here for reminiscence or rekindling, and, in remembering why she was here, she almost let her smile drop. She kept it in place by sheer force of will, though it made her cheeks hurt, and when her muscles began to twitch, she stood hastily.

"How about that house tour?" she asked, reaching for the bottle and topping up her glass.

"Of course," Daniel enthused, getting to his feet. "Follow me, and bring the bottle. We can finish it off in the backyard afterward." He laughed. "I guess I'm not doing any running tonight."

"There's always tomorrow," Heather said. "Which is what I've been telling myself for the past few weeks."

"You run?" Daniel asked, leading them out into the entrance area.

"Every day," Gabriel said, speaking for her proudly. "She got me into it, too."

"The smoking doesn't hold you back?" Daniel inquired, likely not intending to be judgmental. It just came naturally to him.

"I quit last year," Heather retorted, pretending to be offended.

Daniel smiled, and there was that glimmer again. She knew what he was thinking. Here was the woman he'd always wanted her to be: no longer a drunk, no longer a smoker, no longer a depressed lump on the couch. She was accomplished, confident, in shape, and looked the best that she ever had. He was thinking that he'd made a mistake. It was a confidence boost and an insult all at once, and though it made her cheeks flush, it also made her stomach twist. The idea of this man wanting her, romantically, carnally, or otherwise, was painfully disorientating and—if Brittany was right—downright revolting.

Maybe this is all a big misunderstanding, she thought as they ventured up the stairs. *He's happy to have us here and show us around. What killer would do that? Especially if their victim, or victims, were killed recently. Runrabbitrun could've been anyone. Shane makes more sense. A lot more. Aside from timing and circumstance, nothing links Daniel to that account. Surely, I—the woman with the borderline magical intuition—didn't fall in love with a murderer.*

Daniel looked over his shoulder and winked, telling inside jokes without a sound, and Heather thought of Julius to ground herself. That was a man who made her feel good all of the time, no matter what. A man who wasn't possessive or jealous. A man who understood who she was and what she did. A man she wanted to be with. Daniel was none of those things. Daniel had been a skeleton in her closet, old bones in her backyard, for longer than she'd loved him, and yet she could feel him reaching out through the veil.

Gabriel coughed loudly. "Sorry, went down the wrong way," he choked, obviously faking it.

"You okay, man?" Daniel asked.

"Yeah, all good," Gabriel replied, his tone cheery but his expression terse.

He was right. She needed to snap out of it, and by the time they reached the top, and she'd recounted all of her darkest moments with Daniel at supersonic speed, she remembered herself and why she was there.

The rest of the house looked much the same as the living room: dark wall colors, framed memorabilia, music posters, photos of family, and stacks of decorative books on console tables. It was nice but a little dull. Similarly to Brittany's home, it was also too clean for Heather's tastes. It bordered on sterile, like something out of a men's magazine article about bachelor living. It made sense. Daniel had known the best restaurants, what cheeses went with what wines, and the differences between forks and spoons, but he'd never been wildly imaginative. Still, as he enthused and told them in detail about everything he'd done to the house, she listened intently and chimed in when appropriate. Fortunately, when there was slack to be had, Gabriel picked it up, talking about his plans to move in with his girlfriend and how he wanted his future home to look.

She had to admit, the bathroom was especially nice with its rain shower, large charcoal tiles, and gold taps. The plethora of fake plants were also a nice touch, as was the bath table, where she imagined him soaking, watching an old movie on his iPad while sipping a glass of wine. She soon wished that hadn't come into her mind, but it was hard to banish. Harder still was joining that version of him to the one that would strangle his fiancée to death in their bed.

We're wrong, she thought. *We must be.* There was nothing out of place. Nothing suspicious. Yes, it was clean, but Daniel had always been clean. Not only that, but his behavior did not indicate guilt. Maybe that was her closeness to him, her old ties, the fact she'd never been able to accurately read him, or maybe it was because he hadn't done anything wrong. He was just happy to be free, and who could blame him?

"Downstairs?" he asked after having finished his speech on Egyptian cotton. "There's not as much to see, but—"

"Sure!" Heather said, "Then we'll finish off this bottle."

"I have another and some food if you two are interested in staying the night. I'll admit I could do with the company and an opportunity to grill some steaks. I know it's a Tuesday—"

"Sure," Heather said, interrupting for a second time. "That sounds great." She wasn't sure exactly what she was hoping to attain by agreeing, but she also definitely wasn't ready to leave just yet. She had to be sure, and right now, she was teetering on a precipice, not nearly ready to dive into guilty waters.

Gabriel played along, though she could tell she was confused. "Hey, I'll never say no to a steak and champagne. Not something I often get with my salary."

"Well, after all you've done for me, just give me your address and a date, and I'll have someone deliver Wagyu to your front door."

"Hell yeah. Thanks, man. That beats a card and flowers any day," Gabriel said, and Heather wondered if he was coming to the same conclusion that Brittany had either been wrong or had led them on a wild goose chase.

Daniel led the way downstairs and entered the kitchen dining room combo. It was L-shaped, with the galley kitchen forming the long bit and the dining room forming the bottom. There was a bouquet of sunflowers and daisies on the table that Daniel said were from his parents. Heather adored sunflowers, but before she could compliment the arrangement, her nose tickled.

The sneeze erupted from within like a shotgun blast. It was dry, mercifully, but painful, and she instinctively reached for a tissue—which she always had in her pockets—and blew her nose with force.

"Sorry," she said, giggling congestedly as she walked toward the trashcan. "Must be the daisies."

She placed her foot on the pedal to lift the lid, and Daniel made a noise somewhere between a gasp, a yell, and a whimper. It was too late, however, and as the lid opened like a hungry mouth, Heather looked inside and saw Brittany Hart's yellow backpack sitting atop a mound of trash.

CHAPTER THIRTY-SIX

THE DETECTIVE

HEATHER FROZE, TISSUE STILL DANGLING ABOVE THE plastic-lined maw. That was definitely Brittany's backpack. Heather had seen it on her shoulders less than a week ago. And now, it was in the trashcan in Daniel's house. Heather hiccupped and swallowed a laugh. It was ridiculous. It didn't make sense. Why was it there? Why, why, *why* was it there?

Heather blinked away the oncoming shock and put two and two together. Brittany had been here, and she had left her most prized possessions—backpack, wallet, phone, recording equipment, and laptop—behind. That was something she would never do voluntarily, not in a million years. Nor would she—always careful and reliant upon it—smash her phone, especially considering it was protected by a pink shock-absorbent case. The way the glass was broken looked as if it had been stabbed by a large knife. Heather hoped the same couldn't be said for Brittany's body.

Heather turned, the world in slow motion, and saw that Daniel's back was already to her. She threw the tissue to the ground and thrust forward, gaining speed as he bolted toward the door.

"What the...?" Gabriel asked, confused, spinning in a circle and drawing his weapon.

The front door opened with a bang, knocking into the wall with force and sending something in a glass-fronted frame smashing to the ground. Considering his head start, Heather thanked her high heel-induced blisters for forcing her to wear sneakers instead of stiff combat boots today.

"Heather, what is—" Gabriel began as Heather shoved him out of the way in pursuit.

"Trashcan!" she yelled.

"Heather!" Gabriel called after, but she was already gone, jumping over the porch step and onto the gravel.

Soon, she was on the asphalt, and there she was in her element, guided by streetlights and driven by adrenaline. The problem was that Daniel was fast, faster than her, with his long legs, years of training, and marathon races. His eight-second head start now felt like thirty, and he was driven by fear. Nothing runs faster or further than a prey animal being pursued. How funny, she thought, that the rabbit chaser was now the one being hunted. Except, Heather didn't feel like a predator. She felt like a dog chasing a car. She didn't know what she'd do if she caught him. She didn't really *want* to do this. It was all instinctual, and the lack of desire was weighing her down.

When she was a teenager, her parents had fostered ex-racing greyhounds. They were incredibly lazy and great apartment dogs, but what they always excelled at was hunting. She'd lost count of the times they'd plucked a bird from the air or a rat from a bush and brought it to her, frightened, a still half-alive animal in their mouth, unsure of whether to bite down or let go.

Black Beauty had been her favorite. So much so that she nearly became a foster fail. She was also the last greyhound her family ever fostered. The guilt of seeing her broken body on the road after a speeding driver crushed her was too much to bear. The driver was apologetic, of course, but not as much as Heather was. She shouldn't have let her off lead so close to the road. That swooping blue jay had just been too tempting not to chase.

Heather had told Daniel about Black Beauty once after they accidentally hit a rabbit, and the sound brought back memories. A body being hit by a car doesn't sound like you think it will. It's not a dull thunk. It's loud. It rattles your bones. She could barely tell the story through all the screaming in her memories, and all her husband could say to comfort her was, "Dumb dog."

A flicker of anger ignited within Heather, and as her speed increased, she realized that anger was the key. She thought back to how he humiliated her at parties, insinuating she was dumb or uneducated. How he blamed her for losing at trivia nights and eventually refused to go. How he was kind to her parents' faces, but rude behind their backs, disapproving of their cooking skills and money management. How he lied constantly about being faithful. How he went through her phone because he was sure that she wasn't. How he cheated and cheated and cheated until she was just a miserable, insecure husk during the worst time in her life. How she hadn't been with anybody since, and how she was barely with him either. He'd stopped touching her a year before the divorce. How it had been so long that being touched again would be like a virginal experience. How she was frightened of that. How all of this would likely ruin anything good coming her way. Because her ex-husband, the man whom she had exchanged vows and shared a home with, was a murderer.

She sped up, feet pounding the concrete, shins, and ankles no longer aching, and as Daniel glanced back at her, he paled. She must have looked as furious as she felt because he also increased his speed.

For a second, she considered shooting him. It would be easy. She would just have to get him in the leg, and all of this would be over. Yet she didn't want it to be easy. She wanted to hunt, to win, to prove herself. She wanted him to feel what his victims had felt. She wanted to scare him so bad that his heart burst. She wanted to use what he'd taught her against him.

"Murderer!" she screamed, her voice hoarse and breaking, the wind whipping the accusation away.

He had killed Katy Graham. That much was obvious. He wouldn't have done whatever he'd done to Brittany Hart if he had nothing to hide. It made Heather sick. He had met her, Katy, the younger model, the troubled girl, under false pretenses. He had lured her in, isolated her, and eventually strangled her. Heather wondered if it was always going to end like that, if he fought as hard as his account implied, or if he'd spent five years playing with his food, like some sort of sick, five-year edging session.

Heather wondered how close she was to meeting the same fate and then remembered Hannah Roy—the local woman who looked just like her—and realized that there had been fantasizing, phantom hands wrapped around her throat for their entire marriage.

Bile shot up her throat, and she swallowed it down, stopping for nothing. Her insides were on fire. They'd been running for at least five minutes now, and though a speedometer would clock them at the same pace, they were still at least fifteen feet apart.

Had Katy even been his first, she wondered. The forums implied it, but maybe he got off on pretending to be a 'virgin.' Either way, he had the bug now, and three women were likely dead. Heather pictured each and every one of their faces. She thought of their lives, friends, partners or husbands, children, and passions. They were people, women, and humans who only got one shot at being on Earth, and he snuffed that one-in-four-hundred-trillion miracle out.

Heather screamed like a mourning banshee. She had never gotten along with Brittany but admired her gumption, dedication, and work ethic. They were things that Heather could relate to, especially when she'd been green. She was also so young, so full of life. She probably had friends, family, and a boyfriend. She had fans. Young, impressionable fans. She was loved. She loved what she did. And now thousands of people were going to be traumatized forever because of the actions of one selfish man. A man who didn't see women as human but as meat. Animals primed for the slaughter. Deer during hunting season.

Heather was mad at herself, too. She hadn't listened. Hadn't wanted it to be him. Now that she knew it was, it was almost too obvious. It had been screaming at her this entire time, and she'd plugged her ears and sang aloud.

The anger had propelled her. She was close to him now, close enough that she could smell his sweat, and with an extended arm, her fingertips brushed his back. With another scream—this one of fury—she launched herself forward, taking both feet off the ground and wrapping her arms around him.

Going downhill and at full speed, they fell hard and far and skidded along the rough road, grating, peeling, and burning skin. Heather felt something crack, and she didn't know if it was her bone or his until she inhaled deeply. It was a rib, and her movement was worsening the break. Yet she still crawled toward him and climbed onto his back before laying down. She'd caught her prey. She was a greyhound with a half-dead thing in her mouth, and she wasn't going to let go, which only left her with one option—biting down.

She wrapped her limbs around him and squeezed. He whimpered and squirmed as she dug her nails in, but he didn't try to throw her. "How dare you," she whispered in his ear.

"Mmsorry," he mumbled, blood in his mouth.

"Don't lie!" she screamed, voice cracking, loosening a hand to pound the road with the side of her fist. "Stop lying. Just this once."

So he remained quiet because he didn't know how to do anything else. At least the quiet was a relief, and Heather laid her head down between his shoulder blades. He didn't smell the same as he used to. He always used to smell like nothing or close to it. Nothing with a hint of vanilla or cologne. Now he smelt acrid, like juice that had fermented or the inside of a compost bin. Maybe that's what happens when you murder for pleasure, she thought. You start to smell like decay.

The familiar beeping of a squad car broke her from her trance, and she turned her head to see two officers jogging her way. "Detective Bishop?" one of them asked. She recognized the voice as Rosie O'Dowell's. She'd been at their wedding.

Heather nodded but didn't speak.

"Jesus. What... Can you move?"

She nodded again, placed her palms against the damp ground, and pushed herself onto her haunches. "Yep," she muttered weakly.

"What's going on here?" a different voice asked. Sgt. Oliver Mulligan. They had never been friends, but he was a good man and a better cop.

"Pursuit of a murderer," Heather coughed, bracing herself against her knees as she stood. "If you follow me back to his house, I'm sure we'll find a body. In fact, my partner probably already has."

There was a rattle of handcuffs as the officers arrested Daniel without question—it paid to have a trustworthy track record—and hoisted him to his feet by his armpits. Heather stared at him, avoiding the eyes. Beyond scuffed forearms, palms, and knees, he looked in okay physical condition, but he was limp as they dragged him toward the vehicle. His mind was gone. He'd been so close to freedom, only to have it all wrenched away.

Once he was locked away, Rosie and Oliver looked at each other, then at Heather. "Do you want to take the passenger seat?" Rosie asked. "One of us can walk. I imagine you don't want to be in the back with the suspect."

Heather shook her head and raised a trembling arm to dismiss them. "I need to walk this off. I'll meet you there. He'll tell you where to go."

Confused, the officers got into the car with a shrug, turned the car around, and drove ahead at a crawl.

Heather felt like crawling, too, but instead, she limped after them, arms wrapped around herself. It smelled like rain, and after a few steps, a cool mist began to splatter her face and rinse the blood from her skin. She waved at the worried onlookers standing on their perfect front lawns and took in the splendor of it all—this nighttime suburban paradise and a sky spattered with stars—with a chipped-tooth, delirious smile. She laughed as she tongued the broken canine. It was beautiful here, and Daniel would never see nor enjoy such beauty again.

CHAPTER THIRTY-SEVEN

THE PARTNER

"HEATHER!" GABRIEL CALLED AFTER HIS PARTNER as she bolted through the front door and took off down the street after the lightning-quick Daniel, who had conveniently still been dressed in jogging gear.

Gabriel moved quickly to the open doorway and watched as the two became specks on the dark horizon before being swallowed by the downhill slope of the road. Gabriel cursed under his breath, not sure of what to do. He was armed, but he'd never catch up to them, and he wasn't a great long-distance shooter. Not that he wanted to shoot Daniel. Not yet, at least. Not until he knew what the hell was going on.

He considered driving after them but soon realized that Heather had the keys to her car in her pocket. So, fumbling with his phone, he made his way back to the kitchen to try to figure out what had shocked Heather and spooked Daniel. She had mentioned the trashcan, so he went there first, placed the toe of his boot on the pedal, and hesitated momentarily before pressing down. He braced himself for body parts—or, worse, a head staring up at him with milky eyes—but instead, there was a yellow backpack, a wallet, recording equipment, and a broken phone.

"Brittany," he whispered. She had backpacks in all sorts of bright colors to match her flashy outfits, but the yellow one was her favorite. She'd been wearing it when she'd last confronted them.

Sweaty and shaky, he texted Julius, "Call police. Daniel's house. Heather in pursuit of Daniel," and pocketed his phone. He knew Julius would get the message and save Gabriel the hassle of calling 911 himself. Julius used his phone as a buzzer for work and was, as he described, constantly harangued by emails from academics at the university and his lab staff. As expected, Gabriel's phone buzzed within seconds. That was good. There was a police station nearby. They could help Heather much better than he could.

Yet, he wasn't planning on remaining idle. He needed to find evidence. They'd already been high and low in the house and seen behind every door. So where could the body be? Maybe Brittany and her car were at the bottom of a lake, as Amanda had feared, but for whatever reason, Gabriel's gut told him otherwise. Maybe Heather's intuition was catching.

He moved to the entrance area and saw a door they had not ventured beyond at the base of the stairs. He tried the handle and found it locked, but all was not lost. He remembered the bowl of keys on the console from his first visit, and he punched the air as he turned and found the ring in the right spot.

He unlocked the door, reached for a light switch, and illuminated the two-door garage. One of the cars—which looked to be a large SUV from the shape of it—was under a sheet, and the other was a brand-new Mini Cooper in pepper white. He knew immediately, without having ever seen her driving, that this was Brittany's car, and his stomach lurched. The backpack was one thing, but this was confirmation. Brittany was dead.

So, he started his search for her in a logical spot—the trunk. He tried her vehicle first and found nothing except for neatly folded reusable grocery bags. Then he ripped the cloak from Daniel's Land Cruiser, pressed a button on the fat black key, and checked inside. It was spotless, professionally detailed, and smelled like New Car. There was no blood, no ropes, not even a receipt. If Daniel had been planning to take a body elsewhere to dump, Gabriel highly doubted he had already done it.

He shut the trunk, looked around the impeccably organized garage, and, for lack of a better idea, began to open and shut cupboard doors, finding nothing except for immaculate tools hung neatly on the walls—a veneer of red-blooded maleness so that Daniel didn't feel embarrassed when a plumber or electrician would come over.

Gabriel re-entered the house, leaving the garage door ajar, and looked around, his head spinning faster than his body. Then he stopped. Something had caught his attention, but he wasn't quite sure what until he stood still and stared. In the nook under the stairs was a narrow bookshelf facing the underside of the staircase, its back up against a small section of wall next to the kitchen doorway.

This wasn't unusual, per se. Gabriel had seen plenty of houses with that sort of nook. He had one in his home, occupied by a chest full of raincoats and boots. However, when he continued into the kitchen, instead of the wall being the same on the other side—i.e., flat—the wall continued out from the doorframe. Gabriel thought this was odd as it made the dining room area small for no reason by several feet, and it meant that there was an almost room-sized section of crawl space between the right side of the dining room and the left side of the garage.

He stepped backward and tipped the bookshelf forward, causing all of the books to fall to the ground. Sure enough, there was a door there. It was smaller and narrower than the kitchen door to its left and had been painted navy like the walls. It was unassuming, and ordinarily, no one would have ever thought twice about it, likely assuming it to be full of linen or perhaps containing a small bathroom. So why hide it? Gabriel already knew the answer as he moved the bookshelf out of the way and hesitated to turn the knob.

As he pulled it open, he swallowed hard. What he was looking at was not a small room but the top of a set of basement stairs. Like the rest of the house, they were new, so not scary in a horror movie sense, but scary like any stairs can be when you can't see what's at the bottom.

Then he thought about Heather, what he'd read about the Paper Doll Case, and what they'd found in that basement. That poor little girl, the last victim, stuffed into the bathroom, her little blue hand poking out through the gap beneath the door. He knew that room still haunted Heather, and he had the distinct feeling that this was going to be his basement. Not that he had a choice to avoid it. This was an amalgamation of his life's decisions coming together. This was an inevitability. This was the job.

He turned on his flashlight and headed downstairs, not wasting any time by hesitating. He knew as soon as he halted that forward momentum, he'd stop altogether. Then they'd find him stuck on the stairs like a child sneaking out of his room at night, too scared to finish their journey to the toilet.

There was no door at the bottom, just a wall of blackness, and he stepped down into oblivion and was pleased to find a flat surface beneath his feet. He slapped at the walls for a light switch and found cold tiles before he found it. The lights began to flicker, and he knew exactly what he was going to see. Somehow, as white light flooded the room, the reality still shocked him.

The white-tiled room was covered in sheets of translucent tarp. It was as clean as a surgical theater and smelled of room caulk and chemicals. There were blue, plastic barrels in the corner, and Gabriel had seen enough crime TV and read enough in his studies to know what they were full of—hydrofluoric acid. On the counter were more tools, except unlike the ones in the garage, these were surgical and destined to be used.

Mercifully, the lack of blood indicated they hadn't been used yet. As did the bodies. The two women lying side by side were intact and well-preserved, and Gabriel recognized them instantly as Hannah Roy and Brittany Hart. They were both unmistakably dead, though Brittany, more recently murdered, could've passed for being asleep. Hannah, on the other hand, was gray, but the cold had fortunately prevented decay beyond rigor mortis.

At least they'll be salvageable for the coroner, Gabriel thought, unblinking. For some reason, that was all he could think about. The funerals. Their families. He wasn't here, in the room. He was looking at the future. He wasn't sure if that was better or worse.

Not wanting to contaminate the scene, he backed away, and as he reached the bottom step, from his slightly higher advantage, he could see the ring of bruising around both women's necks.

He took another step back. They'd been here the entire time. They'd drunk champagne unawares. They almost left. And the entire time, these two bodies had been beneath them.

He'd told Hannah Roy to run through the park.

He'd told Brittany Hart that he didn't believe her.

He hated himself viciously and knew he deserved the hauntings that were coming his way. Yet, somehow, he saw past his failings. He wasn't the monster here. He didn't know this was going to happen. He was somebody who cared, tried hard, and made mistakes but learned from them. There were always going to be monsters; he was just going to have to try harder to drag them into the light.

He didn't feel triumphant, nor did he feel broken. He felt profoundly sad but ultimately motivated. He was going to do everything in his power to send Daniel to prison. Not only that, but he was going to call Jason Fleming and ask him to contact the FBI. Brittany had found something real, something important. She had found a nest of monsters. They wouldn't be easy to track down, but she was not going to have died in vain. Not on Gabriel's watch. The Hart Foundation had a good ring to it, he thought. He had some savings. He was going to put things in motion. He was going to help with funerals. He was going to raise awareness. He was going to make sure this never happened again so long as he wore a badge and uniform.

Instead of shriveling into himself, Gabriel stood up tall as he made the calls he needed to make. He couldn't and wouldn't fall apart. He owed Hannah and Brittany that much. He owed them better, not worse, strength, not weakness, and thankfulness, as well as apology. He owed them everything, and he knew at that moment he would do anything to see justice served.

CHAPTER THIRTY-EIGHT

THE DETECTIVE

A S HEATHER LIMPED UPHILL, BLUE AND RED LIGHTS greeted her before faces did. Then they appeared: the cops that arrested Daniel, other cops, her old boss, CSI, Julius, and Gabriel. She wasn't smiling anymore. There was tape, which meant they'd found the bodies, and as Julius and Gabriel turned toward her, she crumpled onto the neighbor's lawn.

Their faces were etched with horror and panic as they ran to her side, and she realized she must've looked as bad as she felt. As soon as she felt body heat, she fell forward. Into whom, she didn't know as her eyes were closed, but she felt more than two hands on her, checking her for wounds.

"Hi guys," she murmured.

"Nobody told us you were badly hurt," Julius growled. "They said you wanted to walk, so I *assumed* you needed space." His voice was loud, lashing out at those near enough to overhear.

"I did," Heather confirmed. "Ow, careful. Broken rib."

Hands retreated that must've belonged to Gabriel, and he said, "I'll get them to bring an ambulance down here."

"Already on its way. Daniel thinks his hand is broken," Julius said with disgust. "Go grab a wet cloth from inside. She has blood in her eyes."

Despite his saying that, Heather opened her gluey lids and saw two pairs of brown eyes staring at her. "Are you okay?" Julius asked as Gabriel took a reluctant step backward toward the house.

"Never been better. Why do you ask?" she joked hoarsely.

"I'll live," she answered. "God, it sucks falling over as an adult. There's so much farther to go."

"Look at me," Julius said, turning on his phone torch and shining it into her eyes. She knew what he was looking for. He may have specialized in the dead, but he still went to medical school.

"I'm not concussed," she promised him. "Daniel softened my fall."

"Yeah, you seem okay," he said slowly before lowering the light.

Heather blinked rapidly, wiping away wetness, and then focused on Gabriel, whose eyes were far wetter. He'd been crying. "Did you..." she began and trailed off.

He nodded. "Hannah Roy and Brittany Hart. He had a secret basement. You know, like Peter Anderson. Tarp and all. I think he was planning on cutting them up and dissolving them in barrels of acid. Who knows how he got his hands on this stuff. Probably those sick forum freaks."

Heather heard what he was saying, but she didn't really absorb it, or if she did, it was hard to believe it. Strangling your fiancée in a fit of jealous rage was one thing, but premeditated murder, dismemberment, and acid was something else entirely. He'd upped his game, and she wondered if they hadn't been looking so closely, whether he'd ever have been caught.

Then, almost as if the universe was answering her question, Gabriel's phone dinged. He checked it, and his jaw dropped. "Oh my god," he muttered.

"What?" Heather asked, almost shouting. It was increasingly noisy as more cars and an ambulance arrived. Her ears were also still ringing something awful.

Gabriel turned the screen toward her. "New Crime Time episode."

He pressed play, and Brittany Hart's voice spoke out to them from beyond the grave. No music, no advertisers, just her. "If you're listening to this episode, then I'm dead. I've been murdered. And Daniel Palmer is my killer."

He paused it again and looked at Heather in shock. She supposed the answer to her question was yes. Somebody would've caught him. Brittany Hart would've. They had been very wrong about her final episode.

"I want to see them," she said suddenly, straightening, repressing her pain.

"Heather, I think you should wait for the ambulance," Julius advised. Then he sighed, looking at her expression, used his sleeve to wipe cruor from her face, and helped her stand. "Do you need to be alone?" he asked.

"At first," Heather said. "Come save me after ten minutes. Then, everyone can get on with their work. Gabriel, get the folder out of my car and give it to that man over there," she instructed, pointing at the Chief of Police. Then she threw her keys, and despite the lousy toss, Gabriel caught them and took off.

"Alright, let's go," Julius said, taking her arm and helping her stagger into the house.

"Where's Daniel?" she asked as all the swarming cops paused their busy work to stare.

"He's in the squad car," Julius said. "I think..." He trailed off.

"What?" Heather growled.

"I think he wants to speak with you. That's why they haven't taken him to the station yet."

"Good," Heather retorted. "I want to speak to him too."

She heard Julius start to speak, a small sound catching in his throat. She knew what he was about to say. Why don't you wait? Why not tomorrow? Yet he knew that she wasn't able to wait. She wouldn't be able to sleep or eat until this was done. What she needed wasn't rest. She needed to lash her tongue, get closure, and say goodbye.

They stood at the top of the stairs, and Heather heard Brittany Hart's voice again, clear as a bell. For a brief, painful second, she thought that they must've been wrong about her being dead and that she was talking to the police downstairs. Then she realized it was coming from the kitchen and had a distinctly tinny quality to it.

They all paused to listen as the recording played from Brittany's laptop. "Okay, I'm hiding now," she panted. "I broke into his house through the sunroom while he went on a jog. I'm in what I think is the guest room cupboard. Hopefully, he doesn't come in here, and I can sneak out while he's asleep." The statement was followed by silence and then, very clearly, footsteps on creaking floorboards. More silence. More footprints. Then, a scream. Heather knew she was going to dream about that scream every night for the next six months at least.

"Can you get everyone to come upstairs?" Heather asked of Rosie, who was standing guard.

Rosie gave Heather a small smile and did as she asked without question, and as Julius held Heather steady through her adrenaline crash, the three officers in the basement filtered up the stairs. They looked at her with pity as they passed. No one had ever liked Daniel. They'd been happy for her when he'd left. Except, as it turned out, he'd never really left. He'd simply loosened her leash.

She freed herself from Julius's grasp, squeezed his hand, and ventured down the stairs, using the railing to aid her painful leg. Shin splints, she considered, or a twisted ankle. It was hard to tell, hard to pinpoint the pain in her body. It felt like it was coming from everywhere and nowhere. Her chest hurt worst of all, and though her rib was making things worse, it was her heart that was going through a shredder.

She saw the bodies before she reached the bottom rung, tightened her grip, inhaled a shuddering breath, and turned into a body-wracking sob. Slowly, she made it the rest of the way, and once on solid ground, she fell onto all fours onto the icy tiling. Her hand was near a drain, and she pulled it into herself, feeling phantom blood and water circling it.

She dared not move forward, not wanting to contaminate, and instead searched with her aching eyes. The bone saw lying on the counter almost moved her to vomit, but she kept it together and fell back on her haunches. She had been married to Daniel for five years. She'd read the forums. She'd seen the backpack in the trashcan. She'd listened to Gabriel's description. And yet, she was still surprised. She'd read of countless murder cases in which the wife of the murderer claimed to have never suspected a thing. Judith Mawson, for example, was married to Gary Ridgway, the Green River Killer, who was convicted of killing forty-nine women. Or Rosemarie Fritzl, who married Josef Fritzl, who imprisoned their daughter in the basement for twenty-four years. Heather had always taken them for liars, but now she wondered, had anyone ever been in *her* basement? Was he just getting started, or had he been doing this the entire time? She wasn't sure if she could live with the latter.

"I'm so sorry," she cried out to the women, not caring if her voice traveled up the stairs. "I was selfish. I didn't want it to be him because *I* couldn't bear it. I traveled to goddamn London in the hopes of salving my guilty conscience. And I was so happy when he didn't kill that girl. I was so, so happy." She chewed her lip until it split. "I thought it was Shane. I really did. He was violent. He forced his roommate to lie for him. He was abusive. He killed a man. But I ignored my gut. I called it a liar even though it has never steered me wrong. I should have never investigated Daniel. I should have never agreed to help him. He's always been able to convince me that North was South. He makes me weak. I *am* weak. I—"

A hand on her shoulder stopped her in her tracks, and she smelled Julius's cologne on his wrist. She turned, and buried her face into his palm, soaking his skin with her sodden lashes.

"I'm so sorry," he said, using his other hand to comb her blood-matted hair.

"This is my fault," she sobbed.

"No," Julius said firmly. "It's his. And it will always be his." Julius sighed. "He wants to talk to you. Are you ready?"

"It's now or never. Just give me five minutes."

"I'll tell them." Julius removed his hand, but she reached out and caught it like a bottle falling from a table. "Don't go."

"I'm not going anywhere, Heather. I'll never leave you. I love you."

She buried her face back into his hand and cried even harder because she didn't deserve it, his love, but she wanted it so bad. She tried to say it back because it was true, but it got caught in her throat like an oversized pill. Maybe her love couldn't be trusted, considering the only other man she'd ever loved was waiting upstairs, and his victims were strewn out behind her.

CHAPTER THIRTY-NINE

THE DETECTIVE

HEATHER SAT IN THE SUNROOM ON THE PADDED BENCH in the same spot she'd sat in when she'd reunited with Daniel for the first time several months ago. Rosie's words were still ringing in her ears. "It's not just that he wants to talk to you. Daniel says that he wants to confess to you and only you. He wants to speak to you alone, here, in his house, and he wants to enjoy a drink with you. He says if we don't agree to his demand, or more importantly, if you don't agree, then he'll never confess. No matter what."

Heather scowled. Of course, he had to make this even more difficult than it was already. She crossed her legs, reached for a little wooden folding table, and dragged it close to her. She put the tape recorder on the top and pressed record. Then she leaned back, trying to seem calm and relaxed, tented her fingers on her lap, and waited for Daniel to enter.

He emerged shortly after, pushing open the kitchen doorway, holding two large crystal glasses and a bottle of red wine in his hands. Heather tensed. She knew that this was not only his last glass of wine but also hers. She would never be able to sip it again without seeing this room, his face, and the bodies in the basement. Her comfort drink would forever and always taste like death.

He sat at the circular white table, where he'd also sat the last time they'd been in the sunroom, arranged the glasses on the table, and filled them plentifully. He patted the seat beside him, but Heather shook her head.

"Don't push your luck," she said sternly.

Daniel didn't argue. Instead, he stood and padded toward her and handed the drink over before returning to his seat. He surveyed her as if he was a therapist and she was his patient. He was a Shaolin monk. He was unmoved. Tranquil. Vacant. It made her furious. Though at least he wasn't the pathetic blubbering mess that Heather had anticipated. She couldn't have endured that without breaking the bottle over his head.

"Are you okay?" he asked.

"What do you think?" she retorted, gulping wine and then gagging. What she really needed was water, but this would do for now. At least she might be able to sleep on the drive home.

He sighed. "I am sorry. Truly."

"No, you're not," she spat. "And even if you were, I don't think sorry is a big enough word for what's happened here. I don't think any word in the English language could make my disgust disappear."

"I'm sure there's not because what I have done is unforgivable. Still, I'm sorry anyway."

Heather took another sip and sucked her teeth. She had no intention of acknowledging his apology or guiding this session. She was going to listen, endure, and then leave.

"Should I start at the beginning?" he asked.

"Knock yourself out."

"I don't know when I first fantasized about killing. Perhaps as young as fourteen. I killed the family Jack Russell around that time."

Heather grimaced. "You told me that you never had a dog. That you hated dogs. That's why we never had one."

"I lied. I don't hate dogs. At least, not for the typical reason. I hate them because they remind me of what I did to my childhood best friend."

"So he was your first kill?" Heather asked, wanting to know more despite herself.

"He was. Winston. And he was my only kill until Katy Graham."

Heather eyed him suspiciously. "You waited until your late thirties to kill a human?"

He stared into Heather's eyes, and for the first time, she was able to get a read on him. Perhaps because he was letting her. There was no mask on his pretty face today, no double bluffing with false twitches or charismatic smiles. This was authentic. He wasn't lying. There was no point in that now.

"I wanted to kill much, much earlier," he replied. "But I always managed to maintain control. At least until I turned twenty-one. I never told you the real reason why I transferred universities and moved halfway across the country."

"You said there was a hazing incident. You and some frat boys took a prank too far."

"Another lie. One dark enough to be believed as a genuine secret. What really happened was I strangled my first serious girlfriend half to death in my dorm room. My parents paid her off—not that they believed her—but I couldn't stay. That secret died with her and the Dean. Traffic accident," he added. "Nothing to do with me. Though she was drunk. She was almost always drunk, apparently. I suppose you could blame that on me and the trauma I inflicted."

"And then you didn't date again until you met me," Heather said quietly.

Daniel nodded thoughtfully. "The more I love something, the more I want to hurt it. I suppose it's the same as the trophy hunters who take down elephants and lions. They don't do it out of hate. They do it because they think that creature is too beautiful to live. They want to possess it, not only in body but in soul."

"I don't understand," Heather admitted.

"I'm glad you don't. It's a curse. One that I have decided to embrace instead of run away from. A selfish choice, to be sure, but one I felt unavoidable if I was to keep living."

"Then why not die?" she asked coldly. "Why not eradicate the sickness with some pills or a nice dose of carbon monoxide?"

"Because I don't want to die," Daniel answered, and she supposed it was as good an answer as any.

"Okay, so why me?" Heather questioned. "Why get involved with me? Why run the risk?"

"I'll admit I started dating you purely for indulgent, lustful purposes. I had no plan to involve love in the mix. But then I got to know you. I saw how good you were at your job, and I knew that you could keep me in check. I'd never be able to pull the wool over your eyes. I'd never be able to kill without you knowing it, and I'd never be able to kill you without you seeing me coming, either."

"I was your prison guard."

"And my wife," Daniel insisted, a spark of passion burning amongst the monotonous droning. "I saw us as a team. You got what you wanted: a loving husband, companionship, and a ticked box on your list of goals. In return, I got what I wanted: a wife to cease my parents' concerns, a protector of sorts, and freedom to exist. I fear my body count would be much higher than three without you."

Heather drained her glass before asking, "Did you ever want to kill me?"

Daniel stood to refresh her drink, and as he did so, he looked down into her eyes, letting the booze flow freely. "Every day."

Heather flinched and pulled her almost full glass away, causing a splatter of crimson to hit the ground. Daniel straightened, turning the bottle upright. He returned to his seat and sat down hard as if exhausted. Heather supposed he probably was. He'd been busy and was injured worse than she was.

"So why didn't you?" she questioned.

"As I said, I felt I couldn't. Up until the Paper Doll Case, that is. Peter Anderson got under your skin. He turned you into a husk and drained you of the power that you'd once held over me. You were drunk half of the time. It would have been so easy to wrap my hands around your throat while you were sleeping."

"But you still didn't kill me. Why?" Heather asked, leaning forward now, trying to understand the creature that sat before her like a biologist making a new discovery.

"Because I was grateful. You'd unknowingly kept me clean."

Heather chewed her cheek. "You kept me alive as a favor."

"Yes."

"And because you couldn't risk ruining things with Katy?"

Daniel chuckled. "She might've been suspicious if my wife turned up dead, yes."

"And you knew you were going to kill her from the start," Heather stated, not asking.

"I knew it was inevitable, yes."

"And you dated her anyway."

"Yes. Like with the trophy hunters, the hunt is half the fun, and I knew I wanted to possess her forever from the moment I laid eyes on her."

"So, you'd given up by that point?"

Daniel shrugged. "Without you, I knew I was hopeless. So I leaned into my desires, though I managed to keep them at bay for a long time. And I enjoyed my time with her, I really did, but when I felt her straying, I knew it was now or never. So I made my move. I really did go jogging. I really did go to Subway, but there was no olive shortage. I sent those texts to cover my ass. I was on my way back long before my supposed discovery. I let myself in through the back door. That one over there. And snuck up on her. She thought we were going to have sex, and I let her believe that to get her into bed. I bound her wrists consensually, under the guise of trying new things, and then..." His words failed him as he topped up his own glass. "Then I put my hands around her throat and didn't remove them until she stopped moving. Then I unlocked and opened the front door, exited through the back, jogged around the neighborhood, and made my terrible discovery. Just in case the neighbors were watching."

"Okay, and what about Hannah Roy? Were you sleeping with her?"

"I wish," Daniel laughed, which made Heather's stomach lurch. "But no. I was merely an observer of her life. She started jogging in this area a month or two ago. At first, I thought that she was you, which I suppose was half of the appeal."

"And the other half?"

"The other half was that I didn't know her. I'd never heard her speak. So I could project all of my fantasies onto her. Most of them are non-murderous, I should add. I pictured her cooking in my kitchen. I imagined making love to her in the shower. In my mind, she was perfect."

"A trophy," Heather acknowledged with disgust.

"Yes. Exactly. A trophy. I started following her a few weeks ago, and when I saw her head toward the park, I saw an opportunity."

"And I suppose Brittany was just in the wrong place at the wrong time."

"With all the right information," Daniel finished. "I found her in the closet, brought her downstairs, and I was kind at first. I said I wouldn't call the cops if she told me who she was and what she wanted. As it turned out, she knew too much. I couldn't let her leave. Not if I wanted my freedom back. I knew if she exposed me, I'd never be able to kill again. Of course, I acted rashly. I didn't realize she was bright enough to schedule a podcast. I should've simply let her go and laughed off the claims in court. My instincts, unfortunately, are not as bright as I am. It didn't help that she looked so much like my first girlfriend."

"Two for one," Heather replied grimly.

"I suppose you could say that," he mused.

"Is that everything?"

"Yes."

"Then, for the recording's sake, will you state your crimes?"

"I, Daniel Palmer, born October 20th, 1985, killed, of my own volition, and of sane mind, Katy Graham, Hannah Roy, and Brittany Hart. I also attempted to murder Veronica Lane, my first girlfriend."

"Thank you," Heather said, the words burning her tongue like acid. She reached and pressed stop on the recorder.

"I suppose this is goodbye," Daniel said, finishing his glass.

Heather did the same and stood. "It is."

"Well, then. Goodbye, Heather."

"Goodbye, Daniel. Good luck surviving prison."

CHAPTER FORTY

THE DETECTIVE

"ARE YOU OKAY?" THE TEXT ASKED HEATHER, lighting up on her phone screen in the dark, curtain-drawn room. Heather groaned and pulled the blanket over her head, causing Turkey, one of her three dogs, to grumble as she adjusted his position.

She didn't even check to see who was asking. She'd spoken to everyone that she was close to already that day, and the day before, and the day before that. Julius always checked in when she first woke up—he knew her schedule thanks to their brief cohabitation in London–and Gabriel followed up shortly after he had breakfast. Then came her parents, Gene, Karen, and

Tina around lunchtime. It was now after 4 pm, which only left the rubberneckers. The co-workers she wasn't close to. The type of people who pretend to be close to someone when they died for attention.

Perhaps that was unfair, but it was how she felt. They'd never texted or emailed before now. They'd never hung out. Thus, their kindnesses felt ingenuine. Or she considered that this was simply such an extreme situation that they had been moved to reach out. Still, that didn't mean that she had to respond.

She was very much enjoying not thinking about Daniel, his upcoming trial, the media frenzy, and the journalists who kept turning up on her porch. She was also enjoying cuddling with her dogs, binging crappy reality TV, cold beer, long baths, take-out food, and sleeping. Mercifully, her dreams were mostly dark and quiet, allowing her some peace in unconsciousness.

Her phone began to ring. She cursed and threw the blankets off, sending an empty can tinkling to the floor in the process. That felt like a bad sign, she thought. A sign that the cycle had come full circle. Except this time, she had no desire to pick herself back up. At least, not until her vacation time ran out. Fortunately, that was another three weeks away. She wasn't even sure if she'd go back to work when it was over, though that was a bridge she'd consider crossing when it was less hazy on the horizon.

She had enough savings to live on for a while, and then maybe she'd apply to work at the grocery store or one of the many cafes popping up. Something mundane and peaceful sounded good, and she did love coffee. Sherwood's was also always hiring busboys.

The phone continued to ring, and she reached for it, pressed answer, and put it on speakerphone. "What?" she asked, angrier than expected or intended.

"Hello. Is this Heather Bishop?"

"It is."

"Good. This is Dr. Plemmons. I'm a colleague of Dr. Julius Tocci."

Heather sat bolt upright. "Is he alright?"

"He's fine. He suggested I reach out to you. I'm a therapist. I work with the police force in this county."

"Uh-huh," Heather replied, cursing Julius under her breath. Is now a good time?"

"I guess," Heather grumbled, wiping sleep from her eyes. Despite being annoyed, Heather had good things about Dr. Plemmons from Gabriel. He'd had a few sessions with her since his original therapist retired.

"Great. I appreciate it. I've heard about what's happened and wondered if you'd be interested in an online session so that you can begin to process what's happened. At no cost to you, of course."

Heather sighed and looked at her three dogs' alert, sappy expressions. She looked at the beer cans on the floor and on the table. She looked at her reflection on the open laptop screen. She didn't want to do this again. This misery business. This abject wallowing.

"Yeah. Why not?" she asked. "When are you next available?"

"Well, I have some time right now if you're open to it."

Heather appreciated the offer. It was better now than never, and she knew if she didn't do it now, then it would be never. So she said, "Sure. Send me a link, and I'll be with you in ten."

"Excellent. See you soon."

—

Heather attempted to make both herself and her living space look presentable and swapped to coffee as she pressed the link. However, when she saw her reflection staring back at her in HD, she knew she hadn't done enough. Her hair was a bird's nest, the house was cluttered, and a half-drunk bottle of bourbon was on the console in the background. She shrugged. She supposed there was no point in lying to a therapist about being put together. If they were worth their salt, they'd see through it anyway.

The screen flickered, a ding sounded, and a woman appeared on screen, banishing Heather to a small box in the corner. The woman smiled and looked precisely how Heather had expected her to look. She had short blonde but graying hair that looked airy, fluffed up with hairspray as if she was about to have her glamour shots done at the mall. She wore minimal makeup and had perfect skin with naturally blushed cheeks. She was all at once a beauty and stereotypical grandma. Heather supposed the two need not be mutually exclusive.

"Hi," Heather said, her voice surprisingly hoarse from lack of use.

"Hello, Heather, how are you feeling today?"

"Tired," Heather answered honestly. "Really, really tired."

"That seems understandable considering everything you've been through."

"Yeah," Heather replied, unsure how to respond and feeling like the driest conversationalist ever.

"Would you like to talk about the events at the start of the week?"

"I don't know," Heather said, voice cracking. "Sorry," she hastily apologized as tears sprung forth.

"There's no need to apologize. This is a safe space."

The phrasing was cliche, like that of every therapist in every movie, but Heather still felt comforted by the woman's velvety voice. "I don't think I want to talk about it yet," she added, throat tight.

"Okay. Is there something you'd rather talk about?"

"I just... I feel like I made all this progress since the divorce and the Paper Doll case, and he's taken me back to the start."

"How so?"

"Well, I was an alcoholic, I think. Bordering on it anyway. Situational drunk, whatever you want to call it. But then I started getting myself together a couple years back. I made friends, started exercising, learned how to cook, and recently—" She stopped herself, choking up too much to continue. She took a few deep breaths, and Dr. Plemmons waited patiently. "And recently, I found myself opening back up to the concept of love. As in, I fell in love."

It was the first time she admitted this out loud, but it sounded and felt right. She did love Julius. She wanted him. Wanted to be with him. Wanted what she'd had in her marriage but better and more. She knew he could give it to her, too.

"That's wonderful, Heather," Dr. Plemmons replied.

"Yeah, but I don't know now."

"Don't know about what?"

"I don't know if I can be with him after finding out that my ex-husband was a murderer."

"Do you think that love makes you blind?"

"Apparently, it does," Heather stated, clenching her fists.

"Do you think the person that you're in love with could also be a monster?"

Heather shook her head. "No. Never. Not Julius."

"But you're still concerned about your judgment? Or perhaps being hurt again?"

Heather nodded, wiping her eyes with her pajama sleeve. "Yeah," she croaked. "Or that I'm too much of a mess for him now."

"Do you think that fear is rational, or is that the trauma and grief speaking?"

"I don't know. Irrational, I guess," Heather murmured, thinking of how it felt when Julius had told her that he loved her and the sincerity in his voice.

"Okay. And what do you think you could do to convince yourself of that? Or what could he do?"

"He's done enough," Heather confirmed. "I don't know. I think I need closure."

"And you don't think you've gotten it yet?"

Heather thought hard, trying to understand her own body and how it twisted and tightened. "With Daniel, yes," she found herself saying.

"Okay. Then, where are you lacking the closure you need to move on from this painful chapter in your life? It seems to me that you want to start anew rather than fall into old habits. So what needs to happen for you to have a rebirth, so to speak? What hurdles are in your way?"

"Well, I need to open up," Heather said. "Which I guess I'm already doing."

Dr. Plemmons nodded sagely. "You are."

"And I need to let go of the Paper Doll Case."

"Yes, Peter Anderson," Dr Plemmons replied sagely. "You're not the only officer I've spoken to about him, but you are the closest to the case."

"And what did you advise for them?"

"To speak with him in prison. To see what he's become. I think that the more we avoid our fears and pretend they're not there, the scarier they become. Monsters are not easily suppressed. They tend to become tumorous when ignored."

Heather understood. There was a place in her brain dedicated to that case, and if she visualized it, she imagined it to be cancerous, throbbing, and overgrown. It tickled her skull all the time and pressed against it if she didn't do enough to distract herself or dull the pain.

"Okay," she said, weirdly onboard. "I'll try anything. Anything that will put me back on track and allow me to leave all of this behind."

"And do you think you'll stay in Glenville? Once you have closure?"

Heather furrowed her brow. "Why are you asking me that? I mean, surely, if I left, I'd just be starting the cycle all over again."

"Well, sometimes places, people, jobs can help us heal, but it doesn't need to be the rest of your life. There's nothing wrong with a fresh start, so long as you've actually left the baggage behind."

"I don't know," Heather said, not sure what she was replying to. All of it, she supposed. She just didn't know. Not yet.

"Would you like to continue speaking?"

Heather nodded, bringing her coffee to her lips and trying to organize her thoughts in order to continue the session. It was hard to know where to start or end, but Dr. Plemmons guided her accordingly, and once she got going, she couldn't stop. And when she reached the end, she was teary, exhausted, but also determined. It was time to meet her bogeyman.

CHAPTER FORTY-ONE

THE DETECTIVE

TYPICALLY, POLICE OFFICERS CANNOT AND DO NOT visit criminals that they have arrested, especially if said criminal is being housed in a maximum-security prison. Heather didn't know all the ins and outs regarding the world of prisons and had rarely stepped foot inside a lockup bigger than that of the county jail, but she imagined cops rarely visited for the same reason she never had. They never wanted to see these monsters again, and there were very few inmates who wished to speak to the person who had put them there.

Surprisingly, the same could not be said for Peter Anderson, and shortly after receiving Heather's letter, he had her listed on his approved visitor's list as a friend. This in and of itself made her stomach churn. She had been holding out hope that he'd deny her visitation so that she'd have an excuse not to go, but it soon became apparent that there was no backing out now that the ball was rolling.

So, now she was here, surrounded by guards, waiting for the thick metal door to buzz, dressed in a gray casual suit that made her look less Clarice and more librarian. This was on purpose, and considering the terrifying men she had just walked past, she knew that her decision to deter attention had been a wise one. She was also wearing her hair in a low ponytail—something that always made her feel decidedly like a young colonial man rather than a chic woman—and fake glasses from a Halloween party for the same reason. It hadn't worked entirely, but a reduction in leering was better than nothing.

The door buzzed loudly, making her jump and issuing concerned glances from the guard. She had gone from sleeping all day to sleeping very little in the run-up to this visit, and it was making her twitchy. The three coffees she'd quickly downed this morning probably weren't helping. Her heart was thrumming in her throat.

The guard opened the door and surveyed her with what seemed to be suspicion. He must've known who she was and was as confused as almost everyone else about why she wanted to do this. "No touching," he said sternly.

"Wasn't planning on it," Heather retorted and stepped into the room.

It was stark, concrete, with only one barred window set into the right-side wall. Peter Anderson was sitting at a small plastic table, facing it, his expression vacant, his head swaying side to side. He didn't even look at Heather as she approached and didn't seem to notice her presence until she pulled up a chair, dragging it along the ground with a horrible sound, and sat opposite him.

"Ah!" he gasped, moving his hand to his chest.

Heather felt the exact same way. Not because the man before her was frightening but because he was not. Peter Anderson had never been a particularly terrifying figure, at least not to look at. He'd been small, dowdy, with receding brown hair and a penchant for handmade sweaters. He'd worn coke-bottle glasses, was an adult thumb sucker, and his attempts at growing a mustache were pathetic at best. He wasn't a wild animal like Dennis Burke, a charismatic terrorist like Clarence Dixon Jr., or intelligent like Victor Wu. He was and had always been pathetic. Yet there had been menace there, like that of a rabid rat.

What sat before Heather was more than pathetic. He was a husk. His hair was shock white, his form skeletal, and his eyes seemed to stare right through her. He blinked rapidly and smeared fingerprints around his lenses, creating a blurry sheen that couldn't have made it any easier to see. Not that it really mattered; he was obviously bordering on blindness.

He giggled like a schoolgirl, and Heather scowled. "What's so funny?"

"The ghosts are talking about you," he explained, then he matched her unamused expression. "Be polite!"

"I am."

"Not you," he tutted. "They don't like police officers."

"No, I imagine they don't. How do you feel about me?"

"I like you. I'm indebted to you."

"How do you figure?" Heather asked, glancing at the guard, who looked as disgusted as she felt.

"You sent me here. You set me free. Without you, I would've never found Him."

"Who's him?"

"God. Jesus Christ."

"Of course," Heather muttered. "You know, I'm surprised God is interested in a man like you."

"God forgives all if you're sorry enough."

Heather narrowed her eyes. "And are you sorry? For killing those little girls? For ruining their families' lives? For ruining my life?"

Peter didn't reply, and he looked as if he didn't understand or lacked the vocabulary in his feeble state to say what he felt.

Heather sighed. "Why did you invite me here?"

"Because I want us to forgive each other. I want you to absolve me."

Heather almost laughed. "You're looking for a priest. Not a cop."

"Please," Peter said, suddenly launching his veiny hands across the table.

"No touching," the guard warned loudly.

Peter retracted into himself. "Please," he stated again. "You're the only one that can. So that I can go to heaven."

"You don't deserve to go to Heaven," Heather said. "And if I know God, I know that he would never let you in."

"You're wrong," Peter said, though he didn't sound convinced.

"I'm not. I don't know much about the afterlife, but I know you're going to suffer."

"I've suffered enough."

Heather barked a laugh. "There is no suffering great enough for your sins."

Peter looked wounded and toyed with his thin lips with the tip of his thumb. He was heartbroken, dumbfounded. For whatever reason, he thought this was going to go differently. No wonder he made that awful documentary. He must've thought he could make people sympathize with him. He could suck his thumb all he wanted, but it didn't make him a doe-eyed baby.

Look at you, Heather thought. *The bogeyman. The Paper Doll Killer. The world-famous monster. Now you're nothing but a mummy, turning into dust before my eyes. There's nothing left. You have no power. You have no power over me.*

She thought about her list of questions and realized she wasn't interested in his answers because he wasn't interesting. He was a scourge. A disease. A tumor on society. And he had been quashed and cut out. The damage had been done, but there was no more coming. He was as weak as a kitten, and he would die in his cell, alone and unloved.

He had brought her here to talk, and she had no interest in giving him what he wanted.

She stood, and he reached out again. "Wait," he begged. "I'll tell you everything. Then maybe you'll understand."

"You can't make me understand, and you can't make me stay. You have no power over me." It felt so good to say those words, and she repeated them over and over in her head, drowning out his whimpering and begging.

"Please," he whimpered one last time, his loneliness palpable.

"Goodbye, Peter. We will never meet again. Not here, nor in God's Kingdom."

She walked away, and his protests faded into white noise as she walked through the doorway. The Paper Doll Killer was dead; soon enough, his corpse would be too.

In the parking lot, Heather stood momentarily in the misting rain and looked back at the imposing red brick building. It was nothing more than a mass grave for the world's most rotten, but she knew it was far from at capacity. There were cells available, and she intended to fill them. Just not in the way she had been.

She wanted justice for the long dead, the forgotten. She wanted to put away those who'd been able to live their lives unabated, just as Peter Anderson had. He had run a post office and been loved by his community all the while children suffered in his basement, just as Daniel had drunk champagne with corpses below their feet. She thought about how many monsters had been living out their dream lives for twenty or thirty years, thinking they'd never be caught because the cops gave up so long ago. The idea of shattering their paradises motivated her, thrilled her. She wanted to heat up all the cold cases and knew who she had to call to do so.

She pulled her phone out of her pocket and climbed into her car, a triumphant smile on her face. She scrolled through her contacts, clicked Tina's name, and pressed call.

"Hi, Heather. Are you okay?" Tina asked, knowing exactly where Heather had been this morning.

"I'm good. Great, actually," Heather said, surprised at her own enthusiasm.

Tina hesitated. "I don't—"

"Do you have a minute?"

"I, um, yeah. I have a minute."

"Great. I need to talk to you about a promotion."

CHAPTER FORTY-TWO

THE PARTNER

GABRIEL, BEAU, AND BETTY WERE SITTING IN THEIR usual Sherwood's booth waiting for Heather. She'd called yesterday after her meeting with famous child murderer Peter Anderson, otherwise known as the Paper Doll Killer and the man who'd temporarily ruined Heather's life. Despite this, Heather seemed to be in good spirits over the phone and begged Gabriel for a get-together after she 'ironed a few things out,' whatever that meant. She was borderline hyperactive and uncharacteristically rambling. Whatever was happening, it was clearly very exciting.

Except Gabriel didn't feel excited. Quite the opposite, in fact. He felt exhausted, drained, and numb. He rested his head on Betty's perfumed shoulder and could barely drum up the energy to reach for the pitcher to top up his beer. He hadn't been drinking much this past week anyway; there'd been too much going on to risk being hungover or out of sorts.

To start with, there had, of course, been the paperwork. So much paperwork. He'd been the one to find the bodies after all, and considering one was from his neck of the woods, and one was from Seattle, he was doing twice as much as usual. Not that he minded. He went above and beyond on those reports. Paperwork was never fun, but at least he was alive, and he had no intention of being ungrateful for that fact. How insensitive would it be to complain about doing one's job at a time like this? So, instead, he tried to love his job the best he could and tried his hardest every minute of every day. He didn't even mind picking up Heather's slack. It felt good to help a friend who had guided him into being the cop he was today.

He was trying his hardest in his personal life, too; his relationship had never been stronger, and he'd recently hosted a dinner for Betty and his parents that he had cooked so that they could all relax. His fajitas garnered some criticism, but his interpersonal relationships had never been stronger, and he had a feeling that he and Betty would be living together before the end of the year.

He had also been on television several times, talking to journalists and giving statements, not only on the events that had unfolded but on who the three victims were. They were women. They were loved. They were important. All of them were daughters, all of them were sisters, and one of them was a wife and mother. They gave to charity, they worked hard, and Brittany Hart had done what everyone else had failed to do—solve the murder of Katy Graham.

Thus, the KHB Foundation was formed with the help of Brittany's parents, Hannah's husband, and Katy's sister. The foundation's intention was to raise money to help women escape abusive situations, provide funding to those who assisted abused women pro-bono, and raise awareness of cold cases and murder cases to help seek justice for those who needed it.

There was a Crime Time Helpline, which was set up for arm-chair investigators to give information and for those who felt they were in danger to seek immediate help or counseling. It was only the early days, but Gabriel already felt this might be the most significant achievement of his life thus far. He only wished that it didn't have to exist and hadn't been born out of such violence.

This is where the exhaustion had crept in. He was doing well. He was motivated, staying strong, and not letting the guilt hold him back. Should painful thoughts arise, he went to the gym or surrounded himself with loved ones instead of hitting the beers. This, of course, as well as everything else, didn't allow for much downtime, and though he was proud of himself, he was running on empty.

"Hey! Heather!" Beau called out, causing Gabriel to start. He hadn't realized he'd temporarily fallen asleep and straightened before looking at Betty apologetically with a bleary expression.

"You've got a little..." she said, tapping the corner of her mouth and giggling.

Gabriel laughed as he wiped away the drool with the back of his hand and looked at Heather as she unwound her thick scarf.

"Hi," she said breathlessly, smiling at everyone as she sat down and reached for a glass.

"Long time no see," Beau added.

Heather nodded. "Yeah. Too long. Feels like years."

"Somebody told me it was still February this morning, and I nearly screamed," Gabriel joked with a yawn.

"Jesus," Heather said. "How is that possible? London feels like months ago."

"I think I've aged half a decade."

"Well, no offense, but you do look exhausted," Heather said.

"Thanks," Gabriel replied dryly, finally summoning the energy to pour a beer.

"Seriously. When did you last sleep?"

"I don't know, not last night. Maybe the one before."

"Seriously?" Betty asked, looking at him with concern.

He waved her off. "What about you? You're looking fresh."

"I had the best sleep I've had in years last night," Heather admitted. "Full nine hours uninterrupted."

She was glowing, and her hair was particularly silken and shining, and her somewhat signature eye bags were nowhere to be seen.

"What's your secret?" he asked.

"Weirdly, Peter Anderson. Seeing him in the flesh, as he is now, this withered, senile husk... I don't know. It made me feel like he had no power over me. It was like the Paper Doll Killer was dead, and all that was left behind was this mummified Peter Anderson. I used to dream about him all the time, but last night, it was like he had vacated my brain. I couldn't have thought about him even if I tried. It felt like someone had cut a tumor out."

"That's great," Gabriel said, beaming. "Seriously."

"So, how are you doing?" she inquired, peering over the top of the rim.

"I'm good," Gabriel replied quickly, surprising himself. "Or, at least, I think good. I've definitely been doing good things, but I haven't been giving myself a lot of thought."

"Maybe you should take a couple of days," Heather suggested.

"I'd just end up wallowing, and I hate wallowing."

"That makes one of us," Heather laughed.

Gabriel shook his head. "It's eating me up too. I think I just cope by being proactive."

Heather smiled at him. "Which is why you're so good at this job."

"Not as good as you."

"I'm a good detective," Heather reasoned. "And if the article is anything to go off of, a decent writer. But the rest of it? Not so much."

"Don't be modest," Beau said, elbowing Heather in the side, and others nodded in agreement.

"I'm really not," Heather stated as if it were a fact, and it didn't seem as if she was putting herself down or being self-deprecating. "I am great at puzzles. I care about justice. But if I saw another brutalized body in the flesh, it would be too soon. I'm good at my job, but I'm not good at coping at it."

"Maybe it'll be different now that you've had closure on Daniel and Peter Anderson," Gabriel suggested.

"It's definitely going to be different because I handed in my notice today."

Jaws dropped, and it felt as if the whole room went quiet. Gabriel's heart was pounding. He couldn't believe what he was hearing. Eventually, he managed to choke out, "You quit?"

"I did."

"You can't—" he began and then shook his head, frustrated. "You can't quit. Heather, come on. We need a detective."

"You have one," Heather replied, her eyes sparkling.

Gabriel looked at her blankly, and after a lot of staring and some smirking on her part, the penny finally dropped. "Are you serious?"

"Congratulations, Detective Silva," Heather said, raising her glass.

"No way. You're not serious."

"Deadly. Now, don't leave me hanging."

Everyone raised their glasses and clinked, but nobody cheered. It was as if they couldn't tell if she was joking, but it was becoming increasingly evident to Gabriel that she was not.

"Wait, Gabriel is the new detective?" Betty asked, blinking slowly, her drink hovering around her lips.

"He is," Heather confirmed. "I spoke to Tina yesterday. I told her you've more than earned that promotion and that she'll need someone to replace me."

"Big boots to fill," Gabriel chuckled, awe-struck and still in disbelief.

"Damn right," Heather teased. "But I think you'll manage just fine."

"So what are you going to do?" Betty asked. "We have an open spot at Dottie's if you're looking."

"I actually already have a new gig," Heather said coyly. "I said yes to the cold case position in London."

Beau quickly began to protest, and though Gabriel felt his heart plunge to the pits of his insides, he held up his hand to silence his friend. "Congratulations," he said earnestly, putting his feelings aside. "Seriously. You're going to be amazing. You're a city person. You want to solve murders, not micromanage a small town. I get it. This was the right call. I can tell just by looking at you."

"Thank you," Heather replied softly, a slight sadness taking hold in her features for the first time. "I'm really going to miss Glenville, though."

Maybe it was the exhaustion, but a knot was forming in Gabriel's throat, and he focused on his beer to keep the emotions at bay. "When do you leave?" he inquired, trying to be nonchalant as if this was no big deal. As if he wasn't a detective and his best friend wasn't traveling halfway across the world.

"I'm not exactly sure. I need to talk to Julius first."

Gabriel looked up and saw that she was turning red. "You haven't told him yet?"

She shook her head. "I don't want to ruin what's going on between us by taking off to another country. I don't think he's the long-distance type. I guess I'm just hoping that he'll want to come with me."

"He will," Gabriel confirmed. "I've seen the way he looks at you."

Heather combed her long hair through her fingers and nodded. "Well, I guess I'll see tomorrow. Another round, anyone?"

The group replied affirmatively, and as Heather bounced to the bar, followed by Beau the puppy-dog, Gabriel turned to Betty and realized that he was trembling. "That was a lot," he exhaled.

"Yeah, it was," Betty confirmed, her cheeks pink and her smile wide. "Congratulations. You're going to be great. And hey, this brings you one step closer to the FBI."

Gabriel frowned. There was something wrong about what she'd just said, and it took him a moment to figure out what.

"What is it? What's wrong?" Betty asked, reaching out and placing a dainty hand on his shoulder.

"I don't know. Agent Silva has a pretty good ring to it, but I think I like Sherriff Silva even better."

Betty beamed at him, understanding the implication. Glenville was their home. They loved it. And they were going to stay.

CHAPTER FORTY-THREE

THE DETECTIVE

AFTER PACING AROUND IN CIRCLES, HEATHER knocked on the penthouse apartment door, and Julius opened it immediately. He didn't look as surprised as she'd anticipated, and she wondered if he'd been watching her lap the lobby through the peephole. She flushed crimson at the thought and forgot how to speak in her embarrassment.

"Heather," Julius said fondly, adjusting the tie on his pajama pants. She realized she must've interrupted his pants-less TV time and felt simultaneously guilty and amused. Fortunately, he was clearly not annoyed by the intrusion, and his eyes sparkled behind his spectacles. "Sorry, I must've gotten my dates mixed up. I thought we were meeting in Glenville on Sunday? You were going to show me some of the hiking trails. Did I miss a text?" He pulled his phone out, convinced that this was somehow his fault.

Heather shook her head and shut the door behind her. "No, no. You didn't miss anything, and we're still on for Sunday. I just couldn't wait any longer to see you." She flushed. "That sounded less intense in my head. Sorry, I was just feeling antsy, and I like driving when I feel antsy, and I just kind of... drove to Seattle. Then I figured I might as well drop in while I'm here. Do you mind?"

"Of course not," he insisted, turning toward the kitchen counter where a half-drunk glass of wine awaited him.

Heather followed him in and shut the door behind him. "What were you doing before I showed up?" she asked. "I hope I'm not interrupting anything."

"No, no, of course not. I was just winding down for the night and considering watching a movie. Are you staying? Would you like a drink?"

Their energies were equally frenetic, their tongues and lips moving fast, and seemingly, upon realizing this, they both laughed. "Sorry," Heather said. "I think my nerves are catching."

"Why are you nervous?" he asked.

"I—" Heather started. "I don't know; I'm just in one of those manic moods, I guess. Let's have a drink," she suggested and sat down on a modernist black stool at the marble-topped, vast kitchen island.

Julius nodded and poured her a glass from the bottle next to the fruit bowl before topping up his own. He was too quick, and she was too distracted by the jitterbugs inside her stomach to protest. Then it was too late, and for whatever reason, instead of asking for something else, she took a sip.

As the taste spread across her tongue, she was transported to the sunroom with Daniel. For a second, she was filled with hate and almost toppled her glass in panic as the flashback took hold. Then Julius turned sharply, his face full of worry, and she stared back at him and remembered the grounding technique she liked to use, starting with five things you could see. She could see his chocolate-colored eyes, majestic dark beard, salt and pepper curls, honey-toned skin, and muscular arms. She could feel her heart beating, the coolness of the marble, her jeans digging in as she bent forward, and the air conditioner's breeze. She could hear him calling out to her, the distant rumble of a washing machine, and her heart in her chest. She could smell his skin and his cologne. She could taste the wine, and it was delicious. All of the horror evaporated, and she puddled on the counter, realizing that everyone who'd said so was right: love was stronger than hate.

"Heather. Are you alright?" Julius asked for what must've been the fourth time, considering his urgency.

"Yeah. *Yeah.* I'm okay. I'm good, actually. Sorry," she said for what felt like the millionth time and took another sip. It didn't taste like the sunroom anymore. It tasted like this moment. It tasted like right here, right now, with Julius, where she was safe, warm, and loved. She would always hate Daniel, but he wasn't here and never would be. They'd said their goodbyes, and there would never be another hello. He'd ruined enough of the past. It would be a shame to let him ruin the future.

Julius moved up a few seats and sat on the opposite side of the island's corner so that they were facing each other but still close enough to touch. "I know you said you were in the neighborhood, but I have a feeling you're here for a reason," he murmured. "Something that you need to say."

"Okay, so," Heather began, her chest tight. Then, something caught her eye and stopped her in her tracks. There were cardboard boxes piled up in the corner of the room next to an empty bookshelf. She looked at Julius sharply, confused. "Are you moving?"

Julius followed her gaze and dropped his head in dismay. He sighed. "This is why I wanted to meet in Glenville. I didn't want you to find out like this. I wanted to tell you, not surprise you."

"So you are moving? Did you get a new job?" she asked, panicking as if she wasn't here to tell him the very same thing.

"Yes, and sort of. It's actually a very old job if you think about it." He sighed again and removed his glasses to rub his eyes. "I'm taking Jonno up on his offer to open a practice together. I just... I miss London. I didn't realize how much until our visit. I know that it'll be hard... Heather?"

Heather had lowered her head, turning red, tears springing to her eyes, and weird noises emanating from her drawn mouth. Julius quickly extended a hand to her and grabbed her wrist.

"Oh, Heather. I'm so sorry. I know you're struggling right now, and this is terrible timing—"

Heather looked up, not crying but laughing. A guffaw exploded from her mouth, and she clapped a hand to cover her noisy maw. Julius looked as if he'd been slapped or electrocuted. Pure shock coated his face.

"What is it?" he asked.

"I can't... This is so crazy," Heather wheezed. "I came here to tell you that I'm moving to London. I took Helen up on her offer."

Julius's mouth fell open. "Are you serious?"

Heather nodded, hands covering her mouth.

"That's great news! This is—" He stood abruptly, not knowing what to do with himself. "We need champagne or something."

Heather laughed and reached out for him. Once her fingers found fabric, she pulled him back into his seat. "The wine's fine. Great even. Let's just keep talking."

"Okay. God. I've been dreading telling you this," he said, the very definition of relief. "I thought it would ruin everything, but at the same time, I need a fresh start. I love this place, but my ex-wife lived here too. I still see her around town. And the forensic center has ... Well, let's say there's no love lost there. Of course, I'll miss my students and some co-workers, but with Mum going so quickly downhill... She has six weeks left, so the doctors tell me."

"I'm so sorry. And I understand needing a fresh start."

"I didn't want to go without you," he replied. "It almost stopped me."

Heather sipped her drink thoughtfully. "I'm glad it didn't. Don't get me wrong, if I was staying behind and you left, I'd be heartbroken. But I'd rather be heartbroken than hold you back from your dreams. You prioritized you, and honestly, I think that's pretty damn sexy."

Julius laughed. "Oh, really?"

"Really," Heather confirmed.

The atmosphere in the room changed, silence descended, and Heather's heart beat so loudly she was surprised he couldn't hear it. Both of them put their glasses down. Both of them remained still. Both of them failed to meet each other's eyes until Julius reached out and tucked a strand of hair behind Heather's ear.

"May I—"

Heather answered his interrupted question by swooping in, lips parted, eyes closed, her hand on his jaw. He gasped as he parted his lips, allowing tongues to greet each other as she stood, tilting his face upward and deepening the kiss. It was soft, wet, warm. He tasted like wine and mint. When he placed his hands on her waist, she felt heat spread across her body, and fireworks exploded in her chest.

She didn't want to, but she pulled away, and he let go, allowing her to topple backward onto her stool. She looked at his flushed face, and he looked at hers, both of their hair ruffled from exploratory hands. He adjusted his crooked glasses and reached for his glass shakily, looking both sheepish and naughty all at once.

"So, will you be joining me at Farfalla House?"

"Helen has set me up with a 'flat,'" Heather replied coyly. "But if you play your cards right, who knows? I think I'd enjoy being courted."

"Why don't we start right now?" Julius asked with a smirk. "I have some salmon that needs eating. What do you say to dinner and a movie? Perhaps some stargazing on the balcony later?"

"I could get down with that."

"So you're staying?"

Heather reached for the bottle and topped up her glass. "Whoops. Looks like I'll have to."

Julius shook his head and chuckled as he stood. He kissed the top of her head before moving toward the fridge and seemed unwilling to physically part. "This is going to be fun," he said, amused. "Dating."

"Do you feel young again?" Heather asked, spinning on her stool.

Julius paused as he opened the door, then he looked at her. "No. And that's definitely a good thing. I couldn't kiss like that or cook like this when I was young."

Heather thought about it. "Yeah. I feel giddy. But not young. Refreshed but ancient."

"Tired but wise."

"Creaky but happy."

"Yeah. Happy sounds right."

CHAPTER FORTY-FOUR

THE DETECTIVE

THE PARTY WAS ALREADY IN FULL SWING WHEN Heather and Julius arrived, hand in hand. Despite the party being for Heather and it being her last night in Glenville, very few people noticed her arrival. They were too busy having a good time. Everyone was overjoyed Spring had arrived, that it was warm and dry, and that it was the weekend. They were also clearly quite drunk, and a fair few were pushing the boundaries of the word 'quite'.

Heather had never seen this larger part of the Silva's backyard, but it was perfect for a warm evening gathering with its rainbow string lights, large outdoor setting, firepit, and pizza oven. The food smelled amazing, and seeing what filled the large bowls and plates, she knew her nose did not deceive her.

She had once again brought along her old reliable and now signature potato salad, as it had been a hit at Christmas, and she placed it next to a bowl of spicy chicken wings and sweet potato fries. Her mouth began to water, and though she'd had a late lunch and had told herself she'd hold off from eating more for at least another hour, she couldn't resist and grabbed a couple of fries before grabbing a plastic cup. She then moved like a moth to a flame toward the enormous, colorful cocktail dispensers and poured herself something blue that smelled of lemons and limes.

As she turned back to the party, those who were dancing, bustling around, or eating finally noticed her arrival and erupted into excitement, rushing forward for hellos or pulling strings on party poppers. Betty ran forward, holding two inflatable crowns, one embedded with 2D gems, and crowned the couple before hugging them. Then it was Luisa's turn for a hug, then Martin's, Gene's, Karen's, Beau's, and even Tina's. Finally, it was Gabriel's turn, and they embraced each other like old friends, reunited after decades. It felt like more of a goodbye than a hello, and considering the knot in her throat, Heather supposed that it was.

"This is amazing," she said, pulling back and gesturing around. "Seriously, thank you so much." She tried to continue her thanks but was shushed, hushed, and brushed off affectionately.

"Please eat! Drink!" Luisa yelled over the hubbub. "Then we dance!" She was quite clearly tipsy, and though Heather knew she could not risk being over full, over inebriated, or overtired because of her early morning flight, she planned to indulge to her limitations. It was the polite thing to do.

She loaded up her plate with various goodies, and Julius did the same, clearly very excited about the buffet that lay before them. Then they joined some of the others at the table, dug into their dinners, and blended seamlessly into the already rolling conversation. They laughed and licked their plates clean, and Heather looked around as the conversation was ceased by full mouths. Almost everyone she knew was here. Foster Ellsworth.

Missy Higgins. Lisa Simmons. Even Nancy Ellis, who had probably not been to a party this loud in decades, had made an appearance.

Heather tried not to cry, and she succeeded. There was too much joy for that. And she'd be back soon, during every holiday and whenever she felt like it. This was a goodbye, but at least it wasn't forever.

"Who's your handsome friend?" Karen Wells asked, her henna-dyed hair wrapped up in a scarf and her bangles jingling as she ate.

Heather looked at Julius, who was engaged in some sort of debate with Beau and Gabriel about vintage cars, and said, "This is my boyfriend, Dr. Julius Tocci."

Julius must've heard her over the rabble because he turned sharply, wide-eyed, before softening into happiness. He reached out a hand to introduce himself to Karen and Gene, both of them looking as overjoyed as a grandparent might upon hearing their granddaughter was dating again—and a doctor, no less.

"What kind of doctor are you?" Karen asked as Julius retracted and put an arm around Heather.

He hesitated. His job—cutting open dead people—was sometimes off-putting to people, so Heather spoke for him. "He's a forensic pathologist. Best in the state."

Gene's eyes widened. Heather knew he recognized the name from their first argument, in which he'd insisted on using his rather inept forensic pathologist for the case. "Nice to meet you," he said. "I've heard nothing but good things."

"Same for you," Julius replied, though it was partly a lie.

"A forensic pathologist," Karen began before erupting into quick-fire questions, which turned into a rather inappropriate dinner discussion about etymology. Luckily, nobody seemed to mind, and Heather left him to talk while she made the rounds. Though she didn't do so for long, as she knew that in the morning, she'd be saying goodbye to him too. It wouldn't be for long, not with his mother's health in such a steep decline.

She felt awful leaving him, despite his insistence that she head over and get started without him. He said he'd grieved his mother's death long ago, but Heather knew it was going to hit him like a train regardless. Of course, she planned to fly back over for the funeral, after which he would fly back with her, and then they would begin their new life together in London. She just wished her happily ever after didn't hinge on the demise of an elderly woman, but nothing could be perfect, and at least she'd finally be at peace.

She'd miss him too. They'd spent almost every day together these past weeks, but at least she had Poppy and Liam to hang out with and show her around. She'd also found herself coming around a lot to Helen during their correspondence, Especially upon finding out that she was now married to a woman, that her and Julius's relationship had been nothing more than a fling, and that he'd been the one to dump her.

Heather sat back down at the exact moment as Julius jumped to his feet. He held out a hand and pulled her upright despite her protests. "How about a dance?" he asked, waggling his brows.

Heather shoved him playfully and nodded. "Whatever I have to do to stop you doing that with your face."

"Oh, expect a lot more of this face."

"Jesus."

She refilled her cup with more blue, and they moved onto the freshly mown grass dance floor. Julius spun her and danced like an embarrassing dad, unleashing a side of himself rarely seen. He'd nearly gotten to this level at Christmas, but there were still reservations, but now, he wasn't holding back, not at dancing, not at being himself, and not at showering her in affection. Now she'd given him the okay; the love was incessant, and despite always considering herself prickly and unaffectionate, she loved every second of it.

After three songs, she was nearly done, and catching sight of Gabriel—who was watching her and Julius with a sappy expression—she thought there was no one she'd rather have her last dance with. She parted from Julius with a kiss and a whisper and ran up to her best friend, both arms extended and fingers wiggling.

"May I have this dance?" she asked, glancing back at Julius, who had already taken to boogieing with Beau and Betty.

Gabriel groaned, grabbed her hands, and was pulled to her feet with a groan. "Yeah, but let's take it slow. I've had way too many hot wings."

Heather laughed and pulled him with gusto onto the dance floor before hooking her arms around his neck. As soon as they spun, the music turned soft and slow, and they began to sway like siblings being forced to dance for a wedding photographer.

"So, Detective Silva, how's work?"

"Great, thanks to you. The pay raise isn't too bad either. Except now my parents are even more on my case about moving out."

"Not many rentals around, huh?"

"None that aren't two thousand a month. Damned city vacationers. And it's too soon for me and Betty."

"Well, as luck would have it, I have a house that needs an owner."

Gabriel stopped in his tracks. "Wait, what are you saying?"

"I'm saying I want to give you my house."

He dropped his arms and stared at her in disbelief. "Heather, come on."

Heather grabbed at his forearms and forced him to keep dancing. "What? It's already paid off. I bought it with cash at auction with my divorce settlement and Seattle house money. I'd hate to see some money-hungry landlord snatch it up, bulldoze it, and turn it into condos. That place has history, you know. Mine and all the people that came before. That old lady put love into those yellow walls." She laughed. "Not that you have to keep them yellow."

"I will," Gabriel insisted. "I love the yellow walls." He paused. "Are you sure?"

"I'm sure."

"And the dogs?"

"I was hoping you'd look after them until Julius moves over. They'll love Farfalla House but might be cramped in my apartment. I imagine I'll be over at his daily anyway."

"I'd love to," Gabriel enthused. "Seriously. I want to soak up all the dog love that I can. I'm going to miss those little scamps."

"Yeah, me too. But there's no point in trying to get rid of the smell in that place. Believe me, I've tried. So, I guess you might as well get your own furry best friend."

Gabriel pulled her in for a bone-crushing hug, and Heather didn't mind the ache in her still-healing rib. "Thank you so much," he whispered.

"I love you, Buster."

"I love you too."

They parted, and Heather swiveled Gabriel toward a beckoning Betty. "Go on. Dance with your girlfriend."

"Are you sure?"

"Yeah. I'm going to go sit and watch."

Despite the protests of those on the dance floor, Heather made her way over to the table with a topped-up drink, watched quietly, and smiled when Julius looked at her and encouraged him soundlessly to keep going. She sipped and stared, trying to soak in every detail of what would soon become a memory.

Julius danced for another hour, and while he enjoyed himself, Heather tried to talk to, thank, and hug everyone. When she'd exhausted her list, she sat down again, but this time, the emotions and the nature of the party overwhelmed her. As her eyes welled with tears, Julius jogged over, and she looked up at the stars to clear her tear ducts.

"Is it time?" he asked.

"Yeah. I think so," she said shakily as liquid trickled down her nose. She smiled up at him and sniffed, and he leaned over and pulled her close. "If I don't go now, I never will. And I still need to finish packing."

Julius rubbed her back. "It's okay. We'll see them again soon."

"Yeah. I know. It's just a lot."

"Come on," he said softly and helped her to her feet.

"Should I say goodbye?"

"Isn't that what you've been doing?"

She realized he was right. More goodbyes would only mean more tears, and she didn't want to bring the mood down. So, they walked toward the gate, and Heather turned back one last time. Gabriel froze on the dance floor, meeting her gaze. She offered him a small wave, and he responded with a big one before returning to his dancing.

It was perfect, and it hurt, but it was always going to be painful. She didn't want a big, tearful farewell, and he knew it. She wanted to remember everyone at their best, happy, dancing, and laughing. The party had been grand enough. So, quietly, without any fanfare, she unlocked the gate and stepped through with Julius by her side and a smile on her slick, wet face.

THE END

AUTHOR'S NOTE

Thank you from the bottom of my heart for embarking on Heather's journey in *The Good Marriage,* the thrilling conclusion to our mystery series. Your companionship throughout this adventure has truly meant the world to me. I hope Heather's story provided a satisfying conclusion to the intriguing storylines we've explored together.

As we bid farewell to Glenville, know that the memories we've crafted within these pages will linger. While this chapter closes, exciting new adventures await. I'm thrilled to share that plans for another series are already underway, and I can't wait for you to join me on that journey!

And if you're feeling up to another mysterious and thrilling adventure right now. Don't miss out on the *Mia Storm FBI Mystery Thriller* series. In the latest addition to the series, *The Case,* Mia faces a mystery that will send shivers down your spine. When a suitcase washes ashore containing body parts, Mia could have never imagined the horrifying truth that she would uncover. While shark attacks are one thing, this case makes her question whether her island assignment was due to good luck or lack thereof.

As a new indie author, I am incredibly appreciative of your support. Your reviews and word-of-mouth recommendations fuel my passion for writing and for bringing these stories to life. If you could spare a few moments to leave a review for *The Good Marriage,* it would make an immense difference. Your thoughts and feedback play a crucial role in shaping my creative process, enabling me to craft an even more captivating reading experience for you in the next series!

Thank you again for your support, and I hope you continue to enjoy my books in the future!

Warm regards,
Cara Kent

P.S. I will be the first one to tell you that I am not perfect, no matter how hard I try to be. And there is plenty that I am still learning about self-publishing. If you come across any typos or have any other issues with this book please don't hesitate to reach out to me at cara@carakent.com, I monitor and read every email personally, and I will do my very best to rectify any issues that I am made aware of.

Get the inside scoop on new releases and get a **FREE BOOK** by me! Visit *https://dl.bookfunnel.com/513mluk159* to claim your **FREE** copy!

Follow me on **Facebook** - *https://www.facebook.com/people/Cara-Kent/100088665803376/*
Follow me on **Instagram** - *https://www.instagram.com/cara.kent_books/*

ALSO BY CARA KENT

Glenville Mystery Thriller

Prequel - The Bachelorette
Book One - The Lady in the Woods
Book Two - The Crash
Book Three - The House on the Lake
Book Four - The Bridesmaids
Book Five - The Lost Girl
Book Six - The Good Marriage

Mia Storm FBI Mystery Thriller

Book One - Murder in Paradise
Book Two - Washed Ashore
Book Three - Missing in Paradise
Book Four - Blood in the Water
Book Five - The Case

An Addictive Psychological Thriller with Shocking Twists

Book One - The Woman in the Cottage
Book Two - Mine

Made in United States
Troutdale, OR
03/02/2024

18135902R00195